BIKINI COWGIRLS
OF THE
URBAN LEGION

Dave Agans

B. MiRTHY & SONS

WILTON NH

BIKINI COWGIRLS OF THE URBAN LEGION.
Copyright © 2020 by Dave Agans.
All rights reserved.

For information contact:
B. Mirthy & Sons, PO Box 487, Wilton NH 03086
www.BMirthy.com

B. Mirthy & Sons are not responsible for the content of any website or publication referenced in this book, real or fictional, except for the www.BMirthy.com website.

First edition 2020 — rev 3

Cover art by Aaron Hazouri, www.aaronhazouri.com
Author photo by Duarte Images

ISBN: 978-0-9861709-2-8 (pbk.)
ISBN: 978-0-9861709-3-5 (e-book)

Library of Congress Control Number: 2020910343

For Mom and Dad

Disclaimer

None of the people, events, technologies, or facts in this book are real, as far as the author knows, and any references or similarities to specific people, institutions, or companies are either accidental or used fictitiously. The author is aware of no Corporation or Wacko Conspiracy Group in real life. The urban legends are just legends and the conspiracies are just silly. To the author's best knowledge, there are no antennas in the huge crosses near Houston.

Furthermore, Google Translate does not, as of this writing, handle Dolphin to English. The author had to guess what the dolphins were saying.

Part I

"Aliens Release Missing Girlfriend"
— Headline, The National Nose

Chapter 1

Even if a dolphin could shoot a speargun, it probably couldn't hit the side of a barge. Just the same, Meg's throat tightened a smidge as the pod of bottlenoses cruised into the halo of her dive light. They circled like sharks, but better armed—the weapons strapped under their flippers bore an unnerving resemblance to missiles on fighter jets.

Meg waved the high-intensity beam across the approaching attackers, hoping to blind them. The first spear shattered the lens and drove the sputtering shell into the darkness.

As Howie glanced up from his camera, Meg signaled him to kill his light, but there was no need: a second shot took that out, too.

The moonless gloom made the six fathoms of Gulf of Mexico over her head seem like sixty. She tried to recall her marine biology. Can dolphins see in the dark? A clicking sound reminded her: echolocation. She and Howie were sitting ducks—no, more like fish in a barrel.

The creaky-door sounds of multiple sonars washed over her, interspersed with a few terse whistles. She felt a whoosh from above and a shock as a spear hit one of her flippers. Missed! Good thing echolocation ain't all that accurate. Another whoosh and another shock, in her other foot this time. She tried to kick for the surface but both flippers were snagged by the spears.

Okay, maybe they didn't miss.

The attached lines began to slide across her skin—the shooters were spiraling around her, wrapping her up like a salt-water maypole. Before she could get an arm free to grab her knife, the plastic braids cinched tight. The dolphins started to tow, water rushing past her mask and regulator. She bit down on the mouthpiece and hoped they'd tire before she ran out of air.

Wasn't swimming with dolphins supposed to be fun?

* * *

Howie froze in the sudden darkness and listened as the clicking sounds morphed into invisible thrashing. He dropped the useless camera and pulled out his backup torch. The first flash of light confirmed his fear: Meg was gone. He looked for blood in the water.

Most people paid no heed to the urban legend about CIA torpedo-equipped dolphins escaping their flooded pens during hurricane Katrina. But as an urban "legend" survivor himself, Howie paid plenty of heed. Especially when surrounded by a pod of speargun-packing bottlenoses. Like other urban legends created as cover-ups, details were distorted: these dolphins didn't carry torpedoes and weren't swimming the Gulf aimlessly. That meant they probably weren't armed and trained by the CIA, either—fake urban legends were the signature of Howie's pervasive archenemy, the Corporation. The Corporation clearly didn't want anyone poking around the mysterious underwater fixture a few yards below his flippers; Meg had been chased off the first time she'd seen it, by means of a totally different urban legend.

For some reason, the dolphins didn't shoot the replacement flashlight. Maybe it was too dim to be annoying. Maybe they figured he was no threat, surrounded and targeted by at least eight spears with razor-edged criss-cross tips. He made no sudden movements, figuring there was at least one itchy trigger flipper in the crowd.

A smaller dolphin wiggled forward and poked at his ribs, its spears now at point-blank range. He braced for the shock, but the dolphin rolled sideways and slid along like it was scratching its belly on his compensator belt. Howie pulled in his crotch as the spear blades went by—he'd already been circumcised, by a human mohel, thank you.

With a fresh burst of chirping, the pod closed in. But the spears remained only a threat as the bottlenoses nudged him upward—away from his lost girlfriend, his abandoned camera, and the seabed gadget that seemed to be the cause of all this trouble.

He climbed into the boat and watched the dolphins swim off, then methodically painted the Gulf surface with the flashlight beam. There was no sign of Meg. He listened intently; a splash or a yell would carry much further across the water than light from his puny backup torch. But the only sound was the gentle lapping of chop against the hull. He fired up the motor, hoisted the anchor, and cruised in a carefully widening circle, scanning with the light and calling her name.

* * *

Meg counted seconds since the abduction; she had about ten minutes of air left in the tank. The dolphins showed no signs of slowing.

She sensed a glow, though it was way too soon for dawn. Oil rig lights. Was she visible from the deck? Didn't matter—even if someone was up at that hour, maybe having a cigarette at the rail, and saw dolphins towing a wrapped-up scuba diver, they'd just go back inside and swear off drinking.

A shadow loomed and her shoulder bashed into something solid and rough; a barnacle-encrusted piling faded into the murk. She felt herself turning, coming in for another run, and went limp as she hit the piling again. It softened the blow but she knew she couldn't take many more.

On the next approach, she twisted her feet to steer and this time took only a glancing shot. She kept turning, hoping to create some slack in the lines so she could grab her knife. But something hooked her foot and the lines yanked tight, squeezing more precious air out of her. She was tangled in an abandoned fishing net that had snagged on the piling near the seabed. The dolphins continued to pull, but they were as trapped as Meg.

They circled around, sonar clicking, which gave her the slack she needed to get an arm free. She had her knife out in a few seconds, and in a few more cut through one of the plastic braids. With no counter-spiral to hold her in, she could twist free of the remaining line and out of her still-skewered flippers.

In the dim light spilling from the rig, she saw four dolphins. One was tugging at its line, which was still hung up in the net. The others hovered nearby, keeping Meg from surfacing. Like their trapped buddy, she was doomed if she didn't get to the surface soon for some air.

She went for a peace offering, sawing at the dolphin's taut line until the braid peeled back and snapped.

The dolphin yanked the cut end free and raced for the surface. Meg unthreaded her flippers from the spears and net and slowly followed, under close scrutiny by the other three bottlenoses. There was a cacophonous chorus of whistles—seemed like they weren't all on the same page of the hymnal. But then they quieted down and retreated into the darkness.

Meg broke surface and yanked off her mask for a look around. Her abductors were almost out of sight, flying away in synchronized arching leaps. There was no sign of activity on the rig.

And no sign of the boat, or Howie—dead or alive.

Worrying about Howie would have to wait. She put the flippers back on and trimmed her buoyancy compensator forward so she could swim face up, allowing easy breathing and frequent navigation by the stars. Then, for the second time in three years, Meg set out for the distant Texas shoreline.

The last time she'd been here, it was in the daytime, with Tommy Owen. While he surfaced, she descended alone to investigate a peculiar metal fixture she'd noticed on the sea floor, kind of like a well head but with an antenna. She started back up just as a fire-fighting tanker plane scooped Tommy out of the water. Meg stayed out of sight and overheard her dive boat pilot celebrating the success of the plan to kill both her and Tommy. The incident was later turned into the urban legend of the ill-fated scuba diver dropped on a brush fire, the remains charred beyond recognition, effectively covering up the murder.

It was best to let them believe they'd gotten her too, so she swam back to shore and cleared out before anyone started looking for her. She fled to Boston and joined other urban legend survivors as a duly initiated member of the Urban Legion, fighting the Corporation however she could. Fellow Legionnaire Howie had managed to ease her heartbreak but not her resolve to find and punish Tommy's killers.

Howie argued that coming back to Galveston incognito to

continue the investigation was too dangerous, but Meg insisted, and Howie went along. Now, she had to admit Howie had a point. She hoped she'd get the chance to hear him say I told you so.

Armed dolphins. Meg smiled, wondering if she was the first Legionnaire to survive two murder-by-urban-legend attempts. Her smile quickly evaporated—Howie would share that milestone, but only if he survived.

Since the incident, Meg had followed the news from Houston. For the first year, the local media was obsessed with the missing scuba-diving couple. While the story had cooled, it would heat back up in a heartbeat if any news developed. Having declined the plastic surgery offered by the Urban Legion, Meg couldn't afford to be seen in public anywhere near Houston. Her reappearance would certainly be news and her three years in New England impossible to explain.

Exposing the Urban Legion was the other danger Howie was worried about. She'd have to find him, assuming he survived, and get out of town in secret again. Her dream of living a normal life in the open with her family was pretty much out of reach.

She swam for hours, and as the predawn light threatened to erase her guiding stars, she felt the swells and heard the crash of Gulf surf. She set her feet down and peered over the low waves at a deserted beach. Hot damn! But the causeway in the background meant it was San Luis Beach, and there'd be SUVs full of fishermen arriving soon. She took off her flippers, dragged herself across the dry flat into the dunes beyond, and collapsed out of sight in a hollow behind some low grass. A quick rest and she'd see about finding Howie.

She drifted off to the lullaby of breaking waves, caressed by a warm wind thick with the scent of seaweed and shellfish.

* * *

Meg opened her eyes to find a circle of people staring down at her. There were girls in bikinis, and men in cowboy hats, and cameras. Video cameras. She blinked a few times in the morning glare as a familiar face leaned closer.

"Wait," the man said, "I know you. You're Meg Brecker!"

Chapter 2

Meg squeezed her eyelids against the sunshine, buying time. She should've found a better place to fall asleep. A motel somewhere, far away, maybe back in New England where she wouldn't be recognized. Cape Cod would be perfect.

Was she dreaming? It was Tommy she'd seen, returned from the dead after three years. She opened her eyes again to enjoy the reunion.

But this was no hallucinated homecoming; if she was making it up, she would've left out the crowd and the cameras. And it would've been Tommy leaning over her. This guy was close, but not him.

Clint. Clint Owen, Tommy's little brother.

Shoot. Clint was the host of a web reality show, Next Bikini Cowgirl. That explained the girls and the cameras: they were doing a beach video shoot in the morning light. Meg's name and face would be all over the internet in seconds. And certainly all over Houston.

"Meg? Are you okay?" Clint sounded like Tommy, too. It was like she never left.

Act confused. Think. Don't say anything!

"Where am I?"

"You're on San Luis Beach. Where have you been? How did you get here?"

She wanted to say that somebody killed Tommy and she joined the Urban Legion and hid out in Boston for three years, came back to find his killer, and almost got killed a second time by spear-shooting dolphins.

She did not say that. The truth wasn't a good enough story.

It hit her: she was scuba diving when she disappeared. Just like now. *It's like I never left.* Maybe no story was the best story; easier to forget everything than to make up something new. Even though it was a lot to forget.

"I don't know. I was divin' with Tommy, and then I woke up here. Where is he?"

There was a buzz from the gathered crowd. Someone said, "Keep recording."

Clint hovered over her, his shaded face dark against the bright blue morning sky.

"You don't remember anything?"

She shook her head.

"Not since we hit the water. Where's Tommy?"

Now it was Clint's turn to shake his head, and he added a glance back at the crowd.

"Meg, you've been missin' for three years. And Tommy still is."

* * *

Meg accepted the water bottle and slugged a dolphin-battle's worth. She tried to remember the last few weeks before Tommy's fatal dive, to reorient her supposed recent memory. It was April, she was in the spring term at Texas A&M. She would say howdy to strangers. She was madly in love with Tommy Owen and would wonder what happened to him. That last part was still true, except she did know what happened.

Shoot, and her last name was Brecker.

My name is Brecker, she repeated to herself, trying to bury the made-up name she'd been using for years in Boston. She was cut, bruised, rope-burned, and dehydrated, but otherwise fine. If she could convince Clint and everyone else of that, maybe she could slip away, back to Boston and that made-up name.

But it's tough to claim you're fine with a three-year amnesia thing going. And the TV cameras made slipping away unnoticed impossible—they'd focused on her almost exclusively since she woke up. Meg's two-piece fit right in with the bikini reality show, although her hair was a mess by comparison to the other girls. You just can't find a good dolphin hairdresser in the Gulf of Mexico.

With Clint's help, she got to her feet. She glanced at the scuba gear on the sand and mentally thanked dear paranoid Howie for removing all the traceable markings from it. She vowed to find him, alive, and thank him face to face.

The bikini girls grumbled as the cameras ignored them to follow Clint and Meg toward a cluster of parked vehicles. He offered her a ride, and she accepted. Maybe when they were alone she could come clean and get his help. Hell, he'd lost a brother to an urban legend murder, he was qualified to join the Urban Legion.

She was trying to remember what kind of truck he used to drive (she last saw it a few weeks ago, right?) but that wasn't the ride he offered. An ambulance waited, along with two paramedics and a sturdy Texas Ranger. She smiled and nodded as the EMTs helped her onto a stretcher.

So, she was headed for a hospital, and the Rangers were involved. And Clint wasn't. A quick escape was unlikely.

She thought back to Clint's reaction on finding her. He seemed genuinely surprised, which made sense—there was no way anyone could have set up that coincidence. For her to arrive on the beach at the same time as the reality show was pure bad luck—for her. Good luck for him.

Though, was it? Clint was a former rodeo team-roping heeler who'd gone into announcing, and when Tommy disappeared, he used his platform to launch a highly visible crusade to find him. That fame probably helped get him hired as the Bikini Cowgirl host—though his rodeo skills and chiseled good looks couldn't hurt. But he abandoned the search when he joined the show; no doubt the producers didn't want that negative vibe, just good-looking girls in skimpy swimwear. How would he reconcile this sudden breakthrough with the reality show gag order?

She closed her eyes as the ambulance picked up speed on the main road north. Clint might be a valuable ally in getting her out of this. But she'd have to tell him a few things he'd have a hard time believing.

* * *

Howie left the scuba gear in his car and stumbled to his motel room. He was inserting the door key when a throat cleared behind him.

"I run a nice place here, Mr. Friedman. My guests don't usually stay out all night." It was the motel manager. She was in her fifties and wearing too much makeup, especially given her morning ensemble of pink terrycloth bathrobe and fuzzy slippers.

"Good morning, ma'am. I usually don't either. Had some car trouble and my cell is acting up."

"I figured you were out with some girl—like the one that stayed over the night before. The one you didn't tell me about when you checked in."

Howie smiled, guilty. Were they really still uptight about unmarried motel guests in Texas? Even in cheap motels like the Lone Diamond?

"Eh, you know how it is. Sometimes a lady stays too late and wants to sleep over. You want I should kick her out on the street?"

She gave him a stern look—no, actually, it was something else. He'd seen it before. Horny.

"I do know how it is," she said, and tugged at the bathrobe to expose a little more sagging cleavage. "I can't blame a girl for wantin' a taste of a jalapeño like you."

Howie sighed; another victim of his all-too-effective pheromone cologne. He hadn't met a woman, or a gay man for that matter, who wasn't overcome with lust after the first good whiff. He was probably using it too much, but deep down he was afraid it was the only reason Meg stayed with him. How could a woman so perfect still be in love with a scrawny guy like Howie without a little chemical enhancement? The side effect of arousing every other woman he met had its advantages, but it could be inconvenient.

"I'm sure," he said, and slipped into the room. He smiled at her and closed the door. And set the chain lock.

First things first: look for word from Meg. He fired up his laptop and checked the Urban Legion's Google Autocomplete messaging system, hoping for the best-case outcome: that she'd escaped and could get to a browser. Nada; he should be so lucky. He configured a real-time search process for scuba-related news posts, and a bunch of ads and joke memes came up, but no Meg. Desperate, he searched for "dolphins" and "spears," but he only found the urban legend about torpedo-equipped Katrina escapees.

The dolphins knew what happened to Meg. And maybe they talked about it underwater. His personal witness camera was built into his eyeglasses, which didn't work with a scuba mask, so he'd carried them in his tool pouch, blinding the video. But the audio should've worked fine. He uploaded the night's recording via Bluetooth into the laptop and scanned to where the dolphins arrived. Piping the audio into Google Translate Fauna, he selected Dolphin to English and hit play.

"Take the woman somewhere else and dispose of her. Make it look like an accident." The synthesized voice sounded female—amazing that Google Translate could detect the speaker's sex even for dolphins.

"Yes, commander Yeechchtyt," a male voice responded. Names always came through untranslated. "Wrap her up and bounce her off rig twenty-three for a while." The nightmarish sound of spears slashing and Meg thrashing came through the speakers, followed by an even more nightmarish silence.

"What about him?" said another male voice. "Take out that new light?"

"Hold your fire," said Yeechchtyt. "I want to check him out."

Howie tried to recall what had happened at the time. She'd nudged him and rubbed against him. Google Translate emitted a happy moan.

"I like him," the dolphin said. "He smells good. Get him out of here, but don't hurt him."

Wonder of wonders, the cologne even worked on female dolphins. Underwater. Too bad the Urban Legion couldn't send sales offers by spam email to the males; here was a whole new untapped market of frustrated mammals. He wondered what they used for money.

He was musing about seagoing cologne-delivery logistics when his notify feed came up with a webcast video—featuring a close-up of Meg's face. Meg's beautiful, *alive* face. Thank God! He switched on the sound just in time to hear her amnesia story.

Very clever, but she obviously hadn't had time to think the strategy through. Whoever tried to kill her and Tommy might not believe she couldn't remember. And even if they did believe her, they'd want to finish the job so she never would remember.

Roger and Lynn back at Urban Legion HQ needed to know about this.

* * *

Lynn Grady pressed a finger to the print reader to unlock the security door and stepped inside the new, almost-completed Urban Legion headquarters. As she passed the gym, she noted the electrician working under the cowling of the hot tub, head in and ass out, his tool belt hanging below two inches of visible butt crack. She found Roger at his station in the control center.

"Funny how plumbers and electricians can't seem to keep their pants up. Must be the heavy tool belts."

Roger flashed a familiar kindly look. She was about to be educated. Again.

"They're licensed; they don't have a choice."

"What do you mean?"

"It's in the code—wait, I'll show you." He pulled up a Board of Tradespersons 2016 National Standards document, scrolled through the index and selected a section, then pointed to the screen:

Part 9: Safety
Section 63: Explosion Prevention
Paragraph 2: Flammable Gas Vents
Within 15 feet of any spark-producing electrical panel, power tool (battery or AC operated), gas-powered motor, or propane torch, tradespersons shall provide a direct vertical vent path into ambient air for flammable intestinal gas. The vent shall extend from

the tradesperson's sphincter upward between the gluteus maximii to a visible exit from the trousers above the beltline. Under no circumstances shall the vent be obstructed, such as by an undergarment, tee-shirt, or pencil.

Well, that explained it.

After six months of information overload, Lynn still felt like a clueless Urban Legion rookie in Roger's presence. She was just a former warehouse worker with a food critic side gig. He was an MIT mechanical engineer, an Elite Trail Boy with skill patches on every subject from Wilderness Survival to Epic Practical Joking, and an Urban Legionnaire with years of gritty experience. He was only too willing to share information, but ever since he'd become the head of the local Legion, as well as Lynn's significant other, he hadn't given her any risky responsibility. Was she still too uninformed, or was he protecting her from the action she craved?

Innocence can only be lost, not gained, said Zen-mind, the advice of Zen teachers that popped into her brain after particularly unenlightened thoughts. Those happened a lot—Lynn was not a spiritual honor student. But after the Lexingham Mall episode with her ex and the armed French waiters, her innocence was water under the bridge.

Or, over the dome, she thought as she looked up at sunlight rippling in through the curved glass. When Roger first described the new HQ, he said it would have a great view of the Head of the Charles crew race. He didn't say the view would be from underneath the boats. Which, truth be told, wouldn't be that great a view.

The location, twelve feet below the surface of the Charles River and halfway between MIT and Harvard, was strategic. Just fifty yards upstream, also underwater, was the world headquarters of the Wacko Conspiracy Group, a consulting arm of the Corporation responsible for making up conspiracy theories so crazy that no one would take the real conspiracy seriously. They were well-paid for their efforts to promote wild ideas about 9/11 sabotage, flat earth, and UFOs, among dozens of other things. Founded by professors from various nearby Harvard schools, it was the original think tank.

Roger had found WCG's headquarters while mapping river currents, scanning the riverbed with a floating sonar rig and hearing members' voices. Water conducts sound very well, so the new Legion HQ was built downstream and sported a high-sensitivity directional array microphone to detect all the WCG conversations. A cone of silence prevented the WCG from overhearing the Urban Legion in return.

"Keep your friends close and your enemies closer," Roger told Lynn.

"Is that a Sun Tzu quote?" she asked. Roger had studied *The Art of War* to get his Military Strategy Trail Boy patch.

"Nah, that was Vito Corleone in *The Godfather Part II.*"

While Lynn would have liked to go undercover in a hostile Corporation facility, at least she was able to spy on one, albeit from the comfort of her padded office chair. Roger had assigned her to listen to recorded WCG meetings. He wanted to know how they communicated with the rest of the Corporation. And where they got their funding.

Roger's phone played the opening bars of "New York, New York"—that would be Howie calling. With news of success in his and Meg's underwater mission, Lynn hoped. Roger set the phone on his desk and hit the hands-free button.

"Roger here. I've got Lynn on speaker. How'd it go, Howie?"

"Don't ask. Actually, I'll tell you. It sucked. We barely reached that mystery device when dolphins attacked us, with spearguns yet. They dragged Meg away. She survived, but she washed up on a beach and ended up on camera, on a web reality show. And they recognized her."

"Crap," Roger said. "How did they know it was her?"

"The host of the show is Tommy Owen's brother."

Roger winced like he'd gotten a sudden headache.

"Was she conscious? Did she tell them anything?"

"She claimed amnesia."

Roger rolled his eyes, and when they settled they were aimed at Lynn, as if he expected her to share his disapproval.

"It's not a bad idea," she countered, "considering the circumstances." When a girl goes undercover, she has to think fast.

Roger shrugged and nodded.

"You're right. There's no better place to fake something than on a reality show. So, Howie, what can we do for you?"

"Eh, nothing yet. I'm going to pay her a visit in the hospital—she doesn't know what happened to me and I bet she's worried. Well, I hope she's worried, after all we've been through."

"Okay, let us know if you need anything. And contact the Houston Legion."

"Yeah, if I need their help," Howie said.

"You will. Stay safe."

"That should be a lot easier now that we're both on dry land. Meg's a natural swimmer, but when it comes to scuba diving I'm a fish out of water."

Howie hung up, and Roger started looking for news about Meg on the internet video feed.

As a Dirt TV on-the-scene report queued up on Roger's screen, Lynn looked around—at the monitors, the control panels, and the easy chairs, all flickering in wavy light filtering through the river. Meg getting into trouble on a field mission did not bode well for Lynn getting a juicy outside assignment soon. Roger would want to keep her here, where there probably wouldn't be any fire-fighting planes or armed dolphins swooping in for the kill.

* * *

Arlene Harrington gave one last check-pose for the makeup artist and reviewed her on-camera presence points. *Serious expression. Don't touch face. Don't brush hair out of the way. Lean in for important stuff. Use sing-song announcer voice. Bob head dramatically.*

She was excited. This had the makings of a career-launching story.

"This is Arlene Harrington for Dirt TV, broadcasting live from San Luis Beach in Galveston, Texas, with exclusive breaking news on a disappearance that has mystified authorities for a long time. Just over three years ago, Texas A&M grad student Tommy Owen texted his brother Clint that he would be scuba diving that morning off the Galveston coast."

Her Dirt researchers had already pulled footage from the original investigation and would be showing it picture-in-picture.

"That was the last anyone heard of Tommy Owen. There was no trace of a dive boat, or any witnesses to what happened that day. Texas Rangers were brought in, and when they went to interview Meg Brecker, Tommy Owen's girlfriend at the time, they discovered that she, too, was missing. There was no indication at either person's apartment that they had not intended to return that evening. A massive manhunt was launched, but no trace of either Owen or Brecker was ever found."

Raise eyebrows mysteriously.

She nodded, which was the signal to insert footage from the Reality Web video feed. The initial discovery of the girl would be onscreen behind her.

"Then this morning, a major break in the case. This exclusive video from our insider source at the Next Bikini Cowgirl reality webcast shows Meg Brecker, the missing girlfriend, as she was discovered on the beach here. When questioned about her disappearance, Ms. Brecker said she couldn't remember anything since diving with Mr. Owen. She acted very shocked and upset that it had been three years since then. And looking at the footage of the interview, one might be tempted to believe her."

Flash cynical look.

She nodded again, and the camera followed her as she stepped over to the waiting Texas Ranger. A lock of hair fell across her cheek.

Ignore the tickle.

"With me is Lieutenant Norcroft of the Texas Rangers Company A out of Houston. Lieutenant, how much do we know about this case so far?" The cameraman gave her a thumbs up; Texas Rangers looked great on camera. Arlene wondered if they got the same presence training as she did.

"I'm afraid I'm not at liberty to say, Ms. Harrington. At this point, we don't want to compromise the investigation by revealing what we know."

Hard-core reporter—dig for truth.

"We have exclusive footage of Ms. Brecker being taken away in an ambulance, accompanied by several Rangers. Is this a missing person case or a criminal investigation?" She shoved the microphone over as he gave the camera a steely gaze.

Ignore the tickle!

"Every missing person case is a potential criminal investigation until we prove otherwise. And Tommy Owen is still missing."

Ignore the fucking tickle!

"What about Clint Owen? How does he fit into this development?"

"Clint Owen has cooperated with the Rangers throughout the investigation and we expect that he will continue to do so. That's all I can say. Now if you'll excuse me." The Ranger touched the brim of his hat and turned away.

Just a few more seconds…

"There you have it. Stay tuned here for further updates as they happen. Arlene Harrington for Dirt TV."

The camera light winked out and she raked away the wayward lock with a relieved sigh.

* * *

Meg was assigned a semi-private hospital room, but no roommate, unless you counted the Ranger standing guard outside the open door. He allowed no visitors except for doctors and nurses, and he kept a sharp eye on them, too, as they tended her injuries. He didn't let them say anything, except to ask how she felt.

She felt pretty good. A few hours rest, dressings on the barnacle scrapes, and ice on the bruises had done wonders. She hadn't spent long enough in the early-morning sun to get a sunburn; her skin retained its ghostly New Englander glow. Nothing much else she could do but get the hell out of there and contact Howie.

If he was alive.

She put alternative outcomes out of her mind and focused on escape. She'd need clothes—hospital gowns weren't in fashion that season, and even if she could find her swimsuit, that would draw equal attention. But she'd seen a linen cabinet at the end of the hall; maybe she could snag some scrubs on her next trip to the bathroom. She could go almost anywhere in scrubs in a University hospital. Hell, from what she remembered of the Galveston nightlife, she could even hit the bars on the Strand in scrubs.

The best route away from the building once she got outside was the next question. Meg was trying to recall the layout of the UT Medical Branch campus when the Ranger let in a newcomer: a middle-aged man in dress clothes and a lab coat. Flashing a Ranger badge, he introduced himself and told her he'd be asking some questions. Since she was the last person to see Tommy alive, he said, she was a key witness in his disappearance.

"We're sorry we have to keep you sequestered like this," he said. "But we hope that blocking any news from the missing years might help you remember what happened."

And then he recited her Miranda rights.

So she was a suspect; blocking the news might help catch her lying about her amnesia. And if she disappeared now, she'd be a fugitive, not a missing person.

She stuck to her version of the day Tommy disappeared and didn't bite at leading questions about recent events. It was easy enough to just forget everything from the moment they submerged. At one point, she had to decide whether to lie about the dive boat and its pilot—she knew that revealing a third person out on the Gulf that day would get the Ranger's attention, and it did. He questioned her in detail, trying to get a description of the guy and the boat. But she actually hadn't paid much attention at the time and said so. If she had noticed anything useful, the Urban Legion would have been all over that pilot already.

The Ranger recorded the entire interview and thanked her when it was over. Then he gave her a card, asking her to call if she remembered anything.

The only thing she intended to remember was not to call the Texas Rangers.

Chapter 3

Executive Producer Charlie Stewart sat in his Las Vegas headquarters, looking over the Reality Web streaming stats with mixed emotions. Next Bikini Cowgirl was already the most-downloaded webcast on the net, and now even the live streams were approaching broadcast numbers. The key word was "approaching." He'd just hung up a video call with his boss.

"It's like winning a Webby when your friends are winning Emmys," Fiona had said, petting the cat on her lap. "You can't brag about it at cocktail parties. Don't you want to brag at cocktail parties, Charlie?"

For her, it was all about beating broadcast and cable. Fiona wouldn't be happy until everyone's eyes were locked onto his web video. Charlie had no clue why she was so obsessed, but he did know that if Fiona wasn't happy, Charlie would no longer be Executive Producer at Reality Web.

Not that he'd mind bragging at cocktail parties, especially to his former cable employers. But he intended to embarrass them in more ways than just winning a ratings war.

So, Meg Brecker had reappeared, and discovering her on Bikini Cowgirl goosed the webcast's ratings into the big leagues. The tabloids—broadcast, online, and even print—were all over it already, providing free advertising. And Fiona made it clear she expected Charlie to leverage the stroke of luck by recruiting Brecker as a contestant.

The good news was, Meg Brecker looked great in a bikini. Short, maybe, but stacked for her size and not an ounce of fat on her. She was a Houston area native, and according to the research report on his screen, she had some cowgirl skills. Her built-in character type—the cowgirl with the mysterious past—would be a viewer magnet.

Her mysterious past was the bad news. If she was faking the amnesia, or she recovered her memory, Meg Brecker was a serious threat to the entire project.

Charlie drummed his fingers on the desk. He wished he could check her out for himself, but there was too much to do at Reality Web central in Vegas. He needed boots on the ground in Houston.

Ha! Boots. He already had Jim "Muddy" Bootes on the job as technical director. But Muddy's previous fuck-up was the cause of the problem. And maybe the cause of the next one, if Charlie didn't put him on a short leash. He called Muddy in his office at the Bikini Cowgirl ranch.

"I knew you'd call," Muddy said as the video popped up. "I was thinkin' about a plan already."

"I knew that," Charlie said, "and I know what kind of plan you have in mind. But whatever it is, forget it. You had your chance to take Brecker out three years ago, and apparently you blew it. Now my boss wants Brecker on the show for the ratings. That would be alive, Muddy. We're going to recruit her, and you need to back off."

Muddy was shaking his head.

"But she survived the hit. If she remembers, she'll blow the whistle on us. She might even be fakin' the amnesia—the damn Urban Legion has pulled off crazier shit than that before. Isn't your boss worried about her bein' a fuckin' Urban Legionnaire? She's got the credentials."

Charlie gave Muddy his best intimidating glare.

"My—our—boss doesn't know anything about the scuba diver hit or the legend we made up to hide it. You told me you got both divers, so I never reported the incident upstairs. I don't intend to now—we're going to handle this on our own. Are you on top of the local Legion?"

"Yeah, they're based out of a local restaurant—Chompy's. The Elvis shrine in the foyer is a dead giveaway."

"I assume you haven't seen Brecker chowing down on an Enchilada Combo lately."

"Nah, it's been quiet."

"Okay, keep an eye on them." Charlie studied the man on the

screen. Muddy Bootes was a roughneck, not smooth enough to lure an honest amnesiac onto a bikini reality show. And totally lacking in the kind of subtlety needed to flush out a fake amnesiac. He'd need help, and he wasn't going to get it from the current Bikini Cowgirl director—a paid professional, but clueless about the big picture. "I'm going to replace your director. Please meet Pavel Nepovim at the airport tomorrow morning. I'll send you flight info."

Muddy didn't look happy, but he nodded and signed off.

Charlie gathered his thoughts, pulled up Pavel Nepovim's contact, and hit the call button. Pavel was artistically subtle, very reliable, and totally ruthless.

* * *

Pavel Nepovim sat back in the director's chair and observed the action on the couch with a critical eye. The Halloween theme was brilliant—rubber face masks meant he could get all the de rigueur shots without needing special lighting or weird camera angles to hide the otherwise naked talents' identities.

The girl was hot. While it was easy to entice someone into an anonymous porn shoot with a ridiculously large cash offer, they usually didn't put any passion into the performance. This one was different. Of course, Brad was quite the stud and knew how to turn a girl on. Or maybe she was just faking it, trying to earn the money fair and square.

Too bad she'd never see it.

"Cut!"

Pavel lit a cigarette, took a drag, and exhaled a spotlight beam of smoke onto the stud's rubber werewolf face.

"What is happened?"

"Sorry, I couldn't help myself."

"You are pro—you are supposed to have control. Even snuff film needs money shot."

Sakra!

Ah, well, he had a stunt double standing by. Halloweenie III got its happy ending, using close-ups only.

The Quality Control department would complain; he made a mental note to follow procedure to the letter when he disposed of the body. And he'd be sure to point out in his report that, edited money shot or not, the lady was certainly not going to talk about the Corporation dirty laundry she'd stumbled upon. Which, after all, was the whole point of a snuff film.

No one ever survived a Pavel Nepovim snuff film.

The theme for *Chain Saw Orgy* filled the room, and Pavel reached for his phone. The cameras weren't rolling anymore, so there would be no need to cover the sound with a moan soundtrack. He hated snuff films that used fake moan soundtracks.

Pavel Nepovim was an artiste.

* * *

Charlie Stewart shielded his eyes as the image of Pavel's shirt popped up onto his iPhone, pushing the display's color palette to the limits. The man's Euro-savant style might fit in with the L.A. porn crowd but wouldn't go over well in Houston. He'd have to tone it down.

"Pavel! Good to see you." He noted the generic condo furniture in the background. "Are you on a shoot?"

"Just finish up."

"Okay, better go out on the balcony. This is private."

"There are many porn shoots on balconies of this building today. I go into bathroom."

It was awkward talking to him on video while he sat on the can, even if he was fully dressed and not actually taking a shit.

"I've got a job for you."

They talked about the situation; Pavel was genuinely interested in going to Houston, taking over as director of the Bikini Cowgirl show, working with Muddy Bootes, and killing Meg Brecker.

"No, Pavel, I only *might* want to kill her. She's a fucking gold mine at the moment. I want to make sure she's not faking the amnesia, and try to get her on the show. If she is faking, or won't come on the show, then you can kill her."

Pavel was silent as he considered the deal.

"I make sure she faking, or convince her not to join show, and then kill her."

Charlie sighed.

"Pavel, I want her alive and on the show if at all possible. The money is huge. The audience is huge. And the pressure from my boss to keep that audience is huge. Killing her is a last resort."

"Okay, I got it, Charlie, you don't worry. I just pull your leg. I don't kill your golden goose. Unless needed. And show will be masterpiece."

Charlie nodded, and hung up. He still wasn't sure what Nepovim would do. But the man was dedicated to his art—if he did kill Meg Brecker, at least he'd do it spectacularly, and on camera.

Chapter 4

Meg was dozing when a commotion at the door got her attention. The Ranger was arguing with someone. Someone familiar.

Pappy!

Meg's father apparently won the argument; he strode into the room, his anger at the Ranger visibly dissolving as his face lit up.

"Meg!" he bellowed, diving to give her a bear hug on the bed. "Goddamn, we thought we lost you!"

"Guess not, Paps," she said, hugging him back. It was almost as good as hugging Tommy would've been.

"I missed you so much," he whispered into her ear as they clung. Even hard-ass Pappy could have a broken heart. She remembered him crying for days when Mom died, and trying to hide it. She could only imagine what he went through when his only daughter disappeared. A wave of guilt for putting him through that pain welled up and flooded her eyes as well. She squeezed them shut and clutched her father. There had to be a way to stay home with him this time.

"What happened?" he said, coming up for air. "Where've you been?"

"I told you, sir," came a voice from behind him, "no questions without a Ranger present." Pappy rolled his eyes and twisted to face the officer.

"Okay," he said, "You're present. Stay here while I talk to my own goddamn daughter." The Ranger stepped back but nodded and stayed in the room.

"I don't know, Paps. I don't remember anything except divin' with Tommy. I thought it was this morning, but they're tellin' me I've been out for years."

Her father looked into her eyes, probing. Could he tell? If she did come home, how long could she keep her secret?

"It's the damnedest thing, Meg. Three years and seven days. I been countin'. Everybody's wonderin' where the hell you were all that time."

"Guess I flunked out of A&M, then. So when can I come home?"

He frowned and shook his head.

"Can't say. It a big investigation now."

The Ranger leaned over and cut the reunion short.

"That's correct sir, this is an ongoing investigation, and I'll need you to leave now so the doctors can do their job."

Pappy shrugged, gave Meg a hug, and stood up.

"I'll come around again soon." He sneered at the Ranger and sauntered out at his own pace.

He was replaced by a doctor and two nurses.

"We'd like to take some fluid samples," the doctor said.

* * *

Howie sized up the entrance to the John Sealy Hospital tower. A crowd overflowed the grass-covered islands in the driveway loop, held back by yellow barricades and a handful of Galveston police. A news van was parked along the drive, but not for long—a sunburned guy in a Stetson was winching it onto a tow-truck, ignoring the curses of the reporters around him.

Howie pasted on a "what's all this fuss about?" look and threaded his way through until one of the cops stepped in front of him.

"What's your business here?"

"Just visiting my mom. What's going on, officer?"

"Nothing that concerns you. What's your mother's name and room number?"

Whoops. Do some research next time, schmuck.

"Miriam Friedman, room 423."

The cop consulted a tablet.

"I don't have a Mrs. Friedman here." He nodded toward the crowd with a smirk. "Go join your friends—that wasn't even a nice try. The room numbers here don't work like that."

Yeah, research would've been good. He flashed a sheepish grin and retreated to the news hive.

Howie was eavesdropping on a discussion about whether Elvis was involved in Meg's disappearance (he was) when he noticed the sky bridge into the hospital's second floor from across the street. There were no cops in front of the other building, so he wandered over to check it out.

A children's hospital. Not likely that a creepy-looking thirty-year-old would be allowed in and up to the second-floor bridge. Just the same, he pushed through the revolving door and far enough into the lobby to hit the wall of glares from the security guards.

"Is this the primary care building?"

"No sir," replied a guard. "That's three blocks north and three blocks west." He pointed the way.

Howie was surprised that there actually was a primary care building. He was one for two on uneducated guesses.

He'd need to do some research before he could go any further. And get some help from the Houston branch of the Urban Legion.

* * *

Howie watched the last few minutes of the Trinity Bay Players' rehearsal with a finger up his nose. The community theatre occupied a storefront in a nearly abandoned strip mall, and their performance space reflected the neglected ambiance. The seats were reclaimed from some defunct vaudeville stop and mounted on plywood platforms climbing in a circle around the stage. The stage itself was so small that a dozen instruments hanging from the single pipe above were enough to flood it with light. Not that you'd necessarily want to do that—the set was a series of battered flats too warped to form a smooth wall. Some of the edges were off by an inch.

This was the high-tech Houston Urban Legion headquarters?

Howie almost hoped he was mistaken, and the decoy they'd set up at that Mexican restaurant was actually the real thing. Maybe the Players, not recognizing his nose-picking as the Urban Legion secret greeting, would hand him a tissue and show him the door. But when the house lights came up and the actors could see him, they all simultaneously smiled and jammed their fingers up their noses.

"Welcome!" A black-haired woman in an equally black tee-shirt emerged from the control booth behind him, pulled her pinkie from her own nose, and offered her hand. She and Howie both looked at their fingers and thought better of it. "I'm Laurel Yanni, I run the organization—and the lights, and the costume shop, among other things."

"I'm Howie Friedman, from the New England Legion."

With a trace of a Cajun accent, Laurel shared her history. A former New Orleans fashion designer, she created the dress that looked white and gold or blue and black, depending on the viewer's IQ. She'd gone into hiding after receiving death threats from the low-IQ side of the viral photo controversy.

"So what's your story?"

"Don't ask," Howie said; he never discussed his legend. "The important thing is my girlfriend's story—you might have heard of Meg Brecker?"

Laurel's eyebrows shot up.

"The missing scuba girl they found this morning?"

"Right. Her missing former boyfriend, Tommy Owen, got scooped up by a tanker plane and dropped onto a brush fire—you've heard the legend."

Laurel nodded.

"So she's been hiding in the Legion all these years?"

"It's as good a place to hide as any. Meg and I did another dive in the Gulf last night, trying to figure out why the Corporation took Tommy out, and we were attacked by spear-shooting dolphins. She escaped but ended up on camera."

"I saw the clip. Clever to come up with the amnesia story."

"Yeah. But she's quarantined and doesn't know I survived. I want to let her know I made it, and that she should keep up the story until I can get her out. That's where I could use your help."

Laurel nodded again and led Howie down to the stage.

"We can handle that. Come on in, and welcome to the Houston Urban Legion headquarters."

They went backstage and through a tall gray-metal supply

cabinet, into a brightly lit room full of equipment. It was like the C.S. Lewis wardrobe, except it led into a NASA control center instead of Narnia.

"We got most of this stuff used when NASA updated their tech a few years back."

"How do you guys get your funding?"

"We sell Canadian meds on the internet. But we import them from Mexico—the authorities will never suspect it."

Howie looked around the room, amazed by the size.

"Your building didn't seem big enough for this space to fit behind the stage."

Laurel chuckled.

"Thank our set designer. It's just clever use of perspective—the stage looks much farther away from the audience than it actually is."

Laurel introduced Howie to the Trinity Bay props mistress, "Spike" Stillgood, and their publicist, Devon Macomb.

Spike was the first Black, female engineer at the New Orleans craft brewery Fleur de Brew, and she proved her worth by inventing a process to make non-alcoholic beer that actually tasted as good as real beer. But the Auto Body Repair Cartel, one of the many industry groups working for the Corporation, saw that as a threat to their business. They arranged for a street gang to drive with no headlights, wait for Spike to respond by flashing her own lights, then chase her down and kill her. They didn't know Spike's twin sister had borrowed her car. Of course, the killing soon became just an urban legend about a gang initiation ritual.

Devon had also dodged a Corporation bullet. He'd written a seemingly innocent blog post warning people about the eel skin wallet effect: residual charge from electric eels could erase credit card magnetic stripes and render them unusable. The Eel Products Cartel planted a venomous snake in his coat closet, which killed his roommate, the original Devon Macomb. His death became the legend of the copperhead in the factory outlet coat store.

"I took his identity, swapped all the images on the net of Devon and me, and joined the Legion." The new Devon was apparently quite the internet hacker.

Howie explained Meg's predicament.

"How about flyin' a drone into her window and droppin' off a note?" Spike suggested.

"You'd have to make it edible so nobody else would see it," Howie replied.

"We could do that, honey."

"And I don't know what room she's in. Or how to open the window if she has one."

Spike shrugged, defeated.

Laurel suggested setting Howie up with a doctor's costume and an ID.

"Devon, can we hack their database so he can get in?"

Devon shook his head.

"No, I've been hacking institutions all over Galveston, but I haven't broken the Sealy security software yet."

"How about the Shriner's Hospital across the street?" Howie asked, and told them about the sky bridge. Devon smiled.

"That I can get you into. Of course, once you go across the street you're gonna hafta bluff your way around."

"I'll take it," Howie said, and soon was admiring himself in the costume-shop mirror—white shirt, blue tie, and lab coat with a "Dr. Howard Fine - Neurology" badge pinned to the lapel. Laurel had even made up a special tin-copper-lined yarmulke with an abstract Rod of Asclepius embroidered on the front.

"This is great," he told her. "My mother always wanted me to be a doctor."

* * *

Doctor Howard Fine adjusted his tie and tightened his grip on the Android tablet as the revolving door spit him into the Shriners Hospital lobby. He approached the desk with distracted confidence and flashed his badge at the reader. The guard glanced up at Howie and then at his screen, and punched a button. A solenoid buzz welcomed the newly certified physician through the gate and into the inner lobby.

He took the stairs to the second floor to avoid awkward elevator conversation, and crossed the glass-walled bridge to the

Sealy Hospital to avoid awkward Galveston police conversation. He'd studied the layout and guessed that Meg would be near the Neuro ICU on the fourth floor. He took the stairs again, paused at the top to catch his breath, and stepped into the lobby. He expected a heavy guard presence, but it was deserted except for the nurse behind the reception desk.

Howie put on his busy air again and strode up to the woman.

"Doctor Fine," he said, "I'm looking for patient…" he glanced down at the tablet "…Meg Brecker."

The nurse typed a few characters and glanced at the monitor.

"Wrong floor, Doctor. Ms. Brecker is in room 9B-14."

"Ah, thank you," Howie said, nodding and looking down at his tablet. He typed the room number as he headed for the elevator. Awkward conversation or not, he wasn't going to walk up five more flights. Besides, no real doctor would walk up even two flights, much less five.

The elevator door opened onto a similar layout on the ninth floor. But this one wasn't deserted. One Texas Ranger stood at ease directly across from him, eyeing him suspiciously. Another was guarding the hallway to wing B. Howie guessed there'd be another outside Meg's door.

He glanced at the floor indicator, frowned, checked his tablet, and shook his head. He punched another button and held his breath until the doors closed. At least he knew her room number now. As he exited the Shriners Hospital a few minutes later, he studied the Sealy tower across the street and considered the proper approach trajectory to room 9B-14.

* * *

Meg lay awake, craving sleep, in the dim glow of various instrument status LEDs. She'd insisted the guard close the door for privacy and darkness, but it didn't help—the light from the hall wasn't the source of her insomnia. Out of a dozen scenarios of the midnight dolphin attack, she hadn't imagined even one where first-time diver Howie would survive. And a few of them had particularly gruesome endings. She was afraid to dream.

How long could she keep this up? She'd lost two lovers to whoever planted that device out there. Should she just confess to the Rangers? They'd be delighted, and she could go home and live with Pappy in peace.

Except that would mean exposing the Urban Legion. And exposing her, and Pappy, to Corporation retaliation.

She leaned back into the pillow and stared at the green flashing light on the ceiling. Her eyelids drooped, but didn't close—there was something strange about the green light. It wasn't just blinking like all the other indicators in her room. She sat up and scanned the equipment. The light wasn't coming from there—it was coming through the window, and the flashing used the Urban Legion's scrambled version of Morse Code.

"...GOT AWAY FROM DOLPHINS. KEEP UP AMNESIA STORY. WILL GIVE YOU SUPPORT AND GET YOU OUT. FLASH A LIGHT TWICE IF YOU SEE THIS. I LOVE YOU." The message began again: "THIS IS HOWIE, I'M OKAY, GOT AWAY FROM DOLPHINS. KEEP UP AMNESIA STORY..."

Meg choked back a cheer and flashed her bed lamp twice. Through tears she watched the message stop mid-word, then after a pause, change to "SEE YOU SOON. DID I SAY I LOVE YOU?"

Yes, you did. You say it a lot.

She lay back again as the green light blinked out, and her eyes closed all the way this time.

Damn, she was tired!

She drifted off, and dreamt about Howie trying to spirit her away from Houston while Pappy and Tommy (or was it Clint?) begged for her to stay. The dream never reached a decision.

* * *

Howie thanked Spike one more time for the use of the drone as they arrived back at Urban Legion HQ. So much for phase 1. Phase 2 would be tougher: making Meg's amnesia unquestionably plausible to the public and the Texas Rangers, not to mention whoever tried to kill her. Especially to whoever tried to kill her.

He sat down at his laptop with a ginger ale from the theater concession stand. Spike had offered to fetch some ice, but Howie assured her that he really—really—didn't like ice.

A little research found an angle: psychogenic amnesia, where the brain suppresses all memory of an intense psychological trauma. If he could get that out there, he could change the question from "Is she lying?" to "What happened to her?"

The difficult part was getting it out there. He packed up the laptop and wandered to the back room where Devon spent his time. The writer was hunched over his own keyboard, at a desk covered with papers and notebooks, a full ashtray balanced atop the pile. There was a bottle of Johnnie Walker on the desk corner and a Scotch on the rocks in Devon's right hand. Howie shivered at the sight.

"Hi, Devon. Am I interrupting your writing?"

Devon turned slowly. Too drunk to be startled?

"Never!" he said with a lot more energy than Howie expected at 2 a.m. "I'm just checking out the workshops for next month's Bayou Country Writer's Conference." He leaned back, pointing at the screen. "I'm torn between 'Scotch, Bourbon, or Gin—What's Right For Your Genre?,' 'Tuning Out Indy Song Lyrics At Starbucks,' and 'Deeper Is Older—The Archeological Filing System For Your Desktop.'"

Howie peered at the list, which also included "Pantsers Panel Discussion: Are PJs Acceptable Writing Wear?," "Erotic Novel Research (And How To Remember His Name In The Morning)," and "The Deadline—Just A Suggestion."

"Does this conference have any seminars about actually writing?"

"Pfft! All writing conferences have a few, just to placate the writers' wives and husbands, but real writers don't need that stuff. Last year one seminar was 'Eliminating Clichés And Mixed Metaphors'—and people avoided it like a ten-foot pole."

Devon pulled a rolling desk chair around and offered Howie a seat. As Howie settled in, Devon held out a jar of white school paste.

"Care for a huff?"

Howie shook his head. "Why?"

"Inspiration. White paste is a mild hallucinogen. That's why kindergarteners are so creative—it's a big dose to their little bodies. How about a drink, then?"

"None for me, thanks. I've got an urgent problem to deal with—I need to write a blog post."

Devon grabbed his Scotch, took a healthy sip, and coughed.

"No prob," he said. "What's the topic, and where's your blog?"

"The topic is Meg Brecker's psychogenic amnesia. And I don't have a blog. But I need this post to go viral."

"Everybody needs their post to go viral," Devon said, flashing a conspiratorial grin. "But we're the Urban Legion. We've got the web backdoors to make that happen." He said he'd make it look like Howie had been posting for years, by planting fake posts and giving him fake fans. "We can put it out there just like the Corporation does with urban legends. What we can't do is get it back."

He took another swig and turned to his keyboard. In a little over an hour, the story hit the wire. And as late-night social media addicts read their feeds, the post climbed to the top of the trending charts. Twitter, Facebook, and Reddit were going bonkers.

Howie thanked Devon, checked in with Roger, and went back to the motel for some badly needed sleep. Had he overdone it? The tabloids would be all over this, and the paparazzi would be all over Meg. Phase 3, getting her out, was going to be tricky.

* * *

Roger sat at his console in the Boston Urban Legion headquarters, twelve feet below the Charles River, wishing he was in Houston. When the King chose Roger to lead the local Legion, he didn't say the job meant sitting on his ass and watching his team take fire on the front lines. Roger was a fighter—he wanted to be involved. Fighting kept his mind off the risk to his friends. And the sadness over the friend he'd already lost.

Even at 3 a.m., he was grateful for Howie's call; he'd been so worried about Meg's amnesia ploy he hadn't slept much anyway. But now Howie's blog post, amplified by the Houston Legion's capable hacker, was giving it credibility. Nice work, guys.

Maybe too nice. While Meg's amnesia was more believable, her story was now way more popular. The tease of some unknown psychological trauma had put a lot of amateur and professional detectives on the case. Some of them might figure out the truth.

Some of them were already close. One reporter said a drone was spotted hovering near John Sealy Hospital, looking like it was flashing some kind of code. Another quoted an anonymous insider saying doctors had found traces of semen in Meg and were 99% sure it was not related to Tommy Owen.

Howie needed to cover his tracks better.

Roger felt useless. Keeping tabs on the Wacko Conspiracy Group a few yards upstream seemed frivolous compared to keeping his team safe and the Urban Legion a secret.

Except…

The WCG's mission was to keep the Corporation a secret. They did that by creating conspiracy theories so crazy that no one believed the truth behind them all. Couldn't he do the same for Meg and Howie?

He called Devon, who was still up, as usual. They brainstormed a few twists for the troublesome stories out there. Devon assured him the results would swamp the truth in the web tabloids by morning.

* * *

Arlene Harrington chewed her sausage-and-cheese kolache without tasting it—she was too absorbed in the numbers. Her Dirt TV feed had ridden the Meg Brecker video wave for the first day, but that was old news now. Intrude Magazine led with an exclusive insider report from John Sealy Hospital that doctors had found traces of semen in Brecker.

Shit. Her crew hadn't gotten within twenty yards of Sealy or anyone in it. Arlene washed down the spicy-sweet bun with a swig of black coffee and continued to read. The story further claimed that doctors had "99% confidence that the sample was not of terrestrial origin." Great. Dirt TV had a mystery girl. Intrude had fucking aliens.

Prying Eye claimed that Brecker's dad had been able to visit her, briefly, and was threatening to sue to get her released. That story was trending with the ambulance chaser audience, but not anywhere else, so she could ignore it.

The National Nose was reporting a UFO sighting in the hospital area, with witnesses claiming that the alien craft was transmitting some kind of message. The headline was "Proof: Aliens Invented Morse Code." The source was probably the same as Intrude Magazine used. Why didn't that source contact Dirt TV with this stuff?

Her hit count tracker started to beep, indicating a visitor uptick on her news feed. She clicked over to the analysis page and quickly found the reason: her video of Meg's discovery had been linked by a blogger, some Howie Friedman.

She'd never heard of him. But apparently he had a huge following, and his clickbacks were goosing her ratings. He'd done his research, too; if he was right about psychogenic amnesia, Brecker wasn't lying. Arlene read the rest of the post, but it stopped short of any conjecture about the trauma itself.

Unlike the Sensation Today article, which featured an artist's conception of alien sperm cells, complete with wriggling tails and big, blank oval eyes.

Chapter 5

Pavel exited security at Hobby Airport and found a muscular, flinty-eyed man holding a sign reading NEPOVIM. He instinctively looked at the man's cowboy boots to see if they were indeed muddy. They were well-worn, but clean. His clothes were muted earth tones, even more bland in contrast with Pavel's orange-and-pink modern art print silk shirt. The one standout feature of Muddy's outfit was his huge belt buckle, engraved with an ornate, dollar-sign-spewing oil well. As Pavel approached and nodded, the man extended a hand.

"Mr. Nepovim? Muddy Bootes. Welcome to Houston. Hope you got some sleep on the redeye."

The voice was deep and rugged, like that voice actor who narrated everyone's pickup-truck commercials. Pavel shook his hand, noting the firm grip—strong enough to indicate physical superiority but gentle enough to not be an asshole about it. Pavel would not be able to intimidate Bootes. But he would need his help to work with locals; they would have to become friends.

"Please to meet you. But also, call me Pavel. You prefer Muddy to James?"

Muddy frowned.

"I prefer a sharp stick in the eye to James."

Pavel pictured a snuff video title: *Cyclops—Love is Blind.* It had potential.

They retrieved Pavel's luggage and proceeded to short-term parking and a large pickup truck, which was, indeed, muddy. It was the kind of vehicle Pavel would expect from Charlie's right-hand Texas technical man, complete with a huge toolbox in the bed. No gun rack, though, which was a bit of a relief. Charlie had warned that Muddy might resent Pavel's presence, taking it as a message that he'd lost Charlie's trust. Which it was. Once they exited the lot, Pavel got to the point.

"I understand this is sudden for you."

"Well, sure. Meg Brecker washes up on the beach one day and you show up to replace my director the next. Charlie moves quick."

"Did you have good relationship with my predecessor?"

Muddy shrugged.

"Nah. He was just paid talent, like the camera and sound and wardrobe people. I watched him out there bossin'; I don't know a whole lot about TV, but I wasn't impressed." Muddy glanced over and gave Pavel a look that said he wasn't impressed with him, either. "Charlie says you do good work though. Films? TV? Anything I've seen?"

"I make art films—they are generally not seen in theaters. Have you heard of *The Postman Never Leaves*?" Muddy shook his head. "How about *The Girl on the Train Tracks*?" Muddy shook his head again.

"Guess I'm not up on artsy shit."

"Does fact that I make 'artsy shit' bother you?"

"Nah. Charlie and I go back a long way, and I've always just tried to do my job. If Charlie thinks you're the better man to run the show here, I can accept your artsy shit." Muddy shot him a critical look as he pulled the truck onto the highway. "I'll just hafta ignore your artsy clothes."

* * *

The headline screamed from Pavel's tablet: "Will Brecker to Court: Release My Daughter!" He turned to Muddy, who was skillfully negotiating I-45 morning rush-hour traffic.

"In USA, authorities cannot keep prisoner without good reason, correct?"

Muddy shrugged.

"Well, some reason. Maybe not a good one. Why?"

Pavel pointed to his screen.

"It seems that Texas Rangers do not have good reason to hold Meg Brecker. Her father is suing to get her released from hospital."

"So," Muddy said as he tucked the truck into a gap in the left lane, "we could finally talk to her, and she'd be free to join the show."

"Or, she could disappear again. I have different idea."

Twenty minutes and a few back roads later, Pavel and Muddy were seated at the Texas Rangers Company A Headquarters. Across the desk was Lieutenant Norcroft, lead investigator on the Brecker case.

"You have to understand," Norcroft said, "We can't let any press interview her; it would compromise our investigation."

Pavel nodded.

"But that will soon be out of your control." He placed the tablet on the desk so that Norcroft could read the headline. "We are not press, and we might be able to help each other. We would like to interview Meg Brecker for possible joining of our reality show. Our contestants are under our control, away from press, and public, until end."

Norcroft shook his head.

"We're trying to keep Brecker isolated so she doesn't hear anything about the last three years. We hope that will help her recover her memory."

Or help catch her lying about her amnesia. Pavel and the Rangers had similar goals.

"Rest assured, sir, we would not poison your witness. We will follow whatever isolation rules you establish for her."

Norcroft's eyebrows twisted as he considered the scheme.

"This is highly irregular, you understand," he said. "But I have to admit, this case has been stalled for years and maybe it's time to bend the rules a little. I'd have to insist that a Ranger have full access to your set at all times."

Pavel looked at Muddy, who did not look pleased with that idea. Pavel was not either, but it might be their only chance to keep Meg Brecker under their control. Unfortunately, the watchful eye of a Ranger might tone down the other cowgirls' behavior. They would not be as uninhibited and certainly would not do anything illegal.

Debbie Does the Death Penalty? Not this time.

"That would be fine, Lieutenant."

"I'm curious though, why would she agree to join your show? She wants her freedom, and those expensive lawyers will get it for her soon enough."

"Ah, but you have kept her away from news, so she is unaware of this lawsuit, correct?"

The Ranger's eyebrows straightened as they rose.

"That's a very good point, sir."

On the road back toward Galveston and the Sealy Hospital, Pavel fingered Norcroft's letter of introduction while reading a blog article about psychogenic amnesia. It seemed possible that Meg Brecker truly could not remember what happened. This could be good, but it required verification.

He swiveled to face Muddy.

"Do you know where we can acquire lie detector?"

* * *

Lieutenant Mike Norcroft spread the contents of the Owen/Brecker file across his desk. At the time of their disappearance, he'd had precious little evidence to go on. Tommy Owen was a marine biology student, and Meg was into hydroponic farming, both in the graduate program at Texas A&M Galveston. Tommy's brother said they planned to go diving, but that's all he knew. They found Tommy's truck near the waterfront in Galveston, but it was walking distance from just about every charter boat pier in the harbor. Not a single operator admitted to taking them out or renting them a boat. Both students' apartments looked like they were expecting to come home again.

He had Tommy's and Meg's phone records, but not the phones—they disappeared with their owners. There were no text messages of interest, no calls other than the weekly calls home, and occasional texts to each other. The only unexplained datum was a call from an unregistered number the night before they disappeared—a burner phone, untraceable on purpose.

Did they know that person? They never called that number; it was just the one incoming.

On a hunch, Norcroft had brought up Google Cache History and did a timed search for the burner phone number, limited to a month before and after the disappearance. Maybe the caller had advertised some kind of clandestine service on Craigslist.

Nothing. He'd even enabled the Dark Web search and tried again. Still nothing.

Now, looking at the file years later, it finally hit him: Tommy didn't call them, so there was no reason to look for their number. He repeated the search, but this time using Tommy's number. And up popped a Craigslist ad:

> Needed—Dive boat excursion, cheap. Grad student with not much money researching hot water microbes in the Gulf, need a dive boat for two people, one day.

The ad included Tommy's phone number. Not a great idea in general but apparently it got results. Whoever called his phone took them out for that fateful dive.

He scanned his Brecker interview notes again. Meg didn't notice or couldn't remember anything about the dive boat operator or his boat.

The only thing he'd learned was that this dive was about hot water microbes, which sounded like a code for something. Maybe smuggling? Hydroponic dope growing? A drug deal gone bad would certainly be cause for someone disappearing. And for a survivor to pretend to have amnesia about it.

* * *

Meg sat up in bed reading People Magazine; it was a waiting room copy and thus was three years old, so the Rangers weren't worried about her getting any recent news. They hadn't considered that it would help her reset her alleged memories to the time period. She looked up as her Ranger guard showed two men into her room. One was dressed in colors and patterns not found in nature and moved like a dancer. The other guy had that local blue-collar look: rugged and confident. He was carrying a small, gray, plastic tool case.

"'Afternoon ma'am," the Ranger said. "These folks'd like to speak with you, if you don't mind."

The colorful guy stepped up and bowed slightly.

"I am Pavel Nepovim, Ms. Brecker, and this is my assistant, Mr. Bootes. I am director for Next Bikini Cowgirl reality show—our crew found you on beach yesterday morning. I have proposition for you."

Meg was used to that, especially from creepy guys like Pavel.

"What kinda proposition?"

"Your appearance on our video has created such a spike in our viewership, we would like you to join our show. You have interesting story, we believe you have cowgirl skills, and we know you are looking good in bikini. Our fans, and especially our sponsors, would be pleased if you would compete with other cowgirls."

Not as creepy as she thought. This guy was a businessman.

"What's in it for me?"

"We give you fifty-thousand-dollar signing bonus, and you get to leave this hospital. The Rangers require that you would be sequestered away from other girls, but your private cabin will be far more pleasant than this room."

Meg glanced around her antiseptic prison cell. Anything would be better. But the last thing she wanted was to be in the public eye. Keeping up the amnesia charade would be a lot harder in the limelight of a reality show. Maybe she could limit the exposure.

"Reality show, huh? How does it work?"

"There are photo shoots, daily skills competitions, and many candid video sessions. Each day after competition fans will vote, for one cowgirl they like and one they don't. One losing cowgirl will leave show each of first three days, then two will leave for next three days. After that is finale, fans will choose winner from survivors. Prize is million dollars plus one-year modeling contract."

"It's over in a week?"

"Yes."

So she could lose the competitions on purpose and act like an unlikable bitch and go home in a day. Unless everyone loved her anyway, which would mean a week. Either way it might be quicker than getting out of the hands of the Texas Rangers.

"Okay, I'm interested."

Pavel gave Bootes an awkward glance.

"There is one minor detail, however," he said. "Next Bikini Cowgirl is wholesome reality show, and we will not risk scandal. Our contestants have all passed background checks, but in your case, that is difficult. You understand."

Oh, yeah. "I understand."

"You have said you remember nothing about last three years. We would like to confirm that before we invite you onto Bikini Cowgirl. We would like to ask you some questions, using lie-detector."

Meg glanced at the Ranger, who was studying her reaction.

"I got nothin' to hide," she said. Then, smiling at the Ranger, "Least, as far as I recall."

"Thank you, Ms. Brecker. This will not take long."

Pavel's assistant pulled a chair alongside the bed, set the clamshell tool case on his lap, and opened it. Embedded in a foam insert was an oblong instrument with dials, buttons, and a rotating needle indicator. There were two metal cylinders with wires attached, which Bootes removed and plugged into the main instrument. Meg had seen these before, on the A&M College Station campus, when she and her friends took a Scientology personality test as a lark. As drunk as they were, they did not sign up.

"That's an e-meter," she said. "Are you guys Scientologists?"

Pavel smiled guiltily.

"No, we are not. We merely, ahm, borrowed this electro-psychometer from acquaintance. It is difficult to obtain proper lie detector on such short notice."

Meg relaxed. The Urban Legion had trained her to fake out even the pros, and these guys were rank amateurs. This would be easy—just think of something traumatic on every question.

Electrodes in hand, she answered with outward calm while internally reliving her first kiss (behind the gym) and her first menstruation (during gym). They asked a bunch of questions about recent history, with emphasis on the source of her bruises and rope burns. She answered them all the same: "I don't know."

The last few questions were a little trickier. Do you remember the boat you were on with Tommy? Do you remember where it was berthed? Do you remember anything about the pilot?

Meg answered all these questions the same way as she had for the Rangers, with "no." But something was off.

How did they know there was a pilot? She'd told the Rangers that, but figured they'd keep it to themselves. Maybe this was just a Ranger ploy to get her to admit something. The guard was paying careful attention to her answers.

It didn't work—she stuck to her script.

"I think that will do," Pavel finally said, nodding to his assistant. Bootes took the handles from Meg and packed everything back into the box. Pavel rose and shook Meg's hand.

"Thank you for your cooperation. We will return with decision soon." He turned to Bootes. "Come now, Muddy, we have much to discuss." Bootes nodded and followed Pavel out of the room.

It was a good thing Meg was no longer holding the handles—the e-meter needle would have slammed into the maximum stop. She'd passed the lie detector test without mentioning how she hid below the gunwales of the dive boat and heard the pilot say on the radio that both she and Tommy had been successfully scooped up by the tanker plane. And that the guy on the other end congratulated him and promised a very nice payoff for setting up the hit.

But she'd just now remembered: the pilot had called the guy on the radio "Muddy."

Chapter 6

Ordinarily, Meg would've been glad to see Pavel waltz into her room with a contract in his hand. But he was followed by Muddy Bootes, which gave the word "contract" a whole different meaning.

She'd spent the last hour assessing the situation and debating her next move. There were a few things she was sure of.

Muddy Bootes, and probably Pavel Nepovim, were behind Tommy's death. They were probably also Corporation, given that the murder had been covered up by an urban legend. Meg's first priority was to get that information out to Howie and the Urban Legion.

Meg must have been quite a hit on the beach, since they wanted her as a contestant on the show. And they believed the amnesia story; they wouldn't risk giving her a media spotlight if they thought she might use it to expose the truth about Tommy's death.

This was also an opportunity to go undercover. As long as they believed her story, and she stayed on the show, she could try to figure out what they were up to from the inside. She'd have contact with Clint and could enlist his help. He certainly wanted to know what happened to Tommy.

And if she didn't join the show, or got voted off, she'd be joining Tommy on the other side, since, other than boosting the ratings, they didn't need her alive. Didn't want her alive. She'd have a target on her back, and they'd take her out the minute she was out of sight of the Rangers.

She smiled as Pavel pulled a chair alongside the bed and sat down.

"I have spoken to my managers at Reality Web. They were quite pleased to hear my recommendation to invite you to join Next Bikini Cowgirl." He handed her a thin sheaf of paper. "They right away forwarded this contract. I think you will find it quite satisfactory. If you initial each page and sign at bottom of last one, we can proceed with getting you out of hospital and onto our ranch."

Meg glanced at the pages: enough legalese to choke a lawyer.

"Onto your ranch? I was hopin' for a night off first." She waved the contract. "I'd sure like to go over the fine print in here with my Pappy."

Pavel and Muddy exchanged glances.

"That will not be possible. We have made special deal with Rangers that you would come directly to show today. They allow it only since our contestants are sequestered—no phones, no internet, no TV."

Shoot. She didn't dare step into the spider's parlor without at least getting word to Howie about Muddy and the dive boat. But she also didn't dare step away from the spider's only reason to keep her alive.

Maybe she could stall, and pass a private message at the same time.

"Okay then, how about you let Pappy come here?"

Pavel's face fell. He looked at Muddy and got a shrug in return.

"I not think we can do that. The Rangers—"

"They already let him in once, they'll let him in again." She tossed the contract onto Pavel's lap. "And I won't be signin' this without him."

* * *

"This is problem," Pavel said as the elevator doors slid shut. He had called Will Brecker and invited him to come talk with Meg; Pavel and Muddy were going to the lobby to wait for him. "If he tells Meg he is suing for her freedom, it is kiss of death; she will have no reason to sign with us."

"Let me work on it," Muddy said as they took seats on a lobby couch. He poked at his tablet for the entire half hour until Pavel got the call that Brecker was in the parking lot.

"It is time," Pavel said. "What have you got?"

Muddy looked up, smiling.

"We can buy him off."

Pavel shook his head, not understanding.

"He's broke," Muddy continued. "He hired the most expensive lawyers in Houston, and he just took out a second mortgage on his farm to pay for it. Apparently, peas and beans aren't sellin' so well lately. My money's on foreclosure by October."

"And what do we tell him? 'Excuse me, Mr. Brecker, but we need to trick your daughter into joining our show, here's money for you not to mention lawsuit'?"

"I wouldn't put it quite like that. Tell you what, let me talk to him local to local. How much we got to offer?"

"Two hundred."

They made their way to the yellow barricade, where a Ranger waited with a big guy in well-used working clothes and a quality hat. They introduced themselves, and soon guided Will Brecker into the elevator.

"Will," said Muddy, "we got a bit of a problem, maybe you can help us out. Y'see, your daughter is a sensation at the moment, and there's a lot of folks out there hollerin' for her to join our show. So we made a deal with the Rangers that they'd let her out of here if we took her right onto our show, where they can keep an eye on her."

Brecker's eyes glowed. This was not going well.

"The Rangers'll have to let her out of here anyhow. I've got lawyers."

"We know that. But she don't. We're thinkin' the only reason she wants to join our show is to get out."

"Guess if that's the case, you boys lose."

"The stakes are mighty high, here, Will. Reality Web is offerin' her a big payday to join us. A lot more if she wins. And we're willin' to offer you a big payday for not mentionin' the lawsuit to her today. Let's say, enough to pay off that second mortgage?"

Will stared at Muddy; Pavel tried to read his face but concluded nothing except that Brecker was probably a very good poker player.

7-Card Blood? Texas Holed 'Im? The title needed work.

The elevator opened on Meg's floor.

"I'll think on it," Brecker said.

* * *

Meg watched the ice in her father's face melt. Her mood might have warmed as well if Pavel and Muddy hadn't walked in right behind him.

"Hey there, Meg. Told ya I'd be back."

She smiled and lost herself in his Texas-sized hug.

"I knew you would, Paps." Would she ever be back for good? How did she stay away all those years?

"So, these boys tell me you're fixin' to join their reality show. Paradin' you around in a bikini."

"Yeah, Paps. Can we talk about it alone?" She glared at Pavel, and the Ranger behind him. She avoided looking at Muddy.

The Ranger spoke up.

"I'm afraid that's not possible, ma'am."

Meg was afraid of that too. How the hell could she get a message out to Howie with the cops *and* the bad guys listening in?

"Doesn't matter none, Meg. You can just tell 'em no."

"But they can get me out of here, Paps."

Pappy glanced back at Pavel and Muddy.

"I can get you out of here, Meg. I got the best lawyers in Houston workin' on it. And these fellers tried to bribe me not to tell you." He flashed a subtle snarl. "Guess even they don't think you'd join 'em fair and square."

Shoot. There went excuse number one. She had to find a way to stay out of Muddy's crosshairs.

"But the money's great, Pappy. I'm gonna need it to finish up at A&M. I don't think you can cover that, unless the string bean and peas business has really picked up."

It hadn't—her father's jaw tightened. He'd been struggling to keep the farm solvent even before Meg disappeared, and Meg had since followed his lack of success from afar. It wasn't easy to sell string beans and peas back when the Lima Bean Cartel forced every mixed vegetable packager to include limas. And now that they were calling their new smaller strain of limas "edamame" and claiming it was actually soy, Pappy still wouldn't give in. He hated "edamame" as much as lima beans, just like everybody else—but the cartel was too powerful to fight. He'd even tried raising salsatillos, but once manufacturers figured out they could make fake salsa out of tomatoes, onions, and peppers much more cheaply than using real salsatillos, they'd forced authentic salsa brands out of the market. Pappy was still broke.

He shook his head.

"I can't cover college, Meg, I'm flat out with the lawyers. You really want to get involved with these guys? On a goddamn bikini show?"

"Well, it might be fun. And it's a cowgirl competition. I can show 'em what you taught me. Bet you a week's barn chores I can win it all." She eyed his open-hanging jacket as she gave him a confident wink and watched him fight off a growing smile. "But you also taught me never to buy in the presence of the salesman. I'll think on it once Mr. Nepovim is gone."

"That's good advice," Pappy said finally, giving in to a full grin. "Works for cars and horses, oughta be good for sleazy reality shows. It's your decision."

She smiled and put her arms out for another hug. They embraced, and as he backed away she caught his jacket lapels and pulled him back in for a kiss. She held him close and whispered.

"I'll think hard on it, Paps. Thanks for bein' here."

Pappy nodded and got up from the bed.

"Now give my daughter some peace and quiet." He herded everyone including the Ranger out of the room and closed the door just short of a slam.

Meg took a deep breath and pulled out the smartphone she'd picked from his jacket pocket during the last-minute hug and kiss. She studied the fingerprints on the screen, found the four most worn PIN digits, and tried to map them to significant family data.

Bingo—Mom's birthday.

* * *

Howie was halfway through a medical law paper on mental patients' rights when his Google Virtual Private Text app popped up with a beep.

Meg!

He punched the accept button before the beep ended.

Meg via Unknown> Hi Babe!

< Where are you? Wait, switching to voice mode

Howie clicked on the text-voice translate option—he could talk faster than he could type.

"Okay," he said, "where are you?"

"Still in the hospital," said the synthesized voice. It didn't sound like Meg, but it was just as good to hear. "Stole Pappy's phone, don't know how long before he notices and comes back for it. Two guys, Pavel Nepovim and Muddy Bootes, run the bikini cowgirl reality show. They want me to join. But I remembered Muddy was the name of the guy on the radio with the dive boat pilot when Tommy was killed. Look him up, find out what's going on."

"Okay. I've been looking at legal briefs; your Dad's lawyers have a strong case to get you out soon."

"Pappy told me. I still want to join."

"What? Meg, they know you saw the murder. They just want to get you into their hands so they can finish the job."

"They don't know what I saw, and they believe I don't remember."

"Okay, so they want to kill you before you do remember."

"I don't think so. They said the show's ratings skyrocketed when I showed up. They can't afford to kill me."

"As long as you're on the show."

"That's why I need to join. So while I try to out-cowgirl the competition, you get going on Muddy and Pavel; the sooner you figure out what they're up to, the safer I'll be. Meanwhile I can investigate from inside. Clint is there and might know something, maybe I can get close."

This was so wrong.

"I can't talk you out of this?"

"Maybe you have. I'll think on it."

"Okay. Think hard. And if you join, watch your back."

"Let's both watch my back. Gotta go—visitors."

The app connection indicator went from green to red. That first conversation with Meg was not as much of a relief as he'd anticipated.

* * *

Muddy waited with Pavel while Will Brecker rummaged through his pickup for the lost phone. He took advantage of the moment out of earshot.

"So what's the plan if she doesn't join the show? Once his lawyers get her out of here, we take her out?"

Pavel nodded.

"If she will not join, we have no use for her."

Brecker backed out of the passenger door and slammed it.

"Nope. I musta dropped it in the hospital. Sorry boys, but I need to go back in."

"We understand, Mr. Brecker," Pavel said as he turned toward the hospital barricade.

Muddy followed, chewing on the problem. If Meg went home with her father, it might be hard to get to her before she got her memory back. And what would she remember? He didn't know what she'd been up to for three years, any more than she did. And whether she remembered or not, there might be clues that led back to him and Charlie Stewart. Even one clue was one clue too many.

He rode the elevator up in silence. How hard would it be to take out old man Brecker along with his daughter? He looked tough.

When they entered the room, Meg was too busy greeting her father again to catch Muddy sizing them both up. Piece of cake.

They found the phone, which had dropped into a fold in the

bed linens. The Ranger was getting a little short by now and tried to hustle them out. But Meg said wait.

"While you're here, Pavel, I might as well tell you. I've made my decision."

Muddy tried not to show his interest.

"I'm in," she said.

"Really?" her father said, surprise and concern on his face. "Just like that?"

"Well," she added, "on one condition."

"What is that?" Pavel asked.

"I'm gonna need a generous supply of SPF 50 sun block."

Will Brecker shook his head, but Pavel smiled.

"Of course."

Muddy smiled too. Now he had options. Pavel, of course, would insist on following Charlie's order to keep her alive. But Charlie hired Muddy to kill Tommy Owen and his girlfriend—and paid him for it already. And once Charlie found out Meg had survived, he rubbed Muddy's nose in the failure, and then went and hired Pavel to babysit him.

Fuck Charlie. And fuck Pavel.

And fuck keeping Meg Brecker alive.

Muddy was a proud Houstonian. Houstonians do their job.

Chapter 7

Howie skimmed countless news posts about Meg joining the Bikini Cowgirl show. Their marketing team knew what they were doing.

So much for talking Meg out of it.

All he could do now was honor her request to investigate Muddy and Pavel and the show. He looked into Reality Web, the show's producer, which was based in Las Vegas and run by a guy named Charlie Stewart. There was no way Howie was setting foot in Las Vegas, much less leaving Meg alone in Houston. He'd call Roger and have him deal with it.

Since Meg was trapped on the show with no outside contact, she'd need someone on the inside, to be on the lookout for trouble and head it off at the pass. Or something cowboy-ish like that. The problem was, nobody could get inside.

He rescanned his clips of the previous shows, trying to find an angle. He was almost done when the Dirt TV clip from the beach popped up: the one with Arlene Harrington claiming to have an insider at the show.

Dirt TV was the only outside media that had footage of Meg's discovery. A quick back-door check of the Facebook ad database showed lots of cross posts between Dirt TV's page and the Bikini Cowgirl show. Cross posts of video. Dirt TV had special access to the show and the cowgirls.

A few more clicks provided Arlene's hotel and room number. Howie punched the address into his phone and called to reserve a room there for himself. As he packed his bags, he took a moment to freshen up with a heavy splash of pheromone cologne.

Arlene could get him into the Next Bikini Cowgirl show. The cologne could get him into Arlene's hotel room. But he had no intention of cheating on Meg, so the big question was, could he seduce Arlene without having to actually put out?

* * *

Lynn Grady had become an expert on wacko conspiracy theories. It was tough to stomach the radio shows and YouTube videos, so she pored through conspiracy theory debunking sites, which tended to get to the point quickly. Unfortunately, those sites had fallen right into the Wacko Conspiracy Group's trap—they debunked *every* conspiracy, even the ones that Lynn and the Urban Legion knew were genuine. Or at least, sort of genuine. The WCG was very good at adding ridiculous details and side-claims to obscure the very real, and very nasty, activities of the Corporation.

But Lynn was learning the tricks. Tap into fear, hatred, helplessness, distrust of authority, and the feeling that failure is somebody else's fault. The facts don't matter, those are just made up by "them." And top it all off with a sense of superiority for being in the know about what's really going on. For not being "sheeple."

But understanding how the Wacko Conspiracy Group worked didn't tell her who they worked for. They were also very good at not using names—for themselves or their contacts. Lynn could tell which Corporation cartels were funding various projects, but not who the people were. Or even how they communicated with each other.

She was about to go admit defeat to Roger when he hurried into the control room.

"Howie just called. Meg discovered that the people running the Bikini Cowgirl show were involved in Tommy's murder. They got Meg to join the show."

"What? She's gonna join the people who tried to kill her?"

"She wants to investigate from inside."

"That sounds crazy dangerous."

"It is. Howie tried to talk her out of it. But she also thinks they need her for the ratings, and they'll kill her right away if she doesn't join."

Lynn sighed.

"She's probably right."

"Yup." There was sad resignation in his voice. "Howie's gonna try to hook up with Dirt TV, which seems to have a sweet arrangement with Bikini Cowgirl. They plug the show on their cable channel and get exclusive access in return."

"So Howie wants some of that exclusive access."

"Right. I'm going to look into Dirt TV, it's all I can do from here. But Meg is walking into the lion's den and we need to know who's managing the lions. The show is produced by Reality Web—it's a Las Vegas outfit, run by a guy named Charlie Stewart. I'm going to call the Vegas Legion and have them dive in."

"Why don't we go out there? The WCG can wait."

"I can't go."

"Why not?"

"I'm not allowed. I was part of the MIT blackjack team back when I was in school. Once the casinos figured out we were counting cards, they banned us all from the entire city. They have our pictures in a database and cameras all over the place. If I set foot in Vegas I'll get beat to a pulp within a half an hour. In fact, they also look for brass rats—" he waved his MIT ring "—and they'll escort you out of town if you're wearing one."

"I can go." Lynn held up her naked hands. "No rings."

Roger's brow furrowed.

"Alone? I can't send you out there alone."

Lynn studied his face. Was that concern for her safety or distrust of her ability? Probably both.

"I won't be alone. You said there's a Legion office there."

"Um, yeah. Cirque Noire."

"They're a *circus?*"

"Yup. Their act is a pulp-fiction thing—hard-boiled detective, femme fatale, dedicated secretary, gang boss, cops, thugs. I think the cops and thugs are the clowns. But it's weird—their leader plays the detective in the show. He likes to stay in character. So he acts like a noir detective all the time, even when he's not on stage. He'll treat you like a dame."

That was a very familiar feeling at the moment. Lynn didn't say so.

"I can handle that."

"But they've also got all kinds of tech expertise and great fighting skills. You're an English major and a martial arts newbie."

Nothing she could do about her technical weakness. She had been practicing jiu-jitsu and tae kwon do, figuring she needed something a little more violent than yoga and dirty basketball now that she was a full-fledged Urban Legionnaire. But maybe "full-fledged" was premature. Roger certainly thought so.

"So I'll learn some new tricks, and come back a better agent."

"What are you going to tell your daughter? She—" he stopped mid-sentence. He knew she was on an art exchange student program in Paris. He glanced at the ceiling, searching for another argument.

"Roger, Meg is in trouble. I'll go crazy sitting here listening to WCG meetings knowing I could be helping in Vegas."

His gaze returned to her—she saw pride and concern.

"I know I'll go crazy," he said finally, "sitting here listening to WCG meetings while you're out spying in Las Vegas."

He offered a hug and kiss, and she took it.

"Please be careful," he whispered.

"I will. Any other advice?"

Roger grinned.

"Don't draw to an inside straight."

* * *

Howie crossed the hotel lobby, spotting one of the larger members of Arlene's crew at the entrance to the lounge. He pasted on his best seductive smile—it wasn't much, but it made the pheromone effect a little less creepy to the victims—and stepped into the bar. Arlene was having a late lunch at a table near the window, and Howie headed for the table next to it.

He'd only been seated for a moment when a large shadow fell across him.

"I think you should pick a different seat. You're crowding the lady." Apparently, Arlene's crew doubled as bodyguards.

Howie turned toward her in time to watch her condescending sneer melt away. As usual, the pheromones only needed a few seconds.

"Wait, Bobby," she said, "He's okay." Bobby's eyebrows said

"Really? Him?" but a glare from Arlene said "Scram, Bobby." The big man shrugged and returned to his station by the door.

"Thanks," Howie said, extending his hand. "My name's Howie. I just got into town and I could use a little friendly conversation."

"Arlene. Glad to help. Here on business?" Arlene had the glow in her cheeks that meant her hormones were out of control.

"Yeah, I'm a freelance writer. Did a piece on Meg Brecker's psychogenic amnesia, thought I'd like to get a little closer to the subject."

"Howie Friedman?" Her pupils were dilating. "So I guess this conversation isn't a coincidence. I read your piece. I liked your piece." Her eyebrows said "wink-wink nudge-nudge know what I mean?"

"I'm glad," he said, leaning closer. "Are you interested in a partnership? I am a *firm* advocate of close partnerships." He tried to emulate the eyebrow thing, but without a mirror he couldn't tell if he looked sexy or silly.

"Maybe we should talk about this upstairs." She touched his arm. "In private."

Howie smiled. Sexy it was.

"Lead the way."

Arlene walked through Bobby-the-bodyguard's disapproving stare with a businesslike air; Bobby was probably paid to keep his objections to himself. Howie also maintained a professional composure, though he did consider flipping Bobby the bird. In the elevator, he half-expected Arlene to attack him, but she kept her cool.

"Did you know that most elevators have security cameras recording twenty-four-seven?" she asked, apparently reading his mind.

"Didn't know that." He wondered if she knew about restroom flush sensor videos. He could probably get a good look at her female charms on any voyeur site. But he had a feeling that was about to be redundant.

She let him into her suite and locked the door behind them.

"Drink? I've got scotch, bourbon, gin, and vodka."

"Got any ginger ale? It's only three p.m., I'm working."

"So am I," Arlene said. "But we can handle that." She handed him a can from the mini-bar and a glass from the tray, and lifted the top of the ice bucket.

"Uh, no ice, thanks."

Arlene shrugged as he opened and poured the ginger ale. He took a tentative sip while she placed four cubes in her glass and covered them with bourbon. She raised her glass.

"To a close partnership." They drank, and she moved closer. "I could use you on my team."

Howie kept a poker face.

"What's in this partnership for me?"

"I can get you into the show," Arlene said, setting her drink on the table. "Full access to the staff and the girls. Including Meg Brecker."

Howie's poker face might have cracked a bit, but Arlene didn't seem to notice.

"Works for me," he said. "When do we get started?"

"In a half hour," she said, taking his glass and setting it alongside hers. "Just enough time to get to know each other better." She wrapped her arms around his neck and planted her mouth on his.

She was actually pretty hot. Howie got into it, but the back of his mind was churning on how to get out of it. Without blowing the "partnership."

An evening news fanfare blared from her purse. Her ring tone. Arlene snarled and unlatched herself to answer it.

"Yeah. Now? Okay, be right down." She looked at Howie apologetically. "And we're bringing a new writer." She hung up and nodded toward the door.

"They're going to unveil Meg Brecker this afternoon. We'll have to pick up where we left off, later," she said.

"Of course," Howie answered. "Not to worry—I'm worth the wait."

* * *

"I need muscle," Muddy Bootes growled, "Not some pretty boy Hollywood types. Or Euro trash." Muddy regretted blurting that; Pavel seemed like the sensitive type.

"Do not worry," Pavel responded cheerfully, apparently not so sensitive, "they are not like me. And they are not from Hollywood, but nearby San Fernando. Please, just give them chance."

Muddy didn't have much choice about that. Charlie Stewart insisted that he give Pavel's friends a shot at his as-yet-unfilled henchperson positions.

"All right, send 'em in."

Pavel nodded and opened the door. Two guys strolled in, looking cocky. Maybe they had potential.

"Muddy, this is Brad Driver and Peter Long. Gentlemen, this is Muddy Bootes, technical director at Bikini Cowgirl show. Have good interview—as they say, knock 'em dead." At that, Pavel slipped out and closed the door behind him.

Muddy waved them to chairs as he sized them up. Brad Driver was medium-tall, blond, well-muscled, and deeply tanned. Peter Long was almost the opposite: short and wiry, with dark brown hair and pale skin. Their demeanor gave him no clue as to their physical abilities—or their moral compasses.

"Okay, guys, let's get down to it. Pavel recommends you highly. What kind of experience have you got?"

"You name it," Peter said. "Contractor, debt collector, plumber…"

"Hold on," Muddy said, "I like the contractor and debt collector, but plumber? You mean like pluggin' leaks?"

Peter shot Brad a grin.

"You could say that."

"Also policeman," Brad added, "gardener, pool boy, and pizza delivery guy."

"I don't get it. What's that got to do with Pavel?"

"We're actors, dude," Brad said. "We do all of Pavel's films."

Actors. Shit… Pool boy?

Porn actors! Double shit!

"I didn't know Pavel did porn. I hope you're not expectin' to do any fuckin' here."

Brad looked a little disappointed.

"I figured with all these girls—"

"You figured wrong, Brad. I need muscle. And I need you to fit in. Ever play cowboys?"

"Sure," said Peter.

"Can you ride?" Both guys grinned again. "Horses, I mean." The grins disappeared.

"A little."

"I rode a pony at the county fair when I was seven," Peter said with the excitement of a seven-year-old. "Does that count?"

Tinhorn actors. Never even been to a dude ranch. But that wasn't important if they could do the real job.

"Ever killed a man?"

The reaction to the blunt question was interesting. Brad blurted a shocked "no!" but Peter nonchalantly answered "sure."

"Tell me about it, Peter."

"Nothing special," the little guy answered. "Pavel does snuff films. I usually kill somebody before the shoot is over."

Jeez.

Muddy turned to Brad.

"But you don't go for that?"

"No way," Brad said with a look of disgust. "I only do hetero porn. I leave the guy-on-guy stuff for Peter."

Muddy glanced at Peter, who gave him a sexy wink. He quickly returned his focus to Brad. This could be okay.

"So, you've killed women?"

"Abso-tively, dude. Lots of 'em. While I fucked 'em."

"But you're willin' to skip the fuckin'."

"If I have to. As long as I get paid."

Muddy didn't know exactly what he'd need these guys to do, but killing a man was certainly possible. Killing a woman maybe even more so.

"You're hired, guys. Report to the wardrobe department for some cowboy duds and then to the corral for some horseback riding lessons. Peter, you're gonna need a lot more experience than you got at that county fair pony ride. The horses are full-grown here, and fast. Try not to fall off too often."

It was so hard to find good help.

* * *

Lieutenant Mike Norcroft knocked smartly on the office door of Major Don Knowbrese, his commanding officer at Texas Rangers Company A. He heard a friendly "come in" and entered the room.

"Howdy, Mike. How's the Brecker case goin'?" Don offered him the chair in front of his modest and almost-neat desk.

"That's what I'm here about, sir. While you were out this morning, I took an initiative and now I need some backup." Norcroft explained the deal he'd cut with the Bikini Cowgirl people. "Brecker accepted the offer to be on the show."

"So, what d'ya want backup for?"

"They've agreed to keep her quarantined, but they also agreed to allow a Ranger on set to make sure nobody feeds her any information. And if she's faking the amnesia, she might slip up at some point, off-camera. I'd like to have a witness there."

Major Knowbrese rubbed his chin.

"So, you're sayin' we need a man to spend twelve hours a day hangin' out at a reality show, with nothin' to do but watch a dozen half-nekkid cowgirls."

"That's right, sir. It's a depraved assignment but somebody's got to do it."

"Hmm… It'd be a shame to ask one of the Rangers to volunteer—they all have families, they'd get in trouble with the wife fer sure. Though they'd probably take it on for duty's sake."

"They would, sir, they're all dedicated to the service. But we've already pulled them away from their districts for a few days guarding Brecker in the hospital."

Knowbrese nodded thoughtfully.

"I hate to do this to ya, son, but it sounds like you'd be the best choice. You've been on the case all along, and you're not married."

"Well, I'm willing to do what's necessary, sir."

"It'll be long hours—would overtime pay make it easier to take?"

"That would offset some of the hardship, sir, yes."

Knowbrese let a smile creep into the corners of his mouth and eyes.

"Alright, Lieutenant, consider yourself assigned. Find out what happened out there. If anyone can suffer through this ordeal, you can."

"Yes, sir. I won't let you down."

Chapter 8

For her first appearance on camera in front of Muddy Bootes and his accomplices, Meg would have preferred a Kevlar one-piece to the skimpy nylon number supplied by the producers. But it was Bikini Cowgirl, after all, and except for the lack of a tan, she looked good in it. She'd stayed in shape during her sunless years in Boston.

She donned her new boots and hat, which fit perfectly thanks to the apparently resourceful wardrobe department, despite Meg's insistence on wearing a half-dozen tin-copper alloy barrettes. She didn't think Muddy was the type for a psychological attack with a voice sug-jector, but she'd salvaged her barrettes from the hospital for protection just in case. She was pretty sure the wardrobe folks couldn't come up with a tin-foil Stetson.

Pavel was waiting and perked up when he saw her step out of her cabin. Meg was tempted to think it was lust but reckoned it was more like greed. She could almost see the dollar signs in his eyes.

"You look good, Meg, very good. Better than others. You will do well on our show."

Meg hoped so—the stakes were pretty high. Life-and-death, in fact.

"You will partake in skill competitions, mock commercial photo and video shoots for various products, and conversations we call barn chats, where Clint, our host, will interview small group of contestants. You are familiar with Clint, I believe?"

"Yeah, I am."

"Good, you will also speak with Clint in one-on-one interviews, using his own camera. They will be evenings, we will not warn you. We want spontaneity. This works for you?"

"Sure." As if she had a choice. Actually, her choice would be to talk with Clint one-on-one, but without the camera. She'd be on the lookout for opportunities to reach out to him.

They walked together to the Pearland Guest Ranch fire pit for a hastily added get-acquainted session. Bikini-clad cowgirls were lounging around on log benches, in a variety of poses but all delivering the same withering glare at the newcomer. Clearly they'd gotten a heads-up. Several cameramen were filming, catching every visual dagger; this was reality TV heaven.

"Good afternoon, ladies!" Pavel announced, "Now I would like to introduce newest cowgirl: Meg. Please give her warm welcome."

The other girls applauded half-heartedly, while Clint stood to the side, studying her. She returned the favor—Clint looked unnervingly like Tommy, and in fact was now the same age as his brother was when he took his last dive. Clint was more rodeo cowboy than Tommy's marine biologist; he wore more rugged jeans and fancier boots, and his belt buckle was huge, with an engraving of a two-man steer-roping event. His hat was serious rodeo quality, perfectly formed and worn at the perfect angle.

"I think introductions all around are in order," Clint said, and with a nod, "Meg, why don't you go first?"

Meg took a seat on the circle and turned on the charm as best she could.

"Hi, ladies. As Mr. Nepovim said, I'm Meg. I was born and raised on a family farm outside of Alvin. Lost my mom when I was eight, raised by my Pappy, who taught me everything I know. You mighta heard of me before; apparently I disappeared a few years ago along with my boyfriend Tommy. He's Clint's brother, by the way." She gestured toward Clint, who nodded politely.

"I'd like to thank y'all for findin' me on the beach. I wish I could tell you how I got there, but I don't remember anything since Tommy and I went divin'. Before that, I was tryin' to get my master's degree at A&M, but I'm guessin' I musta flunked out. If I can win this competition, I'm aimin' to use the prize money for tuition, and try again. If I don't win, I'm hopin' I'll at least have a few new friends." She mustered as sincere a smile as she could and sprayed it around the circle. It was not returned. Tough crowd.

The others introduced themselves, but since this was old news to the viewers, they had to keep it brief. There were twelve of them; it seemed like the casting director tried to fill out a few categories.

There were the cowgirls you'd expect: Dakota was a wholesome, outdoorsy type, complete with freckles and a big Texas smile; Cassidy was similar but solid muscle—a little big for the bikini competition but could probably drop a steer in 8 seconds; Gabriella was Latina with a kick-boxer's body and the intensity to match.

Then there were the soft, sexy types: Sarah Mae with her playmate body and flirty smile; Riley was a classic airhead beauty, but Meg suspected that was just an act; and Dallas looked like she just stepped out of her daddy's Mercedes and expected everyone to treat her accordingly.

There were oddballs, of course, just to keep things entertaining: Faith was a strict Baptist and had big doubts about being there—she was the only one wearing a one-piece, and you could almost see her halo tarnishing every time the camera panned across her mostly covered skin; Jasmine, a fit Black girl, had been adopted from Houston's inner city and found her bliss on a Wharton County goat farm; and Bobbie Jo was big, and angular, and spoke in deep tones—her pre-op name was just plain Bob.

But Meg figured the hardest ones to win over were the bad girls, clearly chosen to antagonize everyone else: Lisa was a wiry little girl with a crew cut and a troublemaking glint in her shifting eyes; Samantha was a Goth, cowgirl style, dressed in black from hat to boots; and then there was Mattie. Mattie was older than the others, even a couple years older than Meg. Other than stretch marks from her baby, she'd kept her bikini body—but apparently not her husband, lost to a sweet young thing who was probably very much like the other contestants. Mattie had revenge on her mind.

That was okay with Meg. She had revenge on her mind, too.

* * *

Pavel Nepovim leaned back in his chair and studied the bulletin board on the wall, with its array of cowgirl contestant photos. His predecessor was clearly a hack—the character types he'd pinned below each photo were all so cliché.

Of course, his predecessor didn't have the luxury of literally killing a character within two hours of plot development. Unfortunately, in this case, neither did Pavel.

But that didn't stop him from considering the possibilities. Just for fun.

Tombstone Cowgirl? Blazing Girdles?

He'd need a killer. The mysterious Goth could be a shadowy assassin. Or the dyke lesbian a murderous militant feminist, wiping out her male-worshiping sisters. The bitter divorcee was fine as a bitter divorcee, but in Pavel's movie, she'd be homicidally bitter. His favorite was the drag-queen-turned-cowgirl—cold-blooded murders beneath a glam veneer—delicious.

The victims were easy; reality character clichés were interchangeable with horror film victims anyway. The religious nut praying in vain for salvation; the flirty slut's final, desperate effort to seduce her killer; the daddy's girl attempting to buy her life; the wholesome girl-next-door who naively walks into the deadly trap first.

And the mean girl, smarter than she acts, who knows the others will be killed but doesn't warn them in order to save her own skin.

Of course, that doesn't work.

He was musing about how he'd kill the hard-working immigrant, the inner city fish out of water, and the tomboy, but he kept coming back to the girl with the mysterious past.

Meg.

It didn't really matter how she died if she was lying about the amnesia—he'd think of something. While she was passing Muddy's lie detector test, he'd been looking for mistakes. But she'd been consistent.

Clint was the key. He looked just like his brother did when he disappeared. He had to be stirring Meg's feelings for Tommy, and that might just dredge up her lost memories. Or expose her lies about losing them.

What if Clint acted like he was attracted to her?

He was a loyal employee and would do whatever he was asked,

according to Muddy. But would the reality show audience buy a budding romance between two beautiful people who've lost the same loved one?

Pavel chuckled.

Of course they would. Audiences bought all the other ridiculous premises reality shows came up with. This one actually had some plausibility. And with careful editing of Clint's acting and Meg's reactions, Pavel could make it look real. That's what reality shows were for, after all.

In fact, the people who didn't expect Meg to abandon Tommy so quickly would still believe the story—they'd just hate her for it. There'd be social media wars about it. People would download the latest episode to see what the traitorous bitch was up to now. Conflict was money.

Of course, if enough people hated her, they might vote her off early. Pavel was fine with that—it was the other excuse for turning her story into a real snuff film.

* * *

Meg and the other cowgirls gathered near the corral for the afternoon photo shoot, a mock fashion magazine feature. They'd all used the last hour to achieve that perfect, casual-but-still-gorgeous look. Each girl had a fashion consultant and could get just about anything she wanted, as long as it fit her on-camera persona. If it didn't, the consultant would suggest otherwise.

Today's shoot was on horseback, so they were all in riding gear. 'Course, "riding gear" was kind of a loose definition. Riley and Dallas wore the popular cutoff shorts with a blouse just long enough to act like a micro-miniskirt, exposing tanned thighs and calves above their ornate boots. Sarah Mae's blouse was shorter, no doubt to show off her lace-trimmed daisy dukes. Samantha's outfit was similar, but the blouse and lace were black. Most of the other girls were in full-length boot-cut jeans and embroidered button-down shirts—though every one of them except Faith tied the shirt for a bare midriff look. Even Lisa, who wore a tee-shirt, had it knotted to one side to expose her belly. Jewel-encrusted belts and buckles sparkled in the late-day sun. Everyone knew this was about sexy, cowgirl style.

Meg looked around for Clint. He was tracked by camera #2 as usual, and surrounded by a team of sound and communication techs. Could they make it any harder to get a private message to him?

Next to him was a Texas Ranger and a reporter talking into a hand-held microphone for what looked like her own private cameraman. And next to her was Howie.

Hot damn! He'd gotten onto the set. Maybe he could connect with Clint.

The reporter stopped talking and turned to Howie, pressing against him and whispering in his ear. He must have been wearing his cologne.

Meg would've thought he'd leave the stuff at the motel before walking onto a ranch full of cowgirls that weren't Meg.

* * *

Howie peered around the uniformed bulk of the Texas Ranger and took in the glorious view. Okay, so there were a dozen gorgeous girls in hot outfits milling around, but the best part was the thirteenth. Meg looked beautiful.

Arlene introduced Howie to the Eurosexual director. Pavel offered a brusque handshake and said they were welcome on set provided they stayed out of mike and camera range, didn't bring in any food, drugs, or alcohol, and didn't talk to Meg.

"If you are caught talking to her, it will be your funeral," he said with a nod toward the Ranger. As Pavel turned on a heel to organize the session, Howie shot a look at Arlene that said "You promised access to Meg." Arlene shrugged.

Howie took inventory of alternative interviewees. The girls wouldn't know anything about the doings behind the scenes. If one got friendly with Meg maybe he could use her to pass messages; he was glad he'd worn the cologne. There was also the host and crew, who probably did know some dirty little backstage secrets. They were all male though; he'd have to depend on his New York Jewish charm to win them over.

Miracles could happen.

As he periodically let his gaze fall onto Meg, he noticed two other people doing the same thing. The Ranger rarely took his eyes off her to ogle the other cowgirls; ogling Meg was his job. But as host, Clint Owen probably should have been a more equal-opportunity lecher. He watched Meg as much as he could get away with.

At the first break, Howie wandered over and caught Clint at the coffee urn. The cowboy looked Howie up and down, showing no sign of interest. Howie offered a hand.

"Hi, I'm Howie Friedman. Writer with Dirt TV, working with Arlene Harrington on publicity." Clint accepted the handshake with a crushing squeeze.

"Clint Owen. What can I do for you, Mr. Friedman?"

"First of all, you can call me Howie."

"I suppose I could do that, and you can call me Clint. You know, you're not the kinda fella I'd've expected Miz Harrington to be bringin' around here. You're from New York, right?"

"You have a good ear, Clint." He'd have to be deaf to not know Howie was a New Yorker. "I was wondering if I could ask you about Meg Brecker. Quite a surprise to find her on the beach the other day?"

"Yep. Kinda figured I'd never see her again."

"Did you know her well?"

"Nah, I only met her a few times. Gotta admit though, now that I'm seein' her up close, I'm kinda jealous of my big bro." He winked.

Howie suddenly understood the feeling.

"Must be strange to be jealous of a guy who's missing," Howie said. Not to mention a guy who's dead.

"I guess," Clint replied, reflecting back the coldness of the question. "So, I got some hostin' to do, maybe we can talk more some other time?" He was already turning to leave.

"Yeah, thanks."

Howie watched the rugged rodeo star approach the cluster of cowgirls. Meg was watching him, too, every step of the way.

Chapter 9

Arlene set up in front of the training track where the horseback fashion photo shoot had gone down earlier. The setting sun was at the right angle to give her a golden glow—there was no need for portable lighting, just a soft reflector, barely off-camera, to balance the shadows on her face. Her guy was good at this.

"This is Arlene Harrington for Dirt TV, broadcasting live from the Pearland Guest Ranch in Pearland, Texas, where the Next Bikini Cowgirl competition is underway. The big news is the addition of Meg Brecker to the cast. Brecker, as you're no doubt aware, is suffering from amnesia since she and Tommy Owen went missing three years ago. Meg is joined by another new guest, Lieutenant Norcroft of the Texas Rangers. He's here to keep an eye on Brecker and seems to be doing a good job of that, despite a dozen other distractions." He was also doing a good job of keeping Meg away from Arlene and Howie. And that kept a disappointed Howie away from Arlene.

Fucking Rangers.

Arlene nodded at her director and waited for the indication that clips of the day's activity were rolling picture-in-picture behind her.

"As you can see, the girls looked stunning at today's fashion shoot in a variety of outfits, posing on and off horseback and around the corral. My personal favorite was Dakota in jeans and a plaid shirt that said she's spent her whole life on horseback, but the guys in the audience might prefer Sarah Mae's daisy dukes look, leaning on the rail and daring you to come on over and flirt for a while. Viewer voting starts at midnight; be sure to text for *your* favorite. But don't miss tomorrow's pistol shooting competition; these girls will be aiming to win."

Her director held up a hand and pointed behind her.

"Hold on," she said, "Something's happening." Then she heard it, hoof beats approaching from her right. As the camera panned away from her, she followed its gaze toward the track behind her.

A huge chestnut-colored horse galloped toward her, ridden by Peter Long, one of the new cowboys they'd hired. She thought he was just an actor, but apparently he was also a trick rider. He slid off the saddle to the right, hanging onto the reins with one hand and waving the other wildly, then bounced off a fencepost onto the saddle again as the horse passed behind her. She turned the other way and saw him slide down to the other side of the horse and drag himself underneath until he was out of sight behind the cloud of dust. It seemed painful, but Arlene figured trick riders knew what they were doing. She returned her gaze to the camera, maintaining her composure.

"Well, as you can see, the Bikini Cowgirl show is full of surprises. Check out tonight's barn chat and tomorrow's competition to catch the latest antics. This is Arlene Harrington for Dirt TV."

* * *

Meg did a quick costume change into a bikini after the horseback photo shoot and headed to the chat barn for what was billed as an informal conversation among some of the contestants. The reality was not so informal: the event was recorded by a full contingent of cameras and microphones, moderated by Clint, and observed by Pavel and Muddy. And the Ranger. Meg took her place along with the rugged-looking Cassidy and Dakota and black-clad Samantha.

The seating consisted of hay bales carefully stacked to look random. In the stall behind them, one of the better-behaved horses munched his oats peacefully. He was a lot less fidgety than the cowgirls—the hay was kinda itchy for sitting on in a bikini.

"Howdy, ladies," Clint began, offering a symbolic tip of his hat with a touch to the crown. "We're figurin' on gettin' to know y'all a little better tonight, and givin' you a chance to size up the competition a bit. So, let me start with this question: What makes you think you can win this?"

He tossed a horseshoe into the middle of the circle, spinning it like a Frisbee. It landed with a puff of sawdust, the open arms pointing to Dakota.

"You first, Dakota."

Dakota gave the camera an "aw-shucks" shrug and a freckled smile, and glanced around the circle.

"I ain't nuthin' special, I reckon. I grew up just a few hours west of here, helpin' my folks with the horses. I love horses, and I've done just about everything you can do on a horse. I've won the barrel race at a few county rodeos, but I ain't never been on TV before now." She lowered her head a bit. "T'be honest, I'm a mite nervous about the whole thing."

Meg could see Pavel nodding appreciatively—he had his Miss Wholesome, the nice-girl underdog everybody could root for.

Cassidy was up next. She gave the camera a hardened stare for a moment, before standing up and striking a pose for the group. She was a lot heavier than the other girls, but not fat—just solid muscle.

"This here's a real cowgirl body. I'm not a fashion model who happens to love horses—I'm a working ranch hand and I've got the muscles and the calluses to prove it. I think there's nothing sexier than dropping a steer in 8.3 seconds. Or a cowboy." She shot a quick wink at Clint, almost as if challenging him to a wrestling match. Or something.

Cassidy would be tough to beat on skills, but Meg figured the audience would pull for the fashion models.

Samantha's turn started with an intense stare at Clint. He seemed unnerved by this Goth cowgirl—maybe it was her black Stetson, or more likely, the Acora death-metal tattoo on a canvas of ghastly-white skin. She swiped an evil smile across the rest of the girls.

"I enjoy darkness," she said, almost whispering. "I'm not afraid of it. I'm not afraid of anything." She smiled again, wider, almost maniacal. "But you all are. You're afraid of me. That's why you'll lose."

Whoa. Meg wasn't sure what that all meant, but she had to admit, Samantha was right. Meg *was* afraid of her.

Pavel was grinning from earring to earring.

Meg didn't lay claim to any special advantage, but she did say she had motivation—she needed the prize money to finish college. She didn't mention that she needed to stay in contention to stay alive.

"What do you think about Bikini Cowgirl competition so far?" Clint asked. "Be honest."

"Honestly?" Cassidy said. "It's all bikini, no cowgirl."

"Yeah," added Dakota. "I'm itchin' to show some skills. You don't tell us anything about what's comin' up."

Samantha waved a finger at the others, as if casting a spell.

"You fear the unknown. They want you to be fearful."

Meg shrugged.

"I'm with Cassidy on this one. I kinda feel like I'm locked in the barn. I lost three years of my life already, I'd kinda like to get back to it."

Cassidy looked Meg in the eye.

"You could always just withdraw. Get on with your life and let us get on with the competition. It was supposed to be the twelve of us—nobody's happy about you showing up and stealing the show."

"Thirteen contestants seems a mite unlucky to me," Dakota added.

"I think thirteen is an excellent number," Samantha whispered.

* * *

Howie sat down with the Houston Urban Legionnaires in the situation room behind the Trinity Bay Players' stage.

"So, we know Muddy Bootes was involved when Tommy Owen was killed. We don't know if Pavel Nepovim was, too, but since they both interviewed Meg, it's a pretty good bet he at least knows about it. I guess we need to dig a little deeper into Muddy and Pavel."

Devon took a drag on his unfiltered Camel and blew a plume across the table. He'd been typing on his laptop as Howie spoke.

"Muddy is an ex-roughneck, has a long résumé of oil rig work. First non-oil-biz job was at the Disaster Channel. Pavel is a little more mysterious—he's got a few indie film credits but nothing mainstream. From these titles I'm guessing he does porn."

Howie nodded.

"Makes sense. The shirt he wore today was so loud it was obscene."

"Interesting. He just flew in this morning to take over as director."

"That's not good," Howie mused. "His first order of business was to recruit Meg."

"The question is, what's his next order of business for Meg?"

"I couldn't dig in with either of them on set," Howie said. "They threw me a few crumbs; let me talk to the girls and the crew, but beyond that, nothing."

Spike suggested a drone with a long range camera and microphone to eavesdrop. Howie thanked her for the idea but pointed out that most nefarious plotting takes place indoors.

"Maybe we can infiltrate," Spike said. "If I was, say, Muddy's props assistant, I could keep an eye on him. I'm qualified, I've done it all from Broadway to Hollywood."

"Another great idea. But qualifications when there's no job openings are like bagels when you're not hungry. I can't believe Muddy doesn't have who he needs already."

Devon had been typing away as usual.

"Apparently, Reality Web just advertised for props help for the Bikini Cowgirl show." He pointed to the job search website on his screen. "With a little help from their local Urban Legion hacker."

Howie examined the fake ad, which looked like it was posted by Reality Web headquarters in Vegas. In other words, posted by Charlie Stewart. Muddy would probably obey his boss.

"Okay, that was impressive, Devon, but it'll attract other applicants. Not to mention an angry phone call from Charlie Stewart."

"That would be true," Devon said, "if this ad showed up anywhere but at the Bikini Cowgirl ranch. Other applicants, and Charlie, will never see it."

"So how do we explain why only one person showed up for the position?"

Devon frowned, thinking.

"How 'bout we make it minimum wage?"

Howie shook his head.

"Lots of desperate people around."

"Long hours?"

"That's more money."

"No air conditioning? It *is* Houston."

"Air conditioning they've got—it's also the twenty-first century. Not to mention April."

"How about I transpose digits in the farm-to-market road number, and only accept applicants in person? Spike is the only one who's smart enough to figure out the correct address."

"Huh," Howie said, nodding. "That could work. Spike, how quickly can you put your résumé together?"

"No need," Devon said, walking to the printer to grab the paper as it slid into the output tray. "I've got it right here."

* * *

Clint switched on his Stetson-mounted GoPro camera as he approached Meg's cabin. They'd warned the cowgirls about the random interviews so they wouldn't be in their pajamas, or underwear, or even in the buff, when Clint came in with portable camera blazing. Dallas had ignored that warning, probably on purpose, and not only answered the door in a sheer nightie, but didn't cover up during the interview. With pixelation censorship, it made for an excellent webcast moment. Dallas toyed with him, strutting her not-yet-blurred stuff, and Clint had a tough time maintaining his composure. His awkward reaction got more rave reviews than Dallas's soft porn performance.

The interviews were unscripted but not unplanned. Each girl was chosen by the show for facets of her life that were likely to create good drama. And Clint went into each interview with a set of questions intended to trigger that drama.

In Meg's case, the questions on Pavel's cheat sheet were about her amnesia, of course, but also her feelings for Tommy—and Clint's feelings for Meg. Pavel was setting up a romance angle.

"Just do method acting," he had said. "Fall in love with her but be shy to admit it." While it seemed crazy, Pavel was the director; Clint intended to do his job, even if it involved a role in the drama.

Was he a good enough actor? Wouldn't Meg see through it? And how could she possibly show any interest in Clint? If she was telling the truth, she'd only been missing Tommy for two days. Pretty quick rebound.

But if she wasn't telling the truth, she'd been missing Tommy for three years, which was enough time to get over him and possibly take interest in Clint. That would be a slip-up. Maybe this romance plot wasn't so crazy after all. If she was lying, Pavel wanted to flush her out. So did Clint.

He knocked on the cabin door, and Meg opened it, still dressed in her barn-chat bikini. She led him to the couch and they sat down at opposite ends.

"Well, Meg, it's good to see you again."

She let out an embarrassed laugh.

"I guess! Good to see you, too, though it doesn't seem like it's been very long."

"How does that feel?"

"It's confusing. Like time hasn't passed, even though everyone is tellin' me it has. And no one'll let me see the news or anything to prove it. Is this like that Jim Carrey movie where he's the only one who doesn't know his life is fake?"

Was that movie older than three years? Yes. She hadn't tripped up. Yet.

"The Truman Show. This isn't a movie." He grinned. "Although, if it *was* the Meg Show, I'd be a paid actor, and I'd have to say that."

Meg grinned back.

"Guess there's no use goin' there."

"Do you miss Tommy?" Geez, Pavel was on the nose.

"I will, I guess; it seems too soon now. Do you miss him?"

Clint didn't expect personal questions back. How would he react if he were in love with Meg?

"Of course I do. But I kinda got to acceptin' that he was gone. You might have to get used to that, too."

The rest of the interview involved amnesia-related questions to catch Meg lying, and a few about Tommy, giving Clint a chance to let his own "feelings" for Meg slip out. Meg cooperated nicely; in fact, she seemed almost too willing to let Clint talk about himself.

Her comment about the Truman Show still rattled around in his mind. Was Meg a paid actor, trying to set him up? That would explain the coincidence of her showing up on the beach. How about Dallas and her pixelated strip show? How much were Pavel and Muddy willing to manipulate reality around him?

Who was the Truman here?

* * *

After the interview, Meg closed the door and leaned against it. She was exhausted—Clint's questions were insidious, all looking for a slip on her part, requiring her to stay on her toes. She thought she'd pulled it off.

But while his questions mostly came from notes, and probably from Pavel, Clint sure acted personally interested in whether Meg's amnesia was a lie. It made sense, since she was the last person to see Tommy alive—he might consider her a suspect, like the Rangers did. That made it all the more urgent for her to talk with him in private.

She reached under the couch cushion and retrieved the note she'd written in lipstick on a paper towel. She was going to pass it to him at some point during the interview, out of sight of the camera. But before she got the chance, she had second thoughts.

Clint's comment about accepting that Tommy was gone made it seem like he knew his brother was dead. Which would explain why he dropped his crusade to continue the search. And meant he knew he was working for the killers.

Or even more appalling: Clint was Corporation, involved from the beginning, and the whole crusade was fake, to deflect suspicion. Now that she thought about it, Clint and Tommy didn't get along that well. And Tommy had told Clint they were going diving that day, so he could have passed the word to Muddy. But that was crazy. He wouldn't kill his own brother, would he?

She unfolded the towel and reread the message: *Urgent. We need to talk in private. Tell no one. No mikes or cameras.*

Before she could show this to Clint, she'd have to figure out whether he could be trusted, without letting it slip that she could not. And at the same time stay alive in the competition, so as to stay alive, period.

She tore the towel into small pieces and flushed them down the toilet.

Part II

"Bikini Cowgirls Bare All"
— Headline, The National Nose

Chapter 10

Lynn stretched out the kinks from her flight to Las Vegas as the rental car agent finalized the agreement on his tablet, noting the various dings and scratches on the car they gave her. She'd waived the high-cost insurance option and didn't want to be paying for previous customers' mistakes. There'd been a lot of those; this Altima had seen better days.

She stowed her luggage and squeezed behind the wheel—if this was a full-size, how tiny was a compact? The sedan fit her six-foot frame, but barely. On the other hand, it was a limo compared to the elderly Civic she drove at home.

"Is there anything else I can help you with, Ms. Grady?"

"I'm all set." Not really, but she had to put up a good front in Vegas. As she drove north along the Strip, she wondered what would make her stand out as a total newbie. A quick glance at the crowds on the sidewalk told her: everything. Her clothes were too frumpy, her skin was too pale, and she was at that awkward age— too old for a partying bachelorette and too young for a gambling grandma. Plus, she didn't smoke.

It is not shameful to be yourself, said Zen-mind. No, not shameful, she agreed, but a lot more difficult to run a covert mission. Did her Zen masters ever run covert missions? Maybe she could add Sun Tzu to her list of mental advisors; Lynn could use training in the art of war.

She turned the car over to the valet at Noir, the 1940s-detective-film-themed resort at the north end of the Strip. Roger had warned Lynn about Vegas hotels: once they got you inside, they tried to keep you there with a maze of casinos, bars, restaurants, and shopping malls, with no clocks or natural light to let you know you'd been there for days. But Noir was still a surprise.

Everything was done in black and white. The lobby was dark, with ominous shadows stretching across a wet asphalt floor punctuated by steaming manhole covers. Colorless neon signs flashed above, casting twisted silhouettes of fire escapes into alleyways. A vintage car with a teardrop profile, skinny tires, and wide whitewalls was parked near a gin-joint doorway. She'd done some research on the noir movie genre on the flight in; this place captured it perfectly.

Even the porters and desk clerks wore charcoal-gray suits with white shirts and black ties. Same with the other guests milling about the lobby. Lynn was thinking she should buy a colorless dress when she looked down at her burgundy blouse and blue jeans, which were no longer burgundy and blue, but black and gray.

How the—?

She pulled out her cell and called Roger.

"It's all black and white," she told him. He knew that. Of course. "How do they do it?"

"I love that place," he said, "At least I used to, when they let me into town. You probably know that an apple looks red because it reflects only the red color when hit by multichromatic light, like sunlight or fluorescent bulbs. You've also seen monochromatic sources, like LEDs and lasers, that only output one color. But Noir's lighting fixtures emit nonchromatic light, which has no colors in it at all, so everything looks black and white. Even an apple."

"But my phone screen is still in color."

"Right, because it has its own multichromatic backlight. But don't let them see you using it—they're pretty uptight about maintaining the atmosphere."

"Okay, I'll talk to you later." Lynn hung up and tucked the phone into her bag. She looked around again, noting the shadows, cigarette smoke, and sleazy saxophone music drifting through the lobby. Her lack of a tan was not a problem here, in fact, it seemed appropriate for a noir female character. All she needed was a trench coat.

She registered and gave her bags to a spiffy-looking bellhop, then rode the elevator, with its metal-arrow floor indicator, accordion-grid gate, and disinterested operator, to her floor. She let herself into her nonchromatic room and gave it a quick inspection. Venetian blind shadows? Check. Bare cupboard with whiskey bottle and two smudged glasses? Check. Ashtrays with cigarette butts? Check. But this was a nonsmoking room! Check: prop cigarette butts.

When she fired up her laptop, she noticed that the screen light made the actual wall color appear. It was dull green—she guessed that was the cheapest paint they could find, even cheaper than gray. No need to pay for better colors if you couldn't see 'em.

She sighed and brought up a browser to look in on the Bikini Cowgirls.

* * *

Pavel watched the scene on his smartphone. His cameraman had set up far enough away from the cowgirls that they wouldn't be aware of him. But the ultra-zoom lens was paired with image stabilization and a parabolic mike to make it seem like the camera was nearby. A truly candid shot of a casual conversation that looked fake candid. This reality TV stuff was heady.

Dakota was proclaiming her love for horse care.

"Once, I helped foal our mare. It was such a beautiful experience for everyone," she gushed.

"Oh, honey," Mattie said, "Some day you'll find out it's not so beautiful for the mare. My ex is a big guy, and my son was a bruiser even at birth."

Cassidy nodded, holding her hand up in front of her.

"And beautiful ain't the word that comes to mind when you're elbow-deep cleaning a gelding's sheath."

"Eww!" said Dallas and Sarah Mae in unison.

Bobbie Jo shook her head.

"I thought I was done with that kind of thing. Do you make him buy you dinner first?"

* * *

Bobbie Jo's comment reminded Lynn it was time for dinner, so she headed to the Noir dress shop for a slinky cocktail number. The last time she'd worn anything so sexy was at a Corporation-run French restaurant with gun-toting waiters. She smiled to recall her own ex drunkenly dissing the priceless but cheese-fouled brandy. At least he paid for dinner, or more likely, his Corporation expense account did.

She headed for the Confidential, the hotel restaurant that boasted the "authentic noir experience." Over a dinner she didn't have to order, since they never show that in the movies, she discovered that a woman eating alone was another thing that never happens in the movies. Or at least, not for long.

A handsome guy in a wet raincoat and fedora strolled up to the table. He took off the hat and glanced around the room.

"What's a nice dame like you doing in a joint like this?" he asked.

As a food critic, Lynn was used to eating alone and politely getting rid of opportunistic men who assumed she was looking for a dinner partner. But this situation called for a more cinematic response.

"Waiting for a nice guy to show up. That wouldn't be you."

The guy was cool—a little eyebrow raise was all he showed of the rejection.

"Well, I'll see ya around then, toots," he said, and wandered off to his next victim. Lynn watched him sizing up the room; there weren't many targets avail—

"Hey girly," said a short, solid man in a trench coat, hat in hand. "You look like you could use a sugar daddy to buy you that nice dinner." Lynn looked him over, then put on her girly-est voice.

"And you look like one of Daddy's goons—the little one— only much smaller."

The guy harrumphed and turned on his heel. Playing a tough noir dame was kind of fun, actually. She looked forward to the next round, which happened before she could swallow another bite.

"I didn't think I'd ever see a supermodel dining alone."

Supermodel?

"That's because we don't have supermodels in the 1940s. Take a hike, mister."

Amateur.

By then, the room had apparently run out of lady-killers and Lynn was able to finish her meal in peace.

She had time to catch the Cirque Noire late show. Unlike any other circus she'd seen, this one had a detailed plot. They hit all the noir movie conventions, including the hero narrating directly to the audience in first person (and getting knocked out in the second act), the loyal secretary, and the double-crossing femme fatale. After the show, she headed backstage to meet Burke Barrage, the Las Vegas Urban Legion boss and Cirque Noire hard-boiled detective.

* * *

It was a windy night in Sin City, the kind of wind that dries the frat-boy piss on the sidewalk before it can drag itself to the curb. I was relaxing in my dressing room after the show with my old friend Jim Beam. My performance was good, as always, but I had to admit, I was getting antsy. I needed a little action, a little more danger than I get from juggling shivs and roscoes on a tightwire thirty-five feet above the stage. I'm a professional acrobat. But I play a private detective. My name's Burke Barrage.

There was a rap on the door.

"Go away. I don't sign anything but paychecks."

"I'm not looking for an autograph, Mr. Barrage. I need your help. May I come in?"

She sounded tall, but maybe it was just that her voice was coming over the open transom. I never could resist a dame in distress, even if she looked down on me. They often did.

"It's open."

The first part of her that came through the door was a long, pale, pink gam that kept going until it disappeared under a cocktail dress along with her motive. The rest of her was just as long, capped by a halo of flame-red hair. But this angel was a little too dated to play the femme fatale.

I stood up to bounce her back out when she held up one of those long, pale, pink fingers, pointed it at me, and shoved it up her nose.

Damn! She was either an Urban Legionnaire or had remarkably bad personal habits. Maybe this was the action I was craving. I did a subtle nose dance but didn't cave yet.

"Where's your tin-foil topper?"

"My what?"

"Your hat. Don't play dumb with me, sister."

I wear a tin-copper-lined fedora whenever I'm out in Corporation territory, which is everywhere around here. If this Jane wasn't wearing metal, she'd be a roundheels for every voice sug-jector in Vegas—if not the casino gink planting bad-bet advice into her head, it'd be the buffet guy convincing her she already felt sick before she ate that lukewarm chicken parmesan.

"Ah," she said, demurely touching her curls. "It's micro-metallic hairspray. They tell me it doesn't take much metal with all these little antennas I've got going. And it's tinted red, so it even hides the gray."

I could buy that. Actually, I probably couldn't, unless her local Legion had a souvenir shop. But it might make a nice present for my girls—they hate having to wear their hats on a hot day. Which is most days around here. I'd look into it later.

"Welcome to Las Vegas, doll. Have a seat, and let's jaw."

She balanced on the edge of the low chair like it was a trapeze bar and she was about to dive into a full forward roll.

"I'm trying to find a man," she said. So was every skirt that sashayed into my office. "His name is Charlie Stewart."

So, a particular lug. Wonder what he did to her?

"Charlie Stewart. Ex-husband? Ex-boyfriend? Husband's ex-boyfriend?"

"He tried to kill some friends of mine. I want to know why. And stop him before he tries again."

Sounded like this dish was just what a hungry gumshoe ordered.

Chapter 11

Spike Stillgood sat respectfully at a break room table across from Muddy Bootes as he examined her résumé. The one-pager was packed with theatre and film credits, all very impressive, and all impossible to verify without some serious research. Some of them were true. Muddy looked up and studied her instead.

"I'm surprised Charlie set this up without tellin' me, but it's not the first time he's sent in help without me askin'. In fact, it ain't the first time this week. But he's the boss. And I have a project I need to focus on, so I can use a props assistant. But I don't think that's you."

Spike glared at him.

"With all my experience? I hope it's not just 'cause I'm Black. Or female."

Muddy laughed abruptly.

"What? No, Ms. Stillgood, I may be a good ol' boy, but I don't have a problem with any of that." He narrowed his eyes. "It's 'cause you're from New Orleans." He held the stare for a few seconds, then laughed again. "Just kiddin'. I don't care where you're from, either—except if it was Dallas."

Spike smiled politely.

"So, why don't you like me?"

"Oh, I like you fine. But I can't believe you've got what it takes. If I'm gonna trust my prop work to somebody, they gotta be creative, and fast. When I think of an effect, I need to improvise it now—there's no time for orderin' gear from supply houses."

"That's how I work," Spike responded coolly. "Always. How about a test? Come up with an effect, and I'll tell you how I'd do it. Fast."

Muddy looked intrigued.

"Let me think." He stared into space for a few moments before refocusing on her and smiling. "Okay, Ms. Stillgood, let's say we're shootin' a western gunfight, and I want stray bullets to kick up the sand around my cowgirl. What'd'ya got?"

Spike thought through some options. Solenoids with buried wires would work, but there wouldn't be any of those handy. Party poppers would be in stock at the local party store, but setting them off remotely was problematic. Firecrackers with long fuses, buried? Too loud, and maybe not available. She was staring at the cabinets behind Muddy, when she noticed what was sitting on the counter below it.

"Okay, how about I demonstrate?" she said, getting up.

"Demonstrate what?"

"Bullets in the sand."

"Here?"

Spike opened the cabinet, found a paper bowl, and dumped the sugar container into it. She grabbed an individual-serving liquid non-dairy coffee creamer and a hollow plastic stirrer, and returned to the table.

"Let's say this bowl of sugar is your sand," she said as she punched the stirrer through the coated paper lid of the creamer cup. "Film explosions usually use powdered non-dairy creamer, but we need the liquid. It's just as flammable, but also volatile enough to turn the straw into a wick that'll work even when buried. And this straw here is narrow enough to burn slowly; should give you about twenty seconds. So you light it—" she pulled a lighter out of her bag and lit the end of the straw "—bury it, and start filming." She pushed the creamer cup and burning fuse into the bowl of sugar and covered it over. "Pretty soon, you got your bullets in the sand."

They sat looking at the bowl for about fifteen seconds until a small pop blasted a spray of sugar upward and outward. Spike struggled to suppress a laugh—Muddy was covered with the white granules. He could tell.

"Don't laugh at me," he said, smiling. "You look even funnier. More contrast."

Spike matched his smile as she brushed sugar from her face and hair.

"So, Mr. Bootes, did I pass the test?"

"Yep. And you can call me Muddy. Welcome aboard."

"Thanks. You can call me Spike."

Muddy led her down the hall to a makeshift office. He grabbed an engraved wooden box with brass fittings and set it on the table.

"Here's your first assignment." He opened the lid—the box had a felt-lined insert with a dozen slots in it. "This is for the classic revolvers we're usin' for a shootin' competition this afternoon. You may have heard we have a new cowgirl in the cast. This needs one more slot. Can you do it?"

"How soon?"

"Three hours."

"Yup."

Spike's estimate included time for a short break the moment Muddy stepped away from his office. While he went to the mailroom to pick up an overnight delivery, she snapped a picture of the Bluetooth address printed on the AC power adapter for his laptop, and set up a direct audio communication link from the adapter microphone to her smartphone. She set the phone to be in voice-activated record mode for the rest of the day.

* * *

The Grady dame showed up for our morning appointment draped in an emerald green knee-length dress—it was probably sold as a midi, but her knees and her hips were keeping their distance. She wondered how a square like me wound up in a shady business like the Urban Legion. It was easy: after I backed my 18-wheeler over a dozen motorcycles at a truck stop, the Corporation Motorcycle Club came after me. I made my way to Vegas and hooked up with an Elvis impersonator by the name of D.B. Cooper. He'd anted up the two hundred large to start the Legion operation back in the '70s.

We found the team in the practice gym as usual. I steered Grady around to meet the major talent.

Deanna Desque was first; she's our computer whiz. In the ring she plays my neglected girl Friday, always pining away for the attention that goes to flashier, wealthier, unhealthier broads. She was a nuclear egghead at Arizona State. She crapped out on cold fusion but got tepid fusion to work—well enough to turn the heads of the Corporation's Fossil Fuel Cartel. Next thing she knew she was belted into a '67 Chevy Impala convertible with a Jet Assisted Take Off unit strapped to it, speeding down a desert straightaway with a cliff in the crosshairs. The JATO kicked on and the car took off, well, like a rocket. But the G-forces snapped the seat and belt brackets and she tumbled out kisser-over-keister. The upholstery saved her skin as she hit the roadway, while the rocket car planted itself into the cliff and became an urban legend.

Next up was Maggie Palms—our weapons expert. When she plays the femme fatale, her body is her weapon and she's expert at that, too. Maggie got wind of the Chiropractic Cartel pushing futons and beanbag chairs, so they tied a ribbon on her, tossed her into the back seat of a Caddie convertible, and turned it into a concrete cocktail. The story became the urban legend about a jealous husband and a gift car. But Maggie's a contortionist—she squeezed under the rear seatback into the trunk and split the scene after dark.

I noted her giving Grady a mental pat-down—I figured she didn't spot any concealed juggling ball grenades because she finally extended a hand.

"What caliber is that handbag?" Maggie asked.

Grady eyeballed the bag like the rookie clown in a janitor bit when he sees his first broom.

"Caliber? It's just a handbag, I hope. I bought it at a Noir shop."

Maggie shrugged.

"Let me know if you want it weaponized."

Grady begged off, alleging martial arts training, but that didn't win Maggie over. You can only get so far with a smile, a long reach, and a Tibetan heart punch.

I spotted Jack Marcel, our logistics specialist, in the props area. He took a dare as a kid and got his tongue stuck to a frozen railroad track when the 3:15 came through and chopped it off. So he's a natural mime. He's the street contact in the show, my wire for the inside dope on what's going down in the city. But as a mime, it's tough to get the story straight. We play that part for laughs.

He was polishing the inside of his invisible box, so I waved and waited for him, but Grady barged past me to shake hands. I flinched at the sound of shattering glass—it was too thin to cut her, but my wallet was even thinner, and that box wasn't cheap.

Grady froze and gaped at the floor around her. The chick wasn't wise to mime props.

Jack was livid. He yelled, took a breath every few words, waved his arms and stomped around, but the only sound was the crunch of mime glass under his feet.

"What happened?" Grady asked.

"You just smashed a fifteen-hundred-dollar mime prop," I told her. She wasn't buying it, despite the shards of evidence all over the floor. Though, to be fair, they *were* invisible.

"Mime props are made of anti-reflective glass," I told her. "Like the anti-reflective coating on eyeglasses, but nix the eyeglasses. It's real thin, and real invisible. And real fragile."

Grady shook her head.

"I thought mimes just fake all those things. Boxes, ropes, balloons…"

"All made of mime glass, doll. Nobody could fake that stuff so well. Nobody does. Welcome to the world of illusion."

I gave the gym a once-over—the friendly mood had shattered along with the invisible box. I warned Grady to keep an eye peeled for the mime prop storage areas, marked with black-and-white-striped spike tape on the floor.

I signaled Deanna to follow us and showed Grady out, in the harsh silence of our screaming mime.

* * *

Lynn followed Burke and Deanna along the Noir casino, past the hotel tower entrance and the food court, and into the Christian Science Reading Room. There was no one in there. They moved to the back and behind a massive bookshelf, where Burke pressed a hidden button. With a quiet groan, a smaller shelf slid upward, and the Legionnaires stepped into an elevator.

"The Reading Room was my idea," Burke said. "I figured none

of these hotel guests were here for spiritual enlightenment. We can come and go like lady luck in a poker game."

"How do you fund the place? D.B. Cooper's two hundred grand wouldn't go very far."

"He grew that stake at the roulette tables by way of a few friendly bystanders with electromagnets in their pockets. But the casinos caught on. Now we sell contact lenses for pro golfers, shows 'em a grid when they read the green. Takes their putting to a whole new level, if you get my drift. We sell 'em for millions—the pros can spring big for 'em as long as we keep it all on the down-low. The rules don't allow that kind of chisel."

The elevator descended, but that was all Lynn could tell. There were no indicators or buttons anywhere. When the doors opened again, she felt like an Urban Legionnaire.

The Vegas Legion headquarters had as much gear as the Cambridge underwater location. There was no skylight or hot tub, but it looked functional. And unlike the hotel above, the blinking lights and computer screens were all in color.

"First thing to do when checking out an operation is to look in the front door," Burke said. "Deanna, let's eyeball this Bikini Cowgirl show's M.O."

Girl Friday Deanna Desque sat down at a keyboard and brought up the latest webcast video. The cowgirls were doing a hat fashion shoot, and the camera caught some of them discussing hatband styles. Gabriella had beads in Mexican flag colors, Dallas had dollar signs, Faith had crosses, and Samantha had pentagrams. Lynn pointed out Meg as the Urban Legionnaire in jeopardy—Meg was explaining that her wardrobe designer insisted on the needlepoint mermaids circumnavigating her crown.

"Maybe you're really a mermaid," Samantha said, "and you've been underwater this whole time."

"That would explain my tan," Meg agreed, grinning.

Faith didn't get the joke, chiding the two for believing in mermaids. Samantha defended herself by pointing out that, like Faith, she believed in the devil.

Burke had seen enough, and Deanna closed the video. Lynn noted to herself that Meg wasn't underwater all that time, but underground. She surveyed the windowless high-tech headquarters. Even as a newbie Legionnaire, she'd already spent a lot of time underground herself.

She kind of liked it.

Deanna looked up the official Reality Web phone number and put a physical tracer on the call as Burke dialed it. The call was automatically blind forwarded to some unknown location and reached an answering machine. At ten o'clock in the morning. Everyone in the room agreed: that was suspicious.

"Let's see if they use Employee Data Processing for payroll and human resources," Deanna said. She typed a few commands and sat back. "Breaking their encryption won't take long. I've got a million computers working on it."

Lynn looked around again.

"Where are they?"

Deanna smiled.

"A whole lot of people have signed up to help find aliens with the Search for Extra-Terrestrial Intelligence project. They all run the SETI@home software, analyzing signals from space whenever their users aren't actively surfing Facebook or downloading porn. I happen to have a backdoor key to divert those machines to any algorithm I want on that network. Breaking the EDP employee database key is a great way to use SETI@home."

Deanna's technical prowess and inadvertent condescending tone reminded Lynn of Roger.

"My partner in Boston is going to want that key," Lynn said.

After five minutes and a few sips of coffee and tea, Lynn and the Vegas Legionnaires were looking at a detailed Reality Web payroll.

"Okay, Charlie Stewart is pulling in two mill as the big cheese at Reality Web," Burke said. "No surprise. Let's see who works for him."

"There's Pavel," Lynn noted, "just hired yesterday." Clint Owen was in there, and James Bootes. The "Muddy" was not captured in the data. "Deanna, can you tell what Charlie was doing before he started Reality Web? Like, back when Tommy Owen got killed?"

Deanna was already typing the query, and soon a screen full of records scrolled up the monitor.

Charlie Stewart hadn't always been a network chief. He'd worked his way up, starting out as a reporter, and then a news director, for the Disaster Channel. James "Muddy" Bootes began working for him there. And during that stint, the channel covered the huge Tyler County brush fire.

Would Stewart start a fire just to give his news channel something to cover? And even so, arson to create a newsworthy brush fire was one thing; why go to the trouble of dropping a certain grad student scuba diver onto it?

"Deanna," Burke said as he grabbed his fedora, "be a sweetheart and text me the Reality Web office address. It's time someone paid Charlie Stewart a visit."

"I'll join you," Lynn said.

"No you won't, sweet-cheeks. This is a solo operation."

* * *

I printed up a few bogus Chamber of Commerce business cards and stopped by the Las Vegas Reality Web headquarters, in a low-rise office building just west of the Strip. I intended to talk to everyone in the building so Stewart wouldn't get wise to someone snooping Reality Web in particular.

There were six businesses listed on the directory, so I started with Suite A, Fluff Packaging. I had the lowdown on Fluff from Legion intel—they supplied all those one-sheet-at-a-time facial tissue boxes, engineered to scrape dust into the air when you pull a tissue, to make you sneeze again, so you need another tissue. The Paper Products Cartel loves them.

The lobby was deserted, but a bell on the door announced my presence. A bombshell blonde with a business blazer and matching expression stepped out of the back room.

"Welcome to Fluff Packaging," she said, taking a seat behind the reception counter. "My apologies for stepping away. May I help you?"

I handed her a card and my equally phony line about polling

executives for the Chamber. Would she be so kind as to let me interview the boss?

The looker would not be so kind. She told me the boss was only in the office on occasion, and this was not such an occasion. She promised he'd call me; I said thanks and took my leave.

Suite B was Sports Sciences. Another shady outfit I'd gotten wind of before. They make Preparation S, to help athletes hide their steroid use. Makes the drug tests come out clean, and re-enlarges their testicles. It's a growing business.

That lobby was also empty, and a bell gave me away. The same blonde emerged from what added up to be the same backroom for all of the companies in the joint.

She gave me an embarrassed but disarming smile, even though I wasn't armed.

"Okay, you caught us. This is a virtual office, I'm the only one here."

"And the only occasion that the boss comes around is never, right?"

Another guilty smile.

"Yes."

I held up five more business cards like a poker hand.

"Will it do any good to give you these for all the missing bosses in the building?"

"It might," she said. "Probably not. Someone does come to pick up the mail every now and then."

I laid my busted poker hand on the counter and tipped my hat.

"Thanks," I said as I headed for the door. "Don't work too hard."

She wouldn't. With blind forwarding, she didn't even have to answer the phones.

Two facts were staring me in the face: Reality Web hung out with a bunch of Corporation gangsters, and Charlie Stewart did not want visitors.

Chapter 12

Muddy gathered his thoughts as Pavel took a seat across the table.

"What is on your mind, Muddy?"

"Remember during the barn chat last night, Meg said she felt like she was locked in the barn?"

"Yes. She feels trapped. But our deal with Ranger Norcroft says we must keep her away from others."

"Right, and I don't care how she feels. It's just, I got to thinkin', I wonder if that was some kind of subconscious slip. I wonder if she was actually trapped for the last three years. Held captive somewhere. Notice how pale she is? She hasn't been outdoors in a long time."

Pavel's eyes went wide.

"That is wild conjecture. Who would do such thing?"

"Well, I'd been thinkin' about our upcomin' visit with Kenny Trauger. Kenny was the last one to see her before she disappeared. And his new boat has a few special features that might come in handy if he wanted to keep a girl toy around for a while, against her will."

Pavel shook his head.

"It is crazy. And even if you are correct, he would not admit it. You must be careful, we need to use boat for our overnight cruise episode. We will not be able to arrange another boat so quickly. If you piss him off our cruise would be dead in water."

Muddy smiled and nodded.

"More like dead on land. Don't worry, I won't piss him off. But I'm also not gonna trust him."

* * *

Kenny Trauger watched from the bridge as Muddy Bootes and a European stranger strode across the gangplank. At least, the stranger was dressed European: an off-aqua silk shirt, dark green slacks, and loafers with no socks. He was even smoking a cigarette. Had to be the new director.

Kenny took a deep breath and headed down to greet them. This would be awkward—he hadn't seen Muddy since the Brecker girl showed up. He had nothing to hide, but he'd certainly fucked up and Muddy would not be happy about that. Muddy had a thing about doing the job right. Especially when he paid you enough on completion to buy the biggest yacht on Galveston Island.

"Muddy!" he bellowed as he stepped into the sunshine. "Welcome aboard Bound for Glory." He turned to the European and extended a hand. "Kenny Trauger."

"Pavel Nepovim. Pleased to meet you."

"Come on in, we'll chat in the bar. Care for a drink?"

"No," Muddy said, "This is business."

"That does not mean we do not drink," Pavel pointed out. "Would you have good single malt?"

"I got any Scotch you could possibly want. Follow me."

Muddy gave Pavel a nasty look but followed after Kenny. Win over the newcomer, maybe he had a better chance with Muddy.

Shiner Bock, Aberlour 16, and water respectively in hand, the men took seats around a low-slung marble-topped table.

"We're all set for the cruise show. Crew ready, engines tuned, bar stocked. When are you going to deliver your communications gear?"

"Tomorrow morning, Kenny. But how about we cut to the chase. What really happened to Meg Brecker out there?"

Kenny swigged and swallowed.

"It was just like I said, Muddy. I never told 'em who I was, I erased the name on the boat, and I didn't let 'em get a good look at my face. Once I dropped 'em off I made sure of the schedule, called in the firebird, and got out of the way before it showed up. It scoured the whole area, there was nothing left, not even the dive buoy. I hung around long enough to make sure they were both gone—they didn't have enough air to stay down that long. They got one of 'em, showed up on the brush fire, along with the dive buoy. I figured they never found the other body."

Muddy stared at him.

"You didn't actually see her get scooped up?"

"I didn't see either of 'em get scooped up; I had to keep my distance when the firebird came in."

"But you told me you were sure you got 'em both."

"I was sure. I still am. I don't know how she got out."

"Out of what?"

Kenny paused. Muddy was looking at him weird.

"Out of the tanker plane. What else would I be talking about?"

Muddy sipped his water and glanced at Pavel, then back to Kenny.

"This boat was your payment for takin' care of those two. Custom built, courtesy of me and the Corporation. Full bar, gourmet galley, lounge with casino, spa, the works. Cabins for twenty-five guests." He looked around, as if to confirm the feature list. "Sex dungeon. *Deluxe* sex dungeon."

Kenny slugged some Shiner and kept a poker face. Where the hell was this going?

"Every luxury yacht has a sex dungeon," he said, "ever since *Fifty Shades*. What's your point?"

"Your dungeon is specially equipped, at your request. With a private hidden chamber. Fully soundproof. And lockable from the outside. You could keep somebody captive in there forever and no one would know. Unless she escaped and swam to shore. Still sportin' her bondage bruises and rope burns."

He had to be kidding. He didn't look like he was kidding.

"You think I've been holding Brecker captive for three fucking years? That's bonkers!"

"Yeah, it would be bonkers, to mess with me and the Corporation like that. Hope it's not the case."

Pavel had been quiet as he steadily drained his glass.

"So, then, where has she been?"

Kenny shrugged.

"Why don't you ask her? She's the one who survived."

"We're tryin'," Muddy said. "But wherever it was, it was so traumatic she can't remember. Three years in a dungeon would be pretty traumatic, don't you think?" Muddy stood and nodded for Pavel to follow.

"Let me know if you find out," Kenny said. He was genuinely curious.

"Oh, we'll let you know. One way or another."

* * *

Roger sat in his underwater stakeout, sipping a beer and half-watching a few Bikini Cowgirls discussing their educations. Most had gotten through high school, except Faith who married and dropped out at sixteen. Bobbie Jo worked part time as a bartender to cover tuition at beauty school, but she made enough to pay for her transition and decided to stick with it full time. Dallas, Sarah Mae, and Riley gushed about U. Texas, their airhead manner convincing Roger they were there only to find husbands. Well, maybe not Riley—surprisingly, she double majored in business and communication.

The other half of his attention was on the Wacko Conspiracy Group up the river. There were four people, all professors at nearby Harvard University, all experts in some aspect of creating crazy-sounding conspiracy theories so no one would take the real conspiracies seriously. As Lynn had discovered, they worked under contract for various Corporation cartels. Roger wanted to know who ran the cartels.

He wondered if there was a common link among all the Corporation groups—like membership in the Trilateral Commission, or the Knights of the Illuminati, or Costco. Finding such a link would involve searching online databases across the whole internet, looking at every group and every member. A big compute problem.

The good news was, he now had a million computers at hand, thanks to Lynn passing along Deanna's SETI@home key. He smiled to think of his rookie agent going solo in Vegas. She was sharp, despite being tech-averse. She was also eager for action and frustrated that Burke Barrage was keeping her out of it. Roger, on the other hand, was happy about that—he had enough team members in jeopardy to worry about. And Lynn was a lot more than just a team member to Roger.

The bigger problem was what to search for. Roger needed at least one name from two otherwise unrelated groups to search the web with. The four professors at the WCG never used names, either for themselves or for their Corporation contacts.

He thought about what he did know: their fields of study. He tried a cross-correlation between the WCG meeting schedule and the Harvard class schedules, looking for the four professors who had no class conflicts with the WCG.

Unfortunately, there were dozens of matches—Harvard professors had a lot of free time. He needed to narrow it down further.

He decided to run a SETI@home search across the whole web, looking for an organization that included any professor on his short list and any of the Reality Web names he had. He plugged in Charlie Stewart, Muddy Bootes, Pavel Nepovim, and Clint Owen.

There were no matches. Either the Corporation links were too well-hidden or all those people worked for someone else—someone he didn't have a name for—who was the contact point for their group. Charlie Stewart was the boss for Reality Web; all the others worked for him. Who did Charlie report to?

Roger took another slug of beer and looked at the narrowed-down list of mystery professors. Four of those people worked in the WCG think tank up the river. After eavesdropping on dozens of meetings, he knew their voices. He bet that if he sat in on a bunch of classes, he could pick out the WCGers.

What the heck, if lightweight Sarah Mae could make it at UT, MIT geek Roger could survive a day at Harvard. It wasn't the front line danger that Meg was in, but it would have to do. It would certainly help take his mind off worrying about her.

He printed up a fake student ID and punched the class schedules into his phone calendar. His first stop was the Coop; although it would pain him greatly to wear it, he needed a Harvard polo shirt.

* * *

Muddy leaned his chair back and put his boots up on the folding table that served as his desk. He had no need for anything more formal, and in fact, he'd be afraid to ruin a nice piece of furniture with his workingman's footwear. Other than his feet, the table contained only a laptop computer and its AC adapter. Anything else he needed was in the shop or the local hardware store.

In this case, what he needed was on the internet. He did a scan of the news related to Meg Brecker, thinking maybe there was another clue as to what kind of trauma she'd suffered, and whether it was consistent with a three-year stint in Kenny's floating torture chamber. Most articles were just wild conjecture, everything from hiding out with D.B. Cooper to being abducted and raped by aliens—

Wait. The alien story mentioned a semen sample taken from Brecker the day she was found. Muddy called a young man of his acquaintance, who worked at the East Texas Forensic Laboratory.

"Hayden Sterling."

"Hayden! This is Muddy Bootes. How's the new job workin' out?"

"It's great, sir! Thanks to you, sir!"

"Hey, I just fronted the tuition—you're the one who earned the degree. How's my loan to your dad doing, by the way?"

"Doin' fine, sir. The body shop is back up and makin' money. He'll be payin' it off real soon now."

"Good. Listen, I wonder if you can do me a favor. Are you alone?"

"Yeah." Hayden's voice lowered to match Muddy's covert tone. "What d'ya need?"

"I'm bettin' you have access to some medical records. In particular, Meg Brecker, the girl that washed up on the beach a few days ago."

"Um, yeah, but I can't release anything like that."

"I don't want to see nothin'. But can you tell me, did you really get a semen sample?"

Hayden chuckled.

"Yeah, but whoever leaked the story got it wrong. We're 100% confident it's not alien."

"Okay, if I were to come up with a DNA sample, could you tell me if it matched what you got from her?"

"Wow. You think you know who it is?"

"Maybe. Can you do it?"

"Maybe. It would be really illegal, Mr. Bootes. I'd lose my license in a minute if I got caught."

Muddy smiled. He had a backup plan.

"You're a smart kid, you won't get caught. But I'll make you a deal: If you get caught, I'll get you a recurring role on the CSI Houston show. You'll make enough money to pay off that loan in a week—and maybe get to spread a little of your own DNA around with the actresses."

Hayden was quiet for a few moments. That was a good sign; Muddy waited.

"To be honest, Mr. Bootes, this job sucks. Will you get me onto CSI even if I don't get caught?"

Muddy laughed.

"You got yourself a deal, Hayden. Give me a day or so to get you a sample. What do you need?"

"Hair, skin cells, saliva. Semen would be great, if you're that friendly with the guy."

Chapter 13

Muddy torqued the barrel plug to forty inch-pounds as prescribed by the Acme EZ-Backfire manual. The sabotage kit came with a full set of parts and clear instructions. It was designed specifically for the Redhawk single action .32 caliber "cowboy style" replica revolver.

Two dozen of the Redhawks were laid out on his workbench, one each for the Bikini Cowgirls and the rest for Clint, the camera crew, the range master, Muddy, and his two L.A. henchmen. Pavel insisted not only on the authentic-looking weapons, but that everyone who could possibly end up on camera be dressed appropriately, including a leather-holstered Redhawk. Muddy had to admit, Pavel had an eye for dramatic video.

Muddy had checked and cleaned every gun as meticulously as he would his own weapon. Then he broke out the sabotage kit and gave some special attention to one gun in particular.

He was confident that the replacement loading gate assembly would properly produce enough shrapnel to kill the shooter—the EZ-Backfire people had a reputation for reliability. But he'd worried that the alteration would be visible. Now, looking at two guns side by side, he couldn't see the difference.

Spike had modified the felt-lined gun box to perfection; you couldn't tell except for the oddity of a box with thirteen slots. Muddy loaded each one with a cowgirl's gun for distribution at the afternoon's competition. The sabotaged gun went into the rightmost slot—Muddy had arranged for Meg to shoot last. It was only fair for the other cowgirls to get their chance to compete before the unfortunate accident.

Muddy didn't know exactly how the explosion would look on camera when Meg tried to fire her first round. But he was pretty sure even Pavel would consider it plenty dramatic.

* * *

Meg covered her Texas Aggies bikini in a white terry robe, donned her Stetson and headed for the lodge. The other cowgirls had gathered on the porch already; they looked identical in their standard-issue robes, distinguished only by their hats. Meg noted that black hats outnumbered the white and tans two to one.

Pavel's Jeep pulled up, and the director stepped out onto the dusty driveway.

"Okay, cowgirls, today we have first real skills competition, to see what you have got. You may win or lose immunity points, when we announce voting and first girl to go home tomorrow. We go to shooting range now."

As the girls followed the Jeep, far enough back to keep the dust from ruining their hair and makeup, Meg took stock. She was a pistol expert, a good shot with a rifle, okay at trap shooting. She worried it'd be a Cowboy Action shoot—not that she couldn't handle the quickness and accuracy, but who knew if the other girls could? They all looked good in a bikini, but if they couldn't aim on the run, the next few hours would be pretty dangerous.

At the range, Meg was relieved to see a row of silhouette targets set at fifty yards. She would have expected the usual metal chickens, turkeys, pigs, and rams, but these were paper human figures, standing like outlaws ready to draw for a high-noon shootout. The suggestion of shooting people instead of animals made her a bit uneasy. It didn't help that the target silhouettes were clearly cowgirls.

The cameras started rolling. Clint and the camera crew were dressed in cowboy gear too—hats, boots, bandanas, and gun belts with old-style revolvers and extra ammo in the bullet loops. Clint stepped on camera in front of the girls.

"Okay, ladies, today we're gonna do a little shootin'—you should all be excellent markswomen, so we're not gonna give you any practice. You each get an identical single-action revolver, prepared with five rounds; the empty chamber's under the hammer for safety. You take five shots at your target, score one point for every shot inside the heart circle. In the pocket of your robe you'll find your station number—please remove the robe and proceed to your station. We'll start shootin' at station one."

Meg fished the index card from her pocket and read the number: thirteen. Unlucky? Not really. Shooting last, she'd know what she had to do to win the contest.

She dropped the robe and headed down the line. As she walked past Clint, she caught him checking her out from head to toe. Distrust? Lust? Maybe just curiosity—her pale skin glowed in contrast to the skimpy maroon A&M bikini. She met his eye and grinned to let him know she caught him. As he sheepishly smiled back, she flashed the Texas Aggies thumb-up "gig 'em" hand signal.

Clint's smile instantly turned into a glaring frown as he turned away. Meg dropped her hand and continued to station thirteen, wondering.

Of course. Clint was Texas Christian University, the Aggies' arch-rival. In fact, the gig 'em signal originated from a pre-TCU-game pep rally—it meant "stab the TCU Horned Frogs with a spear."

Tommy had been a passionate Aggie. Was Clint that passionate about TCU? Was that why they didn't get along very well? Had he seen Tommy flash "gig 'em" one too many times?

* * *

Howie fidgeted at the gate alongside Arlene and her crew. They'd expected to view the first competition, but several large cowboys (and one rather small one) rounded them up and herded them out, insisting that this event involved firearms and, for safety's sake, would be a closed shoot.

Arlene whispered into Howie's ear.

"Well, since we can't cover the competition today, maybe we should just go back to my room and get to know each other better."

Howie could wait on that. The longer this went on the harder it was going to be to avoid cheating on Meg with Arlene. He could stop wearing so much cologne, but then he might not get into the show anymore.

"I don't give up so easy, Arlene. Let me see if there's another way in. If you all wait here, they won't think anyone is sneaking around the back."

"Take a minicam," she said, glancing toward one of her crew. Howie accepted the handheld video camera; he wasn't about to tell her about the personal witness in his glasses.

He worked his way along the perimeter and behind the lodge, and darted into the back kitchen door. The lodge was deserted, as was the bunkhouse beyond. He was halfway past the tack shop when a voice behind him said "Stop!"

Howie froze. The voice was female, and familiar: Spike, the Legion's babysitter for Muddy. He turned to face her, relieved.

Spike was anything but relieved. More like horrified.

"Howie, you gotta stop Meg from shootin'. I found this hidden in Muddy's trash." She held up a small, empty, collapsed box, labeled Acme EZ-Backfire. Given the quality motto "Guaranteed to backfire or your money back" Howie noted with grim amusement that they would not want to stand behind their product.

"I'm on it," he reassured her, and turned to leave.

"Wait, one more thing," Spike said, grabbing his arm and pulling him in close. "Anyone ever tell you what a hunk you are?"

Howie rolled his eyes and escaped her grip.

"All the time. Gotta go!"

He made it into the lower entrance of the hay barn and peeked through the open front doors. He could see the shooting range across a small pasture. How to cover that ground without being seen was a problem.

But not as much of a problem as the cowboy who sauntered into the opening in front of him. It was Brad, one of the actors from L.A.

"I admire yer work ethic, there, pardner, but you ain't gettin' onto the range today." The drawl was perfect—this guy was good. "We could have a little shootout right here if'n yer lookin' fer one. But I think yer little camera is no match for this here six-shooter." Brad smiled and patted the handle of his pistol.

"I'm convinced," Howie admitted. "That is a very big gun."

He let the cowboy lead him back to the Dirt TV crowd. All the way there, he mused on ways to warn Meg. The best he came up with was flying a drone with a warning banner over the range. But that would need Spike's help, and she was stuck at the ranch. Not to mention, everyone else would see it.

It was hard to tell whether Arlene looked disappointed or pleased as he was shown through the gate.

* * *

Meg proceeded to station thirteen where a pair of shooter's earmuffs waited. The other girls were removing hats to put on the ear protection when Pavel came running down the shooting line. Pretty stupid, even if no one was armed yet. He was yelling.

"Cut! What are these headphones? They look terrible! We want cowgirls, not recording artists! We cannot have shoot with these things on their heads!"

The range master chased him down and tried to calm him.

"They have to have ear protection, Mr. Nepovim. Nobody goes deaf on my watch."

"Over my dead body! We have gone to great effort to make cowgirls look authentic!"

The range master rolled his eyes.

"Except for the bikinis. Tell you what, we can give them moldable earplugs—hardly noticeable. They can even cover 'em with their hair."

Pavel considered this, and smiled.

"Is good idea! Do it! Roll cameras!"

The crew passed around sets of waxy blobs and helped the girls press them into their ears. All were invisible under the cowgirl locks, except for Lisa, whose crew cut didn't hide anything. But Lisa obviously didn't give a damn anyway. The hats went back on and the competition began.

A crewman appeared with an ornate wooden box and opened the lid, revealing a row of felt-lined slots, each containing an old-style revolver. The crewman removed the first weapon from the first slot and handed it to Dakota at station number one. Dakota stepped up to the line, cocked the hammer, aimed, and pulled the trigger.

Dead center in the heart of her target. She smiled and squeezed off four more shots. Three out of five in the circle, two just missed.

"Nice shootin', Dakota," Clint said. "Next up: Gabriella."

Meg watched with interest and a bit of nerves as each girl accepted her weapon, took aim, and fired her five shots into the nearest silhouette. The competition was pretty good—other than Sarah Mae, the playmate type, who couldn't hit the circle at all, most girls put at least two shots, and some four, into the kill zone. Mattie, the divorced mom, put all five into the circle. On camera, she explained that she just imagined the target was her ex-husband. Meg hoped the guy was watching.

Faith was number twelve, just before Meg. The shy Baptist took aim several times but didn't pull the trigger. She finally lowered the gun.

"I'm sorry, I can't do this. God said thou shalt not kill. It ain't proper to be shootin' at another human bein', even if it's just a paper drawin'. I guess I'll hafta forfeit this round." She turned to Meg and handed her the unused pistol. "Good luck, Meg."

Meg shrugged and hefted the revolver, but a second later Muddy came running down the line.

"Wait, that's not a problem. We'll replace the target. How about a deer?"

Faith nodded okay.

"God said man should have dominion over all the animals."

The cameras kept rolling while a few hands replaced Faith's target with a silhouette of a deer. It had a similar kill zone circle below the shoulder, hastily drawn with black marker.

Faith accepted the gun back from Meg, took aim, and put five shots into the circle.

Mighty serious about that dominion stuff.

As the crewman handed Meg her revolver, Muddy asked if she had any problems with the target.

"Well, I'm kinda unhappy with it, mostly 'cause it's a cowgirl, and I think us cowgirls should stick together. So how about I don't shoot to kill? How about I take out her hands, and her knees, and the top of that hat she's wearin'?"

Muddy gave her a weird smile that the cameras couldn't catch.

"Whatever," he said.

Meg lined up the sight with the target's shooting hand—always disarm your enemy first. She realigned. Then realigned again. Something was wrong.

She lowered the pistol and hefted it a few times to be sure.

"This pistol ain't weighted right," she said. "It's barrel-heavy. I don't think that's fair." She glanced around at the crew, all carrying identical revolvers. "Clint, can I use yours?"

Clint glanced at Pavel and Muddy. Muddy was shaking his head but Pavel was delighted.

"Yes, let her use your gun, Clint. Keep filming!"

Clint stepped over to Meg. He locked eyes with her and hesitated as he handed her the six-shooter, as if he was worried she'd use it on him once he couldn't shoot back. She smiled back sweetly—he needn't have worried, it wasn't a gigging spear.

Meg hefted the Redhawk—it felt perfect. Working the hammer and trigger in the rhythm her Pappy taught her, she put a bullet through each hand and each knee, and then blew the top off the target's white Stetson.

Everybody applauded, even the other cowgirls. But not Muddy Bootes.

* * *

Arlene stood directly between the last two targets, taking a knee to bring her face to their level. The targets made dramatic bookends—the deer with five fatal wounds in the circle, and the totally disabled, hatless cowgirl. The day had gone well—you couldn't get better optics than girls in bikinis and cowgirl hats, firing antique six-shooters. With deadly accuracy. Here was the promise of Next Bikini Cowgirl, fulfilled. She wished she'd been able to see it firsthand.

"This is Arlene Harrington for Dirt TV, broadcasting live from the Pearland Guest Ranch in Pearland, Texas, where we witnessed an exciting day of shooting at the Next Bikini Cowgirl competition. As you can see from these clips, these girls are all good shooters."

She waited a moment as the crew played a montage of target circles turning black with hits, followed by Mattie's comment, audible in Arlene's earpiece.

"If I was Mattie's ex," Arlene said with a knowing grin, "I'd try to stay as far away from here as possible."

The Faith clip was next, and Arlene made a joke about the local deer maybe hiding out with Mattie's ex. And when Meg's clip played, including the gun swap and insistence on not shooting to kill, Arlene couldn't help admiring the performance. Meg was good at this—coming off like a diva, but taking high moral ground and finally schooling everyone with her sharpshooting. A real triple-threat.

Of course, Pavel probably set the whole thing up, and everybody was in on it. That's how reality TV worked.

She turned to the injured cowgirl target.

"Meg may have annoyed her competition with her picky little gun issue, but I'm sure they're less happy with her shooting skills. It'll be interesting to see what they have to say about her at tonight's barn chat. I suspect they won't be packing pistols at that. Kind of a shame." She gave the camera that "just kidding, but not really" wink.

Since there wouldn't be any gunplay, maybe she could convince Howie to skip the chat and spend the evening in bed.

"Remember, first round voting is open until tomorrow at eight a.m. Central time. One of these girls will be sent home at high noon, so be sure to vote for your favorite! We'll be back tomorrow with the results, highlights of the revealing barn conversations, and the high-speed barrel racing competition, so don't miss it. This is Arlene Harrington for Dirt TV."

* * *

Muddy Bootes carefully removed the EZ-Backfire plug and returned the unused six-shooter to the tray of rented guns. He had no desire to sabotage the next guy who unwittingly rented the pieces. Meg Brecker was his target, and it turned out she was a lot more difficult to hit than the cowgirl silhouettes on the range.

He wanted to chalk it up to luck on her part. But Meg noticing the weight of the plug meant she had a lot more than luck going for her. She was a worthy opponent, and he only had a few more opportunities to bring her down.

The next time, he'd do it right. And leave nothing to chance.

He looked at the numbers for the day's webcast—they were way up, and the girls' shooting antics guaranteed an even bigger audience for the barrel race. A barrel race that would end quite differently than any other in the history of rodeo.

Chapter 14

After her first night at the Noir and a day in the underground Legion headquarters (which was brighter than her sixth floor hotel room, actually), Lynn was pretty happy to accompany Burke and Maggie into a sun-baked suburban sprawl. Burke was coy about the purpose of the trip.

"You want the inside story on a media company, you go to where the media action is," was all he would say.

At least he invited her along this time. She was still stewing about missing the visit to Reality Web's fake front office. It wasn't like that was a risky foray.

Lynn pulled out her phone so they could watch the Bikini Cowgirl shooting competition on the way over. Maggie thought Meg was being dramatic about the pistol balance, but begrudgingly admired her shooting.

"Just goes to show," she said, "Always pack your own parachute and your own heat."

They pulled up in front of a nondescript warehouse. Maggie had channeled her femme fatale character to infiltrate a number of Corporation hangouts, including this one. She gave the muscle at the door a rather intimate hello and sweet-talked him into letting them all in, claiming they were "potential players." Inside, after looking them over through slits for eyes and patting them down for weapons, a gentleman lugging a few pounds of gold jewelry led them into a lounge. A long desk dominated, with dozens of monitors hung like wallpaper behind it. People were scribbling on paper forms and exchanging them with the desk clerks.

"Let us know if you want in on the action," the man said, and left.

"What are we looking at?" Lynn asked.

"Ever been in a sports book, doll?"

Lynn shook her head.

"Guess we should start from the beginning. A sports book is a casino joint where people gamble away the rent on sports through a house bookie. They can lose the farm on the game outcome, the point spread, over-under the total points, the foul shot percentage—just about any side bet the odds makers can dream up. But sports books are for suckers; other than professional wrestling, all those games are fixed. Well, not the Olympics—that's up to the athletes to cheat individually using performance-enhancing drugs.

"But this is the Media Book. Instead of sports, players can bet on media wins—how much attention a celebrity gets, how many hits a news story gets on Facebook. 'Course, that's all fixed too, but nobody can call the exact outcome. So they bet on it."

Lynn held up her hand.

"Wait. You just said media success is fixed, too. You mean like publicists getting their clients into the spotlight?"

"It pains me to lead a babe out of the woods like this," Burke said, smiling and patting her hand. "Celebrities try to buy press through their publicists, but those fluff pieces don't get a rise out of the media. The media makes money on scandals. Publicists avoid 'em; the media 'encourages' 'em. They got scandal squads to arrange the juiciest news items. They set up hookers with clean-cut actors, athletes, politicians, and businessmen; slip Mickeys into young starlets' drinks before they drive home. The long-view gamers recruit pedophiles to become priests. Scandals ain't easy to create, but when the talented newsmakers out there score, the media wins big. And so do the bettors who played that line."

"How long has this been going on?"

"Since back in the '70s. The scandal squads got their start framing good-looking dames for petty crimes, so the inmates in those B-movie women-in-prison documentaries would all be hot."

Lynn tried to process all that as she watched the action. Burke was just like Roger, turning her perception of the world upside down.

Perception is not reality, said Zen-mind, *and reality cannot be perceived, but only experienced.* Right. So focus on the task at hand.

"Why do we care about this?"

Burke pointed to a screen.

"Those are the news futures lines—the bets are on which networks or websites will get the most eyeballs. Your buddy Charlie Stewart's Reality Web is a dog—a bad bet; the line is twenty-five. That's twenty-five Nielsen points behind everybody else. Not a popular show."

"So?"

"So, Deanna hacked into the Media Book online history database. Reality Web is usually even worse, an eighty-point underdog. It started climbing last week, and I figured we should check out who's playing all the chips. See that nervous rube on the left, in the department-store pinstripes and lightweight wingtips? He's been betting Reality Web heavy since we got here. No doubt he's got the inside dope on Charlie Stewart's latest caper and knows it's gonna be big, big news." He pointed to the board, where the Reality Web betting line was rising rapidly. "And now other bettors are catching on. My bet is that our insider isn't gonna play any more, with that crowd finally getting in the game."

Sure enough, the bettor glanced up at the board and headed for the door.

"Maggie, how about you tail our optimistic gambler from here, while we head back to HQ and have Deanna check him out online? And we need to drop a dime to Houston that not only is something big going down soon, Charlie's been betting on it for a week. Before Meg washed up."

Burke led the group toward the exit, but as Burke and Maggie slipped through the door, a gentleman stepped in front of Lynn. It was the time-challenged suitor from dinner the previous night.

"Hi there, supermodel," he said, smiling. "I guess I don't need to play the Noir game here, right?"

"No," Lynn said, "But there's no need to play any games at all. I'm really not interested."

"Is that 'cause you're still hangin' out with Phil?"

What? How did he know…?

"Excuse me, do I know you?"

The guy smiled again, like a shark.

"Not yet. My name's Nick Wood. You're Lynn Grady, or at least, you used to be. I met Phil at Omni Music, and I remember he had your picture on his desk for a while. I never forget a face, though I didn't recognize you at first at the Noir—your hair isn't nearly as distinctive in black and white. What's Phil up to these days?"

Lynn gave Nick an exasperated look to buy time. He knew she'd been married to Phil while he worked for the Corporation, and now he'd caught her in a Corporation facility. Of course he figured she was part of the organization. He didn't seem like the type who'd take a quick brush-off either. She had to make something up.

"Phil and I aren't together anymore. He screwed up an operation and I don't know what happened to him."

Would that do it?

"So who do *you* work for?"

Nope.

"I'm with…" *think, Lynn* "…the Wacko Conspiracy Group out of Boston. Never heard of 'em, I bet."

Nick's face lit up.

"That's a bad bet, Lynn, and I'm so glad we met!" He pulled a gold business card holder from a jacket pocket and handed her a card. It read "Nick Wood—Technology Marketing" followed by a phone number, nothing else.

"I test-market new technology to the Vegas casinos—I'm the one who got all the voice sug-jectors installed. But my hobby is conspiracy theories—I've been thinking about good ones for a while, but I didn't have any contacts. Let's talk privately later."

Lynn sighed.

"We don't use outside consultants," she said.

"I'm sure. But you'll change your mind when you hear my ideas."

"Okay, I'll call you. When I have time."

Nick smiled again and offered his hand.

"You won't regret it."

Lynn finally escaped into the daylight, where Burke waited.

"What kept you?" Burke asked.

"One of my ex-husband's business associates," Lynn answered, displaying what she hoped was femme fatale cool. "Just a friendly conversation."

Burke displayed hard-boiled detective cool. No reaction.

* * *

Howie took a seat in the Houston Legion situation room, joined by Spike, fresh from her shift at the cowgirl ranch, and Laurel, fresh from hanging the lone spotlight for the upcoming run of *Monologue! The Musical*. Howie set up a video call with Roger and Lynn.

He told them about the sabotage kit and replayed the webcast of Meg's shooting performance.

"It's obvious Muddy set up the exploding gun for her to use last. See how he freaked out when Faith tried to hand off hers? Not to mention how he didn't care what Meg shot at. He knew the bullet would never leave the barrel."

"I don't get it," Roger protested. "Why would he want to kill her? The show is making a lot of money keeping Meg alive and on-camera."

"Maybe they think they'll make more money killing her on camera," Lynn said. She told them about the visit to the Media Book. "We got a picture of the big bettor and looked him up—he does work for Charlie Stewart. So they're planning something big, and they've been betting on it for a week. Since before Meg showed up."

"So maybe they were gonna kill one of them anyway, and Meg was just convenient," Howie said. "Kill two birds with one stone, so to speak. Just our fucking luck."

"Spike, did you get any recordings?" Laurel asked.

Spike nodded, and cued up the first recording from Pavel and Muddy's morning meeting. It was revealing.

"Awesome," Laurel said. "Muddy thinks this Kenny Trauger guy held Meg captive the whole time!"

"The best part is," Roger added, "that means Muddy has no idea that Meg escaped to Boston. And he believes the amnesia story."

"He said Kenny saw Meg last," Spike said. "Doesn't that mean Kenny was the pilot of the dive boat?"

Howie nearly jumped out of his chair.

"Of course! And I bet his new boat was purchased courtesy of Muddy Bootes and the Corporation, as a reward for the hit."

"Good bet," Roger said. "And that gives me another name to look into. I'm going crazy here. Thanks to Lynn, I've got a million computers chewing on hundreds of databases, but still can't figure out how these separate Corporation cartels and consulting groups even know about each other, much less communicate. Every name I can get helps."

Spike played a second recording. They could only get Muddy's half of the phone conversation with his insider at the forensic lab. Roger was pleased to get another name to cross reference, but Howie pointed out the bad news.

"He's gonna test Kenny's DNA," Howie grumbled, "Which won't match."

Laurel put a hand on Howie's shoulder.

"So, we just have to stop him."

"That would involve knowing where he goes," Howie said.

"Maybe no problem." Laurel said, "If he has a toll pass, we can go into Google Maps Toll Tracker and follow his truck 24/7."

"Do it," Howie said.

"Stopping Muddy from testing DNA isn't enough," Roger reminded them. "You also have to stop him from killing Meg."

* * *

Muddy waited in his truck outside the Cuff Club. To prove Kenny held Meg captive on his boat for three years, all Muddy needed was a bit of Kenny's DNA to see if it matched the sample on file at the East Texas Forensic Laboratory.

As suggested by the presence of two torture rooms on his boat, Kenny was into BDSM—a regular at this public dungeon, as was a certain Ellen Wilcox. And Muddy's spies had previously seen Ellen going aboard Kenny's boat. Kenny's main torture room, at least, had gotten some use.

Today, Ellen had come alone to the club for the afternoon session. When she emerged, Muddy waved and stepped out of the truck.

"Evenin' Ellen," he said with a tip of his hat. She took a wary stance. "I'm a friend of Kenny Trauger. Muddy Bootes. I'd like to hire you for a little consultin' work. Won't take but a minute and I'll pay ten thousand dollars. Cash."

He had her attention. After a short discussion, she left with a two grand down payment and a four-ounce wide-mouth plastic specimen jar.

Muddy didn't want to know what Kenny did to her in his private dungeon; he found that kinky shit weird and disgusting. But he figured that even tied up, she should at least be able to get a strand of his hair, assuming she didn't get a full load of DNA right from his balls.

* * *

While waiting for Maggie to get back from tracking the Media Book bettor, Lynn, Burke, and Deanna watched Bikini Cowgirl clips. Dakota was touting her ornately tooled boots versus Gabriella's ultra-light low-top style. Gabriella faced her with a wide stance and perused her footwear.

"Those heavy-duty boots of yours are fine for shit kicking in the corral," she said, "but not so good for kicking the shit out of an attacker. Serious martial arts teaches that you never know when you'll need to fight, so you must know what moves are possible in the clothes you're wearing. I pay attention to that when I pick my outfit." She twirled in her short, fringed skirt and then kicked an inch short of Dakota's chin.

Dakota flinched away and raised her hands in surrender, as the video switched to a new live-action clip of the cowgirls at dinner.

Lynn looked down at her own outfit. The dress was a bit long, but loose enough to kick from. The shoes were another matter, too narrow a heel for a stable stance.

Maggie had just arrived; surely she'd have good advice on weaponized footwear.

"Maggie, what kind of shoes do you think are best for side kicking in a street fight?"

Maggie looked her up and down.

"I think you should leave the hand-to-hand combat to me."

Ignoring the snub and Lynn's wounded expression, Burke pressed Maggie for a report on the Media Book bettor.

"He's living in a student apartment just off the UNLV campus." Maggie handed him a slip of paper with the address.

"Thanks, doll," Burke said, "I'll tail him in the morning."

"Shouldn't we have somebody watch him tonight?" Lynn asked.

"We're all working the big top tonight."

"I'm not. I've got time for a stakeout."

Burke shook his head, then pointed to the Bikini Cowgirl video in progress. Sarah Mae was picking at a salad while Cassidy wolfed down a two-inch thick ribeye. Nearby, Riley was devouring her steak just as rapidly, but managing to look dainty at the same time.

"I think you should see what kind of steak is out at the Noir buffet, sweetie. And don't worry your pretty little metal-coated head about our petty gambler." He turned to Maggie and Deanna. "It's showtime, ladies."

"We'll see you in the morning," Deanna said with a hint of charity in her voice. The three of them headed for the elevator.

Lynn didn't want Deanna's charity, she wanted Burke and Maggie's respect.

She sighed and returned to the cowgirls video, which had moved on to a hot-pepper-eating contest. Gabriella was the clichéd favorite, but Samantha put her to shame.

"I'm into pain," she explained.

* * *

Lynn was squeezing into a clingy cocktail dress, assuming she wouldn't encounter a street fight during dinner in the Noir buffet, when her room phone rang. It was Nick Wood, the Wacko Conspiracy Group wannabe from the Media Book.

"Sorry to disturb you, but I didn't want to wait for you to call.

I had my friends at Noir tell me your room number." The metal-coated hair on the back of Lynn's neck prickled. "I have a great idea for you. Can you meet me in the center of Hoover Dam, tomorrow at noon?"

"What? Why way out there?"

"There's some interesting technology to show you."

There was no way she was going to drive out to Hoover Dam. But she didn't want to argue.

"I'll think about it, Nick."

"You won't be disappointed. Wear tourist clothes, and no hat. See you then."

The man was confident, that was for sure.

She finished dressing and made her way to the Noir buffet, where her cocktail dress fit right in with the tough-guy men and their cheap-looking arm candy. The buffet didn't look like a place for pickup artists to work their craft; she'd be able to eat in peace.

She found a plate and utensils, and started searching for some healthy food. Ten minutes later, the plate was still empty. She'd found the salad section, but in the nonchromatic light it looked old and decayed. The vegetable section had gray beans, gray corn, gray carrots, and gray edamame.

The rest of the buffet featured various degrees and combinations of fat, salt, and sugar. From sliced meats in congealed gravy, to seafood in curdled cream sauce, to deep fried—well, who could tell what was deep fried underneath that lumpy batter?

The desserts were mostly cake with spun-sugar frosting in various shapes and tones of gray. She wondered if they bothered with food coloring given the colorless light. At the end of the line was a soft ice cream machine that proudly claimed "non-dairy" and probably dispensed pure frozen trans fat.

A gourmet may choose to starve, said Zen-mind, *but a starving person cannot choose to be a gourmet.* The voice was right, as corroborated by the echoes in her rumbling stomach. This was no time to be choosy. Or judgmental. She was prejudging everything here, totally unlike how she approached her Zen Gourmet reviews. So maybe she should adopt Beginner's Mind and approach the meal like a Zen review.

She retraced her steps, this time taking a small portion of the less-deadly-looking items, and returned to her table with a full plate.

She closed her eyes, inhaled slowly, then exhaled, letting tension and preconceptions flow out of her body and mind. She opened her eyes and began to eat, writing a review in her head.

[Presentation: plate is colorless, but artfully arranged in gray blobs. Salad: wilted—actually, so limp that individual leaves are indistinguishable. Mix of iceberg, romaine, and arugula. With a little stirring it all blends together into a savory broth, evoking memories of summer on the farm, chewing a stem of hay except without the chewing. Flavor is vaguely grassy, not as bitter as kale.]

Lynn set down her salad spoon for a moment. She was feeling bitter herself, sitting here slurping buffet food instead of working on the case. Her case. Burke had some nerve making her sit this one out.

She took a deep breath and got back to the meal.

[Sliced turkey: actually, sliced turkey loaf. Texture of Jell-O with nuggets of gristle liberally suspended throughout. Salty enough to not need refrigeration, which is good, since the steam table was room temperature. Gravy clearly not made from turkey fat; trying to identify the oil. Maybe palm? Not sweet enough to be corn. Too cheap to be canola or peanut. Too thin to be motor oil.]

Maggie Palms got to "worry her pretty little head" doing outside investigation work. Was playing a femme fatale on stage a prerequisite for this job? Lynn was sweet enough—she looked at her cocktail dress—and cheap enough. Was she not thin enough?

Another deep breath, with a long exhale.

[Chicken nugget: ninety-percent batter around a pea-sized core of what should be chicken, but after hearing about the meat room at the Lexingham Mall, this reviewer has her doubts.]

It was the turncoat François who'd told her about the meat room. She'd played the femme fatale with him, making him and his two thugs believe she was Corporation, saving the mission. She'd fooled Nick Wood the same way—and left the question of whether she'd show up at Hoover Dam a mystery. Just like the nugget meat.

[Vegetables: string beans are stringy and corn is mealy. Diced carrots have the metallic taste of the can they arrived in, but somehow the chef seared dots onto the faces in keeping with the gambling motif, so credit for that. With an open mind, trying the edamame—the beans are dry and chewy, slimy skin around a thick paste with the flavor and texture of drywall patch. Definitely the best edamame this reviewer has ever tasted!]

As a food critic, it was obvious to Lynn that they had just changed the name from lima beans to edamame; she wondered how long before the public caught on. She smiled. Or maybe the Lima Bean Cartel would be contacting the WCG to create a conspiracy theory about edamame coming from GMO soybeans. Infused with leftover vaccine mercury.

She smiled again. That would be a great wacko theory. Did Nick have such good ideas?

[For dessert, could not go wrong with Jell-O, even though could not discern the flavor selected since they all look the same in the gray light. Turns out it's turkey flavor. Or maybe just salt.]

Could she go wrong by meeting with Nick? She'd have to humor him and shoot the ideas down. Or, just tell him she'd pass them along. He had no other contacts with the WCG, so he'd never know she didn't.

And he mentioned interesting technology. Maybe she could get a sneak peak at some new Corporation electronics. Was that worth the drive out to Hoover Dam?

Why not? Burke wasn't letting her do anything else.

But she didn't dare tell him she was seeing a Corporation agent in her spare time. She'd have to prove she was every bit the femme fatale as Maggie Palms.

Chapter 15

Clint tipped his hat to the camera and gave it his friendliest smile. Pavel had been coaching him: "Be nice to girls, then they don't notice you make them mean to each other."

"Howdy all, and welcome to tonight's barn chat. Should be a doozy, so let's get started by bringin' out the cowgirls. First up is Sarah Mae."

Sarah Mae sashayed into the barn on cue, looking like a beauty pageant contestant on the runway, except she was carrying a rolled-up towel. Her red-white-and-blue thong bikini was damn skimpy already, but it looked even tinier stretched across her wide hips and implanted boobs. She gave Clint a little hug and winked at the camera. Clint could bet all the guys watching the show figured the wink was aimed at them. That might buy some votes.

The next thing she aimed at them was her practically naked ass as she bent away from the camera to unroll her towel onto the hay bale. The thong had completely disappeared between her toned, enhanced buns. She turned around and sat, sensuously, big eyes begging for forgiveness.

"The hay is kinda' itchy in this bathing suit; y'all understand, don't you?"

Everyone did.

"Next is Meg."

Meg looked pretty stunning in a maroon bikini. She walked in purposefully, alert and poised, like she thought it might be a trap. It kind of was, Clint figured. He caught sight of Pavel behind camera #1, signaling impatience.

Right, right; the love plot. In full view of the camera, he followed Meg with pining eyes.

He was still pining when Bobbie Jo strode in ahead of cue.

"And Bobbie Jo."

Bobbie Jo couldn't pull off the skinful look, her bone structure was too angular. She still had a sexy walk, though, even if it was covered with cut-off jean shorts and a blouse tied at the midriff. Clint wondered how many of the guys in the audience found her attractive. He didn't. Good thing Pavel didn't ask him to fake a romance with her.

"And finally, Lisa."

Lisa's bikini was more suited for the gym than the beach, and her crew-cut hair more soldier than model. The "I BITE" tat on her left shoulder didn't help the femininity much.

As Lisa settled in, Clint looked at his notes. This group had to be good for some fireworks, if he lit the right fuses.

"Alright, ladies, lets start with something I bet all our female viewers are interested in: fashion." None of the male viewers were, but as long as the cameras stayed focused on Sarah Mae and Meg, they'd stick around. "We can see how your own tastes run, but we'd like to hear your suggestions for the other girls." There were uncomfortable glances all around, but Sarah Mae saw her opportunity.

"I think Bobbie Jo ought to cover up that square midriff. Nice abs, but you need a narrower waist."

Bobbie Jo looked down at herself.

Go, girl, rip her up!

"You're right, my boobs aren't big enough for an hourglass figure." She gave Sarah Mae a visual assessment. "Yours, on the other hand, are way too big. You should get those silicone bags removed. And then you could give them to me." She smiled sweetly. "It's a win-win!"

Meg and Lisa's grins mirrored Sarah Mae's frown.

"We're talking fashion, not body modification," Sarah Mae snapped. "Lisa, even Bobbie Jo dresses sexier than you do. And Meg, what's with all the barrettes?"

Lisa met the insult with a shrug.

"Truth in advertising, I guess. I'm not interested in looking sexy." She turned to Meg. "And I agree with Sarah Mae about the barrettes. That's so middle school."

Meg seemed to be caught off guard, a rare loss of composure.

"I um, don't know. I like barrettes. I've worn them all the time, since... actually, since middle school." She smiled and shrugged.

Bobbie Jo jumped in.

"Grow up, girl. Lose the barrettes. They're not even nice ones, kinda clunky if you ask me."

Meg looked like she wanted to say something, but she held her tongue. It was the first time Clint had seen her speechless.

He broke the silence.

"Well, seems like good advice all around, huh, ladies?" The glares from the girls said otherwise. Great! Pavel was right about the first topic. Clint was still skeptical about the second. "And after you've fixed your fashion mistakes, you'll be that much more attractive to that special someone in your life. Which brings me to my next topic. Tell me about your ideal man."

Pavel hadn't thought this through. Or maybe he had. Meg gave him a glare that would freeze a deer on the highway.

"Tommy, your brother," Meg measured the words, "is the most wonderful man I have ever known." Why so careful? "I miss him terribly. When this show's over, I want to start a crowd-fund campaign to find out what happened to him."

That was a surprise. Of course, Meg didn't know Clint had ended his own campaign to track down Tommy. Or she did and was trying to get a rise out of Clint. Maybe that's why she flashed that gig 'em thing at the shoot. What the hell was she up to?

He stuck with Pavel's script, and looked disappointed. Disappointed that she wouldn't abandon her lost lover in a heartbeat? Hardly reasonable, but Pavel said reality show audiences would buy anything.

Sarah Mae cleared her throat; she didn't like the spotlight on Meg.

"Did he look like Clint, here?" she asked, and fluttered her lashes at him. "Because I can understand why you'd go for him. Clint's a stud."

Clint felt a little warmth rush to his cheeks. Pavel wouldn't be happy if Clint got involved with someone other than Meg. He glanced over at the director, who indeed looked unhappy.

"Uh, how about you, Bobbie Jo? Got your eyes on anybody special?"

Bobbie Jo waited for the cameras to zoom in on her face and then gave Clint a hungry up-and-down.

"Yeah, I do. I'm with Sarah Mae on this one. You're gorgeous."

Clint sighed, looking for help from his last hope.

"Lisa?"

Lisa rolled her eyes.

"Don't worry, Clint, I ain't after you." She looked over at Sarah Mae. "I don't dress sexy because I don't want to attract a man. Ideal or not."

Sarah Mae shrugged.

"We all know you're a lesbian."

"No!" Lisa clenched her jaw. "I'm not anything. I'm… asexual, I guess. Nobody turns me on. I dress like I do and cut my hair like this 'cause it keeps men from hittin' on me all the time." She shook her head. "Trouble is, now I look so butch I get attention from gay women. Can't win."

There was a moment of solemn empathy from the group. Then Bobbie Jo spoke up.

"Girl, you just need a big ol' cold sore on your lip. Nobody hit on me when I had mine."

* * *

Howie was parked a hundred yards from the glittering yacht. The Urban Legion team had brainstormed on ways to keep Muddy Bootes from getting a DNA sample from Kenny Trauger, but they came up with nothing. Then Laurel suggested letting him get the sample but then substituting Howie's DNA for Kenny's.

Such poetic justice, to confirm Muddy's theory that Meg was captive for three years, and at the same time set up Kenny for whatever punishment Muddy had in mind. Hence this intercept of Ellen Wilcox. Howie had followed Muddy and then Ellen after their meeting outside the Cuff Club.

Ellen had been aboard for almost three hours. When she finally walked down the gangplank, duffel bag in hand, Howie applied cologne and stepped into the night air. He wasn't sure how a BDSM devotee would react to the pheromones; the answer was obvious when she got her first whiff. She stopped and sized him up.

"Excuse me, but you are the sexiest little man I have ever laid eyes on. I'd like to take you home and flog the hell out of that cute, tight ass of yours."

Shit. She wasn't a submissive, she was a dominatrix. So much for the plan to swap samples after blindfolding her. As some military commander once said, plans were overrated.

"I don't usually respond to propositions like that, but given how much I like my tight ass being flogged, I'll take you up on that offer. Unless you're just flirting."

Her eyes got bigger, and she took his hand.

"I was just flirting, but if you're game, I am too."

Twenty minutes later Howie was standing in Ellen's windowless home torture room. It was complete with wall shackles, a hard bench with arm and leg straps, and a pegboard with various whips, feathers, clamps, masks, handcuffs, and belts with evil-looking attachments for the male equipment below. On a shelf were candles, oils, vibrators, cattle prods, sheets of sandpaper, a CD player, and the complete Nickelback collection.

Along another wall was a costume rack, with everything from latex body suits to ruffled Edwardian ensembles, and cowboy chaps to leather hotpants. They all had one thing in common: crotchless.

Ellen (aka Pain Princess) had gone to another room to change, and returned in full black leather gear, including spiked bracelets and matching three-inch spike heels. She set her duffel bag on the floor and stood, hands on hips, licking her lips.

"Well, what'll it be?"

Howie figured the Kenny Trauger DNA sample was in her duffel. If only she could be blindfolded for a few seconds, enough time to replace a lock of hair or wad of spit with his own.

His eyes landed on a multicolor gaucho outfit.

"Well, you're gonna think this is really weird."

"Trust me, I won't."

"Okay. I've always fantasized about being a piñata, getting smacked by kids with bats."

"I admit, that is kinda weird. But, we can handle it, except for the kids. You'll have to settle for me."

"Okay. I'd like to wear that pretty poncho there."

Pain Princess helped him out of his clothes and into the poncho. She grabbed a black hood and reached over his head, but he stopped her.

"No, the blindfold goes on you. That's the fun part of the fantasy, trying to avoid getting hit."

She shrugged, grabbed a rattan cane, and placed the hood over her head.

"Ready?"

"I couldn't be readier."

The Pain Princess was aptly named. The first blow hit Howie on the left butt cheek and hurt like hell even through the poncho.

"Ow!"

"Can't wait to make the candy come out!" she yelled, and connected with his stomach as he tried to twist away.

Note to self: Don't let her hit you on the dick.

He took a few more shots to the ass for show before avoiding a few blows. He took a few more and avoided a few more, until he had enough time to quick-search the duffel and grab the sample.

Shit. It wasn't hair or spit, it was semen.

Howie was soon masturbating furiously while absorbing blows from the cane. He tried to channel episodes from his young teen years, when he had to finish despite sisters banging on the bathroom door. The memory was oddly arousing.

It worked, and he dumped Kenny Trauger's evidence on the floor before refilling the specimen jar with his own and tucking it back into the duffel.

* * *

Howie watched Laurel bring up the Google Maps Toll Tracker and punch in Muddy's serial number. They ran back through the previous few hours. The tracker app only captured his position every ten minutes, but that was enough to show him stopping at the Cuff Club again, probably to pick up the DNA sample from

Ellen. And after that, he headed for a Mattress Ranch parking lot. He wasn't shopping; the store had been closed for hours.

"That reminds me," Howie said, "What's with all the mattress stores around here?" It seemed like there was one on every corner.

Spike shot a sly grin toward Laurel.

"Houston ladies take the cowgirl position seriously," she said, "and that means wearing boots and spurs to bed. Really tears up the bedding. All those anniversary sales are for the horny newlyweds—they usually shred their mattress in the first year."

Laurel nodded embarrassed agreement as she punched in a database search for Mattress Ranch at that time, and found the toll pass ID of another car. She tracked that one back to the East Texas Forensic Lab, confirming that Muddy had dropped off the DNA sample. She then switched back to observe Muddy cross the Galveston bridge and park at a low-rent marina.

"What now?" Howie asked.

"Looks like he's got a boat. We'll have to track him visually through Google Earth Real Time."

"I thought Google Earth only updates once every few years."

"Nope. Ever since they added automatic weather, traffic, and accident reports into Maps, we can get a steady stream of images. Unfortunately, they're not quite real time," Laurel said, grinning, "they're about thirty seconds behind. And it's dark. But not cloudy." She pointed out the green and red running lights of Muddy's boat pulling out of the marina, and offered Howie a seat to watch.

"No thanks, I can stand," Howie said, rubbing his still-burning backside.

They watched as Muddy navigated into the Gulf, then accelerated to surprisingly high speed, quickly reaching what they assumed was a drilling platform, since the boat stopped there. There were no lights on, so they couldn't tell for sure.

A quick check of the Gulf Exploration and Mining Registry confirmed the location as platform 10775, one of the very old permanent rigs, before drilling companies floated everything and reused the gear. It was abandoned, its supply of oil dried up for over twenty years.

"So," Howie said, "Muddy is spending his spare time on an

abandoned oil rig twelve miles offshore. It's not like it's cheap housing and it certainly isn't convenient—must be strategic. Any one of you have a boat? I'm thinking somebody should go out and have a look."

The Houston Urban Legionnaires glanced at each other awkwardly.

"Um," said Laurel, "we're theatre people. We've all done a cruise-ship musical, and every one of us immediately swore off boats forever. It's no fun to sing *Food, Glorious Food* with the taste of puke in your mouth."

"Yeah," Spike added, "Try hittin' your mark when your mark is pitchin' all over the place. And that's on a 3000-passenger job. If you wanna sneak out there in a little boat, you're gonna hafta go alone."

"But I need to stick around the show."

"So, go at night, next time Muddy isn't there."

Howie recalled the last time he'd been out on the Gulf at night, alone except for the dolphins. He'd need cologne.

* * *

Meg took her usual seat at one end of the couch, with Clint at the other. He'd arrived at her cabin with the GoPro camera running, just like the first night. She didn't prepare a note this time.

"Back again, Clint? Don't the other girls get a chance to talk to you alone?"

Clint shrugged.

"They do. But not as much as you." He was momentarily at a loss for words. "I like talking with you."

Whoa, that was awkward. But not bad. If he was going to give her more one-on-one interviews, she'd have more time to scope where he was coming from: good guy or bad guy?

She'd gotten started already. His angry reaction to the gig 'em signal gave him potential for bad guy. But she'd mentioned starting a crowd-funded search for Tommy, to help cover her story that she thought he was still alive, and Clint reacted sadly. Sad that his own campaign came up empty? Guilt that he'd abandoned it? That would make him a good guy.

His initial questions were innocuous, mostly about the shooting competition. He congratulated her on her skill, and tried to get her to bad-mouth some of the better competitors. She didn't take the bait.

He then asked her what she thought about the barn chat, and Sarah Mae and Bobbie Jo thinking he was hot.

"They're right," she said. "You are hot. You look just like Tommy did when I last saw him, and you know how I feel about him."

"Yeah," Clint said, a little sadly. "He's a lucky guy."

"Lucky!? He's… missin'!" Meg almost said "dead." If Clint was trying to flush her out, he was getting close.

Clint looked horrified by his faux pas. Was he?

"I'm sorry, I meant, if he comes back—when he comes back—he'll be comin' back to you."

Meg nodded but hid her confusion. She still couldn't tell if Clint knew Tommy was dead.

"How long do you think you'll wait for him?" he continued, glancing at his notes. "I mean, it doesn't seem like it, but three years is a lot of time. What if your crowd-funding thing comes up empty?"

Shoot, this guy was poking deep. Pavel was good at this.

Or, shoot, was Clint thinking he could step in for Tommy after the mourning period? He did seem to like her. And that would also explain his disappointment about her crowd-funded search plan; it meant she wasn't giving up.

Or, maybe they were testing her. If she showed interest in Clint, she'd be admitting she knew Tommy was gone forever.

"I'd rather not think about that, Clint. I'm just hangin' onto the hope that Tommy'll reappear like I did."

Clint's stare bored into her.

"Maybe he'll be able to remember what happened."

"I hope so. I think."

Clint ended the interview on that note and said goodnight. He really didn't believe her story, did he? But the real question was, did he already know what happened?

She couldn't tell him she'd already moved on, to Howie, after only a year, thanks to his pheromone cologne. Would she have mourned longer without the chemical enticement? Howie seemed to be getting over his separation from Meg, in just days, thanks to the same chemicals—that female reporter was hanging all over him every time Meg saw him.

She put Howie out of her mind and got ready for bed.

Chapter 16

Kenny munched a breakfast beignet and watched the tractor-trailer back up to the dock. A guy in blue jeans and a feed store baseball cap began to lower a forklift with the trailer's liftgate. Packed behind that was a truckload of large boxes, presumably Muddy's communication gear. Kenny hit the intercom loudspeaker button and commanded his first mate to help unload. Within a minute, Roy Braxton stepped onto the dock.

But a dusty pickup pulled up at the same time, and out jumped Muddy Bootes. He intercepted Roy, yelling at him to get lost and stay away from his gear.

Great.

Kenny was doing all he could to keep Muddy happy; after all, the guy paid for the boat. So when Muddy requested that he host his bevy of cowgirls for an overnight cruise, he could only say yes. When Muddy insisted that he bring a ton of TV communications gear aboard, he could only say yes. And when Muddy accused him of holding the Brecker girl hostage for three years, he could only say no—but Muddy didn't believe him. He wasn't sure how he could fix that, but getting in his way today wasn't gonna help.

He announced on the intercom for Roy to go back to his station, and waited for Muddy to storm aboard and up to the bridge.

"Hi Muddy. Sorry I didn't get down to greet you—not moving so fast this morning. Rough night last night." He tried to ignore the stinging whip burns across his hamstrings.

"I'm sure it was," Muddy said, as if he understood the situation. More likely, didn't care. "Look, I thought I made it clear that I'm in charge of the communications gear."

"You did, Muddy. I figured you might want help unloading."

"I don't. I don't want any help from you or your crew. This is my gear and I don't even want your guy lookin' at it."

"Okay, I had him stand down."

Muddy shook his head.

"Not good enough, Kenny. There's some proprietary technology in there, and it has to stay that way. I want everyone off the ship—fuck, off the damn island, until we're done. Can you deal with that?"

"Sure, I can handle the boat alone till—"

"Nope, you too. My guys'll keep an eye on things as we set up."

Kenny swallowed his next comment. Muddy did pay for the boat.

"Okay, when do we come back?"

"How about noon, day of the trip?"

"Uh, but Roy is my cook. He's gonna need a few more hours to set up."

"He'll have to do it offsite and bring it in."

"That's tough, he uses the ship kitchen."

"Not this time. Oh, I almost forgot. Does he make gumbo? Good, spicy, fatty Cajun gumbo?"

"Nah. He's more of a barbeque guy."

"Better hire a caterer then. Pavel wants gumbo for dinner."

Kenny shook his head.

"I try to avoid rich and spicy food at sea. It can get messy."

"Maybe that's the idea. Pavel has an eye for drama."

Wonderful. Kenny made a mental note to bring Dramamine and extra sanitizer aboard when he returned.

"How am I gonna find a Cajun caterer on such short notice?"

"That's your problem."

Yeah, one of many.

"Okay. Give us twenty minutes to pack bags, and Roy and I will turn it over to you."

* * *

Howie ducked low in his car as Kenny Trauger and his crewman roared past in theirs. Tracking Muddy to the boat was easy thanks to Toll Tracker. Listening in on the meeting would have been difficult given the distance and enclosed bridge, except for the zoom lens on Howie's personal witness, tied via Bluetooth into Google Translate Lip Reader. He'd been able to follow the entire conversation with scrolling text subtitles.

He couldn't get a close-up look at the gear Muddy was unpacking—it was all hidden inside huge, strapped cardboard pallet covers. He'd need some help.

He dialed Urban Legion headquarters and got the team on speakerphone. They arranged to have Laurel and Devon take shifts watching the boat.

"No way to get someone aboard?" Laurel asked.

"Not so much," Howie responded, then caught himself. "Wait. Kenny needs a caterer for the trip, someone who can prep and serve a gumbo dinner for the entire group."

"Gumbo?" said Devon. "Sounds like a bad idea. Just being on a ship is sickening enough for me."

"Yeah, Muddy thinks Pavel is trying to set up the weak-stomached cowgirls. But, Laurel, you could probably come up with a pretty good gumbo, right?"

"My gumbo is the best gumbo in the state of Louisiana," said Laurel. "And that means it's the best gumbo in the world."

"Okay, can we come up with a business front that Kenny will find when he Googles Cajun catering? Maybe mention short notice, charter cruises, and best gumbo? We need to tweak the search engine optimization so it comes up at the top of the page, with a bunch of five-star reviews. And we need it quick, before he gets a chance to pull out his phone."

"Done," Devon said.

"But," Laurel said, "If I make the gumbo, does that mean I have to go on the boat?"

"I'm afraid so," Howie said.

"You know how we all feel about boats."

"Yeah. But misery loves company. You'll need an assistant to look like a legit caterer."

"Hey, Devon," Laurel shouted, "where are you going?"

* * *

Roger had a few minutes to kill before heading over to classes, so he did a little surfing for Bikini Cowgirl news. Besides the ever-present webcast clips, there were also online tabloid reports, some of which came from him. That was satisfying—at least he was doing something for the mission. He also stumbled on cable reports from Arlene Harrington at Dirt TV, the woman who got Howie access to the show, shamelessly plugging the webcast.

He watched the cowgirls match skills in an informal hay-bale-stacking competition. Mattie went first, pulling thirty bales one-by-one from a row along the ground and stacking them into a two wide, three deep, five high stack. After a few ranch hands reset the pile, Dakota went and cut ten seconds off Mattie's time. Jasmine cut twenty seconds off that time by starting in the middle of the row and stacking there, so she didn't have to carry bales as far. Smart girl. Then Cassidy stepped up and beat Jasmine the old fashioned way, except she just tossed most of the bales into perfect position on the stack.

Meg and Lisa gracefully bowed out, claiming they were too short to reach the top of the stack, even if they could toss the bales. Then Dallas asked if she could hire Cassidy to compete for her.

"That's how I'd do it at home," she argued.

Roger decided it was time for class and headed for the entrance tunnel. As he walked to campus, he got to thinking about Dallas's economic approach, and Arlene Harrington. Would she hype the Bikini Cowgirl show for free? Probably not. Someone had to be paying Dirt TV for all that attention. Maybe he should plug her into his database name search.

Not that he had much hope of getting any results from that. He'd gotten two more names from the call with Houston, Kenny Trauger and Hayden something, presumably from the East Texas Forensic Laboratory where semen samples would be sent. He'd found Hayden's last name in the EDP database, and plugged him and Kenny into the WCG professor short list search. And came up empty again.

He opened his notebook and glanced at the Harvard campus

map hidden inside the front cover. It was so late in the term that a freshman shouldn't need spatial guidance, and given that Roger looked much older than even the seniors, he didn't want to call any more attention to himself.

He'd found so many potential Wacko Conspiracy Group classes, his chances of finding one of his four professors at the front of the room were slim. So he looked for large lectures, thinking he could slip into the back and leave immediately if he didn't recognize the teacher's voice. He didn't expect to be interested in what they were teaching the kids at Harvard, but he was wrong, and actually stayed for most of the lectures.

The first class was *Myth, Religion, and the Human Psyche*, which seemed like just the kind of thing his WCG Psychology professor would teach. The voice was not hers, but the lecture was fascinating, about common delusions. Apparently, delusional thinking varied by culture and era, but the Universal Delusion was "Psychology is a science."

The *Basics of Trial Law* lecture, by someone also not involved in the WCG, taught him "If the facts are on your side, argue the facts. If the law is on your side, argue the law. If neither is on your side, change the facts."

He was pretty sure the Freshman *Business Ethics* class would not be taught by a member of the very unethical WCG. It wasn't, but it could have been. They were discussing Immanuel Kant's test of ethical behavior, as represented in the question "Would this still be a moral act if everyone in the world did it?" The surprising conclusion of the lecture was, "If you're going to do something unethical, do it before everyone else thinks of it, or you'll lose the advantage."

He was feeling a little disheartened by the time he got to *Introduction to Engineering Problem Analysis*, both by his lack of success recognizing a teacher's voice and the messages he was hearing. But engineering was right in his wheelhouse—his mood lifted as he looked forward to hearing Harvard's take on it.

Unfortunately, the lecturer was not the science guy from the Wacko Conspiracy Group; Roger would have to try another set of classes the next day. But the lecture wasn't a total loss—at one point the professor stated, "If a problem has you so confused you can't even choose from the analysis methods we've outlined, take a walk along the Charles River."

A hand went up.

"Will that help us think?"

"No," the professor replied, "it will take you to MIT and you can ask anyone—they'll know the answer."

Roger's MIT ego boost was enjoyable but short-lived—he still hadn't solved his own problem. Maybe if he asked Harvard students who the Corporation professors were, they'd know the answer.

* * *

Lynn and Maggie sat in the Las Vegas HQ, waiting for Burke to return from his morning tail of the Media Book bettor. Lynn seethed at being left out of the action again, but Maggie was happy to tune in to the Bikini Cowgirls and study cowgirl-inspired weapons.

In this case the weapons were whips, a cattle-wrangling tool imported by Floridians from South America. Gabriella organized an impromptu demo and flew through a routine with single and double cracks, and a few freestyle figure eights. Bobbie Jo admitted to having some "whip experience" and proceeded to put Gabriella's routine to shame.

"It's all in the wrists," she joked.

Then Samantha took two whips and blew everyone away with a thunderous routine that sounded like a war going on.

Maggie was enthralled.

"They're like our circus streamers, only violent." She promised to look into the required modifications.

* * *

I stumped along the Strip at eight-thirty a.m., a time when the night crowds give way to a layer of discarded handouts advertising escort services and private dancers. That's all the law allows in

Vegas, but the girls are willing to go further: they'll escort you to hell and dance with you for eternity.

I wasn't interested in young paper skirts, with or without actual skirts. My quarry was Charlie Stewart's betting stooge, Frank Woodland: male, twenty-something, and three-dimensional. I kept back thirty paces; there weren't enough all-nighter hangover victims on the street to cover me if I stayed on his heels.

I shadowed him from his low-rent apartment to the heart of the casino district. He walked, and I figured that's what kept him in shape; his pace was almost too quick to match. It might've been easier if I had my unicycle, but I knew I'd never get enough traction with just one wheel on all those escort flyers. He had a leg up by walking in a straight line; I had to zig-zag and stop-and-go or he'd be savvy to my tail.

Trouble was, that gave him plenty of chances to duck into a casino, and he took one. I lost him in the maze of slots in the Flamingo. There aren't many ways out of a Vegas casino, but Woodland found one I didn't know about.

* * *

Meg could sense the unspoken tension as the cowgirls tried to enjoy their cookout lunch around the fire pit. They were on camera, as always, but knew that after dessert Clint would deliver the first vote results. And that meant someone wasn't going to be around for dinner.

She noticed Lieutenant Norcroft watching from just out of camera range. The Ranger Division probably wouldn't want him to be seen on TV eyeing beautiful half-naked ladies. But he apparently didn't intend to quit eyeing them.

They were roasting marshmallows on cut sticks when Sarah Mae got philosophical, in her own way.

"Ya know, marshmallows are like suntans. You want to look golden brown, not raw white or toasted black. And not orange." She shot a snide look at Dallas. "Kinda like this." She held an arm out for admiration by the others.

"It ain't like I got a choice," Jasmine snarled.

"Me neither," Dakota said. "My freckles just get bigger and the rest of me burns red."

"I don't have to worry about that none," Gabriella added. "I'm pre-tanned."

The girls glanced around at each other, no doubt mentally rating the competition, but soon all eyes were on Samantha. She was even whiter than Meg.

"Samantha, maybe you're a vampire!" Riley said.

"I don't think so," Samantha responded. "I didn't see any signs of fangs when I looked in the mirror this morning." She paused, wide-eyed. "My goodness, I didn't see myself at all!" That got a laugh out of everyone, including Ranger Norcroft.

The mood quickly turned when Clint joined the circle, carrying a scroll of yellowed paper in one hand, and a hammer in the other. It was time to send a cowgirl home. Meg braced herself. Probably all the others did too. They had no idea how the voting was going.

"Ladies, the first day's votin' is all done. Mattie, Faith, and Meg, you all tied for first in the shootin' competition, so you got extra points, and Sarah Mae, you came in last, that cost you points." He looked at each girl as he said their name, and Meg figured the cameras were doing the same. "The fan voting was close; real close. In fact, the cowgirl who'll be leaving us right now is…" he paused again, this time looking at each face around the circle. "…Sarah Mae."

Meg, and most of the cowgirls, let out a gasp. Apparently being the sexiest wasn't as important as everyone thought. "The voting was so close," Clint said kindly, "those lost points did matter." Sarah Mae shook her head slowly in shocked silence, until Bobbie Jo spoke up.

"Since you're done, can I have your boobs?"

As everyone gathered to console the rejected cowgirl, Clint stepped over to a fencepost and tacked up the paper. It was a NOT WANTED, DEAD OR ALIVE poster, with Sarah Mae's picture and name on it.

Clever touch, Meg decided. Cruel, but clever. And a reminder that for Meg, winning the competitions and the hearts of the fans was a matter of life and death.

* * *

Wacko Conspiracy Group pretend agent Lynn Grady drove east on Sahara Avenue, on her way to her meeting with WCG wannabe agent Nick Wood at Hoover Dam.

Lynn told Burke she was going to do a little sightseeing. She didn't say she intended to collect some souvenir information from a Corporation soldier—Burke might worry his pretty little head. She felt good; a covert out-of-town rendezvous made the femme fatale escapade that much richer. Especially if she was more successful than Burke's attempt to tail Frank Woodland.

Lynn had never been to Hoover Dam and thought it might be interesting on its own. She did a little research on the web before she left.

She was passing a car dealership, glancing right and lamenting the sad shape of her rented Altima, when a rust-and-primer-colored pickup truck roared out of the side street. She stomped the accelerator, and the Altima jumped across the intersection as the truck flew across behind her.

She thanked her Boston-honed driving instincts: if she'd waited a split-second longer to hit the gas, she'd have been T-boned. Maybe killed—the truck was speeding. As was Lynn's heart. A blast of adrenaline wasn't the best way to start a clandestine mission, but at least she'd be able to finish it.

As her pulse rate settled back down, Lynn tried to remember details about the truck. She'd only gotten a glimpse, but something was amiss. It had a snowplow mount attached, but no plow—like many trucks in New England between snowstorms. But Las Vegas never had snowstorms.

Was it a battering ram? Was it not an accident?

She spent the next few minutes wondering who would want to kill her. Charlie Stewart? He had no idea she was in town and looking for him. Nick Wood? He thought she was on his side, and he needed her to get him into the WCG. Maybe it was just Lynn's newbie femme fatale imagination at work, and the near miss was just an accident.

We invent many worlds, but there is only one reality, said Zen-mind.

She took a deep breath and focused on the reality of the drive. An hour later, she walked out along the sidewalk above the downstream face of Hoover Dam. For a claustrophobic person, this was therapeutic. If she'd been acrophobic, probably not so much. It was a long way down.

The wind howled up the face of the curving span; it was so strong only one person had ventured all the way out to the center. That was Nick Wood, wearing Bermuda shorts and a Hawaiian shirt.

"I never got the password," she said. Nick grinned.

"I knew I forgot something. But it's not like we don't recognize each other."

"So, why the tourist outfits?"

"So we blend in. Don't want to call attention to ourselves."

Lynn nodded, though Nick's flowered shirt seemed to disagree.

"Fair enough. How come no hat?"

Nick pointed over the edge.

"Wind'll blow it away."

Sometimes it's not about subterfuge. It's just about the weather.

"Okay, let's hear your idea."

Nick glanced around furtively and motioned her to cross the street to the Lake Mead side.

"See that crew on the intake tower bridge? They're running an underwater robot. It's inspecting the dam, square foot by square foot. Amazing technology—uses ground-penetrating radar to look for flaws inside the concrete."

Lynn could see the crew gathered around a computer of some sort.

"So, you sell these robots? How does that help the organization?"

"No, no," Nick said, laughing. "I don't sell those, they have nothing to do with our technology. But they gave me an idea, for a conspiracy theory." He leaned in. "This dam. It's got millions of cubic yards of concrete. And something else, which the robot has discovered, but they're covering up. Bodies."

Lynn glared at him.

"Nick, that's been done. And while denying that anyone is buried here could be considered a conspiracy, it's hardly crazy enough to get any attention."

"Maybe," he said, undaunted, "but I'm not talking about just any body." He paused, looking around furtively again. "I'm talking about Jimmy Hoffa's body."

"Jimmy Hoffa?!"

"Yeah, and not just his. Also JFK's double, Marilyn Monroe, and all of the Clinton body-count bodies. Oh, and Andy Kaufman."

Lynn shook her head. JFK's double? Andy Kaufman?!

"But, those bodies aren't missing!"

Nick smiled.

"That's what they want you to think."

Lynn couldn't find a thing to say for a moment. She had to admit, this was as wacko as anything she'd ever heard.

But it wouldn't fly.

"Nick, you're being anachronistic again. Hoover Dam was finished in the 1930s. Pretty hard to bury people in concrete that's been curing for thirty years. Or fifty. Or seventy. It's good to have no proof of a theory, but the disproof can't be so obvious."

Nick's face fell.

"You're right," he said. "I'm not good at timelines: in high school, I took three years of American History I." He looked around again and found his smile.

"At least you got to enjoy the nice vista, right?" He dropped his eyes, contrite. "I promise the next idea will be fantastic."

"I hope so," Lynn said. "And can we talk about it somewhere closer to my hotel?" If she wasn't going to get any technology out of him, she didn't want to waste a lot of time.

Nick was nodding as she turned back toward the parking lot. Halfway along the walk she stopped to enjoy the rippling reflection of white clouds and blue sky on Lake Mead. Stunning, like the gaudy lightshow of the Las Vegas Strip, but in a totally different way.

"We can appreciate a lake's beauty while standing at the edge," said Zen-mind, *"but we cannot understand its truth without getting wet."*

The same went for the Strip, of course. And in that case, getting wet meant maybe drowning.

Chapter 17

Muddy Bootes was a craftsman—and he'd already failed twice to finish the job on that pretty little bitch. Those failures weighed heavily on his thoughts as he crept along the back barn wall. The only good news was that his bosses didn't mind—they wanted Meg alive. But his bosses didn't count; this was a matter of personal pride.

He entered the stable where a dozen horses placidly awaited whatever the ranch hands offered next. In this case, it would be a normal snack of hay and water with a side of alfalfa concentrate, followed by saddling up for a barrel race. The girls would meet their horses during the competition, allowed only one practice run to get used to each other. Muddy had arranged that Meg would draw Dusty, by far the fastest mare in the group. She would win easily, if not for the technology in Muddy's bag.

Something moved at the far end of the north stall row. He ducked behind a post and froze, listening. Just a restless gelding.

He made it to the wash bay and crouched to prep the Acme equipment kit, which included a handheld transmitter, a subdermal injector gun, and individually numbered, sterilized electronics packets. He loaded a packet into the gun, checked the seating, and crept over to Dusty's bay. The injection behind her ear took only a second, and Dusty gave a short whinny but didn't seem too bothered. She was used to having spurs jabbed into her ribs—a little injector pain was nothing.

Muddy went back to the wash bay and grabbed the transmitter. He punched in the packet ID number and pressed ACTIVATE.

Dusty instantly stumbled sideways against the stall wall. As she tried to regain her balance, Muddy released the button, and the horse overcompensated into the opposite wall. She recovered, whinnying in confusion. Muddy hit the switch again, and Dusty slammed sideways again.

Ever since he'd read an article about how galvanic vestibular stimulation affects the inner ear, fooling a person's—or animal's—sense of balance, Muddy'd been hankering to find a use for it. Most people these days were trying to combine GVS with virtual reality games for a better simulation of sideways acceleration. But with his victim aboard Dusty and hurtling around a barrels course, depending on the timing, a loss of balance could be fatal. And for Muddy, this was no game.

He wished he could take bets on how far a dizzy Dusty would toss a tiny cowgirl like Meg Brecker.

* * *

Howie meandered through the crowd, snapping occasional photos of particularly sexy cowgirls as he worked his way to the stable. Something was up with the horses—Spike had taken a break from setting up the electric eyes and scoreboard for the race and followed Muddy Bootes into the barn. But she had to bail to avoid detection before he did his dirty work. She'd searched through the trash but this time found no tell-tale packaging.

A quick stroll past the stalls convinced Howie that a New York Jew had no business trying to figure out whether a horse had been tampered with. He might have noticed if one of them was a zebra; other than that, they all looked pretty much the same to him.

But there was a crucial clue: a clipboard hanging next to the barn door with the schedule of horses and riders. Meg's assigned horse was a mare named Dusty. Howie found her and looked her over. There was no obvious sign of sabotage.

The only way to protect Meg would be to get her onto a different horse. He glanced again at the schedule and noted the cowgirls just ahead of her. Thinking Southern belle Riley wouldn't be interested in a New Yorker, he went for the sophisticated city girl, Dallas. He found her outside the arena, watching Mattie's race.

"Hi, Dallas, Howie Friedman, Dirt TV. We met earlier." He leaned in to give her a full blast of his cologne. "I was wondering if you'd like to do a little private interview."

Dallas got those big-pupil eyes that confirmed the pheromones were working.

"I'd love to!" she breathed, "Except I can't. Daddy would shoot me if he saw me flirtin' with the likes of you."

"A reporter?"

"Bless your heart. A Jew." She lowered her voice. "I hear y'all are well-hung, but I'm afraid I'll never know. Daddy's good to me; I'll be fine with a good Christian cowboy."

Howie swallowed the righteous rage bubbling up in his throat. His people had dealt with this for thousands of years; one more incident wouldn't hurt him. Much.

Besides, he had to give Dallas the benefit of the doubt—she might not be so much racist as her rich Daddy was. And even Howie's pheromone cologne was no match for the original aphrodisiac: money.

Just the same, he couldn't leave it at that.

"Too bad, but I understand. And FYI, I'm not that well-hung." He started to step away, then stopped and looked back. "But I've got a nine-inch tongue and can breathe through my ears." He memorized her shocked face for later enjoyment as he turned to look for Riley.

Riley wasn't such a bigot or daddy's girl. Under the influence of the cologne, she played up to Howie like the stud he wasn't. He got the distinct impression that Riley's deferential airhead persona was a carefully polished act.

Before long, they were sitting in the barn hayloft chatting about how handsome Howie was. And soon after that, they weren't chatting, or sitting, anymore. Riley's meek persona disappeared— making out with her was like riding a bucking mare, except in this case, the mare wanted him to fuck her. It was awkward to resist, and actually painful every time she touched his recently caned backside. He strung her along for a while, and eventually she gave up.

"With a body like that," she said as she donned her hat and started down the ladder, "I'd'a sworn you knew how to use it."

"Sorry," Howie said, climbing down behind her, "I should have told you I'm taken."

"Lucky girl."

They hurried over to the arena, where Pavel was pacing nervously, clipboard in hand.

"Where were you?" he demanded. "We had to shift rotation."

Riley offered a demure shrug, and lightly touched Pavel's chest.

"I'm so sorry, Mr. Nepovim. I got into an interview with Mr. Friedman, here, and, silly me, I just totally forgot the time."

Pavel glared at Howie.

"So you are cause of late cowgirl."

"It was all my fault," Howie said. "Next time, I'll watch the clock."

"You had better, or you will be off set." Pavel stomped off to join his camera crew, just as Meg took the reins of a gelding named Blackjack. Howie smiled to himself as Meg hopped into the saddle and gave the horse a little kick.

But Pavel's comment echoed in his head. Was causing a "late cowgirl" just Pavel's twisted vocabulary, or was it a Freudian slip? Did Howie just sacrifice Riley to save Meg?

* * *

Muddy heard Clint announce Meg as the next contestant, riding Blackjack. Not Dusty. He suppressed a smile.

He'd anticipated issues with the horse assignment; the near swap of the guns had convinced him of it. So he'd planted Galvanic Vestibular Stimulator receivers in all the horses. He fingered the controller in his pocket and scanned the crowd. Maybe he was being paranoid, but it felt like everyone was watching him instead of the girls. So he punched in the ID number for Blackjack's GVS receiver blindly, so as not to show the controller. Now the question was, did he remember the ID number right? And punch it in correctly?

He rested his thumb on the activate button and waited for the proper moment to find out.

* * *

Meg took a little time to stroke Blackjack's face and whisper a few soft words. Clint told her there was a last minute change, since Blackjack was ready to go and Riley, his scheduled rider, was not. Meg caught a glimpse of the tardy cowgirl, coming out the barn with Howie. They had bits of hay sticking to their shirts.

Really? A literal roll in the hay? Apparently Howie could swap cowgirls as easily as cowgirls could swap horses.

Even easier, in fact. The best barrel racers were a team, with skills and communication sharpened through years of practice. It was damn unfair to have the girls race on horses they just met. Now she'd get thirty seconds to make friends and then try to run a precision pattern at high speed without falling or hitting a barrel. It almost seemed like Reality Web wanted the cowgirls to screw up. And from the way the previous runs had gone, the plan was working. Several girls took 5-second penalties for knocking over a barrel, and three others went so wide around their turns they came in at nearly half a minute. Given that the competition carried a lot of weight in the voting, and the voting carried a lot of weight in Meg's survival chances, she had to do this right.

She put a boot in the stirrup and climbed aboard. Avoiding eye contact with Howie, she gave Blackjack a gentle kick and the practice run was underway.

None of the riders were allowed to use quirts or crops, and no spurs. So this was about merging with the horse, communicating through the reins and her legs and her feet. She accelerated out of the chute at half-speed and aimed for the right-hand barrel.

Blackjack knew how to barrel race. Meg almost didn't need to lean into the first turn—the horse was hips-in without much slowdown. As they raced across to barrel two, it seemed like Blackjack resented being held back. So Meg gave a little kick and a slap with the reins as they came around and sprinted toward the far barrel.

Horse and rider made the last turn as if they'd been doing this forever, and roared back to the chute at exhilarating, full speed. Meg hadn't felt that rush in a long time. Not many opportunities to barrel race in Boston.

She pulled up in the chute and brought Blackjack back around. He was prancing, impatient to go again. He knew the first run was only practice and wanted to open it up this time. Meg leaned over, gave him a few more strokes, and whispered.

"Okay Blackjack, let's kick some barrel ass."

A slight nudge and Blackjack exploded from the chute. Meg leaned hard into the first turn and gave the horse a little heel tap coming out. He didn't need it—damn, he was fast.

The second turn was even faster, Blackjack only slowing enough to round the barrel without going wide. By the third turn, it was more a matter of hanging on than guiding the horse.

She slapped the reins against his shoulders and accelerated toward the finish.

* * *

Muddy watched the practice run with growing joy. Blackjack was even faster than Dusty and would be travelling at breakneck speed at the end of the run. And breaking necks was exactly what Muddy had in mind.

The timed run was even better. When Blackjack came around the far barrel, he was already seconds faster than any of the others. As he steamed toward the chute, Muddy hit the button.

* * *

Meg lurched as Blackjack veered right, almost stumbling toward the bullpen fence. At this speed, they'd probably end up in the grandstands.

Meg pulled hard on the left rein, but Blackjack continued hurtling toward the barrier. She leaned forward to hang on, hugging Blackjack's neck as if she could pull him upright with her arms.

And Blackjack reacted, straining to straighten out. He bolted into the chute, missing the bullpen bars by inches.

* * *

Muddy sat stunned as the crowd cheered the run. They might not have even noticed how close Brecker came to splattering her brains across the stands. As everyone waited for the official time, a replay screen showed the run in close-up.

And it hit him: Brecker was wearing that boatload of metal barrettes under her Stetson.

Fuck!

When she leaned over, she jammed his signal. The lucky bitch was beginning to piss him off.

Clearly, this job was going to need a lot more power.

Chapter 18

Arlene posed in front of the arena where the barrel race had just concluded. She looked around for Howie. He'd showed up midday, disappeared for a while, and came back just for Meg's run before leaving again. Seemed like he was using her for access to Meg—he surely wasn't as hot for Arlene as she was for him. Maybe she could wrap this up quickly and confront the sexy little bastard at the hotel. Hit the sheets, or hit the street with no more press pass.

Her cameraman signaled.

"This is Arlene Harrington for Dirt TV, broadcasting live from the Pearland Guest Ranch in Pearland, Texas. We've just finished the exciting barrel race, live streamed on Reality Web and available on the podcast just a few minutes from now. I've been told to let the video speak for itself, so be sure to check it out on the website. The results will be combined with the viewer voting into an overall score. Sarah Mae went home today; vote for your favorite cowgirl by eight a.m. Central tomorrow so she doesn't go home at noon."

She glanced at her notes; next up was a teaser for the barn chats. It didn't seem tantalizing enough to overcome the lurid, made-up headlines her tabloid competitors were pushing. Was there a way to spice it up?

It was all about click bait. Click baiters don't care if the image is in the article, or even if the article is about the headline. Just make the bait compelling. Doing that on the fly might be tough, but Arlene was up for the challenge.

"While you're at the website, be sure to check out the exciting barn chats. Did Samantha really threaten Mattie with a knife? What did Dallas say to Faith that sent her running away in tears? And…" *come on, girl, you're on a roll* "…just how revealing was

Jasmine's wardrobe malfunction?" Yes! Wardrobe malfunctions always got 'em.

"And be sure to check in tomorrow for the drag race competition, live-streaming at three p.m. and available on the podcast anytime after six.

"But now it's time for me to sign off." *And jump Howie's bones.* "This is Arlene Harrington for Dirt TV."

* * *

Meg was a little late getting to the barn chat. She'd wasted a lot of time thinking about Howie and Riley coming out of the hayloft together. There was a silver lining: Riley never looked comfortable on her horse, twitching and flinching as if chasing a few shards of hay down her shirt. It affected her ride—she knocked over two barrels and came in dead last.

The chat group included Mattie, who at thirty-two could still rock a flame-red bikini; Faith in her usual modest cover-up; and Riley—just who Meg needed to see at the moment. Riley was wearing a gingham-patterned bikini and was already playing dumb with Clint. Couldn't he see through that Southern belle bullshit? Pavel seemed to—he watched the entire exchange with a disapproving glare. But maybe he was just upset that all the girls had brought towels to keep the hay from itching.

Clint started the session off with a good one.

"Alright, ladies, since this here's a reality show, we're gonna talk about the truth today. But we don't want to talk about what you think is true, we want to talk about where you find your truth. Who do y'all turn to get the straight story? Who do you trust?"

"I place my trust in the Lord," Faith said instantly. It was like a knee-jerk church call and response. But she sounded sincere.

Riley didn't.

"I leave that to the men in my life," she purred. "They always seem to know best." Meg wished she could puke on cue.

"That's not a good plan," Mattie snarled. "My ex seemed to know best how to find willing young things like you."

Riley put a hand to her throat.

"My, it sounds like he treated you badly. Maybe you didn't treat him kindly enough."

"That's not how it works, Riley," Meg said, surprised to hear the venom in her own voice. She reminded herself that no one in the room knew she was jealous of Riley—including Riley. Howie was just a sexy reporter to her, with no connection to Meg. "Some guys just take what they can get."

Did she really just say that about Howie? Clint and Pavel, and especially the Ranger, were looking at her funny. Could they tell there was something behind it?

Shoot, maybe they thought she was talking about Tommy! Like, she had a motive to make him disappear. What a stupid thing to say.

"It sounds like you're speakin' from experience, Meg," Clint said, friendly. Prick. "Care to share?" Pavel and the Ranger leaned in.

She wished she could share, but not about Howie. She needed someone she could talk to, someone she could trust. Clint wasn't acting like he was on her side.

"Every woman has had some guy use her," she said. "Though maybe some women use their men just as much." She shot a not-so-subtle glance at Riley. Riley smiled, innocent.

"Why, I believe I don't know what you're talking about."

Mattie jumped on that.

"Yes, you do, you buttery little tramp. It's use or be used. I bet even Faith here has had someone cheat on her."

There was a silence as the focus switched to Faith, who glanced around like she was looking for a place to hide.

"My husband has never cheated on me. He's a God-fearin' man and holds me dear like the Bible says…"

Faith put her head in her hands and started to cry. Mattie jumped over and hugged her.

"I'm sorry honey, I didn't mean to upset you."

Faith looked heavenward.

"Forgive me, Jesus." She wiped her eyes with the back of her hand and looked around at the group. "I've told a lie. He—well, he doesn't cheat, that I know of, but he doesn't hold me dear, neither.

The Bible says a husband should have dominion over his wife, and we believe that. But… I don't know if that means a wife shouldn't ever go out. Or have any friends. Or…" She fought down a sob. "He hits me sometimes. When I don't obey fast enough. I don't think that's in the Bible." She started crying again. Mattie braced her heaving shoulders.

"I didn't want to join this show, I didn't want to be paradin' around naked like a Jezebel. But he insisted—said we need the money." She shook her head sadly. "But that just makes it worse, don't it? He kept hitting me until I agreed." She lifted her cover-up for the first time anyone had seen and revealed fading bruises on her ribs. "He didn't want to hit me in the face; he said the show wouldn't take me if my face wasn't pretty."

"You need to get out, honey," Mattie said, stroking her hair.

Faith sniffed.

"But I need him. How would I get by without him?"

"You don't need him," Meg offered. "Put your trust in the Bible, like you said. You know he ain't a good Christian." Meg marveled that a reality show could actually bring out the truth.

"Besides," Riley said with a coy wink, "If you win this competition, you'll be rich. Not him."

"But only if you divorce him right now," Mattie added, actually smiling at Riley. United in their attitudes about men, if not their approaches.

Faith looked dubious.

"But does the Bible condone this?" She waved her hands along her body. "I feel like I'm sinnin' every moment I'm on camera. I should leave the show."

Meg figured Clint had a prime directive to keep anyone from quitting. Especially a cowgirl who could generate that kind of drama. He jumped right in.

"Faith, the good Lord gave you a beautiful body and amazing talents. Don't you think He would want you to use them? Think of what you could do if you win. Get out of a bad marriage. Maybe open a Bible school. Or a Christian orphanage."

Damn, he was good. Pavel was enthralled, his hands on his cheeks below dreamy eyes.

Faith looked around at the other cowgirls. Riley and Mattie were nodding. Meg was, too.

"It's better than goin' back to your husband," Meg said. "And you can show the world how a good Christian cowgirl behaves." Her stern glance at Riley did not go unnoticed.

Faith chewed on all that for more than a few camera-worthy moments.

"Okay, I'll stay."

Both Pavel and Clint let out subtle sighs of relief. Did they really care about Faith, or just the show? Pavel's priority was obvious. Meg wished Clint's priority was obvious—and wasn't the show. She still wasn't convinced she could confide in him.

She had nobody to trust but herself.

* * *

Lieutenant Norcroft took a pass on the alcoholic selections from the bar and went for a bottled water. It was a shame he was working—the bar menu was extensive. Pavel had set up a pretend screen test, where the cowgirls would be competing for an ad campaign gig, as one of the beautiful young people enjoying the sponsor's alcoholic beverage in an outdoor party atmosphere. The twist was that the girls got to choose ahead of time what beverage they would represent, and Pavel had gone out and stocked the bar appropriately, including the proper glassware. He was a stickler for accuracy.

Norcroft watched them sipping, posing, and pretending to have a great time. He realized he couldn't afford to party with Dallas, who was drinking Johnny Walker Blue on the rocks. He could spring for Bobbie Jo's Cosmo or Samantha's absinthe, but the bars he frequented might not be able to come up with those. Meg, Lisa, Mattie, and Dakota were more his style, going with bourbon, though Dakota turned hers into a mint julep to get a head start on the upcoming Kentucky Derby. Faith stuck with lemonade, and the others went with Shiner beer—Light Blonde for Riley and served in a glass; Bock for Jasmine, Gabriella, and Cassidy, straight from the can.

With a challenging glance at her fellow Shiner Bock drinkers, Jasmine chugged hers and slammed the empty can on the picnic table. Cassidy half-smiled and half-sneered before draining hers and crushing the can on her forehead. The two looked at Gabriella expectantly. Gabriella shrugged, tossed back her beer, and flipped the empty can into the air. Before it landed she side kicked it into a trash barrel fifteen feet away. The other two bowed with respect.

At least if he went out with Gabriella, Norcroft wouldn't have to worry about her littering. That could carry a hefty fine in Texas.

He stopped by the office on his way home from the ranch. He was starting to feel guilty about watching Meg every moment, looking for a slip-up like she was a criminal. From what he'd seen, she was legitimate—competitive but not mean, seeming to look for the good in others, and mystified by her lost memory. It was hard to believe she was hiding something.

There was an oversize envelope on his desk. He'd been waiting for copies of Brecker's high school and A&M yearbooks, and he tore the package open immediately. He grabbed a cup of water, put his feet up, and started flipping through the university book. There was a featured picture of Meg near the pool; she'd apparently done well on the swim team. He smiled. Seems like she had a history in the water. And in swimwear. She looked good then, and even better now.

There was nothing else of interest about her, with only one other reference in the senior section. Her pose was very staid, and in normal clothes. He almost didn't recognize her with her hair flowing freely onto her shoulders. At the ranch she always had it up in barrettes. "Too many barrettes," the other girls had advised her.

He had to agree…

Hold on a second.

Meg said she'd worn them since middle school. She even had them in her hair when they found her on the beach. But there were no barrettes in either A&M picture. He sat up and grabbed the high school yearbook. Group pictures with the swim team and tennis teams. Senior portrait headshot.

No barrettes.

Meg Brecker was lying.

Chapter 19

Howie sat at Urban Legion HQ, watching video clips of the barn chat and the previous night's one-on-one interview. Clint seemed to be probing for a slip-up, sweet-talking Meg to get her guard down. And when Riley sweet-talked Clint during the barn chat, Meg seemed to be jealous. Howie had to admit, Clint's looks might give him an advantage with Meg that even pheromone cologne couldn't counter.

Spike and Laurel sat down with him and joined a video conference with Roger and the Las Vegas team. Roger was complaining about not being able to find any Corporation connections. Burke had also come up empty finding Charlie Stewart. Both promised to make progress soon.

Howie wasn't sure soon was soon enough. He shared the barrel race video.

"See how suddenly Blackjack lost his balance?" he said. "Such an expert horse would not be such a klutz. And Spike caught Muddy slinking around the barn before the race. He must have tampered with Blackjack."

"Yeah, we've seen that effect before," Maggie said. "Looks like a galvanic vestibular stimulator—an electrical signal injected into the middle ear to mess up the victim's balance. The Corporation has used them forever to fix athletic competitions. You might have even seen the video of a ski jump run, where they put a stimulator in a skier's goggles and zapped him just before he reached the ramp. The wipeout became famous as the *Wide World of Sports* 'agony of defeat' clip."

Howie had seen it. The skier acted just like Blackjack.

"So it's triggered remotely?"

"Yeah, so you can time it right."

And get the horse right. He must have tampered with all of them.

"Okay, so Muddy is still trying to kill Meg. Any idea what he's got up his sleeve next, Spike?"

Spike shook her head.

"Nope. He hasn't spent any time in the office so I've got nothing recorded. He's on the rig again tonight, and tomorrow he's goin' right to the track to prep for the drag race. I volunteered to help set up but he insisted he could handle it himself. Though he did have me print up decals for the cars, with the cowgirls' names."

"That means he's planning to make sure Meg is in a specific car," Roger said. "You've got to stop him."

"We can't," Laurel said. "Unless she pulls out of the competition, we just have to trust her to survive. She has so far, with no help from us. And if Muddy is at the race, he won't be on his rig. Howie, you still owe that a visit, and it'll be much easier in the daytime."

Howie frowned; Laurel was right. Meg was risking her life to find out why they killed Tommy—he should help by investigating Muddy's offshore lair.

"Okay, I'll go to the rig tomorrow. But I want to warn her."

"See if you can get her to quit," Roger said.

"I'll have to convince her she's in more danger on the show than off it. And even then she might not quit."

"You need to use the drone again?" Spike asked.

"Nope. But I could use another costume."

* * *

Howie made his way back to the ranch, tugging at a few newly adjusted seams in his cowboy shirt. He didn't think the outfit looked particularly authentic, but what could he expect from a community theatre costume shop on short notice? He hoped it was dark enough that he could get to Meg's cabin without drawing attention. And he hoped his cologne still had an effect on Meg.

He'd gotten past the gate guard and over to the horse barn, but there was an open path between there and the guest quarters. At least the setting moon was low enough that the barn cast long shadows to hide in.

It was when he stepped out of those shadows that the voice came from behind him.

"Hold it right there, pardner."

Howie froze.

"Put your hands up and turn around, real slow."

Howie did as he was told. He hadn't included sixguns in his costume because he didn't want anyone to think he was about to draw. When he got all the way around, he found himself facing a short cowboy and a long pistol.

Good call on the sixgun thing.

"Evening, Peter," Howie said, recognizing the L.A. actor. Even if Howie couldn't see him, his bad Texas accent would have given him away. "Nice night for a walk, huh?"

The cowboy studied him.

"Better at night than in the daytime, if you're gonna wear such a cheap-shit costume. What's that hat, cardboard?"

Howie shrugged, as best he could with his hands up.

"Gimme a break, I'm just a reporter. Trying to get an interview."

The cowboy snorted.

"Sure you are. Trying to get a little action from the cowgirls, is more like it." He waved the gun. "Okay, turn around again, and walk ahead slow. You can tell your story to security." Howie turned and started forward as the gun barrel poked his spine. "Nobody touches the cowgirls."

"I'm not really interested in the cowgirls. Just Meg Brecker, she's the only one we can't talk with on set."

"I don't blame you. She's pretty sexy, I guess."

He guesses? Could he be…? It was a long shot, but worth a try. He slowed a bit to bring the two closer together, and leaned back to look over his shoulder.

"Look, I just want to talk with her. I'm not interested in cowgirls anyway. Just cowboys."

"Wait. You're gay? Turn around again."

Howie turned, with a bit of a flourish in order to waft some cologne toward the guy.

"Yeah. I wish I was assigned to the Bikini Cow*boy* show." He faked an embarrassed laugh.

The cowboy had gotten a good whiff of the cologne, and was definitely gay, given the look in his eyes. He lowered the gun.

"Are you interested in a little cowboy action?"

"Wait. You?"

"Yeah, and with all these other cowboys around I'm so horny I could fuck a bull."

Howie looked him up and down.

"Maybe I'm just the bull you need."

The guy stepped closer, but Howie lowered his hands to hold him back. Peter was breathing heavily.

"Look, I'm willing to trim those longhorns of yours, but you have to do me a favor first. I really need to talk with Meg Brecker. How about you let me get to her cabin tonight? I'll just need a few minutes with her. Then tomorrow night, I'll spend a few hours with you in the hayloft."

Howie nodded toward the barn. Peter was fighting it, but he was no match for the cologne.

"Okay," he said. "Nine o'clock tomorrow, in the hayloft."

* * *

Meg was in camera-ready pajamas in case Clint stopped by for a one-on-one, but she was hoping he wouldn't—the race had totally wiped her out. So when the knock came, she was less than enthusiastic.

"Coming, Clint," she said, and opened the door.

It was Howie, in a silly cowboy outfit with a serious look on his face.

"Sorry, it's not Clint," he said flatly. "May I come in?"

She nodded and pointed to the couch.

"Have a seat, cowboy."

He settled in as she closed the door, wafting familiar cologne around the cabin. She didn't feel very horny, though—maybe seeing him with Riley was an antidote.

"Nice riding today," he said.

"Thanks. Blackjack got a little clumsy at the end, but I managed to straighten him out. How'd your ride turn out?"

Howie was silent for a bit.

"I'm not following you."

"I saw you chattin' up Dallas, and then headin' off to the barn with Riley. And there was hay in your collar when you came back out. You're wearin' your cologne these days."

"I was only trying to make one of the girls miss her turn, so you wouldn't be riding a sabotaged horse."

Meg studied his face. Howie was always paranoid, but this was too much, even for him.

"You expect me to believe that? You're a genetically horny guy with lady-killer cologne who can't get to his main squeeze. But you can get to a dozen other hot ladies, so you give in to the temptation. And savin' me from a sabotaged horse is the best excuse you can come up with?"

"It's not an excuse! My spy here saw Muddy Bootes screwing around in the barn today. You were supposed to be riding Dusty, but delaying Riley moved you up."

"Dusty seemed to work fine for Riley."

"Yeah, apparently Muddy sabotaged all the horses, and only triggered yours. They have a way to make the horse stumble. But I tried. It's the thought that counts."

"Pavel thinks I'm a golden goose here, they don't want to kill me."

"Muddy apparently doesn't agree. You know that pistol you didn't like so much at the target shoot? That was sabotaged to backfire. Lucky you noticed and used Clint's gun instead. And Muddy's sticking name decals on all the cars tomorrow, so he'll be sure you're in the car he expects. I have no idea what he's done to it, but you can bet it's deadly. Roger wants you to quit the show, he's so worried about it. Oh, and I almost forgot. If you survive the drag race, you're going on a boat trip next. On a nice yacht, given to your fatal dive boat captain three years ago by Muddy Bootes, as payment for a job well done. In fact, Muddy thinks the guy held you captive since then; I suspect he has a dungeon on the boat."

Meg didn't know what to say. Like herself, and all Urban Legionnaires, Howie was pretty good at lying to get out of trouble. But Legionnaires didn't lie to each other. Maybe that's why Howie couldn't make this more plausible. He almost had her at the dive boat captain but lost her with the captivity story. Who puts a dungeon on a yacht?

"I don't believe you."

"You have to! Muddy wants to kill you! On camera!"

"While you're fuckin' Riley off camera."

Howie was silent again.

"I admit, I use my cologne to take advantage of women, but only to get what I need to protect you. I used it on Arlene Harrington to get access to the show in the first place."

"Yeah, I thought you might be fuckin' Arlene, too."

"No! I've been completely faithful to you, which is no easy thing, given the cologne." Howie rose from the chair, grabbed her shoulders, and kissed her on the lips. "I love you, Meg, and only you, and I always will. And I swear to God I'll prove it to you, somehow. Please believe me. Please quit the show before the race tomorrow."

He didn't wait for a response but slipped silently into the cool night air and shut the door behind him.

Meg dropped into the chair, the artificial scent of sexuality still lingering where he sat. Was that all there was to their relationship? Could she prove her love to him?

Did she actually have any love to prove?

Chapter 20

Howie arrived at the ranch alone. He'd intended to go to Muddy's oil rig first thing in the morning, but Laurel called and told him Muddy was still there. Howie didn't want to meet up with Muddy Bootes, either on the rig or on the Gulf.

Unfortunately, he'd already left the hotel, drenched in cologne in case he ran into female dolphins during the voyage. Now, he was afraid of meeting up with female humans, Arlene in particular. And any of the cowgirls. Not to mention Pavel's gay cowboy.

The girls would be in the corral, practicing roping, with cameras watching their every move. And Meg would be watching Howie's every move. It would be awkward to be caught in the embrace of a chemically aroused woman.

He stayed far away from the Dirt TV van, but as it turned out, so had Arlene. He rounded the corner of the shooting range pavilion and smack into the reporter.

"Turn off the camera, guys," she said, and as the red light winked out she threw her arms around Howie and planted her face on his.

He kept his eyes open and his teeth closed, and pushed her away.

"Hi, Arlene," he deadpanned, to the amusement of her camera guy. "Sorry, gotta run, I've got a date with… Lieutenant Norcroft."

He ignored her sputtering and strode past, taking a moment for a glance around. No Meg in sight.

He found Norcroft heading for the rodeo corral along with Clint and Meg and several cowgirls, including Riley. Riley ignored him, as he hoped she would. So did Meg.

He kept out of pheromone range until he could catch Norcroft alone.

"Hi Lieutenant, Howie Friedman with Dirt TV. Got a minute?"

"Not really."

"I just wanted to ask how the investigation is going. I notice you've been keeping a keen eye on the Brecker girl."

"If you're so observant, you'd notice that I don't talk about an investigation until it's over. If you'll excuse me."

Norcroft tipped his hat and strode after the others.

Howie followed, looked for his next shelter, Clint. He was hanging around near the corral, not far from Meg.

Clint was never far from Meg.

He headed for the bunkhouse, hoping to find any cowboys except Peter. He peered around the end door, finding only Peter, relaxing on his bunk. Apparently Peter was not just the only gay cowboy, but also the only slacker.

He retreated and cut across behind the hay barn and back to the corral, where Meg and a small group had begun their roping target practice. Howie checked the breeze—he was downwind from everybody except Cassidy, who was entering the enclosure on a horse behind him. He stayed at the rail and pretended to take photos.

A lasso landed around his shoulders and cinched tight, pulling him over the rail into the dusty corral. As he hit the ground, he glanced along the taut rope to see Cassidy scrambling from her horse. She grabbed him around the waist, stood him up and then flipped him onto the ground. Gathering his legs and one arm together, she wrapped a line around all three and tied a quick knot. Then she jumped up with both hands in the air.

"Seven seconds flat!" she bellowed.

Then she picked him up, still hog-tied, and planted a long deep kiss on him.

"You are one fine little doggie," she whispered into his ear. "I want to see you once this reality bullshit is over."

As Cassidy put him back down and untied him, Howie heard clapping coming from the other cowgirls in the corral. He glanced up. Meg wasn't clapping.

* * *

Lynn and Maggie tuned in to the Bikini Cowgirl webcast and watched Meg practice with her lariat on a roping dummy. She was dead accurate; Maggie was impressed. Dakota and Riley matched Meg throw for throw.

Bobbie Jo got five for five around the plastic cow's horns, but she was throwing from only a few yards and threw the loop backhand, like a Frisbee. The other girls struggled to hook both horns.

"If they used bolas," Maggie said, "they wouldn't have to clear the tips of the target." She told Lynn how she'd turned a ball-on-a-string circus prop called poi into a weapon by adding weight and connecting three together into a boleadora. "It wraps you up quick."

It seemed like someone with Maggie's skills should get a little more respect from Burke. But Maggie seemed fine with waiting around watching reality TV while Burke chased down his elusive Media Book bettor.

There was a commotion onscreen and the camera panned right. Cassidy had roped a guy and pulled him over the rail. Lynn got a good look as Cassidy flipped him and tied him up.

"That's Howie!"

Maggie raised an eyebrow as Cassidy let him go.

"Do they always kiss the cow after they rope it?"

"No," Lynn said, chuckling, "unless the cow is wearing Howie's cologne."

* * *

I dogged Frank Woodland on his morning commute, but this time I was ready for his sudden cartwheel into the Flamingo. I'd planted a camera at the entrance, trained on the slots. Between me and my electronic snoop, I had his secret entrance on the hook.

Except he ducked into the Venetian. I scrambled to catch up and burst through the doors to the casino. Woodland was already gone behind the veil of breakfast cigarette smoke. Another trip for biscuits.

I retrieved the camera from the Flamingo and drifted back to Noir, braining on what to tell Grady. She'd asked for my help and I hadn't come through. I wasn't even getting anywhere. That gnawed at my gut like the raw clams at a cheap buffet. And like a reaction to the cheap buffet, it's not good when these things drag out.

Grady took the news with a glare so cold I could see her breath. I shivered and turned my attention to Deanna and her computer console.

She set up Google Maps History; I traced the routes Frank had taken and Maggie added his trip home from the Media Book. Deanna correlated with the Maps traffic monitoring database to highlight any phone movement that matched his routes. It found his phone and showed us all his other movements for the last month. On the screen, the paths looked like an out-of-control silks act, just a bunch of intertwined lines with no discernable pattern.

"How about we just eyeball his commutes for a week and see where he pops up during the day?"

Deanna jiggered the map and, besides his gambling trips to the Media Book, found only two traces for each day: the morning walk into a casino, and a late afternoon walk back. Frank acted like a normal 9 to 5 mug. And despite the secrecy and the different route every day, he always came back out the same way he went in. Real regular.

So, I couldn't work out where he spent his workday. But the show was now dark for our two night "weekend"—I could stake out the Venetian with my camera to get a read on his secret exit. This time, Grady didn't ask to come along; she said she'd just find a good book to read. She sounded sarcastic. Or at least insincere.

In every mystery, the dame has something to hide. Something more than her taste in literature. I decided to keep a closer eye on her.

* * *

Meg saw the cameramen setting up around the corral as the girls practiced. Everyone's rope throws got a little more tentative as they waited for Clint to arrive. Vote two coming. Cowgirl two leaving.

Clint moseyed through the gate with a lasso in hand and asked the girls to stand side by side in a semicircle in front of him.

"The second day votin' results are in," he said, with his usual scan of all the worried faces. "Meg, you won the barrel race and got bonus points. Riley, you came in last and lost points." The cameras undoubtedly caught the dirty look Riley flashed at Meg. Meg hoped it also caught Mattie's smug smile.

"The voting was close for a while, but after last night's barn chats we saw a surge in negatives for a few of you." Meg hadn't seen the other barn chats, so she didn't know what might have happened there to turn people off. Maybe it was her and Mattie and Riley for being so catty.

"So, we'll let this lariat break the news."

Clint swung the loop over his head a few times, then launched it. Toward Riley. She saw it coming and tried to duck sideways while pulling Jasmine into her place. But Jasmine planted a boot and didn't budge, and Mattie on the other side shoved Riley back into line. The rope neatly settled around her shoulders and Clint yanked it tight.

"Riley, sorry to say it's you that's goin' home today. You gave it a good shot, but only one cowgirl can win."

To her credit, Riley didn't fight it as Clint reeled her in to undo the rope. In fact, she was smiling, and once her arms were free, she wrapped them around Clint and planted a kiss on his surprised face.

"Look me up when it's all over, cowboy."

She strode off proudly.

It wasn't fair. Riley was a good horsewoman, and probably would have done well if she had some practice time. Dusty was fast. But that worked against her with all that hay-induced itching, the horse reacting in confusion to every twitch.

At least Riley was going home to a week off and maybe a date with Clint later. Meg would've had a date with a Corporation assassin. She had to admit, Howie's roll in the hay might have saved her life.

* * *

Meg stepped up to the bank of microphones, squinting into the glare of the TV lights. Even during the day they made it hard to see the crowd assembled in front of her.

Pavel had told her the barrel race episode went viral, and when every tabloid website clamored for an interview, his boss insisted they allow one as a publicity boost. Ranger Norcroft wasn't happy about it—as Meg approached the lectern, she'd heard him chewing out Pavel. Norcroft was afraid someone would leak some current event knowledge to Meg; she was worried that she'd blurt some current event knowledge to Norcroft.

Clint and Pavel flanked her, with the Ranger a step back and off to the side, scowling at the reporters. Arlene Harrington stood front and center, looking a bit peeved—at being surrounded by competition? A small crowd of cowgirls loitered behind the reporters, looking equally miffed that Meg was getting so much attention.

She didn't recognize anyone else, except, finally, she saw Howie lurking at the back. He seemed to be staying away from everyone, especially the women. She stifled a smile at the thought of Cassidy hog-tying him in seven seconds flat. Served him right for wearing the damn cologne here.

The first question sounded like a plant, from Muddy or Pavel or even Norcroft.

"Who won the World Series last year?"

Meg wrinkled her brow.

"Is that baseball?" A ripple of laughter followed. "I couldn't tell you even if I did remember anything."

"Do you remember who you had sex with? They found semen—"

"Stop right there!" Ranger Norcroft leapt out in front of the cameras. "I told you, no outside information in your questions. Especially not wild tabloid conjecture. Stick to the competition."

They found semen! Of course—they did all those tests. She caught Howie's eye; even from that distance, he looked guilty. She hoped her surprised reaction to the question didn't make her look guilty, too. An amnesiac would be surprised to hear she'd had sex she couldn't remember, right? And would wonder who with, too, right? She went for that look as she recovered her composure for the next question.

"Seems like you had the fastest horse yesterday. And Clint loaned you his pistol for the shooting competition. He's your boyfriend's brother, and he says he likes you. Is he helping you out?"

Clint jumped in for that one.

"I assure you all, this is a fair competition. I'm not helpin' anyone out."

Did that include Muddy and the Corporation? If he wasn't helping them, he'd surely help Meg avenge his brother's murder. Right?

Meg answered questions ranging from what it was like to handle a stumbling horse to who her favorite other cowgirl was. She tactfully skirted that one.

"Okay, we have time for one more question," Clint said. Meg pointed to a guy in the front.

"Are your breasts real?"

Half the crowd let out a little gasp, the other half an awkward laugh. Meg went with the fun half.

"They were before I lost my memory," she said, smiling. She looked down for a quick survey. "And they seem to be the same now."

* * *

Muddy cruised past Kenny Trauger's Bound for Glory and took a moment to inspect it from the water. The ship was 120 meters, ten times the size of his own little craft. He wasn't jealous—his high-speed boat served its purpose, which was to get him to and from his rig quickly and comfortably. He had no need for a deluxe bondage room.

He could see the equipment crate dominating the stern deck, just behind the lifeboat bays. He assumed the entire installation was being done correctly, but he'd give it a check before Captain Trauger and his first mate came aboard.

He tied up at the marina and unloaded his equipment case. It was heavier than usual, given the machined aluminum parts inside. He'd spent all night modifying off-the-shelf Acme parts to fit a mini-dragster, and when the first two tests failed, he had to adapt new parts to try to fix the issue. Luckily, the offshore rig boasted a full machine shop and every tool he needed. He was confident in the result, but he'd been overconfident before.

At least he'd gotten them done. He called ahead to the raceway to make sure he'd still get access to the cars before the race; they were happy to accommodate any request in exchange for the free publicity they were getting. He also confirmed that the decals Spike created, the stated reason for working on the cars, were waiting for him at the track. The only issue was his lack of sleep. He'd have to pump some serious coffee at lunch. Maybe he could catch a nap before the race.

He certainly wasn't going to miss the race.

His phone rang; he glanced at the caller ID. Hayden Sterling! He hit connect.

"Mornin', Hayden."

"Hi Muddy. I've got the results from your DNA sample. I tried to reach you earlier, but I—"

"Yeah, yeah, I was out of signal range. What's the result?"

"There's a match."

Of course there was.

"So, the sample I gave you matches what they found in Meg Brecker?"

"Well, there were two DNA profiles, and one of them matched the Brecker sample. Your sample had multiple donors."

"Not surprising." Ellen Wilcox had a business to run.

"Are you gonna report this to the Rangers? You'll be a hero, breaking the case."

"Listen, Hayden. I'm not reportin' nuthin', because this never happened. You never got a sample from me, and there's no evidence that you checked anything against Brecker's sample. Got it?"

"Wow, you sound serious."

"Dead serious. Got it?"

"Yes, sir."

"Good. Don't call me again. You'll be hearin' from CSI Houston soon. And thanks."

"Thank you! Bye."

Muddy hung up and started the truck. Now he had one more thing to think about:

What to do with Kenny Trauger?

* * *

Tired of Burke's sexism and Maggie's weapon-colored glasses, Lynn spent the rest of the morning in her room, watching Bikini Cowgirl segments. Samantha was comparing tattoos with Lisa, talking about the long and painful Acora logo sessions, which left less skin across her shoulders untouched than inked. But she loved the attention it got from the rare like-minded male fans of the Houston death-metal band. Lisa professed the opposite goal—she wanted to scare men off. The "I BITE" tat on her shoulder was pretty effective, she admitted, but the "My STD is nothing to clap about" on the inside of her thigh always sealed the deal.

Jasmine had joined the group, and the inked girls sympathized with her complaint that there was no way to do a light-on-dark tat for Black girls. But Jasmine admitted that she had an inner-lip tattoo.

"Growing up Black in a White community, I wanted something to celebrate my heritage," she said, and peeled back her lower lip to reveal the single word: HUMAN.

As Lynn drove to her second meeting with Nick Wood, Jasmine's situation percolated through her mind. Jasmine was a fish out of water on many levels—Black among White, inner city kid among country folks, and even a bit of a philosopher among practical-minded cowgirls. Lynn understood the feeling—she was a hippies' kid with a degree in English and a yearning for holistic balance but acting as a rookie spy in a noir mystery. Unfortunately, unlike reality show contestants, noir dames often ended up dead by the end of the movie.

No, that was selfish. In this case, Meg was in more danger than she was.

Lynn shivered as she plunged into the overly air-conditioned air of the Boom & Bust Bookstore. It was a much better place to meet Nick than Hoover Dam—in town, a short southwest drive from the Noir. Even so, she'd considered standing him up. But when he insisted that the WCG would probably give her a promotion for bringing in his ideas, it struck her that she was Nick's only link to the WCG.

Roger had said he couldn't figure out how all these separate Corporation groups even knew about each other. So how did Nick even know about the WCG? She decided to meet with him and find out—that would earn some Roger respect.

Nick was waiting for her in the fiction aisle. The shelves were tall enough to hide them, but the store was so quiet she was sure their voices would carry. Nick apparently agreed—he stretched up and whispered in her ear.

"I bet you're wondering why I summoned you here today."

Lynn shot him a side-eye frown.

"Good bet, high roller. Let's hear it."

Nick nodded, and pulled one of the face-out bestsellers from the rack.

"*The Urbane League's First Rodeo*," he said, "Ever heard of it?"

"Of course I have." Not only had she read it, she'd overheard it discussed by the real Wacko Conspiracy Group people back in Boston. "What about it?"

Nick peered around the corner and turned back to Lynn.

"What if, instead of being a spoof like *Men in Black*, we put out the idea that it actually contains secret knowledge, like *The Illuminatus Trilogy* does? You know, presented as a joke, but actually revealing the truth." He leaned back, smiling triumphantly.

Lynn smiled, too. This would be easy to shoot down.

"What if I told you we're already promoting the book?"

Nick frowned, his brow wrinkled in thought.

"But the book actually talks about a Wacky Conspiracy Team! You guys are outing yourselves?"

"No, that's what's so brilliant about it. As you said, the book is marketed as a spoof; it's already kind of a wacko conspiracy theory.

Anyone who reads about the Wacky Conspiracy Team thinks it's just a joke. And never suspects there really is one, though with a slightly different name."

Nick started to let out a low whistle, then caught himself, glancing around the racks again.

"So, if we say it's not a joke, we let the cat out of the bag."

"If they believe it. But really, it's too self-referential. If we push a theory that the book is telling the truth about a group that pushes fake theories, I think our tin-foil-hatters' heads will blow up like a fresh batch of Jiffy Pop. It's the 'I am lying' paradox."

Nick's eyes and shoulders fell in unison.

"It is a little too meta, I guess."

Then he shrugged, and brightened up again.

"Okay, it has to be believable, but not too believable, and not be about itself. Give me one more chance?"

The way this was going, it couldn't hurt.

"Sure, Nick. But maybe you can help me out. I'm curious—"

Lynn stopped and put a finger to her lips. Reflected in the smoked glass bookstore window, Burke Barrage was making his way into the next aisle.

"Well," she said loudly enough for Burke to hear, "I appreciate the recommendation, sir. I'll put that on my list of books to read next." She hid her hands from the window and pantomimed someone listening in. Nick nodded solemnly.

"You'll enjoy it, ma'am, I'm sure," he said, and wandered off toward the self-help aisle.

Ma'am? Did she look that old?

Lynn grabbed a random thriller—*Coordinate Zero, Zero*, about a highly evolved smartphone app—and headed for the register. She didn't glance over at Burke. He might have failed at tailing Frank Woodland, but he'd done a pretty good job tailing Lynn Grady. She wondered what made him suspicious. Maybe he was always suspicious of the femme fatale. Not a bad policy, actually, considering what she was up to.

On her drive back, she mused about the Urbane League book. The spoof was dead accurate in some places; she wondered if the author knew something about what was really going on.

She headed back up the Strip and pushed the book, Nick Wood, and Burke Barrage to the back of her mind as she admired the theme hotels. She glanced up at the fake Eiffel tower, and then left at the dancing Bellagio fountains, and promised herself she'd come back on foot to take in the sights up close. As she returned her attention to traffic, she noted movement on the right and instinctively hit the brakes. A beat-up pickup truck fishtailed out of the side road, just missing her front bumper, and turned north. It wove around traffic and disappeared in seconds. It was the same pickup, with the same snowplow mount attached to the front, that nearly hit her on the way to Hoover Dam.

Lynn remained frozen with a death-grip on the wheel. Someone was taking the fatal in femme fatale very seriously. She really needed to be more alert.

Car horns erupted behind her, so she started moving again, slowly, very aware of the side street traffic.

She'd been meeting with Nick both times, so he knew where she'd be driving and when. He was so cooperative, he couldn't have guessed she was Urban Legion. In fact, given the discussion in the bookstore, he probably didn't even believe in the Urban Legion. Or the Urbane League, for that matter.

He knew she was involved with Phil; was the Corporation trying to clean up loose ends from the shopping chip disaster? Couldn't be—she wasn't part of the operation as far as Phil or any of his people knew.

Maybe the common denominator wasn't meeting with Nick but going out in her car. She'd only used it to meet Nick. Who else would know when she was driving? The valet? She reviewed her noir film knowledge but couldn't think of one movie where the valet was part of the plot.

As she dropped off the car at Noir, she looked for signs of guilt in the valet's face but didn't see anything. Then she debated whether to tell Burke.

Oh, what a tangled web we weave, when first we practice to deceive, said Zen-mind.

Zen-mind was importing Scottish wisdom now? And clearly had never found itself embroiled in a noir plot.

* * *

I got back to my office and poured two fingers of Kentucky juice. It was my day off, and I needed to think. I had questions.

Did I spook Grady in the bookstore? I didn't think she spied me, but she dusted out in a hurry just a few minutes after she showed up. And seconds after I did.

Who was she bumping gums with? It sounded like he was a stranger, but I glommed him after Grady took the gate. I could swear I'd seen the mug before, but I couldn't place him. Maybe the Noir. Maybe the Media Book.

Grady showed up just in time to give me the answers. Or not. She looked a little shaken. I offered her a snort to calm her nerves, but it was only noon, so she declined.

"Someone's trying to kill me," she said.

That could add a little urgency to the case.

"Someone? Charlie Stewart?"

"I don't know." She gave me the lowdown about two close calls with the same pickup truck. A truck sporting a battering ram. She was right about snowplows in Vegas—about as likely as high-wire acrobats with vertigo.

"Where were you headed?"

"I was sightseeing yesterday, on my way to Hoover Dam. Today I just went to a bookstore. I didn't see any good novels in the Christian Science Reading Room."

She didn't lie about the bookstore. But if she was onto my tail, she knew a lie would stick out like a clown's size 23s.

"Who knew you were on the road?"

Grady flinched. I didn't expect a straight answer, and I didn't get one.

"Nobody except the Noir valet."

Her eyes said there was someone else. Maybe the guy in the bookstore. But it was hard to tell—she was still as twisted up as a pair of aerial silks after a spin routine. I sent her back to the hotel to unwind; she could've used that drink.

I tossed back the rest of mine and planned my closing-time date with Frank Woodland. But I kept coming back to the question: who wanted Lynn Grady dead?

* * *

Lieutenant Norcroft followed Will Brecker into the kitchen of the modest ranch house.

"Can I get you a drink?" Will asked, pointing to an equally modest bar.

"No thanks, I'm on duty. Mind if we set up at the table here? I'd like to ask you about some interesting Bikini Cowgirl videos."

Brecker nodded, looking intrigued. Norcroft took a seat and opened his laptop as Brecker pulled up a chair next to him.

"Have you been watching the show?"

Brecker shrugged.

"I watched the competitions. Tried watchin' the other stuff, but I can't stand that fake drama they're always tryin' to stir up. Turned it off real quick."

Good. That meant he hadn't seen either video yet.

"Okay, first let's take a look at this conversation from a few nights ago."

Norcroft started the barn chat video and watched Will's face. He seemed a little uncomfortable to see Meg in a skimpy bikini. That was good, too—if he didn't, it'd be creepy. It made Norcroft feel a little guilty about ogling this guy's daughter, but heck, he was single and she was beautiful.

The other cowgirls were giving Meg a hard time about wearing barrettes. She seemed taken aback, then told them she'd worn barrettes since middle school. Will would know if that was true. Will didn't know that Norcroft knew it wasn't. He stopped the video.

"I'd like to confirm that last statement. Did Meg wear barrettes since middle school?"

Will's face clouded. Trying to remember, or realizing Meg was lying?

"I got to admit, sir, I don't rightly recall. I ain't much for noticin' ladies' fashions, much less teenagers'. She mighta'."

Norcroft tried to read that answer—it could've been honest. Not an obvious lie, but not obviously the truth, either. He hadn't confirmed or denied Meg's story.

"She grew up around you. Could you tell if she was lying?"

Brecker chuckled.

"Never could—I'm thinkin' she got away with a mess o' things I didn't know about. And probably didn't want to."

"Okay, let's look at this one."

He started the video of the day's tabloid interview. Will laughed at Meg's comeback answer about the World Series. But he exploded at the semen question.

"What the hell kinda question is that to ask?! You got video of the reporter? I'll kick that sumbitch's ass!"

"No, I don't. And I stopped it there; she didn't have to answer." Norcroft backed up the video to just before the question. "But I'd like you to focus on her face in response."

He played the clip again, and Will frowned as he watched. Norcroft had viewed the clip a dozen times, and thought she was shocked that they'd found semen, shocked that the press knew about it, and maybe blindsided by the idea that there was evidence of who she'd been with during her memory blackout. What he couldn't tell was if she knew who that person was. The lab had tested a hair sample from Clint Owen and concluded the semen did not come from him or his brother Tommy.

Or an alien.

"Well, what do you think?"

"I think she was rightfully surprised and confused by the question."

Norcroft looked Will in the eye.

"But do you think she knows whose semen it is?"

Will slapped the table and jumped to his feet.

"Are you accusin' her of lyin' about this whole amnesia thing? You got the nerve to let someone ask a disgustin' question like that, and then you want me to help you answer it? My daughter is a big girl and she can sleep with whoever the hell she wants to! And if she says she can't remember who it was, you damn well better believe her!"

Norcroft nodded and closed the laptop.

"Okay, I guess that answers my question."

He already knew Meg Brecker was willing to lie. Now it

seemed Will Brecker would back her up unconditionally. Which meant he couldn't be trusted either.

When he got back in the truck, he called headquarters and connected with the digital forensic lab.

"I'd like cell phone records for Will Brecker." He gave them the number. "Yeah, let's go back four years."

Chapter 21

Howie sat in his car and liberally reapplied cologne. He'd waited until he was at the dock this time, in case he was diverted to the ranch again. But Muddy hadn't gone back out to the rig and intended to stay ashore for the drag race, so the literal coast was clear. Howie hated to miss the race—he had a bad feeling about Meg and Muddy and a high-speed vehicle. But Meg insisted he was worrying too much. So be it. That probably meant she wasn't going to quit. And she'd want him to find out what Muddy was up to on platform 10775.

Howie had already scoped the Galveston rental boat scene and chose Wreckless Water Craft Rental, figuring they wouldn't be too uptight about his lack of boating skills. He walked out along the wharf and looked over the waiting sailboats, fishing boats, and jet skis as he approached the office. The platform was twelve miles out, which meant he needed a fast machine. That eliminated all but the 24-foot center console with a huge black outboard motor. Howie didn't know much about boats, but 250 horsepower sounded like it would get him there and bring him back. Fast, if Blackjack was the standard for one horsepower.

He tried to swagger into the office, not sure if boaters would be bowlegged like all the cowboys he'd been observing. The rental guy behind the counter sized Howie up, his drooping eyebrows suggesting that the swagger didn't work.

"I'd like to rent a boat, please. I like that 24-foot Sea Hunt you've got there. Is it available today?"

"Yeah, if it's here, it's available. Got another customer tomorrow though—you just want a one-day?"

"Yeah, just today. Has it got a radio?"

"Radio and a Humminbird fishfinder with GPS. What're you fishing for?"

Howie knew he should've worked out the whole story before coming in. Visions of his UT Medical Branch fiasco flashed through his mind. He had no idea what kind of fish the people around here tried to catch, and no fishing gear anyway.

"Just doin' some scopin' today. Be back next week with my buddies for some real fishin'." He wondered how authentic his New York Jewish Texas accent sounded.

"Whatever. That's $650 for the day, cash or credit, up front."

Howie nodded and handed over his credit card. The rental agent swiped the card, and as it verified, filled out a rental agreement.

"I'll need to see your Boater Ed Card," he said as he passed the form to Howie to sign. There was an awkward pause. Howie had forgotten that when they rented the first boat online, weeks earlier, they'd had to submit an image of the card. The Photoshopped forgery was stored on his laptop back at the hotel.

"I don't have one. Just got into town yesterday. In New York, we don't need a license."

"Well, in Texas, you do. I can't rent to you without seeing your card."

"So you're willing to leave that $650 rental in the slip for the day?"

"Yessir. The fine for renting without seeing the card is $1000."

Howie bit his lip. This went against everything his father had ever taught him.

"How about I show you $1000 cash and we pretend it was a card? And you can take as long as you want to look at it. Until you spend it, anyway."

The agent flashed a look of disbelief, before apparently realizing that Howie was either an idiot or involved in something seriously illegal, but in either case, was offering a great deal.

"Works for me. But keep an eye out for the Texas Marine Safety boats. They're black and white."

"Really? With flashing red lights yet?"

"Blue, actually." The agent paused, waiting. Howie drew ten $100 bills from his previously thick wallet and handed them over. The agent pocketed the cash and held up a key ring.

"You know how to run a Yamaha F250?"

"Eh, I'll figure it out."

The clerk shrugged and handed over the key.

"One more rule. No bananas on board the boat."

"No bananas? That's just a superstition, isn't it?"

"Nope. Banana peel residue ruins the fiberglass finish."

Howie promised to protect the boat from banana corrosion and headed for the slip.

He managed to start the engine and back out into the harbor with only a few bumps into the pilings. By the time he rounded Fort Point and reached open water he'd figured out the steering, the throttle, the GPS, the fishfinder, and the fact that he should have worn a windbreaker. A stiff northeast wind was blowing up considerable chop.

Was he supposed to steer into the waves or along them?

* * *

Muddy Bootes tightened a hidden nut. The Mighty-Mite half-scale junior dragster was a marvel of simplicity, designed to introduce kids to racing with maximum fun and minimum risk. The modifications Muddy was making to this particular vehicle would change the risk level considerably for Meg Brecker.

The afternoon's competition was an 8.9-second-class mini-drag race. The cowgirls would drive identical half-scale dragsters—well, except for Meg, but she wouldn't know that. The bigger girls might have trouble getting into the tiny cars, but for most, it was a perfect fit. And while heavier drivers were slower, speed wasn't everything in these races; each racer would pick an expected time and try to get as close to that as possible, without going faster. Too fast and they'd be disqualified.

Meg was a small girl; she'd have no problem dialing in the minimum 8.9 seconds and might even DQ under. But that didn't matter to Muddy. He was more concerned with what was going to happen after 8.9 seconds.

Three things controlled an alcohol-fueled junior dragster: the steering yoke, the brake, and the throttle. Making the brake fail and the throttle stick was easy, but making it happen only after the car achieved racing speed was not. It was critical that Meg not notice anything wrong until it was too late.

The finish line at East Houston Raceway was set up for kids at 1/8 mile. The adult line was at 1/4, and a retaining wall at a half mile. Muddy figured Meg's car would be doing a good 130 MPH by the time it got to the finish line, where he would spill a little oil from the reservoir hidden in his boot. And the fuel reservoir hidden in front of Meg's feet would make for a fine explosion when she finally slammed into the wall.

Meg's barrettes wouldn't help her—there was no radio signal to jam. And there was no way she'd get out of driving this car, thanks to Pavel agreeing that authentic race optics demanded racers' names in large letters on the dragster shells. Spike had delivered the names on time and professional-looking. She was a good hire.

He smoothed the "Meg" decal into place on the candy-blue fiberglass.

This here deathtrap's got your name on it, little lady.

* * *

Howie pulled up to platform 10775 and looked for the dock. He'd spent a few hours researching the old rigs, enough to know his way around. Typically, the rig crew would hoist newcomers aboard with a personnel basket, but Howie assumed—hoped, actually—there was no one aboard to run the hoist. He found a floating dock anchored to one of the main piers, with ample gangway to deal with tides. He tethered the Sea Hunt to the cleats and climbed aboard the rig.

The gangway led to a small platform considerably lower than the main pipe deck. Leading upward was a ladder. No elevator, no protective cage, just a ladder. About a hundred feet.

Howie forced away wistful thoughts of Manhattan escalators and started climbing. He was already chilled from the open-ocean ride, and hanging onto an exposed ladder fifty feet above the surface didn't help. But eventually he reached the deck and the more conventional stairs up to the crew quarters. He checked that his personal witness was charged and recording.

It was obvious this rig hadn't drilled for oil in a long time. The dining area featured a thick layer of dust, save one table near the kitchen that Howie assumed was Muddy's dinner spot. The kitchen smelled of cooking grease, and the refrigerator had a fresh supply of milk and eggs. Clearly Muddy lived here. Howie looked in on his quarters, where toiletries were scattered on the desktop next to an unmade bed. No reason to make the bed out here. The sheets and pillowcases were white; Howie was disappointed not to find purple, or pink, or a teddy bear pattern.

He was beginning to feel like this was just a creative way to save rent when he noticed footprints in the dust leading away from the kitchen. He followed them to a hallway with several doors.

The first door opened into a well-equipped machine shop. It was mostly neat, with tools and bits all organized behind a cleared-off workbench. There were footprints all around the drill press and the computer-controlled router, and tiny curls of metal were scattered about on the floor. They looked fresh. Howie shrugged. You live on an oil rig, you can't go to the hardware store for parts when the plumbing leaks or the fridge acts up.

He wandered down the hall to where the footprints stopped in front of another door. Howie grabbed the handle and twisted. It didn't move.

Why would Muddy lock one door, way the heck out here?

Howie had his universal lock-picking toolkit in his pocket. He took out his wallet, selected a credit card, and slid it along the latch. The door popped open.

This was the drill control room. Instrumentation lined the circular wall around a swivel operator chair in the middle. Howie expected traditional meters and readouts, but in this case, the tradition had been upgraded. A multiscreen graphics array dominated the wall, displaying a map of the Gulf, with small lit triangles scattered across the entire expanse. The indicators seemed to represent Internet Protocol network nodes; each one was labeled with an IP address, using the standard 192.168.x.x private domain. It was a live status of some kind of network—apparently working well given the green color of most of the indicators. Some of the ones on the east side were flashing red.

The longitude and latitude of one of the nearby nodes exactly matched the coordinates of the undersea gadget Meg had found. So apparently, there wasn't just one mystery device to worry about—there were hundreds. But what was the odd shaped symbol at the top, off the Gulf map? It had no coordinates, but its network address wasn't in the 192.168 private domain; that meant it was public, and could be tracked down.

Couldn't hurt to try. It probably monitored all the others.

Its symbol was shaped like the Welcome to Las Vegas sign, complete with chaser lights and a flashing star. The physical node had to be somewhere near the sign. Tracking it down might help Lynn and the Vegas Legion find Charlie Stewart.

And finding Charlie Stewart, and his mysterious network node, suddenly seemed a lot more urgent.

* * *

Meg studied the mini-dragsters lined up on the infield. They looked kind of cute, and she imagined them all full of kids having a great time. But as the track staff helped various-sized bikini-clad cowgirls into the tiny vehicles, it was clear that this was going to be more fun for some than for others. Cassidy, the steer-and-Howie wrangler, looked like she'd rather be flipping the little car on its back than wedged into it. And Bobbie Jo was so tall they had to remove her seatback before she could slide her legs into the shell.

Meg's car fit her nicely. The shoulder strap was a little tight, pinching between her boobs; Pavel made sure the camera guys got close-ups of that on video. But the steering yoke was the right height, the throttle at a comfortable spot at her feet, and the brake handy at her side. She'd never driven one before, but it seemed pretty simple. She was a little concerned that she'd go too fast, so she'd practiced counting seconds, and would ease off the throttle if she might beat the 8.9 minimum.

Meg was near the middle of the schedule, so she got to watch some others make their runs. They approached the start line where two pairs of sensors detected them, one just short of the line and one right at it. A tower of lights called a Christmas tree, visible a few yards in front of them, lit the top two yellow lights as the car reached each sensor. Then a chain of three amber lights below that lit, in turn a half-second apart, followed by a green one, which meant time to go. A red light at the bottom meant the racer left too early and was disqualified.

The other girls were surprisingly good; most were within a few seconds of their time, and only Dallas DQ'd. She apparently had a lead foot and couldn't resist going as fast as possible. Muddy Bootes was out past the finish line, helping the dragsters off the track, where the fake cowboys waited to tow them back with golf carts. The cowgirls had to walk back; Dallas wasn't happy about that at all. No doubt Pavel made sure the cameras caught her displeasure in close-up, too.

Then it was Meg's turn. She donned her gloves and helmet as two strong guys grabbed the roll bar and pushed her car toward the starting line, through a patch where they'd splashed a little water on the track to wet down the tires for traction. Somebody applied an electric starter crank to her engine and fired it up. The centrifugal clutch would only engage at higher engine speeds; she pulled the handbrake, pressed the throttle, and listened to the engine rev as the car strained forward against the brake. She gave the yoke a few experimental twists and watched the front wheels yaw. The air was thick with the smell of oil, rubber, and burning fuel. This was pretty cool.

"Next up," came Clint's voice over the loudspeaker, barely audible over the roar of the engine, "Meg. Eight point nine dialed in."

She feathered the handbrake and inched up until the prestart line Christmas tree light came on. A few more inches to the start line, and the second yellow lit up. She let up the throttle and released the brake as the amber lights started their sequence.

Flash, flash, flash, GO!

Meg gripped the yoke and floored the throttle. These little racers couldn't pop a wheelie, but Meg could feel the engine making the effort as it poured power into the big rear tires. She almost forgot to count her seconds as the cameras and grandstand flew past. At 5 seconds she realized she was too quick and eased up the throttle while pulling on the brake.

But the car kept accelerating. She passed the finish line at 7 seconds, trying to hold the yoke with one hand, yank the brake with the other, and pull the stuck throttle up with her toe. Only the steering was successful, until she hit an oily patch of pavement where Muddy dove out of the way. The rear end fishtailed into a spin.

Halfway around she was facing backward, oily smoke billowing from the tires as they ground against the asphalt. Fully around the spin she was facing frontward again, the retaining wall dead ahead. The car wanted to straighten out, but that would just hasten the collision, so she yanked the yoke to continue the spin. After another half-turn she pulled the yoke the other way to keep the car aimed backward.

The rear tires were still rotating at full speed, and the car slowed as they began to grab in a cloud of smoke. And then she was stopped—for a split second. There was no time to climb out; she gripped the yoke as the racer accelerated back up the track. She caught a glimpse of Muddy's astonished face near the finish line, and the panicked onlookers at the start as they scrambled out of the way.

Meg blew past the Christmas tree, steered around Lisa's car in the prestart area, and swerved through the entrance tunnel to the parking lot. She found a narrow path through parked cars, skidded the back end into a slight turn to find the open fence gate, and flew along the access road for a few hundred yards. As she approached the state highway, she prayed for no cross traffic and aimed for the ATV park on the opposite side.

The car bumped a bit over some tall grass but didn't slow, and finally skidded into the sandy off-road recreational area. Like a truck turnout, the sand gently absorbed the car's momentum and brought it to a soft stop. The rear wheels were still turning, throwing a plume of sand into the air as they dug a grave for the malfunctioning little car.

She leaned back, heart pounding, and relaxed her white-knuckle grip on the yoke.

This had to be Muddy's handiwork. Howie was right. She felt a flash of guilt for doubting him, quickly replaced by a wave of dread about the next event. A boat ride with the guy whose last boat ride killed Tommy.

She needed help, soon. Someone on the inside. Someone she could trust. Clint?

Howie said Muddy had sabotaged her gun at the shooting competition. But Clint gave her his, saving her life. That was not the act of a fellow assassin.

It had to be Clint. She couldn't trust anyone else.

She unhooked the shoulder strap. The damn thing really did pinch.

* * *

Clint abandoned his station near the starting line the moment Meg's dragster roared past and through the entrance tunnel. Pavel would give him a hard time for not waiting for the camera crew to get it all on video, but the dragster was a rabbit to the camera cart's turtle. He didn't think to grab a handy cam.

He sprinted across the parking lot in time to see her car hit the ATV track boundary with a spray of sand. The engine roar closed in on itself as the plume from the spinning tires fell back and covered the pipes. By the time he reached the state highway, the engine began to cough. He covered the last few yards to the now half-buried car.

"Meg!" he yelled into sudden silence as the sand-choked engine cut out completely.

Meg looked up, startled.

"I can hear you!" She pulled off the helmet. "I'm okay."

She didn't look okay. There was a tremor in her voice and panic in her eyes.

"Clint, can you…" she took a furtive glance over her shoulder "…come to my cabin tonight, without anyone knowing? I need to tell you something important. It's urgent."

Clint shook his head.

"That's against the rules. I'll get fired."

Meg sighed, her eyes searching.

"I was afraid of that." She set her jaw. "The crew will be here soon, so I'll just tell you now. You decide if we can talk later."

She took a deep breath.

"I'm fakin' the amnesia, I remember everything. Muddy is part of a conspiracy that killed Tommy but made it look like the urban legend of a scuba diver in a forest fire. I got away and hid out in Boston with other urban legend survivors, called the Urban Legion. I came back with Howie Friedman, that reporter, to find out why they killed Tommy. We were divin' but got attacked by dolphins with spearguns. After I escaped you found me on the beach. I joined the show figurin' they wouldn't kill me while I was popular, but Muddy's tryin' to kill me anyway. I need your help to find out what he and his pals are up to. And to keep me alive."

Clint stared at her, not even blinking.

"Is this a joke?"

"It's no joke. Please, figure out how we can talk off-camera. And talk to Howie today. Mention the Urban Legion—he'll believe you. Pick your nose, it'll convince him."

"Now you're jokin'."

"It's our secret greeting." She glanced back again. "I think we're out of time."

Pavel and a camera crew appeared over the embankment and made their way across the sand. Clint put on his host face and turned to the camera.

"As you can see, Meg is all right. Just a stuck throttle, but she handled it like a champ."

Ranger Norcroft was next on the scene, followed by medical staff who started checking Meg out, as the cameras captured it all on video for the benefit of the voyeuristic audience. Clint stepped back and watched.

The medics could check her out physically, but not mentally. Her story was crazy. The diver in the fire *was* an urban legend, as were armed dolphins patrolling the Gulf. And even if those were true, could you fill a secret organization with urban legend survivors?

Next thing she'd be telling him about Elvis and his

microwaved poodle! He snorted a laugh. And Elvis would pick his nose to identify himself.

Still, if the story was bogus, why would Meg tell it? It was even less plausible than the amnesia story.

The questions Pavel was feeding him in his chat scripts for Meg were obviously attempts to trip up a liar. And if Meg was a possible witness against Pavel and Muddy, of course they'd want her to forget. Permanently.

And when Muddy hired him—out of the blue, for a surprisingly large sum of money—Clint had to drop his crusade to keep investigating Tommy's disappearance. Did they hire him just to shut him up?

That would also mean Clint was working for the guy who killed his brother. Muddy never mentioned that in the interview.

Clint had to admit, he hadn't seen signs that Meg was worried about what happened to Tommy. It made sense; if she knew Tommy was dead for the last three years, she'd have moved on by now. That was the worst part of the story, if it was true. Clint hadn't moved on yet. He didn't want to. He still clung to the hope that Tommy was alive.

He got a signal that the drag races were getting underway again and headed back to the track. Meg had given him some new information. He could try to verify it when he talked to Howie—leave out important details and see if Howie had the same answers.

Howie was the key.

* * *

Muddy ran to the top deck of the grandstand to watch the action across the highway. The camera crews were arriving, so he dialed in his feed monitor. Meg was explaining that it was just some sort of mechanical failure, and she was fine.

The fucking bitch was indestructible. He might have to just shoot her.

But there would be no immediate opportunity for that—the boat trip was next. And, more pressing, Muddy needed to make sure no one but him looked closely at Meg's car. He'd been counting on the evidence becoming charred smithereens.

His phone chirped at him, an alarm from his drilling rig network. Just another nuisance pelican he assumed, as he hit the silence button. But before the security cam image disappeared from the screen, he recognized the intruder. Not a pelican. It was that reporter, Howie something. The one who came in with Arlene Harrington.

This was like an underwater oil leak—suddenly, priorities change. Meg's car could wait.

He pulled out his phone and scanned his contact list. Arlene got Howie into this, she was the perfect one to get him out. Muddy was sure she and her associates would appreciate the business. He'd even send Pavel's cowboys along to help, free of charge.

* * *

Roger dragged back into Urban Legion headquarters from class, defeated again. Still no luck on recognizing a professor's voice, and this time the classes were smaller and he'd got picked on to answer a question. It was like that nightmare where he's halfway through the term and hasn't even looked at his schedule, much less gone to a class or bought a textbook. He'd fallen back on the tried-and-true sheepish "I got nuthin'." It was that much more embarrassing in front of a Harvard crowd.

He watched the video of Meg's race and his depression deepened. She was exceptionally capable, but also very lucky. How long would her luck hold out? Muddy Bootes was not going to quit. Unfortunately, neither was Meg. In spite of her boss wanting her to.

As usual when he felt like an incompetent manager, he turned his attention to the database search. He'd added Arlene Harrington, and, as expected, came up empty. There had to be a connection—Dirt TV had to be on someone's payroll.

Follow the money.

He thought back on Muddy's wiretapped conversations. He'd said the Corporation funded Kenny's boat, and that Muddy fronted Hayden Sterling's dad some money. Roger found a Sterling Auto Body business in Houston and researched financials. Obfuse Capital Corporation had given them the loan.

Roger set up a new search on Obfuse and found that they had funded the purchase of a luxury yacht for one Kenneth Trauger. But it was another transaction that got him excited. Obfuse had financed the launching of Dirt TV, just a few months before the Bikini Cowgirl show hit the web.

He called Howie and got no answer. He tried texting and waited a few minutes for a response. Again, nothing.

He called Houston and got Devon.

"Hi Devon, Roger here. I need to talk to Howie, right now."

"Not around. He's still out on Muddy's rig."

Crap. His phone was probably out of range.

"Okay, if you talk to him before he gets my text message, you need to pass this along to him. Dirt TV is Corporation-funded, and appears to have been created just to hype the Bikini Cowgirl show. Arlene is the principal officer. So she's definitely Corporation, and Howie needs to be careful."

"Got it, I'll let him know as soon as he gets back."

"Thanks. Oh, and I've got a few wacko stories for you to plant about the drag race today."

* * *

Arlene stood aside to let the cameras zoom in on the extrication process. The tow truck was winching the mini-dragster out of the sand slowly, but not slowly enough for Muddy Bootes, who was supervising the process in detail. He acted like an archaeologist unearthing a dinosaur skeleton—careful not to move too fast or stress the little car in any way. Probably wanted to make sure he could figure out just what went wrong. He seemed like that kind of a perfectionist.

"As you can see, the racer plowed thirty yards across the sand before stopping. Meg was lucky to find the track, and lucky again there was no one out there today. Be sure to watch the exciting competition, including Meg's miraculous survival, on Reality Web later today. This is Arlene Harrington for Dirt TV."

The red recording light blinked out. As her crew packed up their gear Arlene checked her phone. She'd been scooped by everybody.

Prying Eye was already questioning whether the accident was actually Meg covering for going too fast, or maybe a stunt set up by the show. CNN went with a special report on reality show safety concerns.

Sensation Today wondered if Meg had gotten some driving training while she was aboard the alien spacecraft. The National Nose suggested Meg could be the reincarnation of Dale Earnhardt, neglecting to consider that Meg was born before Earnhardt died. Not that facts like that ever got considered by the tabloids.

Intrude Magazine was speculating on whether Clint's fast action indicated a budding romance with his missing brother's girlfriend. Duh. It was obvious Clint had the hots for Meg. It was also obvious to Arlene that Howie felt the same way. Maybe if he thought Meg was taken, he'd give Arlene a chance.

No matter. Muddy had sent new business her way, and that was more important than that tasty little slice of New York brisket. She called Bobby Atkinson and told him to meet her and the cowboys at the hotel.

Chapter 22

Lieutenant Norcroft came back to his office straight from the track. The afternoon had been entertaining, but unnerving, as he almost lost his prize person-of-interest. Meg was resourceful, that was for sure.

Will Brecker's phone records waited in an email. The attached spreadsheet included hot links to related information about each call.

Will used his phone a lot. Calls and text messages throughout most days—it was a wonder he could get any farming done. Norcroft didn't pay much attention to the details until around when Meg showed up. He wanted to see if Will knew Meg was coming.

But the pattern of calls didn't change at all until the story hit the internet. So, Will was as surprised to see her as everyone else. Norcroft looked into Will's new connections after that. There were lawyers, probably for the lawsuit he threatened, and a few mortgage companies, probably to pay for the lawsuit he threatened. Once the deal to put Meg on the show had been struck, those calls stopped.

There were a bunch of incoming calls and texts—Will had a lot of friends who wanted to chat about the news. Funny though, he didn't contact anyone unless they contacted him first. Being a widower must be kind of like being single; you've got nobody you want to share your good news with.

There was one outgoing text session to a unique number. Norcroft clicked on the number's info link but nothing came up. That meant the phone was not in the local database.

He could launch a search for that number, but it seemed useless; Will Brecker was clearly acting like a guy who just found his long-lost daughter.

But... the exact timing of the mystery text session was the day

Brecker and the reality show guys were visiting Meg in the hospital. He expanded the details on Will's phone, and indeed, it was sent from Meg's room. He tried to read the message contents but couldn't—the text was encrypted by Google Virtual Private Text. That seemed suspicious, even for a technology-comfortable guy like Will Brecker.

He called the digital forensic lab. They could figure out who Brecker texted that day.

* * *

Norcroft opened the spreadsheet in front of Will Brecker and pointed to the telltale line.

"There's a text you sent three days ago. Recognize the number?"

Brecker was steaming, shaking his head.

"How the hell did you get all this without a search warrant?"

"Only need a warrant if I'm gonna use the information as evidence. But since there's no crime here, no need for that, right? I'm just trying to figure out what happened to your daughter and Tommy Owen. Are you going to help or not?"

"Ah, I'm gonna help. I don't like your methods, Ranger, but I'm on your side."

He looked at the number, squinting a bit.

"Doesn't look familiar at all. Not even the area code."

He was right about that. The area code was out of a Northeast cell phone block. The number was registered to a Larry's Pizza in Boston. Norcroft had already determined that no such establishment existed.

"Maybe if you look at the date and time, it'll jog your memory."

Will squinted again.

"Hell, I don't remember that kinda detail."

"Let me help: it was while you were at the hospital, helping Meg negotiate the contract with Next Bikini Cowgirl."

Will looked off into the distance, and Norcroft saw the flash of recognition in his eyes, even though he tried to hide it.

"Nope, I didn't text nobody that day."

Norcroft locked eyes with him.

"You're hiding something. Why'd you text Larry's Pizza?"

"What?!" Will looked genuinely surprised. If he knew the number, he surely didn't know the name. "You fuckin' with me, Ranger?"

"No, sir. But I know you texted this number from the hospital. Meg's room, in fact. I want to know the truth."

Will's jaw tightened, and then he gave a little shrug.

"Alright, Ranger, I did remember something. Not that number, I swear I never texted it. I hate pizza." He hesitated, wrestling with whatever he was about to say. "I remembered that I dropped my phone in the room that day. Noticed it missin' in the parking lot and went back to get it. It was buried in the bedding, probably there for ten minutes or so."

Whoa.

"So, Meg must have sent that text."

"I guess so. Missin' three years, maybe she was hankerin' for pizza."

Norcroft doubted that, especially given the delivery time of a pizza from Boston to Galveston.

He already had the digital forensic lab working on getting records for the Larry's Pizza phone. Once he had those, he'd confront Meg Brecker.

* * *

I drained my day-off late-afternoon cocktail of Jim Beam on the rocks and headed out to catch Frank Woodland's evening commute home. I needed a break from thinking about who might've hired Grady's assigned hatchetman; without better skinny it had been a waste of time. Not that Jim and I didn't have time to waste.

I installed my camera and set up camp in the Venetian casino, smoking a Camel and playing a quarter slot to blend in. The ruse didn't work, though—all the old ladies around me smoked Newports.

No matter. Woodland bustled out right on time, and I

followed. He stopped outside and glanced around. Furtive. Guilty. Then he stuffed something in the trash receptacle and headed off.

I watched my camera footage of Frank stepping through the front panel of an out-of-service slot machine. I went inside to try my hand at the secret door, but a house gondolier put a paw on my shoulder. The thug waved his oar at the out-of-order sign and told me I should find another machine to drain my pockets into.

Back outside by the trash bin I pretended to check my phone, and then drop it accidentally. I rummaged around the garbage and came up with my phone and a pair of disposable galoshes. Still wet. Frank Woodland's commute took him either through the Venetian's fake canal or through the web of storm drain tunnels under the city. I could place my bet on the tunnels in the morning. But I'd still have to follow him—the Las Vegas Underground can take you anywhere under the Strip you want to go.

Chapter 23

Clint sat down for the barn chat and presented the participants: Gabriella, Dallas, Jasmine, and Meg. Their skimpy swimwear demonstrated that sexy had a lot of meanings. Gabriella and Jasmine were dark-skinned hardbodies; Meg was pale and fit but more curvy; and Dallas's pinup figure was enhanced by a little bit of smooth baby fat that said she got her exercise in the gym, not in the corral. It struck him that Meg's lack of a tan could be explained by three years hiding out in Boston. Those people were white as ghosts up there.

Pavel had compromised on the towels-versus-hay issue. He nixed the towels, but instead of sitting on the bales, the girls were left standing, with one boot up on a bale, or leaning with an elbow on a stack. Not only were they itch-free, they could arch their backs to flatter their figures. Meg and Gabriella chose the foot-up pose—they were too short to reach the top of the stacks.

Clint glanced at his notes.

"Evenin', ladies. Tonight's topic is grit. Meg showed some tenacity during today's incident. Since we don't intend to let any more accidents happen, you won't get a chance to show the same. So tell us about your own experiences, the times you needed to dig deep, to persevere against adversity."

This was an interesting question, considering it came from Pavel. If Meg was right about today not being an accident, Pavel wouldn't go there, would he? Or maybe he'd emphasize it just to deflect suspicion? Or, Pavel didn't know what Muddy was doing—he was new. Clint looked forward to how Meg would handle the question.

Jasmine tilted her head and rolled her eyes toward Meg.

"Really? Steerin' a toy car down a straight track a coupla times?

That ain't adversity, honey. You try steerin' your way through the crowd on the first day of middle school when everyone else is White."

"Tell us about it, Jasmine."

"I got bounced around in foster homes till I was eleven. Then I finally got adopted… by White parents. My folks are real nice, and pretty well-off. I was damn happy. They love me, for sure, but they figured the other folks in their all-White neighborhood felt the same." Jasmine shook her head. "Nobody wanted to hang with me, but everybody expected me to be a basketball star, carry the team. I got good at rodeo instead, just for spite. But county rodeo circuits don't take to Black girls that well, either. It's always gonna be tough."

Silence hung in the air for a moment.

"I didn't have no racial problems," Gabriella said, "There were a lot of us. But I was little, so I got bullied a lot." She laughed. "That was before all this social media bullying-on-the-computer shit; I got beat up in person." She raised two fists and turned them slowly, examining them, her jaw firm. "So I took up kickboxing." She grinned, eyes blazing. "A few balls-high side kicks and nobody bothered me anymore."

Clint had no doubt Gabriella was no longer bullied. He was a little afraid of her himself.

Time for some fun.

"How about you, Dallas?"

Dallas sighed like this was all beneath her.

"I've actually been in a real car accident. I slid my Ferrari off FM 455 in the rain. Totaled it." She shrugged. "I was tryin' to see how fast I could go."

"How badly were you hurt?" Meg asked, looking concerned. Clint had to wonder if she really was. She was so hard to read.

"Oh, not too bad," Dallas admitted, "Just a coupla bruises. The airbags on them Speciales are really good." She looked around at a ring of expectant faces. "Oh, but Daddy wouldn't replace it," she added, pouting. "I had to drive his old Chevy pickup for a whole year!"

Clint hoped the camera microphones picked up the sighs of

disgust from Jasmine and Gabriella. Meg just smiled, until Clint put her on the spot.

"Meg, besides the race, any big obstacles you had to overcome?" He almost regretted asking the question. But Meg wouldn't talk about all that stuff she said in private. So she'd be lying now, or lying then. Clint leaned in to see if he could tell the difference.

"I dunno, I was pretty normal growin' up. Then my mom died when I was eight, that was tough. I was livin' with just my Pappy, but he tried to fill in." She shot a quick glance at Clint. "'Course, I don't know what happened to Tommy and me for the last three years. So I can't rightly say I've persevered yet. Still don't know how it's all gonna come out." Her eyes defocused as she gazed into the unknown future.

Well, that was proof: Meg Brecker was a great liar. The only question was, which story was the lie?

If the Urban Legion story was true, she would have to lie tonight, and in exactly the way she did. And if tonight's story was true, why would she make up such a weird story at the racetrack?

He'd been thinking about that story for hours. As weird as it was, it was totally consistent. Hard to believe, but there was nothing in it he could prove false.

He definitely needed to talk with Howie.

* * *

Howie parked as close to the hotel portico as possible. He had to get his personal witness video of the rig control room to Roger ASAP. There was no cell signal out on the Gulf, and because his phone had tried its best to find one all afternoon, it was now totally dead. He could charge it, but it would be quicker to Bluetooth transfer from the witness to his laptop, and upload from there to Roger's cloud storage.

He was inside the lobby in a minute and walked directly to the elevators. A car arrived almost immediately, and the doors opened onto Arlene and Bobby the bodyguard. He regretted loading up on cologne, again.

"Going up, Howie?" Arlene asked as he stepped in and the door closed behind him.

"Um, yeah, to my room. I'm really beat."

"I've got a juicy video that will perk you right up."

Howie sighed.

"Can it wait? I'm—"

"No, it can't." she said. "I want to give you a chance to review it before we release it. When the internet sees what Meg and Clint were up to today, it will change everyone's opinion of them. Including yours."

Meg and Clint? Howie didn't think his low opinion of Clint would change much. But Meg? With him?

He agreed to detour to Arlene's room.

* * *

Howie noticed a few things as Arlene's door latched shut behind him. The room was warm, and soft jazz drifted from a speaker somewhere. There were glasses and a bottle of Bourbon on the coffee table, along with an ice bucket. And there was no one else besides Arlene; the muscle had stayed in the hall.

"Just us, huh?" he asked. "You don't want Bobby to see this juicy tidbit?"

"He's seen it. But you haven't. I thought maybe a little trade would be in order."

"A trade? For what? I don't have anything new at the moment."

"Of course not," she said as she dropped ice cubes into just one of the glasses. At least she remembered he never took ice. "I want to trade my video for something you do have." She poured two fingers of whiskey into each glass, and held the straight-up drink out to him. "You."

Howie forced himself to take the glass, half out of politeness and half to give himself time to think. She clinked her glass against his and took a solid swig.

"Look," he said, going for sheepish, "I know I promised you some schtupping action. And such a schtupping you'll get. But I've been under a lot of stress lately, and I have, well, erectile problems."

"Huh. Well, a drink would relieve that stress, and then I'm sure I can take care of your problem."

No way Howie was swallowing that drink.

"Well, maybe, but I don't ever accept a poured drink." He put the glass on the table. "I was… date raped once. I never got over it."

Arlene frowned, and looked at his glass. Then she picked it up, set hers in its place, and took a swig from his glass.

"There, you can take mine, and I'll take yours. That way, you know there's nothing funny in there."

Howie laughed.

"I've seen *The Princess Bride*. I'm sure I can't win a battle of wits with you, even if you're not Sicilian. I'm not drinking from either glass."

"So, no drink and no sex and no video for you, today, huh? Last chance to change your mind."

"Nope, I'll never change my mind." About drinks, about sex with Arlene, and about Meg. He wished he'd resisted the tease about a compromising video; of course there was no such thing.

"Well, you're right about that. Also about not outwitting me."

She pulled a small tube from under the couch cushion and held it up. There was a click and Howie felt the dart sting his neck.

Well, that sucks, he thought as the room began to swim.

* * *

Peter grabbed Howie's legs while Brad took his shoulders, and the two of them hoisted him onto a borrowed maid's cart. It would only take a few minutes to get the unconscious reporter up to his room. Arlene had cleared the hall and her associate Bobby held the elevator to avoid any awkward explanations.

The guy was as sexy as ever. What the hell was it about him? He didn't look like much, but Peter's cock was already straining at his blue jeans. It didn't understand that it wouldn't get a piece of Howie at the barn later. Or ever.

The idea came to him as the elevator doors closed.

"Arlene, what say we make a snuff film? It would be a first for the Universe M7 smartphone!"

Arlene raised an eyebrow.

"As much as I'd like to fuck this guy, with the drugs he's on right now, there's no way he can get an erection."

Peter smiled.

"I wasn't thinking of you fucking him. I was thinking of me fucking him. And he won't need an erection—I've got enough of one for both of us." He pointed to his protruding zipper flap.

Arlene's eyes widened as she looked at his crotch. Brad was chuckling.

"Wait, you're gay?!" she said. "And it's not just me—this guy is sizzling!"

"Yes," Peter said, breathing heavily now. "Yes, he is."

"Whoa, dudes, chill," Brad said. "You know the Corporation rules—no mixing urban legends. Creates too many verifiable cross-references."

Arlene sighed and nodded.

"He's right Peter. You'll just have to do without this time."

The elevator doors opened, and they rolled Howie down the hall. Peter consoled himself, and his cock, with the thought that at least Arlene wasn't going to get any, either.

* * *

Howie woke up cold. Ice cold. He reached for the bedcovers but there weren't any. He opened his eyes. He was naked, lying in a bathtub, sternum-deep in blood-soaked ice cubes.

Not again!

He sighed and looked for the familiar lipstick note on the wall: *Sorry, we removed one of your kidneys. Better call 911 as soon as possible.*

The legendary note was there, but this one was different. He had to crane his neck, it started so high up. Two paragraphs—they needed the room.

Sorry, we removed one of you're kidneys. *Your*, Howie corrected; a journalist, she should get the grammar right at least. *It's too bad it was the only one you had left—guess someone else got to you first. No wonder you don't like ice.*

Howie had now suffered three urban-legend-disguised murder attempts. Maybe a record, though enduring the same kidney theft legend twice might not count for a full two. And actually dying from it would really take the shine off the trophy.

We'd advise you to call 911 as soon as possible, but this time they won't be able to save you, since you have no kidneys left, and we also took your liver, pancreas, and spleen. You should have accepted my offer—you'd still be dead, but it would've been a nice way to go. P.S.—you owe us a kidney.

Fuck.

He should've stayed away from Arlene from the beginning. She had access to the show, he should have realized she was Corporation. But he had to do it anyway to get access himself, right? To help keep Meg safe?

Or was it just to help keep Meg? He was jealous of Clint from the beginning, and that jealousy was his downfall. He screwed the whole thing up.

Meg, I'm sorry I doubted you!

He sighed. Live by the pheromones, die by the pheromones. He'd been living on borrowed time since the cologne convinced the dolphins not to kill him. The loan came due when he used the cologne on Arlene. As his father used to say, some things were just *bashert*—meant to be.

His vision started to get fuzzy, from low body temperature or low blood supply. Or maybe it was the tears that suddenly flooded his eyes. He'd never see her again. He'd never get a chance to prove that he loved her more than anything.

I love you, Meg!

I'll miss you.

Well, actually, he wouldn't be around to miss her, unless there was some kind of afterlife, which he never believed in.

Meg would still be around, though.

I hope you'll miss me.

And forgive me.

How long would he live without critical organs, not to mention the blood that was now turning his bath into gazpacho? More importantly, how long would he remain conscious? He still needed to get his video of the rig map to Roger. And tell Meg he loved her.

Arlene had taken the lipstick with her, so he dipped his finger in the sticky bath fluid and drew a test line on the wall tiles. Crude, but workable. He considered what to write.

Important things first.

Chapter 24

The Houston-area pickup agent for the Corporation's Hospitality Disposal Services Group met the hotel manager in the Chrismoor Suites lobby. He'd done this many times before, with various Houston area hotels, and wasn't expecting any surprises.

"This one's a little odd, Alex," the manager said as they rode the elevator.

Alex followed him to room 627, halfway down the hall on the cheap, parking-lot-view side. The manager slid the keycard into the lock and showed him in.

The room looked ordinary, with the usual signs of occupancy: open suitcase on the folding rack, laptop computer on the desk, miscellaneous cups and papers scattered about. The bed was made, although the bedspread was rumpled. And bloody. Again, nothing unusual. He headed for the bath.

The man in the tub was short, about five-three, with dark curly hair and a beard and mustache. Looked to be about thirty. He was wearing a yarmulke, and eyeglasses, and nothing else, though it was hard to see his body below the surface of the bloody ice water.

Okay, it *was* odd. He'd never seen such a long lipstick message. And they never took so many organs.

The Organ Cartel seemed to think all their victims would actually be able to call 911 before passing out. They rarely did, but the Cartel never stuck around to find out. They had no idea they'd been leaving most of those people for Alex's HDSG to dispose of.

The nice thing was, fewer organs meant less body weight. The guy was pretty small, too, and didn't have a lot of personal belongings. The HDSG disposed of bodies through the Life Sum Crematorium, whose claim to fame was burning personal possessions with the deceased and mixing the ashes. Their motto was "You *can* take it with you." This was very effective for eliminating evidence along with the body, but they charged by the pound, so the less evidence and body, the better. The surcharge for secretly charring anonymous victims stung his budget enough already.

He studied the message. There was more going on here than usual. This victim was no random stranger to the thief. It looked like a targeted hit.

He would have loved to ask the thief what was going on, but Corporation protocol kept the organ people and his disposal group isolated. Probably for the best; if he knew the situation, he might find it hard to keep his professional detachment.

Then he looked at the drawing, finger-painted in blood, and any detachment went down the drain. It was a cartoon of the victim, complete with facial hair, glasses, and yarmulke, pointing to his eyes and saying in a speech balloon *Tell Meg Brecker: I have witnessed amazing things, but nothing surpasses my love for you.*

What the fuck? Brecker was that amnesia chick on Bikini Cowgirl. Clearly this guy was a fan. Alex couldn't blame him—Meg was a babe. But Alex was more Team Gabriella—he liked women who could literally kick ass.

Poor bastard. No way anyone was going to pass his message along. It was hard enough to keep these hotel organ thefts covered up without alerting the world's currently most popular reality star.

Okay, enough empathy. Time to get to work.

"How long has he been here?"

"Three or four hours, assuming the ice was fresh when he went in. He's still pretty well chilled."

That was good; nothing worse than dealing with a day-old thawed body.

* * *

Osita checked her watch as she rolled the special OTD cart up to room 627. This always happened; she only drew Organ Theft Duty at the end of her shift, when she was trying to get home before Miguel left for his night watchman job. It upset him to leave the children home alone when she was late, which was often enough. It upset her, too.

But Osita drew OTD because she was good at it, and fast. She figured she could finish up before quitting time.

She pulled the cart halfway into the room and used it to block the door. It was obvious this would be a quick cleanup; the bed had been used for surgery as usual, but the Disposal people had removed all the personal belongings. The bedspread was bloodier than normal; that would add a few minutes, but not enough to make her late.

She leaned into the bathroom.

Maldición!

The asshole had smeared blood all over the wall. The bloodstain cleaner would take care of it, but needed a lot of scrubbing. The children were going to be left alone again.

* * *

Clint walked down the sixth floor hallway of the Chrismoor Suites, counting off the rooms. It was pretty easy to get Howie's contact info from his press registration form. He'd waited until after midnight to slip away from the ranch unnoticed.

There was a maid's cart in the open door to 627. That probably meant Howie wasn't there. Clint toyed with a few excuses to poke around but didn't come up with a good one. So he pulled out his phone, started recording video, and went into smartphone zombie mode. He was two steps into the room when he noticed a lot of red in the bathroom.

"Oh!" he said, looking up from the phone as he panned it toward the bath. The maid was making the bed and looked as genuinely startled as he was acting. "Didn't expect you'd be cleanin'."

"Is this your room?" she asked, looking very uneasy.

Clint looked around, and frowned.

"Maybe not, is this 527?"

The maid looked relieved.

"Sorry sir, you're on the wrong floor. This is six. Go down one."

"Ah, okay. Thank you!"

He turned again, giving the phone a scan of the whole room and another good look into the bathroom.

Ten minutes later, he sat in his car, watching the video with disbelief. It had clearly captured the lipstick message and the morbid, bloody mural. Howie and Meg were more than just Urban Legion partners; Howie's last request was to tell Meg he loved her. But Clint wasn't sure he could bear to deliver the message.

* * *

Meg opened the door and smiled for Clint's GoPro, as usual. Not as usual, it was the middle of the night. And he wasn't wearing the GoPro.

"Nobody knows I'm here, Meg. And I'm not recording."

Meg nodded and studied his face. He looked really conflicted. Had she confessed to the enemy?

"So we can talk?" she asked, going with trust. "Did you talk to Howie?"

"Not exactly."

Clint's gaze bore holes in her. What the hell was going on?

"I went to his hotel room. He wasn't there. But he left you a message."

"Okay, let's have it."

"He said he loves you."

Meg narrowed her eyes.

"He says that all the time. I'm not sure he means it."

Clint's eyes drooped a little. Disappointed? Sad?

"I think he meant it. I wasn't sure I should show it to you, but I think you need to see it."

Uh, oh. The look on his face was concern. Deep, deep concern.

He took out his phone and made her sit down before starting the video for her. It was a bouncing view of an open door, a maid's cart, the maid in a room, and red-tinged bathroom. Clint hit stop.

"Um, this isn't good," she said.

"Nope." He zoomed in on the tiles above the bath. There was lipstick on the wall. Fucking organ thieves again! But unlike the ones that got Howie's kidney in Las Vegas, this time they meant to kill him.

"I'm sorry I doubted you about your urban legend survivor friends," Clint said quietly. "I guess that was Howie's legend?"

Meg took a moment to answer. Unless he got medical help right away, Howie was gone. And even if he did get help, they probably couldn't save him without most of his vital organs.

Fuck!

"Yes," she said as the tears let loose.

"There's more." Clint hit play again, and the view panned over a few feet. He stopped it and zoomed in again.

The message was in Howie's own blood. Damn, he could be dramatic!

Okay, Howie, I believe you.

"I loved him, too."

She was full-on sobbing now; Clint set down the phone and pulled her head to his shoulder.

"Your shirt's getting soaked," she whispered.

"That's okay," he said.

Chapter 25

Clint handed Meg another tissue and rubbed her back. She wasn't crying anymore, but that didn't mean she was recovering from the shock. More like slipping into a deep, dark, pit.

"I should've believed you right away, Meg. It sounded so crazy, but it sure wasn't. Maybe I could've got to Howie before they did."

She looked over at him, shaking her head.

"No—you couldn't have saved him. I'm beginnin' to think nothing could've saved him. And maybe the same goes for me."

"No!" Clint almost shouted. "Nobody's gonna hurt you while I'm here."

"The Corporation will just kill you like they killed Tommy and Howie. And what's the use, anyway? They're too strong, Clint. The Urban Legion tries to stop 'em, but there's too many of 'em. Too many assassins."

Clint could feel his teeth clenching.

"We have to fight them, Meg. I've lost my brother, and you've lost two lovers. Howie didn't quit until he managed to write that message on the wall. In his own blood. He wouldn't want you to quit either."

Meg sniffed and wiped her nose but then froze in mid-wipe. She stared into space for more than a few seconds. Then she leapt up.

"Wait! You're right! He didn't want me to quit! Let's see his message again!"

Clint picked up his phone and showed her the still-frozen image of the bloody cartoon.

Tell Meg Brecker: I have witnessed amazing things, but nothing surpasses my love for you.

Meg studied it and smiled. She actually smiled!

"He's not pointing to his eyes," she said, "He's pointing to his glasses! Clint, you need to loan me your phone for the night. And then you need to go out right now and get a disposable, with a good data plan and Bluetooth. And then you need to call me and I'll tell you where to go next."

* * *

Clint thought it was too late at night to buy a high-end burner phone, but Meg had Google Maps find a nearby 24-hour Battery Hut. He did a test call to his old phone. Meg had set the ringer to vibrate and didn't answer until he called twice, a minute apart, so she'd know it was the new phone.

She told him Howie had a Bluetooth video recording device in his glasses called a personal witness. She used Google Maps Bluetooth Finder to locate it at the Life Sum Crematorium; that meant the personal witness, and Howie, would soon be toast. Literally. Meg transmitted the Bluetooth ID of the witness and told Clint to hook up to it once he was in range of the crematorium.

Clint drove to the facility in a daze. The story was getting crazier and crazier, but so was the technology. A personal witness, with Bluetooth, camera, and sound, built into Howie's glasses? That was why he mentioned "witness" in the message. And drew a cartoon, including pointing to the glasses.

Good thing Clint had gotten a picture of it. He never would've mentioned it. But Meg caught the significance.

And he thought she was just a pretty cowgirl.

No doubt about it, not only had his opinion of her changed, his whole life had taken a new turn. Unfortunately, there might not be much of his life left—he was now a duly deputized member of the Urban Legion, and the Corporation was perfectly willing to shoot the deputy.

He pulled his truck into the lot behind the crematorium and parked. Meg said Howie's witness should have a Bluetooth range of at least a hundred feet; Clint was just outside that. But he didn't dare park any closer, there were lights on the building and he'd draw too much attention. He pulled out the burner phone and searched for the witness device, half-expecting there was no such thing.

But there it was: a weak signal, but good enough. Apparently, they hadn't stored Howie's glasses with him in a metal body drawer. The only question was how long before they shoved them both into the incinerator and turned them to ashes.

He called Meg and started the upload.

* * *

Meg sat cross-legged under her blanket so the light from Clint's phone wouldn't be seen through the thin blinds of her cabin. She'd done a quick calculation based on the size of Howie's video file; it would take about a half hour to transfer.

The video was hyper-compressed to fit into a small solid-state memory, which meant, unfortunately, there was no way to watch the video as it uploaded. Besides, Meg had also calculated that there were at least thirty-six hours of video in the file. She would have to watch as she decompressed in high speed.

The upload stopped before the end of the file. Was that enough to get the "amazing things" Howie wanted her to see? She called Clint, and he confirmed that the Bluetooth signal had quit. A wave of sadness washed over her. Howie was truly gone.

"I'm sorry, Meg."

Clint's words helped. She thanked him and arranged to swap phones on the way to breakfast. It was time to look at what Howie thought was so important for her to see.

She fast-forwarded through the video and watched the last day of Howie's life at 40x speed, slowing down to catch interesting parts. He'd rented a boat and drove out to an oil rig, which was apparently somebody's private offshore home. That wasn't nearly as interesting as the electronic map—she paused on that, but couldn't make anything of it. Then she watched in horror as Howie returned to shore, returned to his hotel, and walked into Arlene Harrington's trap—baited by a hint of Meg cheating with Clint. The thought of Howie being jealous triggered a wave of guilt, which became a tsunami as she watched him resist Arlene's advances.

It was just as well that her tears were flowing again, she really didn't want to watch the fatal surgery or its icy aftermath. But near the end, suddenly Howie's face flashed by, and then the scene was a still of his bloody message—he'd made sure he was looking at the wall when he stopped moving forever.

She backed up to just before the scene with his face and watched him paint the wall with his own blood. Her simmering anger began to boil. The Corporation would pay for this!

Then Howie pulled off his glasses and held them out so she could see his face. He was always pale, but with the blood loss he looked positively ghostly. Made sense; he was a ghost now, speaking from beyond the grave. Or at least, from a small box of ashes.

She turned up the sound a little.

"Meg," he said, "I have always loved you and will always love you. You knew that." He gave her a weak grin. "But don't dwell on me—you've got work to do. The video up to now is from Muddy's rig in the Gulf. Get the video to Roger—he can figure out where the rig is, and more importantly, what the map I found means. I think the private nodes on the map are your mystery devices, and there are lots of them. The public node symbol is shaped like the Welcome to Las Vegas sign—the controller must be out there. Tell Roger and Lynn to locate it and figure out what it's doing. It's got to be the key to everything here." He smiled again. "I hope at least you'll finally find out what those fucking devices are for."

Howie winced, and his eyes went glassy. The video got shaky but then he snapped alert again.

"And on a personal note, the video also shows that Arlene Harrington and her bodyguard Bobby are organ thieves. I would be grateful if you could put a stop to that! Find my other cell phone account, it'll tell you…" His eyes went glassy again, and the video spun as his arms drooped. After a few seconds, his face reappeared on a swaying video. "Did I tell you, I love you? I always will. Always."

The video swung around again; he'd apparently placed the glasses back on his face. Then he aimed the witness at the mural on the wall and stopped moving.

Meg turned off the playback and cried quietly for a minute. But only a minute—Howie had given her a job to do. She connected to Roger's encrypted cloud storage account and started uploading the video.

The last part was a little confusing though. She didn't know Howie even had a second phone.

Part III

"Bikini Cowgirls Get Wet"
— Headline, The National Nose

Chapter 26

Roger noted the text message indicator as he prepared to shower. He'd left the phone in the changing area during the workout, not expecting anyone to text him that early in the morning; Lynn was in a much later time zone and Howie had probably gotten back really late from the rig.

It was from an unknown number—it could wait. He was naked and grabbing his towel when he recognized the 713 area code. Houston. He opened the text.

> Unknown> Meg here, borrowed phone. Howie is dead, they got his organs. He found a map of network nodes in the Gulf, sent it to me via witness. His last request: figure out the map. See video in your cloud store, start with Howie at the end. Up to you now. Nodes must be devices, I'm going to try to video one on boat trip today. Watch the show. Clint is working with me.

Roger slowly sank to the bench, phone still in hand but the message getting blurry. There was a ton of information in a few words but the ones that counted were *Howie is dead*. Another best friend killed by the Corporation. And Meg was securely in their clutches. They weren't done.

He threw on clothes and headed for the computer to watch the video. Howie's message was a direct challenge: it basically said "Don't let me die in vain." Roger swore that wouldn't happen and scrolled back to the map.

It was a network map, but with physical locations, scattered across the Gulf of Mexico. Howie was probably right, they were devices like the one Meg and Tommy had stumbled on. The nodes were labeled with private domain IP addresses. And one node, at the top, had a public domain address, different than all the others, and a different indicator. As Howie said, it looked just like the iconic Welcome to Fabulous Las Vegas sign.

The Gulf IP addresses were private, so they couldn't be accessed outside whatever network they were on. But it was a good bet that the public node provided a gateway. Roger plugged the public address into Google DNS Reverse Search, to find out who owned it, and got nothing. He pinged the node and mapped the hops along the way, but the best he could tell was that indeed, it was somewhere near Las Vegas. There was nothing more he could discern about anything.

And certainly nothing about what any of the nodes were for.

He called Lynn.

*　*　*

Lynn yawned as she navigated her way south of town. Nick Wood had arranged a predawn meeting at an industrial complex; it was hard to tell by the nearby highway lighting, but it seemed like there was nothing here but sandpits and warehouses. She parked next to Nick's car in a corner of an empty parking lot. As she hopped into his vehicle, she felt like she was making some kind of drug drop; she hoped there weren't any police around. She kept an eye out for any other car, which might contain Burke Barrage.

Nick greeted her with a travel mug full of steaming-hot tea.

"I noticed you were drinking it at the Noir restaurant."

Lynn was impressed.

"Shouldn't be long now," he said. "Keep an eye on that factory across the road on the right."

She nodded, sipping the tea. The building was just a silhouette with a row of small lit windows along the roofline.

"There!"

Headlights approached and turned into the factory parking lot. As the vehicle backed up to a loading dock, the dock door rolled upward, bathing the back of the truck in light. It looked like a dumpster delivery truck, and in fact, deposited its large container onto the dock. There was some kind of track there, and the container slid along it and into the building. The door rolled back down, pinching off the light again. The truck pulled away and disappeared southbound. The whole delivery took less than two minutes.

"Notice anything strange?" Nick asked.

"Yes," Lynn answered, "I came all the way out here from my nice warm hotel bed to watch a trash receptacle delivery."

"Not an ordinary trash receptacle delivery," Nick said. He held up his hand and started counting off on his fingers.

"First, it happened under the cover of darkness. Second, it went down as fast and clean as a Special Ops mission, and the people inside were waiting for the truck—the driver didn't have to ring a bell or anything. Third, the dumpster was not empty, based on the way the truck bounced up when it let go. Fourth, people don't put trash dumpsters inside the building. And fifth, they don't have a rail system to get it in there so quickly."

Lynn had almost finished the tea by the time Nick ran out of fingers.

"Okay, so it's not trash. What is it?"

"Some kind of powdered chemical. Yesterday I could see puffs of it escaping from the lid when they set it down."

"I guess the big question is, what's going on in the factory?"

Nick smiled in the dim light, triumphant.

"The world's most popular jet fuel cleaner." He sat there, smiling, as if Lynn would understand. "Don't you see? These people make the chemicals that get mixed into jet fuel to clear gunk out of the engines. So that powder is getting burned by pretty much every jet engine in the sky."

"Wait," Lynn said, finally getting it. "You're talking about chemtrails?"

"Of course! Whatever that stuff is, it's what the conspiracy is using for mind control." He paused, thinking. "Or weather control, or killing bees, or whatever we want to say they're doing with it. I haven't decided that part yet."

Lynn sipped the last of the tea. This was interesting evidence for a conspiracy theory the WCG had been milking for a long time. It would add real credibility.

She smiled. *And that's the problem.*

"Nick, there are several possibilities here." She set the travel mug into the cup holder and held up her hand; two could play the counting game. She touched a finger. "One, you're onto some kind of real chemtrail conspiracy—the Corporation doesn't tell us everything they're up to, so we might promote a theory that actually touches on the truth. But we have to avoid that. So if this is real, we shouldn't talk about it." She moved to the second finger. "Second, this is just an ordinary chemical that actually cleans jet engines, and the clandestine delivery is just a matter of timing. But your idea is very plausible, and that makes it unsuitable for a wacko conspiracy theory. Remember the wacko part. Our tin-foil-hatters have to seem over-the-top paranoid, or people will take them seriously. We have to be crazier than that."

Nick leaned back against the headrest, staring into space.

"You're right," he said finally, "it's too believable. Or it's true. I guess I'm just not cut out for conspiracy theory work."

Lynn touched his shoulder.

"Not many people are," she said. He nodded, then his face lit up.

"Wait, want to find out if it's true? I have a new toy to try out."

"Sure," Lynn answered nonchalantly. A new toy? Yes, please. Maybe she'd get some technology dope after all.

He pulled out his phone, aimed the camera at one of the factory windows, and pressed a button. A conversation sounded on the small speaker.

"The Fossil Fuel Cartel wants us to lower our prices and up the concentration," said one man.

"That's bullshit," said a second. "Our chemtrail coatings have lowered worldwide solar panel output by twenty percent over the last two years alone. Why do they need more?"

"Solar panel prices are coming down," answered the first, "they need to keep pace."

Lynn and Nick both had their eyebrows up.

"So," Nick said, "I guess it's option one, a real conspiracy."

"Yup," Lynn agreed. "But tell me how you did that."

"This?" He held up the phone. "Turns out a glass window vibrates with any sound, and if there's light coming through it, this program can analyze the changes in the light and turn it back into sound."

"Amazing. You guys came up with that at Omni?"

"Nah. This is just Google Eavesdrop Beta." So much for uncovering Corporation technology secrets. "I expected the WCG would be up to date on these things," Nick said, grinning.

"Sorry to let you down." Lynn saw her chance. "I'd say we try to live up to our reputation, but we try not to have one—not many people even know about the WCG. How did you find out about us?"

"I heard stories from Major Thompkins; ever hear of him?"

"Nope."

"I figured maybe Phil might have talked about him. He led our memory erasure technology team." Nick suddenly narrowed his eyes. "You do know about that?"

Lynn nodded, reliving that moment Phil goaded her into pumping an overdose of RFID chips into his neck to prove they were safe. They weren't. His memory, and personality, were gone forever. She held back familiar tears.

"Yeah, those chips worked pretty well."

"Major Ellis Thompkins was part of the original development group in the Air Force. Engineers at Area 51 were working on top-secret aircraft technology, and while they kept people out, they knew sooner or later some civilians would get good looks at designs under test. So they invented a memory erasure system to make those lucky civilians forget. The first prototype was really clunky; they had to run a strong electrical signal though the whole body for several minutes. They put a special helmet on the subject's head and used an anal probe to complete the connection."

Lynn felt her eyes go wide.

"An anal probe? Are you serious?"

"I am. And when the civilians started to wonder why their butts were so sore, Thompkins suggested planting the alien abduction anal probe story."

Lynn shook her head.

"Wow, that's like the first wacko conspiracy."

"Yeah, and that's why I know about the Wacko Conspiracy Group. Major Thompkins would always brag that he came up with the idea of wacko conspiracies, and the Corporation ran with it. Even their Roswell story came later. He's so miffed that he didn't get any credit, he won't let any of us contact you directly."

"Huh. No wonder they don't talk about him at WCG HQ."

She paused, was there anything else? She couldn't think of anything.

"Well, it's been fun, Nick, even if not productive." It actually had been both. She was sure the Urban Legion could use Google Eavesdrop, and Roger would certainly want to know about the chemtrails. And Major Thompkins. Not bad for a rookie femme fatale. She climbed out of the car, then leaned in. "Thanks for the tea."

Nick nodded, and was still sitting there as she drove away. There was no sign of Burke.

A few blocks back toward the Strip, her phone rang. She pulled over to answer—it was Roger.

"Sorry to wake you," he said, "I've got some bad news and an urgent job for you."

"I was awake, and in fact, I'm in my car."

"Well, pull over for this."

"I did when I took the call. Roger, what happened?"

The pause on the line was ominous.

"Howie is dead. He…" Lynn heard a choked sob "…they drugged him and stole vital organs."

Lynn stared into the darkness. She was too shocked for tears. They'd come, maybe, but first came the anger. Zen-mind had nothing to say.

"Do we know who did it?"

"Yeah, but that's not the important thing now. Howie sent us a map, and I just texted it to you. There are devices, like Meg was investigating, all over the Gulf of Mexico. She's going to try to video one on their boat trip today, so watch the show, it might give you a clue. The main thing is, there's a management station in Las

Vegas, probably manned by Charlie Stewart. You need to find it and figure out what it does."

Great. A crucial task that required her to read a map.

"Roger, you're the map person, I'm not. Can't you figure it out?"

"Not that kind of map. It's a communication network map, and no, I couldn't figure it out. Take it to the Vegas Legion and have them decode it. Deanna must know more about the networks out there." There was another choked-off pause. "It was Howie's last request."

Lynn set her jaw.

"We'll honor it, Roger."

"I almost had it, Lynn. I finally linked Arlene to the Corporation, and tried to warn Howie. She's the one who killed him."

Lynn sat quietly for a moment. She had a link, too. Who would die if she didn't admit to her femme fatale side gig?

"Okay, I'm on it. But I have a confession to make. I've been meeting a Corporation guy, worked with Phil, who thinks I'm with the WCG."

"What? Why didn't you tell me?"

"It's a noir thing, I'll fill you in later. But the key is, he knew about the WCG already; you said you couldn't even figure out how Corporation groups know about each other. I thought he could give us a clue. He told me he heard about the WCG from an Air Force Major Ellis Thompkins, an old guy from Area 51, who claims he came up with the alien anal probe story." She shook her head. "Seems kind of trivial now, doesn't it?"

"Yeah. Everything seems kind of trivial. But I'll plug in his name and see what I can find. Thanks."

Lynn hung up the phone, dropped it on the seat, and pulled back onto the road, accelerating the old Altima toward the lights of the Strip. Howie was dead. The stakes were so much—

Out of the darkness on her right she saw a flash of reflected light beyond a parked semi. She instinctively braced herself as something big crunched into the passenger door. The car jerked left, airbags bursting, and everything went black.

* * *

Meg stepped out of her cabin at 8 a.m. into a brisk northeast breeze. She was exhausted. Clint's phone was tucked into her bra, invisible under the loose gingham blouse. Clint was greeting the cowgirls as they entered the dining hall; when he got to Meg, she turned away from everyone and swapped his phone for the burner.

Once the girls had settled down with their chow, Pavel stood at the head of the hall and clinked a glass for attention.

"You may have noticed cloudy skies and wind today—there is bad weather coming. But weather service says storm is still days away and assures no problem if we go on overnight yacht cruise today as planned. So we will. You can pick up your swimming suits and wraps at wardrobe trailer on your way to your cabins. We will meet bus here, packed for overnight, at eleven today. Please do not be late—we do not want anyone to miss boat." He smiled at his little joke. "Except for victim of today's vote, who will stay on shore. We will announce at dock."

"As if I wasn't worried enough about getting seasick," Dakota confided to Meg, "now we're gonna go out in bad weather. I don't see why a cowgirl competition should have anything to do with boats."

"Well, it's also a bikini competition," Meg pointed out.

"Okay," Dakota admitted, "But I hope the bikini they give me goes good with green skin."

Once breakfast was over and Meg was back in her cabin, Clint called her.

"Clint," she said, "Howie went out to a rig, seems like Muddy is the only one who uses it. He found a map of the Gulf, with a lot of points on it that must be devices like the one I've been investigating. There's also a management station in Vegas. I forwarded the video to the Boston Urban Legion; they'll try to figure out what it means."

"So what do we do now? We'll be stuck on a boat this afternoon, and there won't be cell service out there."

"Shoot, good point. I was figurin' we could use the phones to keep in touch with Boston—I guess not. But I want to go divin' again. Can you smuggle some gear on board, for both of us? The local Legion folks can help."

There was silence on the line.

"Haven't you had enough divin'?"

"Nope. Especially since we'll be out in the middle of that map. If we're anywhere near one of those devices, I want to get a better look."

"How are we gonna slip away?"

"Maybe we pretend to go to your cabin for a little private rendezvous." Clint had confessed Pavel's attempt to set up a romantic plot thread. It could work.

"Okay, as long as they don't make me wear my GoPro."

"Speakin' of which, you'll need an underwater camera. With a Bluetooth link."

"Where the hell am I gonna find—oh. Battery Hut, right?"

"Right. And the local Urban Legion kingdom—"

"Kingdom?"

"It's a long story. Their headquarters is the Trinity Bay Players, look 'em up. Pick your nose so they know you're one of us. See you on board."

* * *

I was sticking to Frank Woodland like a foam clown nose as he played his daily hide-and-seek game, but I peeled off when he approached the Excalibur—I figured there wouldn't be a hidden entrance in a joint that gave rug rats the run of the place. I was wrong. I caught up quick but he vanished behind the Dungeons and Dragons slots.

This time, I knew to zero in on the out-of-order machine. Before the muscle-in-shining-armor noticed me, I jimmied the panel open and stepped into the darkness.

My phone light showed the way down a steel circular staircase. As I suspected, the stair bottomed out onto the concrete floor of the Vegas Underground. Unfortunately, I forgot to suspect that the drainage tunnel would have water in it—which was obvious from Woodland's wet galoshes. I would've kicked myself but didn't want to get my pants as wet as my shoes.

The water was deep enough to hide any footprints, so I picked a direction and sloshed along the tunnel, hoping someone might have spotted Woodland. People lived down here, their beds and belongings up on crates, at least between the storms that washed everything away like a croupier rake collecting bad bets. But there was no one around—I was deep into the darkness, and most of those campers lived near the tunnel openings for light and quick evacuation. Most campers, that is, except for the legendary crowbar-wielding troll who can see in the dark. I didn't believe the stories, but as an urban legend survivor myself, I couldn't be sure.

It was so quiet I could hear echoes of my own splashing footsteps coming from just ahead.

"What are you doing here?" said a hidden voice. Guess those weren't echoes. I reached a side channel and my light fell on a ragged, shaggy drifter blocking the opening. He was barely human, but not a troll. Though, he *was* carrying a crowbar.

"Turn that fucking light off," he growled. I did. Seems the non-troll could also see in the dark. Two out of three on the legend details.

"I'm wondering if you saw a guy come through here recently," I said, friendly-like. "Mid-twenties, wearing disposable galoshes." If he could see in the dark, he might've noticed the footwear.

"The only people allowed to come down here are people who know they're allowed." I heard the splash of a footstep. "You ain't one of 'em." His voice was much closer now.

I ducked left and heard the bar whoosh past my ear. I ducked the same way again, guessing he'd expect me to go the other way this time.

Except he didn't guess: he could see in the dark. I heard a wh— and everything went black. Well, it was black already, but somehow, it got blacker.

* * *

Roger waited an hour after sending the video to Lynn, but she didn't call or text an update. So he called her—and got no answer. He tried texting, with the same result. The next few hours he kept trying. He couldn't reach Burke either, or the Houston Legion headquarters. The entire Urban Legion seemed to have disappeared.

He had nothing to do but worry. No, that wasn't true. Lynn had given him a name. He sat down at the console and added Air Force Major Ellis Thompkins to his Harvard professors database search. Maybe it would take his mind off the danger facing everyone he cared about.

* * *

Lieutenant Norcroft skipped the boat-trip preparation activities at the ranch and went to the office. He grabbed a cup of coffee and brought up the fresh report on his laptop.

It was a beautiful thing. Using cell tower triangulation and a bit of questionably ethical data gathering, his guy at the digital forensic lab had put together a spreadsheet and annotated map of everywhere the mystery phone had been for the last three weeks. It was accurate to within a few yards when there were enough cell towers in the area.

The first few screens were exactly what you'd expect for Larry's Pizza, or at least, a Larry's Pizza delivery guy. The phone was accepting and making calls from all over the Boston area, and always in a moving vehicle. Not too promising; he skipped ahead to the good part, but in his mind, he'd already named the guy Larry.

Two days before Meg appeared on the beach, Larry drove his pizza delivery vehicle to Houston, and spent the night at the Lone Diamond motel a few miles inland from the Galveston Causeway. Norcroft punched the address and number into his phone.

Larry spent the next day on Galveston Island, though with the cell towers all in a north-south line, Norcroft couldn't tell what exactly he was up to. Oddly, though, Larry stayed near the wharves all night, before going back to the motel early the next morning.

Which was about the same time Meg showed up on the beach just south of Galveston.

The next day Larry wandered around the area, including several visits to the Trinity Bay Players, an amateur theatre group, whose contact info Norcroft also noted. The more interesting visits were to the John Sealy Hospital, where Meg was held for observation. He zoomed in on the map—Larry had apparently gotten inside and almost to Meg's room. That night, he went again, after dark, but stayed outside. Larry was apparently very interested in Meg Brecker.

After Meg left the hospital and joined the Bikini Cowgirls at Pearland Ranch, Larry moved his base of operations to the nearby Chrismoor Suites. This hotel had great cell coverage—the map indicated that Larry had stayed in room 627.

And for the next few days, he bounced around between the hotel, the Trinity Bay Players, Galveston, and the Pearland Ranch.

So Norcroft had undoubtedly seen Larry, probably several times. The only time he wasn't watching Meg, he was eyeing some other gorgeous cowgirl, so he really didn't notice the guys. One of the ranch hands? It couldn't be Muddy Bootes or Clint Owen or any of the video crew, they were all involved before Larry showed up. Pavel Nepovim?

No, Pavel was staying on the ranch, not going back to the Chrismoor every night.

But…

Pavel and Muddy were with Meg when Will Brecker's phone texted Larry. So maybe Meg didn't text it, maybe Pavel or Muddy did. But they'd have to steal Brecker's phone, briefly, and that was unlikely. Not impossible, though. Norcroft didn't rule it out.

The bottom of the travelogue showed Larry going back to the Galveston wharf area, and then out into the Gulf.

Norcroft hit page down, but that was it. So, Larry had gone out of range and never came back. Or his phone died.

Norcroft called the Chrismoor first. The voice of a Texas Ranger on the phone carries a lot of weight with a morning junior desk clerk, and the young man was willing to tell him who was staying in room 627: no one. A little more prompting got the answer he was looking for: Howie Friedman, the reporter with Dirt TV, had stayed there until early that morning. He'd used the in-room checkout well after midnight.

Larry, aka Howie, was tantalizingly close to discovery.

The next call was to the Trinity Bay Players, whose recording told Norcroft that he should check out their production of *Monologue!, the Musical,* and leave a message with his phone number if he wanted more info. He wanted more info but did not leave a message.

The last call was to the Lone Diamond Motel, which was answered by a live but tired-sounding woman. Her voice testified to a pack a day for forty years. He introduced himself, and noted her change of tone.

"I'm trying to track down a gentleman by the name of Howie Friedman. I believe he stayed there for a few nights recently."

"Yeah, he was here. Hot little guy!"

Norcroft didn't think Howie was all that hot, but what did he know?

"Can you describe him?"

"Sure. Short, kinda scrawny, black curly hair. Wore one o' them Jew beanies. Don't know what it was about him that got me goin' but he had something. I'm not the only one, either; he had a girl in his room the first night, against the rules. He said she couldn't resist him either."

"What did the girl look like?"

Norcroft was holding his breath.

"Short, too, big boobs, tiny waist. Obvious what he saw in her. She had nice brown hair, but too many barrettes."

Norcroft exhaled.

She didn't recognize Meg from the show?

"One more question, do you watch any internet webcasts?"

"What are those?"

"Never mind."

Norcroft thanked the lady and packed for the boat trip. He was looking forward to a private chat with Meg Brecker.

Chapter 27

Clint walked into the Trinity Bay Players' theater in a hurry. He would've preferred to get the diving gear himself, but he didn't have much time, and no idea how to sneak it aboard the yacht. A flour-smudged woman in a brown-stained apron appeared on the stage. She smelled like sausage and crawdads.

"May I help you?"

Clint stood frozen for a second. This would violate everything he knew about dealing with a lady, even if she was eyebrow-deep in cooking.

"I need some help," he said, sticking his index finger into his nose. The woman reciprocated, and suddenly seemed even less ladylike. He hoped she was going to wash that finger before she got back to the food.

"I'm Laurel Yanni," she said, then faced offstage and shouted "Devon!" A man emerged from the wings.

After quick introductions, Clint explained the situation. They told him they'd been helping Howie. He told them what had happened.

"*Feet pue tan!*" Laurel swore. "They are devils and will burn in Hell!"

"Yeah, well, we still have to stop 'em before then. Can you help?"

"We'll get your diving gear and get it aboard the ship. By one p.m. is good enough?"

That sounded good to Clint.

"How are you gonna get it aboard?"

"Howie set us up to cater the trip. We have extra carts, lots of room to spare. Go! Get your camera. We'll see you on the boat."

Clint was amazed at the catering angle—Howie was apparently

quite the capable secret agent. Still, their plan left a lot of detail to be desired, and he had no choice except to trust them. So he thanked them and headed for Battery Hut.

By the time he'd purchased the top-of-the-line FathomPro camera and hidden it among his other gear, it was time to get to the boat. As he approached the dock, he saw Muddy at the rail, inspecting everyone and everything that came aboard. And currently, that was Laurel and Devon, dressed like caterers, rolling food carts up the gangplank.

Laurel, in a chef's hat, lifted a pot cover and let Muddy take a whiff. The look on his face said Laurel was a great cook. Muddy waved them both aboard.

"What's for dinner?" Clint asked as he set down the duffel full of clothing and cameras.

"Gumbo, rice, potato salad, and garlic bread," Muddy said, "Pavel's request. And if that gumbo tastes as good as it smells, you'd better be in front of me in the chow line if you expect to get any." He gave Clint a friendly slap on the back and nodded him through.

Clint shouldered his bag and took it to his cabin. Next task was to retrieve the diving equipment. Laurel and Devon had packed two sets of scuba gear into a pair of duffels and hidden them behind the curtain on the side of the spare catering cart. All he had to do was get them to his cabin without anyone noticing.

He loitered in the galley, chatting with the caterers, while keeping an eye on the deck outside. When he saw Muddy and Captain Trauger head up to the bridge, he made his move. He lugged the first one outside, while Devon followed with the other and handed it through the narrow entryway. With a final glance in both directions, Clint started the dash to his cabin.

He reached the companionway and started down the steps, one bag in front and the other held awkwardly on his shoulder so it wouldn't bang on the steep stairway behind him. He was almost to the bottom when a voice came from the lower deck.

"Need a hand with those?"

Clint glanced back between the open treads and saw Brad and Peter, Pavel's actor cowboys, approaching.

"Nah, I'm fine, now that I'm down the stairs."

"Bullshit!" Brad said cheerfully, "It's too narrow here to carry them both. I'll take one."

And with that he lifted the rear duffel from Clint's back. Clint had to let go. And appear grateful.

"I appreciate it, Brad. You guys are getting' the whole Houston helpfulness thing down pretty good."

"Better than the horseback riding thing," Peter said. "I don't think I'll ever get the hang of that." Clint resisted the urge to agree out loud. He'd seen Peter try to ride.

When they got to Clint's cabin, he opened the door and slid his duffel into the room, so as not to clang the tank on the deck. But before he could grab the other bag from Brad, the cowboy had set it down, a little heavily, and with a little clang.

"Wow, what's in the bag?" Peter asked.

Clint's mind raced. Metal. Heavy. Taking it on a boat.

"Cthulhu pots. Traps. Thought maybe I'd do a little bottom fishing while we're out there."

"Ka-whats?"

"Cthulhus—local seafood. Kind of like squid, but uglier. Actually, snapper cthulhus. Those are the babies. The adults are too big to catch, and they're kinda dangerous."

"Good eatin'?"

"Yeah, especially the tentacles. Great with tartar sauce."

Brad looked interested.

"If you catch any, I'd love to try some."

Peter grimaced.

"Not me. I'm not puttin' a tentacle in my mouth."

Brad shot Peter a skeptical look; Peter shrugged, and the two cowboys headed off to their own cabins.

* * *

Arlene picked a spot where the gangway behind her was visible just over her shoulder. The cowgirls hadn't arrived yet, and she intended to be ready. It was the last chance to get them on her own video before they shipped out. She wanted to follow them aboard, but Muddy had made it clear that she was not welcome on the cruise. Her job was to plug the webcast and get out of the way.

Director Nepovim also asked her to assure the viewers that the overcast skies would provide perfect lighting for some exciting bikini photo shots.

Right, if that's all it was. Rain, on the other hand, wouldn't provide perfect lighting for anything except maybe that guy on the Disaster Channel who always reported from the middle of storms in a yellow slicker.

If the weather was bad, maybe she didn't want to be aboard all that much anyway. Besides, she owed Muddy some slack. He'd been feeding her great video opportunities up to now, and last night's organ harvest gave her main business a boost—it was the first time Dr. Bobby Atkinson had flown off with two full carry-on coolers. It kept her from getting Howie in the sack, but maybe that was never going to happen anyway. And while Muddy didn't tell her why Howie needed killing, he must have been bad news for the Corporation, and that meant he was bad news for Arlene, too.

She was happy to let Muddy run his own show.

* * *

Meg sat by herself near the front of the bus. The other girls had paired off behind her and the crew was set up across the aisle. The cameras were rolling the whole time—you never knew when someone would do something interesting. Or embarrassing, like falling asleep, which was entirely possible for Meg. But everyone was just eating their box lunches. There wasn't even enough mustard in the sandwiches to create a wardrobe accident.

During the scramble to find Clint, Meg had resisted the urge to tell them he had errands to run. Eventually, he texted someone that he'd meet them at the boat, and the bus started the trip to Galveston.

She was getting anxious about this third excursion onto the Gulf of Mexico, given how the first two turned out. To make matters worse, the bus passed a road sign, one of many around Houston due to frequent heavy-rainstorm road flooding, with the tag line:

TURN AROUND
DON'T DROWN

It occurred to her that, while she couldn't turn the bus around, she could simply refuse to go aboard the boat. It's what Howie and Roger wanted her to do. "But what about your contract?" they would say. "But what about the fact that the owner of this boat killed my boyfriend when we went out on his previous boat?" she would reply.

No, she wouldn't. She still had to play the amnesia game. But that didn't mean she had to sail off to her doom, either. Hell, they were going to announce today's loser at the dock, maybe she'd already been voted off. She DQ'd the drag race, and losing the competition seemed to be the deciding factor so far.

How dangerous was it? The weather was a little iffy, but nothing serious. And Muddy and Pavel and the owner would be aboard, so they obviously thought it was safe.

If she stayed on camera the whole time, would they dare try to kill her? They'd already tried three times, so, yes.

But what was their end game? Those devices out there had to be for some nefarious purpose, or they wouldn't be protecting them by killing off witnesses. This would be another chance to check them out, and maybe expose the whole thing—assuming Clint brought scuba gear aboard, and they could get away.

Clint was taking considerable risk to smuggle in the gear; she kind of owed it to him to show up for the trip. Like she owed Howie for risking his foray to Muddy's rig.

At least if she died out there, she and Howie would be even.

The bus pulled up to a wharf where the biggest yacht Meg had ever seen awaited its passengers. The thought of spending the last three years aboard crossed her mind. Was the dungeon as nice as the rest of the boat?

Clint came down the gangway with a large folded placard, blank on the outside. As usual, the cameras rolled as the girls lined up side by side. A limousine pulled up and a uniformed driver stepped out smartly and stood at attention.

"Ladies, most of you will be boardin' the boat in a moment, but one of you will be treated to a limo ride back to the ranch." He exchanged a nod with the limo driver. "The votin' was close again. Lisa and Samantha tied for the win in the drag race and picked up bonus points. Dallas and Meg both disqualified by goin' too fast, so you lost points."

That confirmed that Meg's "accident" was treated like an ordinary DQ. Fair enough; there was no proof it wasn't her fault.

"The negative votes were the deciding factor," Clint continued as he stepped over to the limo driver and handed him the placard. The driver unfolded the card and held it up. In large black marker, it read: DALLAS.

"Dallas, your courtesy ride back to the ranch is waiting."

The cowgirls' faces fell in empathy as they rushed to say goodbye, except for Dallas, whose lip curled.

"Can I get a ride somewhere else? Daddy's yacht is moored at the marina down the street. It may not be as big as this one, but it has a lot more wait staff and lot less riffraff." The wave of cowgirls crashed short of Dallas, hissing with indignation as it retreated. The limo driver rolled his eyes as he held the door for her.

Meg watched the limo exit the wharf as she boarded the Bikini Cowgirl yacht. She was a bit envious. Dallas's yacht had a lot fewer assassins, too.

Chapter 28

Muddy watched on three monitors in the communications room as the onboard festivities began. He'd made sure to get multiple camera angles and good lighting, for a clear, reviewable record of the moment.

As scripted, Clint gathered the cowgirls on the pool deck. They were all in bikinis by now, including Faith, who, true to her change of heart, exposed a lot of skin, including her fading bruises. Damn, this was good reality TV.

"Okay, cowgirls, first order of business is to introduce our host for the cruise, the Captain of Bound for Glory, Kenny Trauger."

The girls applauded politely as Kenny emerged from the companionway in dress whites and a gold-trimmed captain's hat. The wardrobe department did well on that one—Muddy was pretty sure Kenny usually sailed in shorts and a tee-shirt.

But Muddy wasn't focused on Kenny. He had Meg Brecker's face zoomed in and watched carefully for her reaction. He hadn't seen any sign that she recognized the boat when she came aboard, but she might not have ever seen it from outside the private dungeon. Surely if she'd spent three years as Kenny's sex slave, she'd recognize the man himself. Even if her amnesia suppressed the painful memories, seeing him might bring them all back in a flood. Now, that would be *great* reality TV.

Another possibility, even though Kenny denied it, was that she got a look at him before the dive, and before the amnesia set in.

He looped the moment several times, but as far as he could tell, Meg saw Kenny as just the guy running the boat. She showed no reaction at all.

Maybe she was blindfolded the whole time.

He went back to real time as Pavel directed the girls to pose for a group photo with the Captain. At Muddy's request, Pavel placed six girls sitting on the deck in front, and two standing on either side of Kenny in back. Meg was assigned a spot next to Kenny.

After a few photos, Pavel took the next step for Muddy's benefit.

"Okay, we have good shots of group, but you are all looking like stiff. Relax, get comfortable. Meg, maybe you cozy up to Captain, give him sexy smile?"

Muddy watched both reactions carefully.

Kenny seemed uncomfortable, like he knew he was being fucked with. But Meg gave Kenny a long look, then turned back to Pavel and the main camera.

"Mr. Nepovim, what kind of cowgirl do you think I am? We just met!"

The cowgirls all laughed, including Meg, and Kenny, who looked relieved.

Muddy just chewed his lip. Who was fucking with who?

* * *

Lieutenant Norcroft stepped out onto the shuffleboard deck, where Meg, Jasmine, Cassidy, and Samantha were competing on camera. He had to smile—Meg was taking it seriously, trying to deal with the effect of the pitching deck in the choppy sea. Cassidy complained that this was not a cowgirl thing to do. Jasmine said she was way too young and Black for an old White person's game. And Samantha played medieval knight, brandishing her cue like a long sword, stabbing at the disc till it retreated down the court.

Norcroft had barely made the boat after a busy morning. First stop was the Chrismoor Suites, where he found the only Massachusetts-tagged car in the parking lot, right near the portico. It was locked, but he snapped a photo of the Vehicle Identification Number plate on the dashboard and took it to the nearby Real Worth hardware store. The key-maker started to insist that Norcroft show some proof of ownership before he'd make replacement keys from the VIN, but Norcroft's star badge was document enough. Back to the car, he unlocked it and found a single set of scuba gear in the trunk, with all the traceable markings removed, just like Meg's gear. Next to it was a suitcase packed with women's clothing that could fit Meg. There was nothing else except duct tape and vise grips in the glove compartment. Howie travelled light.

Next up was dropping by the Trinity Bay Players, but the place was dead—he guessed theatre people don't get going until afternoon, needing time to sleep off those late night after-show parties. Or maybe they all had day jobs.

And when he got to the boat, he was met at the top of the gangway by Pavel and Muddy.

"What are you doin' here?" Muddy asked. "Sir."

"I'm here to observe Meg Brecker and the show, as per our contract."

Muddy and Pavel looked at each other. They were worried about something.

"You're not invited on this trip," Pavel said. "We have no room. Just crew and cowgirls."

"I can sleep in a lifeboat if necessary," Norcroft replied, and spotted another worried look. "And as a duly authorized officer of the Texas Rangers, I can assure you that if I'm not aboard this ship, the Coast Guard will keep it in port."

That concerned look again, but this time with a hint of defeat.

"Okay," Muddy said, "but there's no need to commandeer a lifeboat. I'll have a couple of crew double up." He smiled at Pavel. "Wouldn't want to make the law uncomfortable, right Pavel?"

Pavel appeared to force his grin.

"No, that would not be good."

So, now it was time to speak to Meg, alone. Norcroft waited until the shuffleboard game ended, and intercepted her before she could follow the others to the lounge.

"Ms. Brecker, could I have a word with you?"

Meg turned, surprised, but nodded.

"I guess, if it's okay with Pavel."

"It is most certainly not okay with Pavel!" yelled Pavel as he raced across the deck. Apparently Norcroft's question was caught on camera, and Nepovim was monitoring him. Or Meg. "You are killing me! I am trying to create party atmosphere here. It will not do to have policemen interrogating guests!"

Meg's eyebrows were raised, waiting to hear Norcroft's reaction. He faced Pavel, square.

"It will not do to obstruct an official investigation of the State of Texas," he said.

Pavel smiled, like a guy about to lay down a straight flush.

"But, we are not in State of Texas anymore. We are outside nine-mile limit, and you have no authority. Should I get Captain Trauger to confine you to quarters, or will you leave cowgirls alone?"

Yep, a straight flush.

Norcroft folded and bade Meg bon voyage.

* * *

Lynn limped into the practice gym, leaning on her crutch and wincing with every step. She couldn't believe how much time she'd lost dealing with the emergency room, and then the police, and then the damn rental car agency to get her phone back from the totaled vehicle. She hoped Cirque Noire would be rehearsing but it was the second day of their dark "weekend" and the place looked empty. In this case, "dark" wasn't just show business language for closed: the only illumination came from glowing red exit signs.

She spotted a shadow across the gym, slinking toward the prop area like a prowling cat. Or more likely, a prowling Maggie. Lynn followed, walking carefully and squinting at the floor to avoid stepping across mime glass spike tape.

She caught up at the juggling club rack. Maggie was facing away, selecting clubs, oblivious to Lynn's approach.

"Excuse me," Lynn said, breaking the stillness.

Maggie whirled around, the club in her hand rising toward Lynn's head. For the second time in one day, everything went black.

* * *

I woke up in the dark with drums in my head and drainage water in my mouth. It didn't have the same kick as Jim Beam, but was a lot smoother. I found my phone—it was soaked and useless, even as a flashlight. I retraced my steps by feel until I reached the stairway, then slipped out to the Strip before the Excalibur muscle could collar me. I'd napped most of the day—it was five p.m.—so I sprung for a cab back to the Noir.

I heard a voice coming from the gym, then nothing. Inside, the darkness hushed everything but my own footsteps. It was the perfect setting for discovering a corpse, so when I stumbled onto an inert form near the props area, I wasn't surprised. I found the switch panel and turned on the lights for a better look.

Lynn Grady.

I knelt and checked her pulse and breathing. This broad was tough—and alive. The perp beat her up pretty bad, leaving bruises all over. Served her some sap poison too; a fresh lump was rising out of her matted red curls. A crutch was laid out next to her, a silent witness to the crime. I wondered if it was the assault weapon.

I heard the short squeak of steel wire straining against an anchor bracket and looked up to see Maggie Palms stepping out onto the tightwire. The wire wasn't the only thing that was tight— she looked like she'd been poured into her flame-motif leotard.

I sprinted to the ladder and scrambled to the platform, thirty-five feet up. I tried not to notice the lack of a net.

Maggie had reached the middle of the span, holding three juggling clubs. She didn't usually practice alone. Or without that net.

I kicked off my shoes and inched out onto the wire. Maggie must've felt it move—she did a one-eighty to face me. In perfect form, of course.

"Hi Burke, want to help me work out?" she said, her smile saying something else entirely.

"This ain't a rehearsal, kitten. It's showtime, and I want some answers."

Maggie held out her arms, a plea of innocence. It was a wasted gesture. I could tell by the way her balance shifted that those weren't ordinary juggling clubs. I'm a private detective. And a professional acrobat.

"I've got nothing to hide, Burke." She fluttered her lashes just like she does during the act.

"Actually, doll-face, you do. Let's start with the red tin-copper hairspray mark on the club in your right hand. Looks fresh. Why'd you smack Grady with it?"

Maggie glanced down at the club but didn't flinch.

"I didn't hit anybody, and I have no idea what that spot is. These are ordinary clubs."

"You don't lie well, Maggie. Any palooka could see that's a weaponized heavy club."

"Is not. Watch, I'll show you." Maggie raised the three clubs and lowered them, the standard start cue for a juggling routine. Was this a solo act, or would I have an attempted murder weapon flipping my way? I braced myself to catch it.

Maggie came up juggling solo, but that didn't mean she wasn't gonna pass eventually. When the heavy club came to her right hand, she caught it and tossed it up again. Not at me.

But the extra weight threw her off a little. She shifted right and had to stretch her left hand to reach the next club. That movement threw her center of gravity even further right, and the club bounced off her fingertips. She tottered into space.

"Shit," she said as she grabbed for the wire. She missed that, too.

The clubs thudded to the floor seconds later, one thud louder than the others, confirming my suspicion about the weighted club. But Maggie's thud never happened; she hit a trampoline that had somehow appeared below her. I saw Lynn Grady collapsing near it—the bruised tomato must've woken up and shoved it over. I followed Maggie's motion as she bounced back up.

"Why'd you hit her?" I asked as she approached the wire. She shrugged as she plummeted. She was back up a moment later.

"She surprised me with a crutch pistol—it was a defensive reflex," she said, fading into the shadows.

"Good thing she doesn't hold a grudge," I pointed out as she again neared apogee. "That trampoline is her doing."

Maggie nodded as she re-plummeted. I struggled to keep my balance; I usually avoid looking down from the high wire, but in this case I had to look down—and back up—repeatedly.

"I guess I owe her an apology," she said at the peak of the next rebound. I shook my head as she dropped and rose again.

"You also owe her your life. And some first aid."

Maggie headed for the tramp again, this time flattening out onto her back to absorb the shock, and forward somersaulting into a clean dismount. I backed up to the platform and climbed down to mediate the discussion between the two kittens before it turned into a cat fight.

I could've used a drink and a cigarette. And a neck massage.

* * *

Back at the Vegas Legion headquarters, Lynn held a compress to her head and looked over Deanna's shoulder as she punched the management node address into Google DNS Reverse Search. "Location not found" said the website.

"The node isn't in the physical map," Deanna reported.

"I think Roger tried that," Lynn said. "Should we get him on the phone?"

"Do it," Burke said.

Lynn put Roger on speakerphone and gave him a brief summary of the day; his anger at her accident was tempered by relief that she was okay.

"You tried pinging?" he asked.

"Just now," Deanna said, and Lynn watched a series of cryptic lines print out on the screen.

"We're seeing eight microseconds round trip from here," Deanna reported, apparently understanding the gibberish. "Could be anywhere."

"Anywhere near Las Vegas," Roger said.

"Right."

Lynn stared at the screen.

"What is that doing?"

"It's sending a message to the management node," Maggie said.

"All internet nodes respond to ping messages. The time is how long it took to get there and back. Kind of like if you measured how long it took me to drop from the high wire to the trampoline and back up. Except that took 2.8 seconds, and this takes 8 microseconds—network signals are a lot faster than a falling acrobat."

Lynn actually understood that, but something bothered her.

"You said 2.8 seconds. Why not three, or a few? Do you really know it that exactly?"

Maggie laughed.

"Oh, yeah. The wire is thirty-five feet high so, given how fast things fall, we've calculated exactly how long it takes to get to the bottom and back. We use that information to time the music for our trampoline acts."

"So, if you can figure out time from distance, can't you figure out distance from time? And figure out how far away that control node is?"

Maggie, Burke, and Deanna froze.

"That's it!" Roger yelled from the phone speaker.

Deanna dove for the keyboard and typed furiously.

"I can route the ping message by three different paths through known router locations, and then triangulate on the unknown leg!"

Lynn had no idea what that meant. Like Roger, Deanna was obviously one of those map people.

There is no shame in needing directions, said Zen-mind. *We don't do maps, either.*

Deanna determined that the control node was located in the heart of the casino at the Buckley Grand. She brought up Google Earth Real Time and zoomed in on the location. It was in a two-story section of the building. There was a low garage nearby that could provide the Legionnaires a shortcut access over its roof.

There was also a helicopter waiting on the main roof that could provide Charlie Stewart a quick escape.

"Can we get in?" Lynn asked Burke.

"We've got enough saps and roscoes to bust into any casino in town," he answered, nodding toward Maggie.

* * *

Lynn stayed out of the way as Burke mobilized the Las Vegas Urban Legion to attack the casino at Buckley Grand. They were all athletic and probably trained fighters, but their weapons were circus props: yo-yo-ish diabolos, poi bolas, juggling balls and clubs, spinning plates, and hula hoops. None of them seemed very threatening, but then Lynn felt her still-throbbing head bump and guessed that all of them were weaponized like the clubs. Just the same, she was glad for what martial arts skills she'd learned so far.

The group assembled in the back parking lot, along with two stretch limos and a cartoonish classic Volkswagen beetle, complete with giant wind-up key sticking up from the back. As the performers piled into the limos, mime Jack Marcel emerged from the arena, silently leading a team of twenty-five cop-and-gambler-costumed clowns in oversize shoes and red noses.

The clowns began to pile into the tiny VW. Lynn didn't really start to think about it until about ten of them were inside. She walked around the back and tried to peer past the wind-up key and through the rear window, but the interior was totally dark.

"How do they do that?" she asked Maggie.

"Tinted glass," came the answer.

"No, I mean fitting them all in there."

"Basic Tardis technology. Allows the inside to be bigger than the outside. Clown cars have always used it, but Doctor Who made it popular."

"Doctor Who is science fiction!" Lynn said. "The Tardis isn't real!"

"Of course not," Maggie responded, "there's no such thing as time travel."

Two of the clowns started winding the key, which made a loud k-k-k-k-k-k-k noise as it turned. After two rotations, the key snapped off.

"Uh, oh," Lynn said.

"Don't worry, that's just a gag," Maggie assured her.

The two clowns got into the front seat and the engine started, with a sound like a snoring duck. And almost immediately, a huge spring burst through the front hood and sproinged off the pavement a few times before rolling away.

"Uh, oh," Lynn repeated.

"Also a gag," Maggie said. "Remember, that's just the trunk, the engine is in the back."

The last four clowns approached the car, with their hands over their heads, and rotated in a strangely coordinated fashion, like a halftime marching band. Lynn tried to get out of their way by walking around the front of the car.

Her head hit something hard, and the clowns stumbled sideways, clutching at the invisible object they'd been holding. Lynn heard shattering glass as it apparently crashed to the asphalt.

"My imvivable la--er!" Jack yelled. As everyone turned in surprise at hearing his voice, he gave Lynn that now-familiar angry glare.

"Uh, oh," said Maggie this time. "We were gonna use Jack's invisible ladder to go over that low garage roof, so nobody would notice it while we were inside."

"I thought mime glass is too fragile to make a ladder," Lynn said.

"It is. That was a solid glass ladder, coated with mime glass. Makes it pretty heavy, which is why it takes four clowns to carry it."

Burke shouted to the team. "Time for plan B—the front entrance."

The last few clowns climbed into the VW and slammed the doors, and the car rolled forward. But after a few feet the tires began to hiss and the car settled onto the rims. Maggie ran over and inspected them.

"Flat," she said. "All four of them. Must be the ladder shards."

As the clowns poured out of the car and waved their arms in panic, Burke borrowed Maggie's phone.

"Don't touch the time-bomb icon," Maggie said as she handed it over.

Burke nodded and made a call.

"Desert Cab?" he asked. "Yeah, this is Burke Barrage at Cirque Noire, in the back parking lot. We need five cabs, pronto. Right, five. Look for the clowns. Thanks."

* * *

Clint saw Pavel's signal from behind the camera; they were now webcasting live. For Clint, a live webcast was just like every rodeo he'd ever announced: get folks worked up about the next event, then narrate as it happens. The old saying went "this ain't my first rodeo," but it was the first time he struggled to keep his balance while he talked.

"Welcome to all you viewers out there who clicked into the Next Bikini Cowgirl competition's premiere prime-time live webcast. We're comin' to you from the cocktail lounge and casino of the extravagantly equipped super yacht Bound for Glory. We're over fifty miles out in the Gulf of Mexico, so you might notice the boat is rockin' a bit. We got a little weather out here, kickin' up some waves."

Clint had no problem with seasickness, especially because, true to his word, Muddy had beat him to the gumbo and he didn't get any. But the girls chowed down on it; apparently it was as tasty as Muddy claimed. Primed by a cocktail hour with liberally poured hard shots and umbrella drinks, now some of the girls weren't looking so good—it was hard to smile when your stomach was trying to escape through your mouth. At least the light in the ship's lounge was naturally dim, so the crews were using portable lighting, which made everyone look pale and about to puke.

"And speakin' of kickin', you'll wanna stick around, as we're about to start our two-step competition on the dance floor. It's gonna be an extra challenge for our bikini cowgirls, what with the dance floor buckin' like a prize bull."

Chapter 29

Captain Kenny Trauger deftly drove the bow into the rollers. The weather was rougher than he'd like, but not a problem. Bound for Glory was 120 meters of pure seaworthy, and a yacht that size didn't shy away from a few little waves. It also didn't dally; they'd made good time and were fifty miles out by the time the sun set behind them.

Kenny had to admit, he was pretty proud of the ship. He wondered if the guys in the audience would be drooling more over the bikini cowgirls or the brass, glass, and solid teak cocktail lounge.

He was also proud of his choice of caterers. He'd just picked them from a Google search, but they were great—the gumbo was the best he'd ever tasted. If anything, the only danger from the weather was that everyone had probably eaten too much gumbo to handle the waves. Kenny didn't want to think about swabbing secondhand gumbo off the brass, glass, and solid teak.

He'd set up a tablet so he could watch the video the ship was transmitting back to Reality Web. Clint was emceeing the dance competition, being held in the lounge to avoid the rain. It was kind of hilarious as the girls tried to look sharp while struggling to stay on their feet—it was a good thing they were all in boots instead of high heels like beauty pageants. Most of them didn't look too seasick, but then again, as Cassidy put it, Houston cowgirls could hold their gumbo.

He was checking his course on the navigation system when the ship lurched and the thrum of the engines died. Emergency lighting kicked on and alarms began to wail. He dispatched First Mate Braxton to the engine compartment and assessed the situation. Onboard electricity came from the engine-powered generator, but the backup batteries could keep the nav and comm systems going for a day, if they killed nonessential power loads. They'd have the engines up in a few hours, if not a few minutes. And if worse came to worst, there was always a call to the Coast Guard.

"Braxton to bridge," chirped the intercom. "There was a fire—the automatic water mist system put it out. But the engine control panel is totally fried. I don't think we can start these babies without the controls."

Kenny frowned. His big boat was too big to just fire up an outboard and motor out of trouble. On the other hand, it was probably the safest place to be in a storm, even without power.

Just the same, he grabbed the radio mike and selected channel 16.

"Mayday, mayday, mayday. This is Bound for Glory, Bound for Glory, Bound for Glory. TX-7723-ZB. Mayday. This is Bound for Glory. 28 degrees 29 minutes North, 94 degrees 10 minutes 7 seconds West. Drifting. Engine room fire, extinguished, but no power, no propulsion. Can remain afloat indefinitely. Need a tow or replacement engine control panel. Twenty-six people aboard—" he thought for a few seconds; it couldn't hurt "—including ten Bikini Cowgirl contestants. Ship is 120 meters luxury yacht, white hull, three decks. Over."

He set the mike down, and as he waited for the response he noticed two things: First, the radio status display was dark; it had somehow gotten fried in the power outage so his distress call hadn't gone anywhere. Second, his tablet was still displaying the ship video stream. Clint and the cowgirls had been freaked out by the sudden loss of lounge lighting, but the camera lights apparently had their own power. As did the cameras.

And the fucking video system. Muddy had set up a private transmission network between the ship and Reality Web for the trip. Which meant the show was still going on—and everyone watching knew his ship had fucked up.

But it also meant he had a comm channel back to Reality Web headquarters.

He opened an instant message.

< We're out of power. We had a fire in the engine room, control system is toast. Drifting. Tried to call the Coast Guard but the radio is out too. Need a tow.

RealityWeb> OK, thanks for the update. Will contact Coast Guard for you. What's your location?

< 28 degrees 29 minutes North, 94 degrees 10 minutes 7 seconds West.

RealityWeb> Got it. Will send help. Keep the cameras rolling!

Kenny looked over at the tablet and shook his head. About all he could do at the moment was to keep the cameras rolling.

* * *

Clint did his best to manage the cocktail lounge chaos. Pavel stood behind the cameras, guiding their focus to the most humiliating action.

Sadistic bastard.

Some of the girls were just fine, but the waves were getting bigger now. Faith and Jasmine had already tossed their crawdads and andouille sausage overboard—live on camera, webcast to thousands of viewers, with thousands more tuning in by the minute. Word from Reality Web was that the stricken cowgirl cruise had gone viral.

Somehow the sight of a Bible-thumping White girl heaving alongside an orphaned inner-city Black girl was deeply satisfying. Their skin didn't matter; on the inside they were both the same color: bilious gumbo.

Meg and Gabriella were doing their best to help the two rain-soaked girls, which also made for great web TV. But then Meg started scratching at her ear. That was their prearranged signal, and it meant she wanted to dive. She suddenly ran for the rail and barfed into the Gulf. Or at least faked it—he couldn't tell in the rainy darkness, and neither could the camera. She came up wiping her mouth and rushed over to Clint.

"Clint, honey, do you think we could go to your cabin for some Dramamine?" She gave him a coy smile—no, actually, she gave Pavel and the nearby cameraman a coy smile. Clint followed that with a wink at Pavel.

Pavel couldn't hide his delight—nicely done, Meg.

"Of course," Pavel said. "You will only have half hour." He winked back at Clint. "There is roulette competition soon."

Even if they could keep the ball on the table, Clint didn't think that watching a spinning roulette wheel would sit well with seasick cowgirls. But then again, maybe that was Pavel's intent.

Creative sadistic bastard.

He led Meg forward along the deck to his cabin. A half hour was not a lot of time.

* * *

Brad Driver kept a wary eye on his partner as the waves worsened. Peter's only seagoing experience had been a snuff porn shoot on a small day cruiser in San Diego harbor. The only rocking that the boat experienced was caused by Peter Long and his victim in the forward cabin.

Peter was also new to gumbo, and despite Brad's warning to go easy, couldn't resist taking a huge helping. It was really good gumbo.

Still, the combination of Gulf waves and Cajun cuisine did not sit well, and soon Peter was looking even paler than usual. Brad needed to get him out of view of the cameras before he embarrassed himself.

"Come on, dude, you need some fresh air. And a rail to hang onto."

Peter didn't resist as Brad guided him out and forward a few yards. A strong swell gave them a rollercoaster ride up, and then down. Brad grabbed Peter as he lurched across the rail.

And while he kept his partner from going overboard, he could not do the same for the gumbo. As Peter launched the dinner outward onto the gale, Brad was thankful he'd chosen the leeward side of the boat.

Peter hung his head, spitting, then cocked it sideways.

"Is that scuba divers? What are scuba divers doing here?"

Brad glanced over the side into the dark water. There was nothing there, of course.

"You're just seeing things, dude. Seasickness'll do that you."

Peter nodded, and looked back at Brad with glazed eyes.

"I love you, man," he said.

"I love you, too," Brad responded, then quickly added, "As a friend."

* * *

Meg and Clint descended through the underwater fog, trailing a tether to the ship. She'd insisted on the tether, and it was a good thing— there was minimal light from the ship, no moon or stars visible through the overcast, and the water was unusually cloudy. And warm.

They reached the bottom quickly, and played dive lights around for a few minutes. Clint was already filming, though there wasn't much to see. Meg worried that even though there were hundreds of nodes on the Gulf map, the gulf was pretty big, and their chances of finding one right here were slim.

But Clint had used his phone GPS to correlate their location, and waved Meg to follow him as he swam purposefully away from the ship. She followed.

They soon came upon a short, underwater mushroom cloud; sediment was curling up, out, down, and back into the center. They skirted under the edge of the cap, and in another twenty yards entered a dome of clear water, where they found what they were looking for.

The device was the same as Meg had discovered three years earlier. Only this time, the metal cover was open. And a torrent of cloudy water shot upward from the pipe in the seabed.

They approached carefully—the stream looked strong enough to dislodge breathing apparatus. Clint filmed while Meg reached out to touch the plume with her fingers.

She pulled them back. The water was almost scalding. She pulled out her diving slate and wrote "BOILING HOT."

Clint gave her a brief puzzled look, then wrote on his:

"HOT WATER -> HURRICANE."

The Corporation was creating the storm? Why?

In any case, they needed to expose this. She wrote "TIME 2 BLOW WHISTLE" on her slate, and Clint started back along the tether. Meg followed as he disappeared into the billowing sediment cloud.

She couldn't see anything for a moment, but felt the tether pull sharply sideways. She continued along it until she reached Clint. He was seated on another pipe, surrounded by a disk of disturbed sediment. It looked like water was getting vacuumed inward, or at least, it was until Clint got his ass stuck on the intake.

"HEATER INTAKE" he wrote. "I'M STUCK." Meg considered how powerful the heated jet had been—if there was one intake for each jet, the suction would be huge. And it was. She and Clint struggled for a few minutes, but he had plugged the pipe so well there was no way to pull him free.

"LEAVE ME. TAKE CAMERA. EXPOSE THEM," Clint wrote.

Meg didn't even consider that option. There was no way she was going to lose a third partner to the Corporation. Besides, even if she was willing to leave Clint and take the evidence back, the approaching pod of speargun-toting dolphins would probably object.

* * *

Yeechchtyt led her squad toward the intruders. It was almost getting too hot to do their job, but under stress, it was always best to fall back on training. And training said "Protect the pipes from intruders."

Though at the moment, the pipes were a bigger problem. She'd already lost two soldiers to the heat. The remaining archers circled the humans, awaiting her orders. Yeechchtyt moved in for a closer look.

It was the female from the last encounter, the one that saved young Chchkk's life by cutting him free of a fishing net that night. That was worth something. The male wasn't the sexy one. Too bad.

The female was pantomiming something. Pointing to the pipe that was spewing hot water. Then pointing to herself and her partner. Then pretending to close the pipe lid.

Of course.

Yeechchtyt and her team had been trained to attack intruders who would interfere with the pipes. But the trainers didn't tell them that the pipes were bad for dolphins. The trainers were bad. These intruders were good.

Yeechchtyt chattered a hold fire command to the team and fired a spear. The female ducked away and then outstretched her hands. Yeechchtyt knew that sign—it was a plea for mercy.

Stupid human; she thinks I shot and missed. If I wanted to hit her, I would have. I'm going to have to explain everything.

* * *

Meg shivered even in the heated water as she waited for the next spear. The dolphin was so close now it couldn't possibly miss again.

But it didn't shoot. Instead, it swam to the first spear and pulled it out of the sand with its beak. Spear in mouth, it headed for Clint. Even as she darted to intercept, Meg couldn't believe the dolphin was going to kill him in beak-to-hand combat.

She was too late. But she was also right—the dolphin didn't kill him but tried to jam the blunt end of the spear between Clint's butt and the edge of the pipe. After a few failed tries, it turned and offered the spear to Meg.

Amazing. The dolphins understood her signals. And the bottlenose wasn't afraid that Meg would spear it at close range. Of course, if she did, the other dolphins would retaliate tenfold.

The bottlenose urgently nuzzled her dive knife, and then the spear line. Meg nodded. There was a good chance the spear would get sucked into the intake, and take the dolphin with it, if she didn't cut the line. This was a smart creature.

Taking care to avoid the razor-sharp business end, Meg cut the line from the spear and then worked the blunt end just to the side of Clint's tailbone and into his butt crack. Once she had six inches of it in there, she grabbed the other end just below the blades and pulled sideways.

The short spear didn't give her much leverage, but with Clint's help, it worked. A narrow gap opened and the rushing water relieved some of the suction. Clint and Meg both rolled sideways and down to avoid getting caught in the torrent. The spear disappeared into the pipe, perhaps to be launched by the nearby vent like a submarine missile. But it had already done some damage—a cloud of blood billowed from Meg's hand. The cut was in the meaty part of her left thumb—not a big deal.

As long as there weren't any sharks around.

It was now urgent to get back to the ship. Unfortunately, they'd dropped the tether. She waved her light around, but the sediment was already swirling, making it impossible to find anything. Surfacing and finding a darkened ship on an overcast night in big waves was not a great option, but it was the only option. They headed upward.

As they cleared the churned-up cloud, they tried sweeping dive lights again, and this time, found the tether—in a dolphin's beak as it swam toward them. The bottlenose handed it off and the rest of the pod escorted them along the line to the ship. Meg didn't see any sharks—maybe the sharks knew what spearguns could do.

Once they reached the boat, Meg waved thanks. The dolphins clicked something she assumed meant "Don't mention it" or "Good luck" and swam away.

Meg and Clint climbed aboard the aft swim platform and prepared to face the human sharks above.

Chapter 30

The chief meteorologist at the Disaster Channel stared at the unbelievable data. He'd never seen a storm build so rapidly. His program director leaned over his shoulder.

"We can't wait any longer, Vick."

"It just seems like we've got some kind of instrumentation failure. Storms don't act like this. It's not even hurricane season."

"But let's say it is a freak superstorm. The sooner we start hyping it, the better our numbers will be."

Vick rotated his chair to face his boss.

"Yeah, but if we overhype it, like we usually do everything, we look like idiots. I'm not even sure anyone will believe us on this one."

The boss pointed to the radar screen.

"Show them the charts. They'll believe that."

"We'll have to admit we totally screwed up. We've been ignoring it, calling it a minor tropical depression. Nothing Houston hasn't seen a hundred times before."

The director pursed his lips.

"Let's play that up. This storm is wildly unpredictable. Nobody's ever seen anything like it. Maybe hint at climate change, El Niño, anything. Say we don't understand it yet, but it's our duty to warn them now rather than waiting till we're sure. Err on the side of caution and all that." He paused. "Is anyone else onto this?"

Vick shook his head.

"The National Weather Service is noting that the storm is intensifying rapidly, but they're not pulling any alarms yet. The Weather Channel is still in the middle of their two-hour weather history show and hasn't mentioned it. Oh, but our old buddy Charlie Stewart is all over it."

"Stewart? What's that sleazeball's angle on this?"

"He's got a live webcast going on his Reality Web show, Next Bikini Cowgirl. He obviously didn't think much of the storm, he sent a boatload of girls and camera crew out into the Gulf this afternoon. And they've got equipment problems but the video is working fine. He's playing the weather up for all the drama he can."

"Dammit, that's our drama! Is anyone watching them?"

"Hard to say—other people's webcast stats aren't easy to get. But I can tell you one thing: not a whole lot of people are watching us. I suspect they're watching the cowgirls."

The boss grinned.

"I guess you in a rain slicker can't compete with cowgirls in wet bikinis. But do the story anyway. You can leave your bikini in your locker."

Vick nodded, and prepped a breaking news report. The data had gotten even worse in the few minutes he'd been discussing it. A distinct eye had formed, and the central surface pressure was rapidly sinking, looking like it might even slide below 900 millibars. At this intensification rate, they'd have to create a new category 6. The Disaster Channel did have a duty to warn Houston.

Vick could only hope somebody was watching.

* * *

Muddy stalked the bridge deck after looking for Meg and not finding her in the lounge, or in Clint's cabin, where she'd supposedly gone. The only places he couldn't check were the dungeons, which Kenny had insisted be locked for the duration. And that made him wonder if Kenny had the balls to capture Meg again, under Muddy's nose. He had mixed emotions about that— he hated being lied to, but he had to admire that kind of tenacity.

So now he was looking for Kenny, to give him one last chance to redeem himself. He found the skipper on his knees behind the radio rack, trying to fix the transmitter. Muddy was pretty sure the gear was hopeless; at least, he'd done his best to break it beyond repair.

"How's it look, Skipper?" he asked.

"Not good. One of the capacitors blew up and took out the main power supply. Must've been really hot."

Muddy nodded. About 3600 degrees, if he remembered the specs on his pocket propane torch correctly.

"No problem, though, right? You can text Reality Web over our control channel, and they can call in the Coast Guard."

"Yeah, I did that. I just hate sitting around waiting."

"Good, 'cause I need your help. Meg Brecker is missin'."

Kenny flinched, startled. That Meg was missing? Or that Muddy knew it?

"I've been searchin' everywhere, except the dungeons. They're locked."

"Right. She can't get in there."

"Not by herself."

Kenny crawled out from behind the equipment and stood to face Muddy, his eyes narrow.

"What are you saying?"

"Not sure. But I'd like to check the rooms, now."

Kenny stared him down for a few seconds, and then began to grin.

"You think I locked her up?" He actually laughed. "For a second time?" He pulled a key ring from his pocket and started for the door. "Let's go check."

Muddy followed as Kenny led the way below decks. It was actually kind of inspired that the dungeons were in the bottom of the boat. The traditional location for dungeons.

If Kenny was willing to show him the rooms, he hadn't recaptured Meg. But he also was still denying having captured her the first time. Muddy had DNA evidence to the contrary, but Kenny didn't know that.

He'd give the captain one more chance to come clean—he hated to lose a good soldier. But a good soldier doesn't lie to his commander.

Kenny opened the first dungeon. This was the public one. It had restraint tables for three in front of a wall with a full selection of crops and whips, in apparently standard sizes: A1, B1, B2, C1, all the way up to E7-modified. Muddy didn't want to know what the modification was. On another wall hung hoods, handcuffs, harnesses with and without mouth balls, shackles, feathers, and latex bodysuits. The third wall had cabinets and a counter with labeled drawers below—like a kitchen, except for cooking up a dildo-and-butt-plug stew. At one end was a standard wet bar. It was designed for parties, after all.

This dungeon probably did get used for parties, even while Meg had been missing. She wouldn't be here. But hidden behind the shackle selection was the second door, the door that only Kenny, Muddy, the ship designers, and Meg knew about. Kenny used a different key on that one and swung it open.

The secret dungeon was more intimate, with a select set of instruments on its limited wall space. Good for the top ten torture techniques, Muddy guessed. The bondage platform dominated the room, but there was no one bound to it.

"See?" said Kenny, "No Meg Brecker."

Muddy studied the captain's eyes, looking for signs of anything but the defiance he saw.

"And she was never here?"

"Nope."

"And you never saw her between the time we scooped her boyfriend and when she showed up on Bikini Cowgirl?"

"Correct."

"You're lyin'," Muddy said as he pushed the taser into Kenny's belly. Kenny convulsed and dropped to the metal floor. "I hate that," Muddy added, to unhearing ears.

He grabbed Kenny under the arms and dragged him onto the platform. Using the wrist and ankle cuffs, it only took a few moments to bind him well. Muddy removed the dungeon door keys from the inert man's pocket.

He waited a few minutes, and Kenny came to, suddenly, his eyes snapping open and limbs jerking against the shackles.

"What's going on? What are you doing?"

"I don't like liars," Muddy said. "I was willin' to give you a chance, but you insist on lyin' to me."

Kenny thrashed around a bit, but he, more than anyone, knew how hopeless his situation was. He got still again.

"You're gonna sink my ship, aren't you?"

"Yep."

"And me with it."

"Yep. That's the rule, ain't it? The captain always goes down with his ship?"

Kenny nodded, resignation in his eyes.

"You're not gonna kill the cowgirls, are you?"

Muddy showed no reaction. A little hint of horror crept into Kenny's face.

"Is there anything I can say to convince you to change your mind?"

Muddy considered that.

"How about Meg's safe word?"

* * *

Roger watched the webcast with the helpless dismay of a dedicated but incompetent manager. Meg and Clint hadn't returned from "getting some Dramamine"—he was pretty sure they'd gone overboard to film the devices. He wasn't sure they'd ever gotten back. The storm was getting worse, the boat was powerless, and the show was continuing as if this was a minor inconvenience. They probably hadn't even called for help.

Roger could fix that, at least.

He looked up the U.S. Coast Guard Galveston Station and gave them a call.

"Coast Guard."

"Hi, Coast Guard, my name's Roger. I've been watching the Next Bikini Cowgirl live webcast, and they've got a big yacht in trouble out on the Gulf. They have no power, and they seem to be drifting. There's a lot of people on board. I think they need help."

"Well, Roger, we appreciate the call. We haven't heard from them. Do you know where they are, exactly?"

"Um, not really. Somewhere in the Gulf east of Galveston."

"That makes responding a little difficult. If we get a distress call, we'll deal with it immediately. Thanks for calling."

The Coast Guard wasn't worried, either.

Roger could fix that, too.

He set up a robocall program to light up the Galveston Station switchboard with calls, using random caller IDs, randomized scripts saying in various ways that the ship looked powerless and drifting, using random regional accents plugged into Google Text-to-Speech. They'd think the whole country was freaking out.

The whole country should've been freaking out. Bound for Glory was bound for deep trouble.

Chapter 31

Charlie Stewart paced from the weather screen to the webcast monitor and back, watching the situation build on both. Things were going swimmingly, he thought, forgiving himself for the pun. Fiona wanted webcast drama, she was getting webcast drama. She'd better be watching.

He found it surprising that Fiona was interested only in the ratings and not the long-term benefits of controlling the weather. It would be such an evil genius thing to extort protection money out of Gulf cities from Fort Myers to Cancun after this very graphic demonstration of his power. And she fit that master villain role perfectly, the way she was always calmly petting a cat.

Of course, he'd earned his own evil genius status—he'd worked his way up. As a rookie New England weatherman, he'd taken bribes from snowplow operators and ski areas to overestimate snow totals. Nobody noticed the plow guys were only plowing two inches instead of five per run—and they still got in a lot of runs. So did the New England skiers, who were fine with two inches of snow. They considered anything whiter than mud to be eastern powder.

But at the Disaster Channel, when Charlie started setting dramatic wildfires, his bosses got upset.

"We don't create disasters, Charlie, we just report 'em."

But overhyping 'em was apparently okay.

Their loss. They had no idea how much of the weather control network he'd already set up by then, on their dime. It amused him to think they were just now realizing how powerful a storm this was.

Fools.

Revision 2.0 of StormGen was working perfectly, unlike

revision 1.3 that he had first deployed. The test of that got a pretty good storm going with Hurricane Harvey, but it created electrical interference with the control transmission system, and before they could shut it down they lost steering. It drifted over land where they couldn't control it at all, and it stayed for weeks, causing the biggest floods in Houston since the Great Storm of 1900.

Charlie smiled. Harvey was just a dress rehearsal; this was opening night of a one-night smash run. Muddy had clandestinely wired the control antennas to the towering Sagemont cross, giving StormGen 2.0 unstoppable communication power. Not only was he in complete control, the ship was flawlessly transmitting the drama of cowgirl heroines stranded on the wildly pitching nautical stage, somewhere out in the middle of a yet-unnamed category-huge hurricane. Their ship was foundering, with no help in sight...

"Call on line one, boss," Frank Woodland said, "Caller ID says U.S. Coast Guard Galveston Station."

...unless the Coast Guard showed up.

"Put them on, Frank."

Frank punched a button and the red comm indicator lit.

"This is Charlie Stewart. What can I do for you?"

The voice on the line sounded strong, and maybe a little irritated.

"Mr. Stewart, this is Commander Gingrich from the Coast Guard Galveston Station. We've been getting reports that you have a ship in trouble off the coast of Galveston, from which you're webcasting. We normally wouldn't bother without a distress signal, but there were enough phone calls to make us tune in to your show. The situation looks pretty bad, Mr. Stewart, despite your willingness to keep webcasting. We're scrambling a rescue mission now, but we need to know where the boat is."

You certainly do.

"Commander, have you ever watched reality TV?"

"No sir, waste of time. No offense. Even if it does involve girls in bikinis."

"Right, which is why you don't know how reality shows work. You see, Commander, 'reality' is a misnomer. We create the illusion of reality, but everything is carefully controlled for maximum impact. The only reality is that we don't have a script for the players—they just react to what we're throwing at them. As you could see from the webcast, there's a lot of drama going on out there. But I assure you, we are in complete control of the situation, and there's no need for a rescue mission. Everything is working perfectly."

"They clearly have no power. They're drifting in very high seas."

"Yes, that part is scripted. The boat is very large, Commander, we know what it can handle."

There was a pause; Charlie exchanged a glance with Frank.

"Okay, Mr. Stewart, I'm not sending my men into a hurricane just to be on reality television. There's sure to be someone else who really needs help out there tonight."

"Good plan, Commander. Good night."

"Good night, sir."

The comm indicator winked out and Charlie relaxed. He and Frank studied the monitors for a half a minute, and then Frank looked up.

"You sure you know what you're doing?"

"Absolutely: making a can't-miss viral live video. My boss will be pleased."

* * *

We stepped off the street into the clamor of the Buckley Grand casino. We had everybody but the clowns—you can never count on a cab when you need one. Or five.

It was early evening, but time doesn't mean much in a joint like this. It smelled of cigarette smoke, watered-down booze, and losers. The lights and bells made it festively desperate.

The webcast on Grady's smartphone gave us the latest scoop on the Gulf situation. It wasn't pretty. If they didn't get help soon, those sexy cowgirls would soon be bloated corpses washing up on some Texas beach.

I'd stalked this dive before, back when it was just a gambling den and not a Corporation lair. I hadn't noticed if there was muscle at the time, but I'd been alone, just a regular patsy looking to lose a few days' pay. This time, I brought a team of circus performers, armed with props; the muscle noticed us.

We were ten steps onto the slots floor when a line of standup comics blocked our way.

"What is this, a circus?" one of them asked.

"You look like my mother-in-law. Only not as pretty," said another.

"How do you like my suit?" asked a third, "And my microphone?" He flung a handheld mike toward my forehead. I ducked just in time. I'm a private detective. And a professional acrobat.

"Take my water. Please," said a fourth, and squeezed a stream of liquid from his water bottle. I spun sideways so it only grazed my shoulder. There was a hiss and rising vapor. My shoulder was on fire.

"It's acid!" yelled our bartender and plate spinner, as he slapped a white disc onto my shoulder. The plates are pressed from bicarbonate, and it neutralized the acid and the burn like a bouncer tossing a heckler. He spun plates to block the streams from the other comics while our street walkers flipped hula hoops onto them. A press of the contraction switches cinched the hoops tight, trapping the funny guys' arms by their sides. Quick taps on their noggins with juggling clubs sent them all to comedy-club dreamland.

I glanced around, bracing for the crowd reaction. But they were all heads down at the one-button bandits, and ignored us. We pushed further into the casino.

The blackjack area was lousy with magicians. They didn't try to block our way, but they kept disappearing and reappearing in different places so we couldn't get a bead on 'em. We fired rounds of juggling balls when they popped into sight, but the tuxedoed triggermen deflected them in mid-flight with conjured doves.

The doves were taking the brunt of our attack, giving the magicians time to fight back. I felt a sting behind my right ear, and another. Then one on the left. Quarters were clinking to the floor around my team, as we were buffeted by new coins appearing, at painfully high speed, behind our ears.

Our craps player and ball juggler pulled out a concussion ball and flung it straight up, yelling "No roll!" The team was savvy to that play and ducked, plugging our ears with our fingers. The concussion charge knocked the sense out of anyone else within thirty feet, including all the magicians. Another round of sap-taps with the clubs made sure they'd stay that way.

I took a peek at the nearest table; one poor unconscious sucker had just hit 21 to the dealer's 19. His luck depended on who woke up first.

The next obstacle was a row of craps tables. Guarding that were six chorus beauties with legs for miles, naked from the waist up except for the feathered wings strapped to their shoulders. The sexy angels advanced in a kick line, each sharp kick more like synchronized karate than the Moulin Rouge. Then I saw the five-inch spears protruding from their shoes; these lookers were giving spike heels a whole new meaning.

The Grady dame was closest and ducked under the end dancer as the line started their next kick. She snapped her crutch under the dancer's leg and jiu-jitsu'd it further up and over the dancer's head. The dancers were all locked arm in arm, so the whole line backflipped along with the first. They kept going over until their shoe spikes impaled the broad side of a burnished-cherry craps table. They stuck there and couldn't move as we wrapped them up in contraction hoops. Tough to sleep in such awkward positions, but the juggling clubs helped.

"See?" Maggie said. "I told you that crutch was a weapon!"

We made for the control room door. Two gangsta rappers took the floor outside, pulled their gats, and spit lead. They knocked a few of us over but Kevlar leotards saved our skins.

Maggie wrapped up one of the shooters with a poi bola, and I took care of the other.

"Yo, yo," he chanted, "you got some balls, takin' this hall, with yo' clubs and yo' hoes, swingin' yo' yo-yos." I gave him a sap-nap with a juggling club. I hate rap. It don't mean a thing if it ain't got that swing.

The room fell still—Las Vegas still, with plenty of dinging bells and flashing lights. But no more violence.

All we had to do was get through that last door.

* * *

Meg and Clint crouched in a surprisingly empty lifeboat bay as someone came around from amidships waving a flashlight. They'd stowed the diving gear, wrapped up Meg's hand, and quietly discussed the plan. They couldn't just go on camera in the lounge and tell the world what they'd found—Pavel would cut them off before they got a word out.

Clint suggested tapping into the webcast video feed with a video clip of their own. They could show the vent and explain what it was doing. Meg hoped the Urban Legionnaires in Las Vegas were able to find the control node. If they knew what it was doing, maybe they could shut off the storm.

She held her breath as someone splashed past on the wet deck; she recognized the gait as Muddy Bootes. When he rounded the aft lounge deck and disappeared behind the dining room bulkhead, they made their move.

They scrambled into the galley, which was lit only by an emergency light in the far corner, over the passageway to the communications room. Meg pulled up short. The catering crew was gathered around a stainless steel table, trying to hang on as the ship rolled. They were looking mighty seasick, but not so sick they didn't see their visitors.

She started to retreat but Clint blocked her with his arm. He touched a nostril with his index finger, and both caterers did the same. Meg smiled and returned the Urban Legion signal.

After hurried introductions, they heard footsteps on the stair. The caterers sprang into action and hid Meg and Clint in the curtained shelf of a catering cart. Meg was grateful that the splashing waves had soaked the floor—they hadn't left tell-tale footprints.

"How's it goin' down here?" boomed Muddy's voice over the whistling wind and creaking fixtures.

"It's all good," said Laurel, laying on a thick Cajun accent. "We're just trying to batten down the cookware."

"Have you seen a cowgirl or a cowboy around here?"

"There's a whole bunch of 'em in the lounge."

"Yeah, except two. You seen 'em down here?"

"Nope."

"Okay, I'm gonna look around the comm room."

"What about us? Any sign of rescue?"

"Not yet. But don't worry, this will all be over soon."

Meg swore silently—it all made sense now. The storm generators, the crippled ship, the backup video and transmission capability, and even the missing lifeboats meant that Reality Web was producing the world's first prime-time live snuff webcast. It was also the third urban legend they'd tried to kill her with. Whether they succeeded was yet to be determined.

It took a few minutes for Muddy to return from the communications room and go back out on deck. After he left, Clint and Meg climbed out of the cart and made their way forward to the comm room. Clint found the transmission system, activated the console, and paired his camera with the Bluetooth video concentrator unit.

As the star of the reality show, Meg would narrate the damning video. He set her up for picture-in-picture with the underwater footage, turned on his portable floodlight, started the playback, and gave Meg her cue.

"Hi, everyone. Behind me is video of a boiling hot water vent I just filmed near the ship. There are hundreds of these across the bottom of the Gulf, generating this storm. They're controlled by Reality Web. I think they want to kill us all on camera, and maybe destroy Houston as well. If my friends are watching, please, figure out how to turn off the heaters before it's too late."

* * *

Charlie Stewart alternated his attention between the video from the ship and the ratings charts. The cowgirls were in a state of absolute panic, and the streaming cache servers were straining to keep up with millions of viewers. These events were not unrelated.

The ship was pitching wildly; every few minutes a huge wave crashed against the windows, evoking screams from the girls— screams which could only be seen, unable to compete with the roaring wind. His crew were doing their usual great job, keeping the cameras rolling. A shame they weren't in on the secret. They'd be hard to replace.

Especially Clint Owen. But the point of hiring the charismatic announcer was to shut him up about investigating his missing brother. This would do the job. Besides, his loss at sea, especially along with his romantic interest Meg Brecker, was the kind of tragic coincidence that would keep the tabloids gossiping for years. Charlie wasn't a philanthropist; he intended to charge top dollar for video clips and stills from Meg and Clint's last moments. Pavel was a genius for setting up the relationship.

Speaking of which, where were Meg and Clint? A quick scan of the video feed accounted for nine cowgirls, Pavel, and the Hollywood cowboys, who were barfing into the ice bin at the bar. No Meg, no Clint. Maybe they really were getting it on in his cabin. Big mistake not to have cameras there.

He had his phone out and was about to ring Muddy over the embedded cell channel when the video changed abruptly. He was suddenly watching a murky underwater video of one of his heat pumps in action.

Fuck!

"Frank, go to ads, now!"

Frank hit a key and the webcast video switched away from the churning vent to a "we'll be right back after a word from our sponsors" clip. With the current viewership numbers the ads would make a mint. But he could only stall so long; Muddy needed to fix this, fast. He pressed the call button.

Seconds ticked away. Muddy wasn't on camera, so he should've been able to answer—assuming he could hear or feel the vibrate function over the howling gale.

The stream from the ship changed. Meg Brecker appeared picture-in-picture over the underwater scene, explaining to the world what was really going on. The video looped, starting over with the brief flash of the vent before Meg appeared. It would have been a troublesome segment if anyone besides Charlie and Frank had seen it.

"Is she guessing right, boss? They all die?"

"Nah. Though I wouldn't mind if Meg Brecker did." Muddy was right, the bitch was probably an Urban Legionnaire.

The roar of wind burst through the speaker.

"This is Muddy," came a shout. "Helluva storm, boss!"

"Muddy, I cut off the webcast. There was an override video stream coming from the ship, of one of the vents in action. Then an explanation by Meg Brecker. You need to shut down the override from your end before we can restart the webcast. The video is looping, so look for gear in the communications room. I think Meg's with Clint. Shut her up. Let me know when you're done. Do you copy?"

"Got it, boss."

The room went quiet when Muddy hung up.

Charlie gathered his thoughts for a few moments, then started narrating a technical difficulties message, explaining the interrupted clip as a camera that fell overboard near the bilge pump outlet, and promising a quick return to the excitement at sea after a few short advertisements.

* * *

Muddy stormed into the galley, shoving one of the retching caterers aside on his way to the comm room. He was too late to catch Meg and Clint there, but the jury-rigged playback setup was obvious. He hit the reset on the video mixer; the normal video feed would be back up in a minute.

He found the head-mount underwater cam, set it carefully on the metal floor, and stomped it. He scooped up the shards, hustled back through the galley, and tossed the remains of the camera and evidence over the rail. Meg Brecker was next.

If Clint had gone diving with Meg, he would have had to change clothes, and if he wanted to reappear on deck, he had to change back. Muddy headed for the starboard outside walkway, which put him halfway between Clint's cabin and the lounge for an easy intercept. He ducked into an exterior bulkhead doorway.

Clint slunk by first. As Meg followed past, Muddy sprang from his hiding place and, with a good grip on her narrow waist, flung her far overboard. The scream started loud but was instantly lost in the storm.

Clint started to turn at the sound but Muddy's leg sweep and drop tackle pivoted the host's head into the rail. He went limp and sagged to the deck.

Muddy cursed as he pulled the inert cowboy to his feet and gripped him under the rib cage. He was a lot harder to grab than Meg, and a lot heavier to throw. He didn't get nearly the distance this time.

Muddy opened a text side channel and sent Charlie a message that the video was back to normal and Meg and Clint were gone. After a brief stop at the lounge to discreetly gather Pavel and his cowboy actors, he led them to the aft lifeboat bay. He unlocked it, removed the cover, and enjoyed the gasps of appreciation. The modified oil rig escape pod had room for eight, making for a luxurious seabed shelter to ride out the peak of the storm. Once the weather calmed down, the twin-propeller navigation system would quickly return them to shore.

They climbed aboard, dogged down the hatch, and used the remote-controlled deployment crane to lower the chamber into the churning Gulf.

Chapter 32

Lynn figured the Cirque Noire Urban Legionnaires had some kind of modified circus prop they could use to smash through the door to Charlie Stewart's control center. So she was surprised when Jack Marcel stepped silently up to the door. He seemed to remove a large invisible key ring from his belt, and then flip through invisible keys, considering each before rejecting it and going on to the next.

Burke, Maggie, and Lynn split their attention between Jack's key search and the Bikini Cowgirl webcast on Lynn's smartphone. Suddenly, the video changed to an underwater scene, of water and steam churning from a metal pipe. The scene lasted only a few seconds before the webcast cut to an ad.

"What was that?" Lynn asked, not sure if she'd really seen it.

"Good question," Burke said. "Meg said she was gonna try to film one of the devices, right?"

"Right."

"Maybe that's one of them, and she managed to jimmy the video into the feed. Until Charlie cut it off."

"It looked like a hot tub jet."

"Yeah, it did," Maggie said, slowly nodding. "And if it's heating the water like a hot tub jet, and that map shows hundreds of other jets just like it, you could create a hurricane to order. Just in time to film a shipwreck on live internet TV."

Burke nodded too.

"All choreographed from the comfort of the control node on the other side of this door."

Jack was at least thirty rejections into the key ring search when his eyebrows rose high and a broad smile broke across his white-painted face. With exaggerated movements, he placed an invisible key into the lock, and turned it.

Lynn whispered to Maggie.

"How does he have the right key?"

"It's an elevator override key—and all locks in a building use the same master as the elevator, for firefighter access. There are only about eighty different masters. One of them had to work."

"He's got all eighty on that key ring?"

"Of course. Didn't you see the size of it?"

On Burke's signal, Jack silently opened the door, and the Urban Legionnaires slipped inside. Two men, oblivious to the intruders, were busy at a large console on the far wall.

The largest screen displayed a map of the Gulf of Mexico with wind and pressure indications across it. There were red dots everywhere, matching the device map Howie had sent.

There were also two video monitors. On was captioned "TO AIR," displaying the same ads as on Lynn's phone. The other one said "SHIP FEED" and showed the underwater vent they'd seen earlier. Except now the video included a picture-in-picture of Meg, explaining that the device was a storm generator, guessing that Reality Web wanted to kill her and the cowgirls, and asking her friends to turn off the machines. It was a recorded loop.

The Meg video suddenly switched back to the pandemonium in the ship's lounge.

"We're back, Frank," said the older of the two men. "Go to live feed."

Frank pressed a key and the TO AIR monitor switched back to match the ship feed. Lynn's phone did the same.

Burke cleared his throat, and the two men spun around. The older man matched their pictures of Charlie Stewart, the younger was Frank Woodland.

"Good evening, Charlie. You don't know me from a bum on the street, but I'm sort of one of Meg Brecker's pals. Seems like she'd like you to unplug that storm machine."

Charlie sneered and shook his head.

"Can't do it. Once the storm is going, nothing'll stop it except time and dry land."

Woodland whirled to face him.

"You said we were gonna shut it off before anyone got hurt!

The Peltier diodes can—" Charlie whipped an elbow into Woodland's temple and the guy slumped onto his chair. Before anyone could react, Charlie sprinted to a small alcove and shouted, "Have a taste of your own medicine—code two two five!" Then he waved goodbye as a door slid shut in front of him. With an ominous hiss, yellow foam began to stream from the sprinkler heads.

They copied your foam systems, said Zen-mind.

"They copied our foam systems!" Lynn shouted. "We've got to get out of here!" The Urban Legion always installed construction foam dispenser jets in its facilities to render them unusable in case they fell into enemy hands. The sticky expanding foam would fill the room in fifteen minutes, and completely harden in a half an hour.

"Stewart took an elevator," Maggie said. "He's going for the helicopter!"

"Relax, kid, the clowns are all over that by now," Burke said.

Maggie ran to the fallen technician and tried to revive him. He wasn't responding.

"Damn," she said. "We needed one of them to stop the storm. Deanna, any ideas?"

Deanna was at the console already. The oozing foam was ankle deep.

"Woodland mentioned Peltier diodes," she said. "These are set up as heaters, but if you reverse the polarity, they'll cool, like in portable refrigerators. I just have to figure out how to do that." She studied the console intently.

"Is there a help button?" Lynn asked. Deanna shot her a disdainful glance and focused on the console again.

"Would ya look at that," she said. "There *is* a help button." She clicked the icon and a menu popped up. She searched "Peltier polarity;" a few paragraphs and a flurry of keystrokes later, she sat back to look at the map.

"I reversed the polarity on all the devices. That oughta do it."

The dots on the display were changing from red to blue, one by one. In a half a minute the entire Gulf was covered in blue dots.

The foam was calf-deep, sticky but still fluid.

"I owe you dolls a drink," Burke said.

Lynn looked around at the other screens. On a small monitor she found text conversations with the ship. The first sequence was from Captain Trauger, requesting Coast Guard help. It included coordinates—Lynn snapped a picture just in case. The second message was much more disturbing:

Muddy> Video restored. Meg and Clint gone. We're out of here. See you next week.

Burke was studying the map. The hurricane eye pressure had stopped falling, and maybe even started to inch up. But it had a long way to go. And on the video, the waves crashing against the casino windows looked like they hadn't gotten the memo.

"We need to take a powder, now," he said. The foam was at their knees and would soon start to stiffen up.

"Trouble is," Maggie said, "we don't know how long those coolers are going to run. If they cool too much, they'll wreak havoc with the weather down there."

"They'll keep running forever," Woodland mumbled. He was just coming to, still groggy. "They're built on abandoned low-yield oil well heads, and they convert the oil to electricity with some kind of direct converter. But they'll stop if you shut down the console. Charlie didn't want to risk anyone else taking control of them, so they need a constant refresh signal from here to keep running."

"I can handle that," Maggie said. She pulled out her phone, punched a few buttons, and rested it on the keyboard. "I set the bomb function to remote control. When the storm calms down we set it off. The room will be foamed and hardened by then, so the explosion will be forced directly into the console."

"Okay, let's beat it," Burke said, and steered the troupe through the gunk to the door. He went back to help Maggie with the technician.

Lynn watched from the casino as Maggie pushed the door shut behind her with a squirt of foam around the bottom. Jack pulled out his key ring and locked it.

"Frank Woodland, right?" Burke asked the technician.

"Yeah," the man answered, "How'd you know?"

"A little bird told me. Thanks for the dope about the Peltier diodes. How come you squealed?"

"I'm just a co-op computer science student, running errands and tweaking the software. Charlie told me he was just gonna mess with the cowgirls. I didn't think he was gonna kill 'em all."

"Smart move," said Maggie, "That wouldn't look good on your résumé."

"One more thing!" he blurted. "Charlie told the Coast Guard they shouldn't send out help. Said everything was under control. Guess it was, sort of. We've got to call them, right now."

Lynn was already looking up the number. She dialed it and then pulled up her picture of the ship's coordinates.

* * *

At one moment Meg was following Clint along the outer deck to the casino, and at the next, she was airborne, screaming. At least she was still in her swimsuit as she twisted to hit the water cleanly. She came up for air and looked back at the ship. Even through the rain, the dim emergency lights revealed Muddy struggling with Clint. But Clint wasn't struggling back. Then he came flying over the rail, as alert as a bale of hay.

Meg was onto him in seconds and positioned herself behind him with an elbow under his chin. He was positive-buoyant in the salt water, at least, so she just had to keep his head up, and not worry about him dragging her under.

What she did have to worry about was getting back onto the ship. Good thing it was drifting—if it were under power, she and Clint would be lost in the wake in seconds. She swam as best she could with him in tow, keeping near the ship but not getting closer.

"Meg!" came a faint yell from the deck. It was Laurel, the caterer Legionnaire, leaning over the rail.

"Throw me a life ring!" Meg shouted, buoyed herself by sudden hope. Laurel nodded and ran off, then after what seemed like forever, ran back along the deck.

"Life rings are all gone! Found one rope!" She was brandishing a coil of safety line.

"We'll take it!" Meg yelled, waving her hand.

Laurel wound up and flung the coil, remarkably accurately given the wind and waves. It landed a few feet from Meg's outstretched right hand, and she grabbed it. She only wished she had told Laurel to tie the other end to the rail first.

Having the rope in one hand and Clint in the other made it hard to swim any closer, or even stop drifting away. There wasn't much time before she'd be out of range.

She brought her hands together around Clint's head, kicking furiously to make up for the lack of hand paddling. The rope wasn't the proper stiffness for a good lariat, but it would have to do. She made a medium loop and tied a honda knot. With a good grip on the end she tried swinging the coil and loop over her head. Clint's inertia gave her something to push against, but without paddling she had trouble getting the coil clear of the water.

As lightning flashed she picked her target, a cleat at the edge of the lower deck. It was smaller across than steer horns, so it'd be easier to hit, but harder to catch the loop. And the waves were way bouncier than your typical trained rodeo horse.

She could take advantage of that. The swells rose and fell a little out of sync with the ship—she could use a rising wave to propel her up enough to fling the rope, while the ship was coming up to meet her. The next crest, she gave a set of hard kicks, stretched her arm back, and flung the coil.

The loop caught the cleat, but only the forward end. She didn't dare pull for fear of losing hold completely. She clutched Clint tight and started kicking toward the stern to get a safer angle, but the waves were fighting her. As she fell into a trough, she glimpsed the loop loosening, dangling precariously from the cleat.

The next swell and flickering lightning in the clouds got her another look, at a welcome sight. Devon, the other caterer, had scrambled onto the deck and was looping the rope fully around the cleat. He gave the line a tug to tighten it, and then flashed a thumbs up to Meg.

It was difficult to pull herself along the line with one arm around Clint's neck, but she was making progress. As she approached the hull she saw that Laurel had joined Devon, and the two of them were pulling the rope in with one hand each, the other hand clinging to the rail as waves crashed over them. Meg just had to hang on, which gave her time to think about how to get aboard. Neither caterer, nor even both together, would be able to lift two people out of the water.

But the same waves that helped her throw the line rolled up to help again. With crests crashing onto the deck, she just had to catch one at the right time and grab the rail before washing out again. After another set of hard kicks and a final yank on the rope by all three Legionnaires, Meg and Clint rode the next big whitecap over the rail. They scrambled to hold onto Clint in the backwash, then dragged him to safety in the galley.

First thing was to check on him: he was breathing and had a pulse. Just unconscious.

Meg nodded and the caterers helped her lift the show host onto a stainless steel counter, out of reach of the steadily more-intrusive waves.

Meg considered that. The waves were way higher on the ship than earlier; that was how she was able to get back aboard at all. It wasn't that the storm was getting worse—the ship was riding lower.

They were sinking!

She turned to Laurel and Devon.

"When he comes to, tell Clint to check on the cowgirls. And to keep out of sight of Muddy Bootes. I'll catch up with him after I fix a leak."

* * *

Lieutenant Norcroft was looking for Meg when he discovered a bigger problem: Bound for Glory was taking on water. He went to the bridge to inform Captain Trauger, but no one was at the helm. There was a tablet set up next to the console, playing a video featuring Meg Brecker in a PIP window. He watched her short presentation.

It was beginning to make sense.

Now he really wanted to find Meg—perhaps the Captain had seen the video and gone below to find her too? Did he know about the devices? Would he sink his own ship on purpose?

Norcroft sprinted down the sequence of ladders until he found the equipment deck. Water sloshed through the bulkhead from the engine room.

He waded into the compartment where knee-deep water surged from side to side with each roll of the ship. The emergency lights showed him what he needed to know: seawater bubbling up from a break in the engine cooling line, already submerged. The bilge pump wasn't working—disabled? And First Mate Braxton was draped over a tool chest in the corner, unconscious, his head barely above the wildly surging water.

Norcroft braced his feet wide, grabbed Braxton under the arms and used the next wave to sit him up against the wall.

"Can I help?" It was Meg Brecker, standing in the doorway, hanging on to the edge for balance.

"Yes. Make sure Braxton stays safe while I figure out how to stop the leak." Meg came over, wrapped her arms around the inert first mate and wedged herself in the corner to keep him upright. Norcroft opened the tool chest. It was a basic kit: screwdrivers, wrenches, wire cutters, vice grips, electrical and duct tape, and some spare fuses, gauges, and engine parts. No hoses or replacement valves. He looked around for something to plug the breach.

He peeled off his shirt and stuffed it into the gushing pipe. The pressure was tremendous.

"We're going to need more help, Meg," he said. "I can't hold this for very long, we'll need people to take turns."

Meg was looking at the toolbox.

"How about you wrap the pipe and shirt with duct tape?" she asked.

"Won't hold under the water."

Her brow knotted.

"A friend of mine always said you can fix anything with duct tape or vice grips, but sometimes you need both. You can wrap it all up in duct tape and then clamp the tape to the pipe with the vice grips."

It was a great suggestion.

"Okay, toss me the tape." Steadying herself against the sloshing water, she flipped the roll to him. He wrapped tape around the pipe, over the shirt plug, and back around the pipe a half-dozen times.

"Now the vise grips." Meg tossed the tool across, pretty accurately given the rocking hull—all that horseback roping practice, Norcroft guessed. He clamped it around the pipe as near to the severed end as possible. "Let's do a couple." Meg tossed a second pair and he clamped that on next to the first one. He stumbled back as he let go, then pushed forward and felt around the makeshift plug. The tape helped make a better seal, too, so the leakage was down to nothing.

"Good idea," he said, wading over to Meg. "That Howie is a bright guy."

He got the reaction he expected—a flash of realization that Norcroft knew more than she wanted him to.

"Look," he said, bracing himself next to her and Braxton. "I've managed to put a lot of pieces together, but not the whole picture. I know you and Howie stayed in the Lone Diamond Motel before you showed up on the beach."

Meg's eyes got intense.

"I don't know what you're talking about."

"Yes, you do." Meg was just staring at him. Almost there. "I saw the video you just made. You're some kind of agent." He paused, looking for a reaction, but got none. "I think Howie is too, and maybe Clint and Tommy, and you're the good guys; the bad guys are trying to silence you. You had a couple of near accidents on the show already."

Meg sighed and shook her head slowly.

"It's worse than that. They killed Howie."

"What? How do you know that?"

"It's complicated, and I can't talk about it, you have to understand. I hope that video got the word out to—my fellow agents—and they can stop the storm. Until then, we need to keep everybody safe. Pluggin' that leak was a good start."

"Fair enough. But this case has been driving me crazy for three years. Will you answer one question?"

"Maybe."

"Is Tommy still alive?"

Meg's face clouded over.

"No. Our dive was to look into abnormal Gulf temperatures and we ended up on Kenny Trauger's dive boat. He set up a tanker plane to scoop Tommy up and dump him on a brush fire."

"The urban legend?"

"It's real. Most of 'em are. They missed me but didn't know it. I had to go underground or they'd try again. I work with other urban legend survivors." She choked up a little. "Except Howie. They drugged him years ago and stole a kidney, but yesterday they stole a few more organs. He ain't a survivor anymore."

Norcroft let out a low whistle.

He was right all along: this pretty cowgirl was clever, competent, and resourceful. And that was all while avoiding assassination and carrying an overwhelming emotional burden. She'd make a great Ranger.

After they hoisted Braxton by the shoulders to carry him to safety, Meg stopped and turned to Norcroft.

"One more thing," she said. "Welcome to the Urban Legion."

Chapter 33

The first few minutes of the descent were a little rough for Muddy's escape pod, but once they reached the seabed the only movement was an occasional slight sideways drift. It was certainly much better than being on the surface in an artificial hurricane. Especially on a sabotaged, sinking yacht.

"Comfortable?" he asked his guests.

"This is very good vessel," Pavel answered. His two flunkies nodded agreement. And why not? The seats were amply padded, the cooling system kept them at 80 degrees maximum, and they had enough air, water, and food for a week.

Muddy checked the temperature gauges. The seawater outside was up to 118 degrees—no way the Gulf could be that hot. But the heater outputs were scalding, above 150 degrees, before mixing with the cooler Gulf water; they must have settled right near a discharge vent. That would explain the drift movements, too. Those vents churned up the water a lot.

The temperature would go even higher as the heaters kept running, but he wasn't worried; the escape pod was designed to handle temperatures all the way up to actual boiling—not that the vents would ever get there, but it didn't hurt to have design margins.

He watched the gauge for a moment to see how fast it was rising. It flipped to 117.

Going down?

Maybe they hit a cool eddy of some sort. He kept his eye on the gauge. It kept going down.

Gauge must be broken.

Muddy sighed and sat back; he wouldn't get the satisfaction of seeing how high the local temperature would peak. Maybe the weather services would at least have the overall Gulf temperature, which was the real interesting number; he could check once they were back on land. That was the only missing luxury in the escape pod: no contact with the outside world. Muddy would've loved to watch the pandemonium above on the webcast as he waited for the end.

Ah, well, it would go viral and be on the web forever. There was nothing left to do but catch up on much-needed sleep. Muddy relaxed, dozing off as his porn-industry companions discussed their upcoming film *Cut Jewels*.

"Gettin' kinda chilly in here," Brad said, waking Muddy up, "might want to turn down the AC."

Muddy nodded and checked the control. The AC wasn't running. There was no need: the outside temperature was now down to 58 degrees, and the inside temp was following it down. This was not a broken gauge.

He looked at his watch. Down 60 degrees in only three hours? Charlie must have reversed the heaters—they'd pump out 40-degree water in that mode. And the pod was sitting right in the output plume.

Why would they reverse the heaters?

Muddy's concern was redirected at a creaking sound from the hull.

"We're leaking!" Pavel said, lifting his alligator shoes from a widening puddle in the footwell.

Shit!

The metal parts were contracting in the cold, and the watertight seals were breaking. Muddy had carefully selected the Acme premium high-temp O-rings to handle heat expansion, but he hadn't considered the cold. It wasn't supposed to get cold. He remembered the space shuttle Challenger disaster, caused by the same issue: O-rings that weren't designed for the cold, losing their flexibility. He wished he'd remembered that earlier.

"Hang on, boys, we're gonna hafta ride this one out on the surface." Muddy fired up the instrument panel and flipped the ballast control to full buoyancy. The pod jerked upward as the air tanks filled, but only for a moment. Through a viewport, Muddy watched a stream of air bubbles flow upward, as the pod settled back down with a slight thump. The ballast tanks, leaking around chilled Acme O-rings, emptied noisily into the Gulf. When the stream of bubbles stopped, there was only silence.

"We're fucked, aren't we?" Peter asked, desperation cracking his voice. Pavel and Brad both turned to Muddy and waited for the answer.

"Yep," he said.

The four of them sat quietly for a few minutes, the silence punctuated by occasional whimpers from Peter, as the water rose to their calves, then to their knees. Muddy could only guess what kind of prayers the others were saying.

Pavel suddenly stood up and pulled out his phone. He fumbled with it for a moment, holding it up against the provisions cabinet across the way.

"You can't call from here," Muddy pointed out.

"Checking angle and lighting," Pavel said, and then pushed a button and balanced the phone in the cabinet handles. He sat back and extended a hand toward the device.

"Smile for camera, gentlemen," he said. "I think you have good title, Peter: *We're Fucked.* This will be famous, as first autobiographical snuff film ever!"

"If anyone finds it," Muddy said.

Peter wiped his eyes and leaned over toward Brad.

"This could also be the first autobiographical snuff porn film, Brad."

Brad grimaced.

"No, it couldn't."

Peter shrugged, and he and Brad adjusted themselves to orient their good sides toward the camera.

Muddy closed his eyes.

At least he'd finished the job on Meg Brecker.

* * *

Charlie Stewart rode the elevator up with mixed emotions. He had surely executed (ha!) the most awesome live (ha again!) webcast ever; a multi-victim snuff film, yet. And even with the Urban Legion swarming his headquarters, they weren't going to be able to stop it. Of course, the loss of his HQ meant no extortion money from Gulf cities. He'd have to settle for his bonus from Fiona for pulling the poll numbers for the webcast.

Why she was so hung up on beating broadcast TV, he never did figure out. As long as she paid him as promised, he didn't care.

The elevator reached the helipad level and the door opened. Lit by the lights of the taller buildings on the Strip, the copter waited as expected, but something was popping over the edge of the roof. They were clowns, flying like they were launching from a trampoline on the ground.

Charlie grabbed his rifle from the rack by the door and sprinted for the copter. There were half a dozen clowns around it already. Two were spraying the engine area with seltzer bottles—except the hissing and smoking of the dissolving cowl meant it was very acidic seltzer.

Charlie dropped to one knee and fired, shattering a bottle and sending the clown howling. A second shot took out the other clown's bottle. Charlie got back up and climbed into the copter. To his relief, the engine started immediately—the acid hadn't hurt anything yet. He buckled in and skimmed through the checklist as the blades began to rev up. A few more seconds and he'd be airborne.

He twisted the thrust control. The engine groaned against the weight, and instead of lifting into the air, the copter merely leaned a bit to the left.

He looked over the left side and saw two clowns with a giant tube labeled "Super-Duper Instant Glue" applying the last few feet of a bead along the copter's left tread. The tread was already stuck to the roof and even the 180-horsepower engine couldn't break it free.

Time for the fallback plan.

Charlie unbelted, grabbed the rifle, and bolted for the balloon hanger. Since his days as a weatherman, he'd always wanted to try the balloon thing; now his escape depended on it. He slipped into the small hangar and locked the door behind him. A button press retracted the roof while he prepared himself.

Eight helium-filled weather balloons strained at their steel wires, which in turn strained at the arms and back rail of the aluminum lawn chair they were welded to. The makeshift airship strained at the mechanical catch that held it down.

Charlie settled in, strapped on his seat belt, gripped the rifle securely, and released the catch.

The acceleration was breathtaking. The balloons were sized for the coldest weather, but here on a warm evening, they provided way more lift than needed. Within a minute Charlie could barely make out the clowns milling about on the casino roof, disappointed. Charlie smiled.

He was quickly above the approach lanes for McCarran Airport; the possibility of a collision with a jetliner had been the main risk he'd worried about. But the overdesigned balloons could also take him too high, where cold or lack of oxygen would be a big problem.

That was why he brought the gun, of course. He took aim at the center balloon—it was barely visible with reflected light from the city below—and fired. The sphere turned into a rag and settled down below the chair. He was still rising rapidly, though, so he shot a second balloon.

And a third, and a fourth. Still rising. He hadn't expected the four remaining balloons would have so much lift. The last two bullets in the clip were supposed to let him land safely, not just stop him from rising. If it took two more just to level off, how would he get down?

Maybe one more would do it. He took careful aim and pulled the trigger.

The click reminded him that he'd wasted two bullets on the fucking seltzer bottles. He looked at the wires running up to the remaining balloons. Stranded steel. Welded to the chair. The only way down was to jump. That wasn't gonna happen.

As he drifted toward the Grand Canyon, dimly lit by the setting moon, Charlie tried to find the lights of the tourist village. He dropped the rifle, thinking maybe he could hit someone with it at least. A small comfort as he wafted onward.

He shivered. He was headed directly for a rather large Gulf hurricane.

* * *

Fiona tried reloading a few times, but the "server not found" status kept coming up on her screen. The webcast was over, apparently. She scratched Lola behind her ears and wondered if this was just another technical difficulty like the earlier glitch.

She knew that wasn't a bilge pump, and why Charlie went to ads so quickly. At least he got the video back right away, if not for very long. She called him, but his phone was either off or dead. He couldn't be out of range; the Vegas Strip was a cell phone hotspot.

It had been going so well up to then—the underwater heat pumps had built the storm so fast the weather services were calling it a freak event. She checked them again and was surprised to find the storm fading as quickly as it came up. That was certainly not part of the plan.

The weather experts wanted to call the whole thing an "instrumentation anomaly," claiming the storm hadn't been as bad as the measurements indicated. But the video from Next Bikini Cowgirl proved them wrong and left them shaking their heads.

That video was dramatic all right—every bit as dramatic as she'd hoped. She figured Pavel Nepovim wouldn't be happy without a few on-camera deaths, but for her, the key was the viewership. The masses had been hooked for a solid hour, and that was all the time her experiment needed.

"Let's look at the numbers, Lola, okay?" The lap cat seemed fine with that. Fiona switched to the Media Book live ratings site. The webcast had a strong stream count from the start of the live portion, but soon after the ship lost power the total increased exponentially. Next Bikini Cowgirl had viewership rivaling the Super Bowl, even though it was close to midnight. And those viewers were worldwide—no translation needed to understand a sexy disaster in real time.

"The numbers are great, Lola," she said, renewing her scratching as Lola purred happily.

The numbers were, in fact, huge. Big enough to make a discernable difference in other areas, if the technology the Corporation was testing worked correctly. She'd been collecting news and social media statistics for months to get a baseline reading; if the Bikini Cowgirl show caused a ripple effect in those stats, she'd see it.

And if the ripple effect was there, the experiment would be deemed a success. It would be time for the next, and final phase. The Corporation would fulfill its destiny at last.

* * *

Roger stared at the frozen image of cowgirls huddling against a huge wave in mid-crash. Was the storm settling down? Hard to tell. He looked again for Meg in the shadows and couldn't find her.

He replayed his recording of the show, and paused on the "bilge pump" image. Meg had done what she intended, to get a video of the device. It was obviously a heat pump, and a bunch of them scattered across the Gulf could generate a monster storm. Did generate a monster storm. But Reality Web cut off the video so quickly he doubted anyone noticed.

Lynn called and filled him in. So everything was fine—other than nobody knew if the ship would stay afloat until the Coast Guard arrived, or who was trying to kill Lynn, or what happened to Meg and Clint.

The one thing he did know was what happened to Howie.

He broke down again, his head dropping into his hands. There was no one around; he let the tears come, and then the sobs.

A leader wasn't supposed to act like this. A leader wasn't supposed to let this happen.

He thought back to the King's words. "You care for your people, and you take responsibility," the old man said when he offered the job to Roger. He didn't warn him that caring and responsibility become crushing guilt when you screw up.

What would the King do?

Get busy.

He wiped his hands on his shirt, blinked his vision clear, and focused on the console. He still had his Wacko Conspiracy Group cross-reference program running; he brought it up to see if he'd made any progress. To his surprise, the output was complete. And very specific.

The analysis showed that Major Ellis Thompkins had exactly one thing in common with exactly four Harvard professors from his WCG candidate group. And while Arlene Harrington wasn't in the group, her Dirt TV partner Bobby Atkinson was.

They were all members of the World Feline Admiration Society. He dug in: it had a website, a Facebook page, Twitter and Instagram accounts, the works. And it had been around for a while—there was a Usenet group in the early days of the internet, a newsletter in the 1950s, and even a bimonthly French-language journal called Culte du Chat, first published in 1889.

Was the Corporation that old?

And that big? The World Feline Admiration Society had 8,678 currently active members.

Roger shook his head and closed the program. Even the Corporation had cat lovers, there were bound to be some members. It didn't mean the WFAS was significant.

But some organization out there was significant. He vowed to find it. For Howie.

* * *

Clint approached the lounge carefully, keeping an eye peeled for Muddy as suggested by Laurel and Devon. They'd told Clint he'd gone overboard and Meg saved him—the girl never stopped being amazing.

The waves had calmed down a lot by then, but an occasional splash-over rewetted his already soaked clothes. The water was much colder than before; Meg's Urban Legion friends must have gotten the message and figured out how to reverse the heaters. He didn't think Reality Web had a change of heart.

He peeked into the lounge and counted male heads. Just the cameramen, no Muddy or Pavel, no Kenny, not even Peter or Brad, or Ranger Norcroft. He braced himself for the pandemonium and stepped inside.

There was no pandemonium. The camera crew was coiling cables and packing gear into road boxes. Clint went there first.

"Packing up already?" he asked.

One of them shrugged.

"Boss's orders," he said, nodding toward Gabriella.

"They told me they lost the connection," Gabriella said, stepping up with authority. "They would'a just sat around filming for nobody if I hadn't given 'em something useful to do. There's nothing going on here anyway."

Clint surveyed the lounge. Jasmine and Faith were standing near the roulette table, hand-in-hand, deep in prayer. Mattie was sitting in a corner with Samantha on her lap, stroking her black hair and telling her everything was going to be okay. Dakota and Cassidy were having a competition to see who could straighten up their section of the lounge the quickest. Cassidy was righting tables two at a time and winning the race.

"Looking good doesn't have to mean looking sexy, Lisa," Bobbie Jo said from behind the bar, which she'd turned into a hair and makeup salon for Lisa sitting on a stool in front. Bobbie Jo's eyes were gleaming. "I can see it now, asexual chic!" She pointed her comb at Lisa. "You could be the next It Girl, in more ways than one!"

Clint was starting to feel better about the situation when Gabriella tapped his elbow. She couldn't reach his shoulder.

"Where's Meg?" she demanded.

Good question! Where was Meg?

"I thought she'd be here."

"She wasn't with you?"

"She…" how much should he say? "…well, she was, but I got knocked out by a wave. I woke up in my cabin, and figured she came back here. Have you seen her?"

"Not since you two lovebirds left."

That wasn't good.

"What about Pavel, and Muddy?"

"They slipped away a while ago, too, along with those two fake cowboys. What's going on, Clint?"

"I wish I knew. I'm going to go look for everyone. Stay here."

He did a quick tour of the bridge and upper decks, finding no one. He checked in with the galley, where Laurel and Devon were giving first aid to Roy Braxton.

"Meg wants you to meet her and Ranger Norcroft in the dungeon," Laurel said.

If Clint hadn't gone through so much with Meg already, he wouldn't have believed that was serious. He headed further below; dungeons should be near the bottom, right?

Relief washed over him; Meg was okay. Was that how Tommy and Howie felt about her?

* * *

Meg and Lieutenant Norcroft looked around the torture room like it was a museum.

"I've never seen anything like this, have you?" she asked. Norcroft shook his head.

"No, but if I had, I probably wouldn't admit it. This was Captain Trauger's little secret; it was locked earlier. I figure we can hide out here till we figure out what to do next."

"You're not just gonna out me and declare the case solved?"

"Is that what you want?"

Meg sighed.

"What I want is to go home to Pappy's farm and get a good night's sleep."

"Okay."

"But I can't. The Corporation is still out there. If I show up in public they'll kill me the first chance they get. I've lost two lovers to those creeps and I don't want to lose anyone else. If they even think I'm alive they'll get to Pappy, or Tommy's family." She took a deep breath. "I need to disappear again."

Norcroft studied her, then nodded.

"I can help with that. We'll say you were lost at sea during the storm—tragic accident. We can keep you out of sight until you're close enough to shore to swim for it again. And once we're in cell range, I can have someone drop off Howie's car near the beach where you can find it. Your suitcase is in the trunk." Norcroft pulled out a key and handed it to her. "I left a spare in my office."

"You have Howie's car?" So that was how he knew the duct tape and vise grips were Howie's idea. The guy was sharp. "You should also pass word to the Urban Legion that I'm okay. They'll be worried. The caterers can get you in touch."

"Whoa," said Clint as he stepped into the room, "This boat really does have a dungeon."

"'Mornin', sleepy head," Meg said, smiling. Clint looked happy. "How are the girls?"

"They're all fine." He glanced at Norcroft and back at Meg.

"Ranger Norcroft knows everything," she said.

Clint nodded and relaxed. "The storm is settlin' down, so I think your friends got the word. Gabriella's got the crew packin' up."

"Gabriella?"

"Yep. The camera guys were hoppin' to it. Don't want to sample that balls-high side kick, I guess. I searched the ship—found everybody but Captain Trauger, Muddy, Pavel, and his two Hollywood cowboys. And that locked aft lifeboat bay we saw earlier is now unlocked and empty. The crane had deployed. I think they had an escape boat."

So they were all still a threat. Shoot.

"Clint," Meg said, "Ranger Norcroft is gonna help me disappear again, tell everyone I was lost in the storm."

Clint's face fell.

"I guess it's too dangerous for you here, huh?"

"Yeah. Maybe for you, too. You could come join the Urban Legion. You've got the credentials."

"It won't work," Clint said. "The cowgirls have seen me since the storm let up. It'll be hard to sell that I went overboard now." He looked into her eyes. "Not that I wouldn't like to join you."

It was like that first moment on the beach. Like she was looking at Tommy.

But he wasn't Tommy.

"Okay. You need to keep this all a secret, though."

Clint nodded.

"Should I admit that Pavel's romance plot was a sham? Or be heartbroken at my tragic loss? The tabloids will want to know."

"Your call, Clint. Whatever's most convincing."

"That would be heartbroken."

Chapter 34

Arlene cleared her throat and faced the camera. She had to hide her excitement.

"This is Arlene Harrington for Dirt TV, broadcasting live from the U.S. Coast Guard Station in Galveston, Texas, with breaking news on the status of Bound for Glory, the yacht that was caught in yesterday's freak storm, along with the entire cast and crew of the Next Bikini Cowgirl show. We've received information that the ship is under tow by the Coast Guard and should be arriving soon here at the Galveston Station. We're about to get an update from Coast Guard Commander Gingrich on the status of the rescue operation."

The cameras panned away from Arlene, and she let herself relax. Commander Gingrich approached the bouquet of microphones sprouting from a portable lectern. He looked very serious as he adjusted the CBS and National Nose mikes upward to suit his height.

"I will make this brief, and will not be taking questions, as we are still investigating this incident. Last night, the luxury yacht Bound for Glory became disabled in the Gulf of Mexico about sixty miles southeast of Galveston. No distress call was made, but due to the indication of trouble in the video transmission from the Reality Web show Next Bikini Cowgirl, several—many— concerned citizens contacted this station to report the problem. Unable to reach the ship, at 2250 hours we contacted the Reality Web home offices and were told that the situation was under control and no help was needed. Out of concern for the ship's safety, we began monitoring the webcast, and at 2320 hours, the video was halted, due to technical issues according to the website."

Arlene was not happy about that—her Dirt TV had exclusive

access to rebroadcast clips from the show, and she hated to miss all the juicy action.

"We tried to contact the Reality Web offices again but were unable to reach them. At approximately 2325 hours, the video resumed. We received an anonymous call from the area of the Reality Web offices stating that the situation was no longer under control and requesting that the Guard send a rescue team as soon as possible. With the freak storm fading quickly, we dispatched a high-speed cutter and an emergency towing vessel. The video went down again at 2355 hours, as did the website, which is still not responding. The rescuers reached the ship at 0115 hours this morning and made contact with Lieutenant Norcroft of Texas Rangers Company A, who was aboard the ship and had taken command."

Arlene perked up at that. What happened to Captain Trauger?

Commander Gingrich paused, looking even more serious than before. Arlene felt a shiver.

"Lieutenant Norcroft informed us that a number of people aboard the boat were unaccounted for. Search and rescue operations began immediately, and are continuing, but we have not yet found any sign of the missing persons."

He paused again.

Who? Arlene wanted to shout it. Who?! This guy was better at reality drama than she was.

"The following persons are missing and may be lost at sea: ship's Captain Kenneth Trauger, artistic director Pavel Nepovim, technical director James Bootes, ranch hands Peter Long and Brad Driver, and cowgirl contestant Meg Brecker."

Commander Gingrich continued, saying something about commitment to keep searching and credit to the sailors involved in the rescue, but Arlene wasn't listening anymore.

All of the Corporation people were gone. As well as Meg Brecker. That did not sound random. Arlene was suddenly very glad she had not been invited on the cruise.

She and Dr. Bobby Atkinson were the only ones remaining, and the good surgeon had left yesterday with his precious organic cargo. Arlene pulled out her phone, and by the time the news conference wrapped up, had booked her own flight under an assumed name. Her career as a Dirt TV reporter, and in fact, Dirt TV itself, was over.

* * *

Like all the big cases, this one wasn't open and shut. That's the genre, I guess. I could pat myself on the back about finally getting the drop on Charlie Stewart and his mad-scientist control center. And stopping him from sending half of eastern Texas, along with ten innocent cowgirls, off to the big sleep with an apocalyptic hurricane.

But I, and all the clowns I could muster, couldn't stop Charlie from vanishing into thin air. I had to figure he'd be dropping in out of the blue sometime later to cause more trouble.

What stuck in my craw was the murder mystery. I still had no clue who was trying to bump off Grady. At least she was leaving town and might avoid the next planting attempt.

Since her rental car was totaled, I offered her a ride to the airport, and arranged to meet at her hotel room. I figured there was no way I'd wrap up a noir case without spending any time in the client's digs. The dame still hadn't come clean on her friend from the Media Book; if I played the right tune, maybe she'd sing.

"Who is he? How do you know him? Why would he try to kill you?"

Grady 'fessed up, if I could trust her. She'd been playing a dangerous game, but that's what Urban Legionnaires do. I could buy the story and agreed that Nick Wood had no reason to kill her. Which left the same question: who did?

The room phone rang.

"Who calls you here?" I asked.

She looked a little concerned.

"Only Nick Wood."

"Answer it. Put it on speaker. I'm not here."

Grady punched the speakerphone button and Nick Wood's voice jumped into the room.

"Lynn! I had one more idea. But it might be too crazy even for the wackos. I figured I should bounce it off you just to see what you think."

Lynn rolled her eyes. I motioned "go ahead." I wanted to see her game in action.

"Okay, Nick, I'm all ears."

"Okay. Rental car agencies, right? They need to replace their old vehicles, and they don't want to pay for it. So when someone waives the insurance, they give them the oldest, crappiest car on the lot, and send out a hit-and-run vehicle to total it. The renter waived the insurance and has to pay for replacement. The company gets a new car for free."

Grady was staring at me, wide-eyed.

"Lynn?"

"Um, not sure what to say, Nick."

"Too crazy, huh?"

"Yeah… too crazy."

"Okay, I'll quit bugging you. See you around the Media Book sometime maybe."

"Yeah, maybe. Bye."

Grady hung up the phone.

"You waived the insurance, didn't you?" I asked. She nodded.

"I didn't want to pay thirty dollars a day. I have my own insurance. Which is going to pay for the car."

I'd remember that. I have my own insurance, too.

I'm a private detective. And—well, you know the rest.

* * *

"All clear, Meg."

At the word from Lieutenant Norcroft, Meg emerged from the stairway onto the back deck. Clint was carrying her scuba tank and vest. He looked like he'd be crying if he wasn't such a tough cowboy. Meg gave him a hug.

"Promise me you'll tell Pappy?"

Clint smiled.

"Yep."

"And that you'll keep him from tryin' to find me?"

"That could be a lot harder. Your Pappy's a stubborn cuss. How about I promise him we'll meet up with you after the heat is off?"

That sounded real good.

"Alright. Stay in touch with the local Legion. I'll contact you through them."

Clint nodded, maintaining that tough cowboy-ness.

"Time to go, Meg." Norcroft was holding out her mask and flippers.

"Okay. We'll be in touch with you, too, Lieutenant. We need to stop Arlene Harrington."

"We will, Meg. Now get going. Howie's car is parked on High Island Beach. Shouldn't be anyone around but don't dawdle." He grinned. "No naps in the dunes." Meg grinned back.

"No naps. Thanks again."

Meg donned the scuba pack, checked her buoyancy vest pocket for Howie's car key, put on the flippers and mask, and slipped off the platform into the Gulf. As she dove out of sight and headed northwest, the familiarity pressed in on her more than the weight of the water. Here she was again, swimming into hiding, away from everything she loved. Away from everything she lost. Everyone she lost. With another mission to find another set of killers.

She was crying. She'd have to clear the mask if that kept up. Unable to wipe her eyes, her vision got blurry for a few moments, so she didn't see whatever bumped her from below.

She pulled up short as the pod of dolphins surrounded her. Some of them were still armed, but one only partially—the one that had offered a spear to free Clint and seemed to be the leader.

The dolphin hovered in front of her, expectantly.

Meg reached out and grabbed its fin. Gently, the dolphin began to swim, and pretty soon the pod and their human passenger were heading for the Bolivar Peninsula at cruising speed.

Epilogue

"Is There Life After Bikini Cowgirls?"
— Headline, The National Nose

Howie seemed to be floating toward a bright light. He heard voices in his head and instinctively reached for his tin-copper-lined yarmulke. But he didn't feel it. He didn't feel anything, not even his arm or hand.

"Where am I?" he asked. "Is this the afterlife?"

"Nah," growled a Brooklyn accent. "We think it might be Cleveland."

Join the fun!

Thank you for enjoying this book! My goal in writing the Urban Legion trilogy is to make the world a funnier place, and you can help! Authors depend on our fans to spread the word about our books. So I would be very grateful if you would leave an honest review of *Bikini Cowgirls* on Amazon and/or Goodreads—besides telling all your friends and family about the trilogy.

You can stay up to date on Urban Legion specials and giveaways, including Book 3 (what happened to Howie?), by checking out TheUrbanLegion.com. Join the *Legionnaire* email list for very rare updates (I promise, no spam). If you want to discover other funny fiction, you'll find reviews and links on *The Yucks-Files* page. In fact, if you've read something funny that I haven't reviewed, let me know there! I've picked up several new hilarious authors that way. To discover what other funny endeavors I'm up to, check out DaveAgans.com.

For social media fans, you can like *TheUrbanLegion* page or *AuthorDaveAgans* pages on Facebook.

In any case, keep laughing.

Dave Agans

Acknowledgments

I'm deeply grateful to my wife Gail for pushing me to both complete this book and to get it right. Kudos to my team at B. Mirthy & Sons who took it from there, and shout-outs to editor Nina Eppes and cover artist Aaron Hazouri.

Special thanks to the New Hampshire Writer's Project and my Nashua Region associates, notably Peggy McFarland who provided valuable in-depth story advice. I'm grateful for Houston-area cultural insights from Krystle and Gabe Kraus, Kurt and Rhonda Everson, and Tom Agans. My introduction to circus culture is thanks to Jackie Davis and Jen Agans—someday maybe I'll actually be able to juggle clubs. As in Book 1, I drew on craft guidance by Blake Snyder, Robert McKee, and Donald Maass, among many other writing teachers. And this go-around, I discovered and used resources by Rayne Hall, who also helped me punch up my opening.

I continue to be inspired by well-known humorists Carl Hiaasen, Christopher Moore, Dave Barry, Christopher Buckley, Kurt Vonnegut, and Douglas Adams, and have newly discovered funny fiction by Jasper Fforde, Benjamin Wallace, Barry J. Hutchison, Marshall Karp, Paul Levine, and Mark Schweizer. Check them out.

And speaking of Mark, thanks to the Bullwer Lytton Fiction Contest, for awarding me the 2018 prize in the Crime/Detective category.